I0581872

The Universe Within

A Cosmic Shores Novel

G. S. Jennsen

HYPERNOVA PUBLISHING
2025

THE UNIVERSE WITHIN

Copyright © 2025 by G. S. Jennsen

Cover design by Vampy1.
Cover typography by G. S. Jennsen.

Hypernova Publishing
174 E Neider Ave #89
Coeur d'Alene, ID 83815
www.hypernovapublishing.com

Publisher's Note: This is a work of fiction. Names, characters, places, and incidents are a product of the author's imagination. Locales and public names are sometimes used for atmospheric purposes. Any resemblance to actual people, living or dead, or to businesses, companies, events, institutions, or locales is completely coincidental.

The Hypernova Publishing name, colophon and logo are trademarks of Hypernova Publishing.

Ordering Information:
Hypernova Publishing books may be purchased for educational, business or sales promotional use. For details, contact the "Special Markets Department" at the address above.

The Universe Within / G. S. Jennsen.—1st ed.

LCCN 2025901574
978-1-957352-28-2

CONTENTS

The Universe Within

PART I:

THE PHYSICIST

1

In a quiet region of space three parsecs from the closest star, a crack in the fabric of the cosmos bolted across the firmament like a lightning strike breaking free of a thundercloud.

At barely a nanometer wide, the crack itself was invisible to the naked eye, the only visual evidence of its existence a faint coral haze spilling out from it into the surrounding void. But Alex Solovy Marano looked upon such wonders with better eyes.

A spectral cacophony concentrated into a sliver of a filament as bands of radiation blinding in their intensity elbowed against one another, fighting to escape through the crack.

"What can you make of the EM data, Valkyrie?" Alex asked.

Her Artificial companion replied over the ship's speakers while manifesting a series of charts above the data center table. 'The bulk of the radiation is a close match for emissions from a typical K5V orange dwarf star. However, I am also detecting numerous narrow-band radio signals consistent with a technological source.'

"Technological? Are you saying there's *intelligent life* on the other side of this manifold tear?"

'I am saying 'consistent with.''

Alex leaned in closer to inspect the data for herself…and had to agree. The scan showed an abundance of tight, narrow-frequency microwave signals layered across the stellar emissions.

Caleb Marano sidled up behind her and rested his chin on her shoulder to get a peek as well. "None of those readings sound like Dzhvar to me."

"No, though squeezing everything through a nanometer-wide slit could be obscuring any dimensional perturbations."

They'd been hunting the Dzhvar for three years now, but the pandimensional life forms were notorious for being maddeningly elusive—right up until they exploded into physical space to devour everything in their path. Planets, stars, the manifold itself. And, of course, people.

Though ostensibly annihilated by humanity's allies, the Anadens, in a galactic war a million years ago, Alex had it on good authority that the Dzhvar would return to resume their universe-eating ways, sooner rather than later. And because neither she nor Caleb were the type to sit around twiddling their thumbs while waiting for doom to descend upon them, they searched the cosmos for signs of the ancient enemy's return. Thus far, they hadn't found so much as an omen or portent.

Their colleague, Mesme, had alerted them several days ago to the sudden eruption of strange fissures in this region of space. As ethereal beings who treated the cosmic manifold as their playground, Mesme and its fellow Katasketousya sensed disruptions in the fabric of space in a way the most advanced sensors could never hope to match. So she and Caleb had raced here in the hope of catching one of the fissures in action.

And catch one they had…but instead of Dzhvar gobbling up the environs, had they discovered something else entirely?

"Even if the Dzhvar aren't present here now, it doesn't mean they didn't cause this most unusual tear in space on their way through." Alex's shoulders lifted as the thrill of the chase revved up. "And if they did, and there are living beings trapped on the other side of it, well…."

"Let me guess: All the more reason to go investigate?" She could *feel* her husband smirking as he moved to one of the storage cabinets, grabbed a bag, and began collecting their exploration gear.

"We'd be remiss if we didn't. You know, when Mesme told me about the fissures, it mentioned a humanoid species used to reside in this general region of space. They called themselves 'Elakri.'"

"Used to?"

"They disappeared over nine thousand years ago. Their entire stellar system vanished. Mesme thought the location was probably a coincidence, but…" she gestured to the charts above the data center table "…something technological is on the other side."

'I said '*consistent with.*''

"Come on, Valkyrie. When was the last time you were wrong?" She leaned against the edge of the table and contemplated the cabin. "I think we can use the Dimensional Rifter to pry the crack open wide enough for the *Siyane* to slip inside."

'I agree,' Valkyrie replied. 'But we should hurry. The two earlier fissures that occurred in this region of space only lasted between fourteen and eighteen minutes before healing.'

"Which is why I'm confident you're already running the necessary calculations to ensure we don't miss our window or get squished during traversal. So you're not going to like this next part—"

'No!' Valkyrie exclaimed. 'Out of the question. You will not leave me behind.'

The Artificial knew what Alex had been about to say, because Valkyrie had read her mind. Lived *in* her mind, as well as in the circuitry of the ship and a half dozen other locations scattered around Concord space. As a merged Prevo pair, they'd enjoyed a connected existence for the last twenty years. Separate and independent when it suited them, but also united as one.

Nonetheless, Alex continued speaking aloud for Caleb's benefit. "It's only so you can rescue us if the need arises."

'And how do you expect me to do that? You're taking the *Siyane* with you.'

Caleb glanced back at her, eyebrow raised, as if to suggest he was wondering much the same thing.

"If we haven't returned to normal space in one week, borrow a ship equipped with a Caeles Prism and a Dimensional Rifter and wait for another tear to materialize. Use the Rifter to hold the tear open the way we're about to, instantiate a wormhole to the location you'll then be able to read from our trackers, and whisk us away to safety."

'And what if this is the last time a tear manifests?' Valkyrie challenged.

"You'll possess all the data we're collecting on the phenomenon.

You and Mesme will figure out a way to force one to open."

'One that accesses the same star we're currently recording emissions from?'

Alex shrugged gamely. "Probably? I have faith in you."

'I don't care for it,' Valkyrie protested. 'This is dangerous.'

Across the cabin, Caleb burst out laughing.

'I mean this is dangerous *even for the two of you.*'

It was endearing how Valkyrie worried. Granted, the Artificial was correct; these momentary tears had appeared out of nowhere a month ago, and there was no guarantee the phenomenon would continue. Also, they had no idea what waited for them beyond the fissure.

"Maybe a little bit," Alex conceded. "But you can't expect us not to go see what's on the other side."

'I don't. I want to see it as well.'

"When we get back, you can review the entire experience as if you lived it alongside me."

'*Almost* as if.' Valkyrie sounded positively morose. 'Fine. One week.'

"If we're not out by then, come fetch us." With that, Alex hurried downstairs to grab her always-packed overnight bag—best to have it close by, just in case—then returned to settle into her cockpit chair.

By the time she sat down, Valkyrie had modified the Dimensional Rifter's operation to nudge open the tear a bit. As it did so, the ship's sensors would gather reams of data on the nature of the fissure and the space it revealed, which Valkyrie would also be recording until the nanosecond she disconnected her consciousness from the *Siyane.*

Caleb slid into the seat beside her. "Are we ready?"

She flashed him a sideways grin as she took manual control of the ship. "Always."

2

———————

A half-consumed sandwich dropped onto the edge of its plate and teetered precariously for a beat before succumbing to gravity, scattering an assortment of luttuga, sliced toma and seasoned carne across the marble floor.

The sandwich's unfortunate demise transpired in concert with Laurent Kovalne leaping up out of his chair in a fit of shock. This sent the chair careening across the room until it bounced off the opposite wall, ricocheted and skidded to a stop near the overturned panite. His knee banged into the underside of the polished glass desk; he didn't notice the jolt of pain, though, nor how his kovfé mug wobbled in a daring feat of balance before settling, miraculously still upright.

Laurent pressed his fingertips onto the desk and leaned forward—then reversed course and stepped away as he flung new readouts out of the center screen to populate the diamond grid surrounding it. Next, he blackened the windows that overlooked the Trenae District outside. Finally he turned off the lights, until he was left with only darkness and the impossibility displayed in front of him.

Anomaly 3181622C—the third such anomaly he'd detected in the last month—had been puttering along, emitting the same faint but distressing radiation as the first two occurrences, when abruptly every emission had increased in intensity…his focus darted to the leftmost screen. *Bonta bae.* Over a thousandfold.

Great Guardian, was the world about to come to an end? The allegedly eternal universe preparing to rip apart into atoms, then fundamental particles, then quarks, until no iota of their existence remained?

The emissions shifted and lost precision, as if partially obscured. But almost as soon as the shift occurred, it was gone again, and in its absence the emissions shrank back to their initial strength. The world continued to exist.

He held his breath, refusing to blink lest he miss the next surprise.

But no further surprises appeared. Anomaly 3181622C lasted for another 1.8 minutes, generating nothing anomalous but its existence, before fading away.

Laurent reached for his kovfé and absently lifted the mug to his lips, but neglected to take a sip as he stood there stubbornly waiting for the arrival of a further revelation.

When nothing else happened after five minutes, he sighed and sat down—

And landed hard on the floor, spilling the kovfé down his silk shirt and soaking the crotch of his pants. *Malede*, it was hot! His right hand rested in something mushy…he lifted it up to discover the smushed remains of his sandwich.

He peered around and spotted his chair sitting halfway across the office.

"Brilliant show, Laurent. Truly." He climbed to his feet, opened the door to his office and called for a cleaning bot, then rolled his chair back to the desk and tried sitting again, this time with greater success.

No longer hungry—and lacking a sandwich in any event—he pushed the empty plate aside and ran standard analytics on the data he'd collected. Before and after the massive expansion in intensity, the emission profile was almost identical to that of the prior two anomalies. But for those few seconds, everything had gone haywire.

He needed better instruments stationed out there beyond Giarnum, needed more sensitive hardware that could detect and measure manifold perturbations to a far more precise level. But in truth, he was lucky to have any instruments operating at all.

His office offered a lovely view of the Trenae District of downtown Ventise, because all corporate and governmental offices offered lovely views, but it was the equivalent of a utility storage closet. Extraplanetary physics was not exactly the most fashionable or celebrated line of study, primarily due to the fact there was nothing of note to study.

Extraplanetary space was, once one got past the Elakrin atmosphere, all but void. Nothing but scattered particles of gas and dust and the solar wind, until it petered out at the edge of the universe; 'The End,' per Khesa Prutet doctrine.

Except the solar wind *didn't* peter out—it vanished in a blink of distance. It was this phenomenon that had first piqued Laurent's interest in extraplanetary physics back in his courses. The 'Universe Overview' program had noted this fact about the solar wind in a dry list of other facts about the rules of the cosmos, then continued on to the next topic. Laurent had paused the program and spent half an hour doing side research, trying to understand the proffered scientific explanation, during which he tumbled into a hole of increasingly conspiratorial conjecture on why certain laws of physics broke down at The End.

He hadn't bought into the conspiracy nonsense, but he had been intensely curious about what struck him as a thoroughly unsatisfactory explanation. This curiosity had eventually led to him becoming one of only three living extraplanetary physicists. Word was he would soon be one of two, as Katia Santon had lost her funding and was searching for a more respectable line of work.

But this, *this* might change everything.

He'd kept the discovery of the anomalies to himself up until now, mostly because they weren't interesting enough (to anyone but him) to share with a wider audience. But that flare! What if it meant the anomalies were poised to grow significantly larger? What would be the impact of such an escalation? His somewhat panicked musing in the heat of the moment about the universe disintegrating might not prove to be so hysterical after all. Obviously, to suggest the universe was not eternal was blasphemy, but religious edicts had no place in science.

Laurent pored through the data analysis two additional times, then contacted his boss.

CS

Laurent,

I'm out of town at my niece's arrival gala, but I glanced over your report, and I agree, your findings are concerning. Still, the readings are more likely the result of a faulty sensor on one of the deep space monitors than a fundamental flaw in the manifold, right?

I was able to schedule you an appointment with a bureaucrat at the Department of Extraplanetary Affairs, since the DEA will have to authorize any mission to inspect or replace the equipment. The details are attached.

Oh, and Laurent? When you get to the meeting, keep it simple. This government functionary isn't a scientist. And for the love of the Guardian, keep your enthusiasm under control, lest you frighten the poor man.

—Alcide

Laurent chuckled to himself as he read the message. His boss knew him rather too well. He'd once been not so politely asked to leave a cocktail party after gesturing excitedly throughout the spotlight violin performance while speaking to a captive business owner's wife. She'd made the mistake of inquiring about the scientific nature of The End. He'd happily acceded to the 'request' to leave, because unlike virtually every other person in existence, he personally found parties, fetes, galas and most of the other social gatherings that were a near-constant feature of proper culture to be frivolous affairs. Dreadfully boring, no matter how much originality the symphonics displayed.

He wasn't ashamed of his passion for his work, even if the rest of society didn't share it.

But discovering the cause of these anomalies was more important than convincing a government bureaucrat that the interaction of subatomic particles as they approached the cosmic edge was as exquisite as the Century Honored Visual. So he spent the next half hour preparing a list of stupid-simple bullet points summarizing the phenomenon and why discovering the truth about it mattered.

Marginally satisfied with the presentation, he left his office to head for High Square.

CS

Every government building was a lavish architectural celebration of Elakri artistic genius, but the Department of Extraplanetary Affairs headquarters was less celebratory than most. Its bronze filigree accents hadn't been refreshed in at least a decade, the fresh flowers lining the sidewalk appeared lackluster in their enthusiasm for the sun's rays, and a few telltale cracks marred the carnation-pink marble entryway.

It made sense, though. Elakrin was the beating heart of the universe; by definition, everything existing beyond its atmosphere was merely an accessory. The exotic resorts on Giarnum enjoyed the bounty of eighty percent of the DEA budget, and most of the remaining funds went to zero-g mining and manufacturing operations.

The Cosmic Sciences Division came in dead last at 0.5 percent of the budget. And of *that*, the Space Physics Institute where Laurent worked received the crumbs left over after a few decimal places. A short list of wealthy donors indulged the institute with enough grants to pay the salaries for Alcide, Laurent and a half dozen other employees, most of whom did the practical work of tracking the interaction of solar dynamics with Elakrin's atmosphere.

Laurent checked in for his appointment, then followed the overlay as it directed him to an upper level and down a winding hallway decorated in frescos of Giarnum and Phaesta, their moons and the sun, but most of all, of the Guardian.

He signaled his presence at the office door, and after a few seconds, it slid open.

"Come in, please." The speaker was a genteel young man sporting mild russet hair that complemented coral irises bleeding to florid. He wore a black velvet longcoat over beige silk pants. Emblazoned on the coat's lapel was a familiar crimson-and-gold starburst emblem.

Laurent hesitated in the doorway. "I'm sorry, I think the overlay directed me to the wrong place. My appointment is with Mr. Khaleen."

"Unfortunately, Mr. Khaleen was called away on urgent business. I'm Insaf Devran. Please, have a seat."

"I don't see how the KP can be of any help—or have any interest—in the matter I've come to discuss."

The man's expression remained as smooth as the silk weaving his pants, but his voice grew a touch icy. "The *Khesa Prutet* deserves the respect of the use of its full name, Dr. Kovalne. And on the contrary, we share an appreciation of the sciences, and of every atom comprising our Guardian-gifted universe. As such, we are happy to consult with Extraplanetary Affairs on a variety of topics. Now, sit."

Laurent found he had eased into the chair opposite the desk without intending to do so.

"Thank you. I reviewed the note your employer sent along. You believe you've identified a problem involving The End?"

"Hopefully not a problem, but definitely an anomaly. A series of them, three so far, though the most recent one was far more notable than the earlier events." He splashed up his bullet points and proceeded to explain his findings.

Devran pressed his fingertips together in a thoughtful pose. "How very interesting. What do you believe is causing these anomalies?"

"It could be malfunctioning equipment. I was never happy with the quality of the components used in constructing the deep space monitors, so I wouldn't be surprised if they're already deteriorating. Still, if this were a malfunction, I'd expect to see unpredictable results. These anomalies have been perfectly consistent—"

"Oh, but you indicated the most recent event behaved quite *inconsistently*."

"No, I said it grew exponentially in size."

"Yet that is inconsistent with the previous events."

Laurent grumbled in frustration. Why was he sitting here arguing semantics with a KP priest? This was physics, not spirituality! "I'm concerned the cosmic edge—"

"The End."

"Of course. I'm concerned *The End* is experiencing a…flaw. A shift in the way the laws of physics behave in the region, or perhaps a…breakdown of some kind."

"The Guardian is not flawed, Dr. Kovalne."

Laurent managed to catch himself before he uttered his initial response and found himself stripped of a job and a home and labeled *scappatu*. "I didn't mean to imply they were. Thus, my request is for a mission to visit the deep space monitors and, if necessary, conduct repairs." *And also get a bird's-eye view of the anomalies in action, the better to investigate more tantalizing possibilities.*

"I see. If the equipment is failing, this should obviously be remedied. Flights are in high demand—or so I'm told—but I'll ensure your request is given all due attention." Devran stood and extended a hand, palm turned halfway. "I appreciate you coming in today."

Laurent stumbled up out of the chair, surprised at the abruptness of the dismissal. "When will I hear if the mission has been approved? I'd hate to spend additional time chasing these anomalies if I'm receiving bad data."

"It will be up to Mr. Khaleen, but I expect you'll hear in a few days."

"Fine. Good." With some reluctance, he placed his palm against the man's extended one. A quick tap, then he spun and exited the office.

A dozen curses raced through Laurent's mind as he stormed down the hallway and out of the building. He was used to his work being relegated to third-class status, to being the final clause in an afterthought appended to all the pageantry of Elakrin life. But to be patronized so by a KP priest? 'Appreciation of the sciences' his ass; the man wouldn't know a quark from a lepton!

If the manifold really was collapsing and all life was exterminated because he'd been given the brush off, the blame's first stop would be at the skeletal feet of Insaf Devran.

3

"I feel like I'm trapped in a shoulder-width cave deep underground. I've never been especially claustrophobic, but right now I kind of want to hyperventilate."

Beside her, Caleb's knuckles blanched white atop the armrests of his cockpit chair. "You're not the only one."

Alex's gaze darted to him. "Akeso?"

"What piece of it I brought with me is still present, but cut off from the whole. Diminished, and a little panicked for it."

"Are you all right? Physically?"

He managed a clipped nod and stood. "Yeah. I'm going to take a walk and try to soothe some nerves. Mine and Akeso's. See what you can learn about this place now that we're on the other side."

Alex's eyes followed him into the cabin until she was sure he was steady on his feet. Then she returned her gaze, but not quite her attention, to the readings splashed across the HUD.

Her husband was special in many ways, but objectively the most notable way was how he shared mind- and body-space with a planetary intelligence. Eighteen years ago, the planet they'd named 'Akeso' had saved his life by using its regenerative abilities to re-infuse his body with life force after he'd drained it dry saving humanity from annihilation. Ever since then, they'd been as one in aspects that were both similar to and wildly different from the bond she shared with Valkyrie.

Akeso's presence within Caleb had proved capable of reaching across any cosmic distance and the most tenacious of quantum blocks, but it appeared the tear in the manifold they'd traversed was far more than a simple dimensional fold.

The fissure had sealed itself less than two minutes after they'd crossed it, and now they found themselves in a completely enclosed space. On an initial analysis, the characteristics of the space matched normal space exactly. Not only were the three physical dimensions present and acting properly, but all the hidden quantum dimensions existed here as well. She could access sidespace without difficulty—but solely in the confines of this pocket. Normally, sidespace allowed her to fling her consciousness to any defined point in the universe, but here she promptly banged up against an impenetrable wall.

The wall bounded a spatial bubble 2.6 AU in diameter, or less than the distance from the sun to Mars. Inside the bubble was a K5V orange dwarf star, three planets with two detectable moons, and a tiny planetoid orbiting on the fringes of the star. Possibly some smaller objects as well, but picking them up was going to require a lengthy and intensive scan.

Alex knew more about the spacetime manifold, the numerous dimensions comprising it, and the prickly primordial entities that frolicked upon it than anyone alive or dead (arguably excluding Mesme), and she couldn't begin to guess how this bubble *existed*.

The Katasketousya were capable of creating pocket universes, but Mesme insisted that without a portal to hold the door open, so to speak, any such constructed universe would be utterly and forever inaccessible from Amaranthe. And the Dzhvar, ostensibly their reason for being here, only destroyed the manifold; they did not create perfectly preserved spheres hidden within it.

Unless the bubble analogy was more accurate than she realized, and upon encountering the Dzhvar, the bubble...popped? But if this were the case, the pocket universe would spill into Amaranthe and become part of the larger cosmos.

A tiny and intermittent hole in the bubble's skin, though, might correspond to the tears. It wasn't a perfect analogy, but it felt close to the correct one.

Caleb reappeared in the cockpit and leaned over her shoulder. "What have you figured out?"

She peered up at him in concern. "Is everything all right?"

He offered a weak grimace. "Akeso's calmed down, I think. It's so diminished, it hardly has a voice at all. Been a while since things have grown this quiet in my head." On seeing the worry in her expression, he lifted the grimace into a smile. "But *I'm* not diminished, so let's go have an adventure. I see there are planets here?"

"You're sure?" she asked, reluctant to so easily accept his platitudes. Still, he looked okay.

"Absolutely."

Sounded okay, too. She decided to play along for now. "Well, good, because the exit closed behind us. Until another tear manifests, I don't have a ready way for us to get back home."

He tilted his head. "Like I said, adventure."

"Uh-huh. Um, yes, there are three planets. Only the second one is conducive to supporting a main spectrum species, though there's a faint technological signature coming from the third one. The second one, however, is singing so loudly that the signals are bouncing off the walls of this little pocket universe. I won't know specifics until we get closer, but I'd guess they're equivalent to twenty-second or early twenty-third century humanity. Which is strange."

"How so?"

"I'd thought perhaps this was the same species that disappeared from the region of space where the tears are occurring, but the details don't match up. Mesme said as of ten thousand years ago, they were as advanced as the Anadens in most respects."

"Maybe Mesme lied."

"*Priyazn....*"

He held his hands up in surrender. "Forget I said anything. Progress does not always advance in a straight line. What if whatever event cast them into this snow globe universe set them back technologically as well?

"I say we dial up the stealth meter, then investigate the second planet. Let's also turn on the spigots and start loading up the data banks with their transmissions, so the translators and Shrouds have something to work with. We should plan to check out the view from the ground. Since we're here and all."

4

A brilliant sunset glinted off the iridescent dome of a building down the avenue and transformed it into a dance of flames. The neighborhood basked in waves of warm apricot light, and for a moment everything shone. The semi-holographic floating sidewalks overhead glittered like gemstones. Pedestrians paused their travels to upturn their faces into the warmth, and a silent reverence swept across the landscape.

Then the angle of the sun shifted, the sunlight faded to a pleasant dusk, and normal activity resumed.

Caleb waited for Akeso to comment on the visual spectacle...but he sensed no murmur of notice in his mind. He forced himself to put away the pang of sorrow the absence evoked. Akeso was safe and healthy back home. It was merely that the fragment residing within him now consisted of little more than life-giving cells harboring minimal conscious awareness.

He was himself, and himself alone, in a way he hadn't been in almost two decades. The sensation was strange, to say the least. His inner monologue would have to be conducted solo, if it was to be with anyone. He told...yep, himself...this was fine; he'd always been quite comfortable with...himself. God, he was already insufferable!

So he forced his focus firmly away from his navel and toward his surroundings. He couldn't afford to devote much effort to psychoanalyzing the newly peculiar state of his psyche, anyway. He and Alex now walked the streets of a thoroughly alien world, and this required all his attention.

The Shrouds they wore—advanced prototype devices out of Concord Special Projects—presented them as Elakri in every physical detail, from the enormous eyes, minuscule ears and wide faces to the disproportionately long legs and pinched waists. They'd fabbed attire on the *Siyane* to match the style of clothing ordinary people here wore. A couple of hours of eavesdropping had resulted in a translation algorithm loaded into their eVis that enabled them to both speak and understand the native language.

All of which did relatively little to decrease the danger they found themselves in. They knew virtually nothing of these people's customs or ways of interacting, nor of their government system or social structure. The body language of a species often took months to learn to mimic, and they had only a scant few hours of surveillance footage. They possessed no currency, and they lacked the necessary information about these people to construct a convincing backstory.

Ah, well. It wasn't as if this was the first time he and Alex had leapt headlong into the middle of an alien world and just winged it. More like the…fifth? Though it might be the first time they'd done so disguised as one of the natives. The Shroud tech was going to open up a plethora of possibilities, both benign and nefarious. Regardless, the faster they picked up on the subtleties of social interactions that allowed them to pass as natives in casual contact, the better.

So he watched and learned.

The good news was, these aliens seemed to be a peaceable sort, displaying a high standard of living and a gentle enough demeanor. Looks could be deceiving, but at a minimum, the streets weren't overtly violent. He was heavily armed of course, but his weapons were collapsed and concealed within his attire, as were Alex's.

This architecture is extraordinary.

It is, he replied to her pulse. *They obviously take pride in their city.*

Other, less charitable descriptions included ostentatious, overdone, gaudy, and so on, but to invoke them would be judgmental on his part. Every building gave the impression of being a renowned art gallery, museum or cathedral, featuring spires swirling heavenward, gilded domes and bronzed archways. At street level, every façade was both pristinely clean and wildly ornate—nearly as much so as the clothes the Elakri wore.

Caleb forced himself not to pick at the filigree trimming his breast lapel. He hadn't worn anything this fancy since a primary dance back on Seneca when he was sixteen years old and madly in love with Loukia Floros. Well, except on his wedding day, but even that suit had been simply tailored, befitting the rustic setting and intimate ceremony.

His lips curled up as he eyed Alex beside him. She wore an outfit far more gaudy than anything he'd *ever* seen her deign to wear, wedding included. Glittering decorative buttons adorned a bright, high-collared blazer and filigree-ornamented flared pants swooshed around her feet when she walked. Their pre-landing survey of pedestrian traffic suggested the attire was rather modest by local standards.

Alex strode a touch awkwardly in the subtly disguised platform shoes; the Elakri were a tall species, and they'd each needed to add several centimeters to their height to reach even 'short' status. The outfit was so wildly out of character for her, he'd laughed aloud when he first saw her getup—then captured a few visuals using his ocular implant to send to family when they returned home. Which might earn him a night on the couch as punishment, but it would be worth it.

He looked equally ridiculous, but he'd spent years engaging in undercover work, so donning a disguise didn't bother him. Alex, though, was as perturbed as a pet dog in a sunflower costume. But because her desire to uncover the secrets of this snow globe universe was greater than her mortification at the outfit, she was enduring, for now.

"How are we supposed to find a museum or cultural center, when *every* building resembles a museum or cultural center?" Alex's voice was low, barely above a whisper, but she spoke the native tongue. It had a pleasant, lilting style to it, and almost reminded him of Italian, the language his mother's ancestors had spoken centuries ago.

"Or a church," he replied.

She shot him a squirrelly glance as they followed the gently curving sidewalk to the right. Up ahead, a series of bridges spanned a river, catching the last light of the day upon its waters. "Church?"

"Or something that serves the same purpose as a church."

"Okay, I give. How is a church going to tell us anything about why these people are living in a pocket universe?"

They passed a group of five Elakri talking with one another as they walked, and he observed their body language. If he were asked to describe it in a word, it would be 'performative.' Everything was exaggerated, as if they were novices acting in a vaudeville play. Their mannerisms matched their extravagant clothing as much as they did the baroque structures lining the immaculate avenue. This was a society which valued appearances.

"Origin myths," he answered quietly.

"But we already know their origin. The species Mesme told me about called themselves 'Elakri' as well, so my initial suspicion was correct. According to Mesme, they existed in normal space until around nine or ten thousand years ago and were an advanced, space-faring civilization. Then they vanished. Into here, it turns out—but they didn't originate here."

He didn't offer a snide retort to her mention of Mesme this time. He didn't trust the (at present) Kat to be truthful on any particular topic, but he did trust that Mesme kept the best interests of the inhabitants of Amaranthe in general—and of Alex in particular—at the forefront of all it did. Those motivations meant their aims coincided, for now. "True, but ten millennia is a long period. On such a time scale, history often becomes myth."

"Fair enough. So how are we going to find—"

He stopped and grasped her shoulders, shifting her attention toward a structure on the left, across the wide avenue. "There."

"A church?"

"Or something serving the same purpose."

On each side of a pearl-white walkway, matching orb-shaped sculptures featured wrought iron lattice frames with red-and-gold waves shooting out like tongues. Beyond the sculptures, the walkway sloped up to a dramatic arched entrance. The building was almost entirely transparent, save for elaborate gold ornamentation decorating the façade. Framing the building was an expansive lawn filled with colorful shrubs and enormous blooming flowers.

"That is the tackiest church I've ever seen."

Caleb chuckled under his breath. He wasn't going to lecture her about engaging a filter on her thoughts when they inevitably interacted with the locals. She knew the drill. But until she had to play a role, she would be herself and nothing but.

As the sky began to fade from dusk to night, bulbed lights gradually brightened to life, painting the streets in a diffuse, warm glow. He considered the possibility they had unwittingly begun their journey in an ultra-wealthy enclave, for thus far the city rivaled the finest Novoloume urban centers for pretentiousness, though it lacked the Novoloume's natural, understated elegance. Offhand, he couldn't think of a human city that compared.

Was this what became possible when one needn't worry about foreign threats? No monsters of the void rising up to destroy all that had been built? No rival colonies competing for resources and power? It all seemed far too perfect to be true. Perhaps across the continent, millions lived in squalor or slaved away in mines. Perhaps underground prisons were packed with vagrants and malcontents.

When they reached the next intersection, they fell into the flow of pedestrians crossing the street in the direction of the dramatic glass structure. He doubted the answers they sought would be printed on a pamphlet a greeter handed them upon entry, but it felt like a place to start—

Up ahead, on one of the bridges spanning the river, a man ran stumbling into the light of a floating globe. As he did, a white laser beam sliced a few centimeters above the man's shoulder, and he fell to his knees with a cry.

Ah, there it is. Normalcy restored. Caleb grabbed Alex by the hand and took off running toward the bridge.

5

L aurent shuffled along the riverwalk, hands stuffed in his jacket pockets and chin drooping toward his chest. All the fiery outrage at the ridiculous meeting with the KP priest had fled him after an hour or so of impotent raging, leaving behind a defeated, forlorn weight to settle upon his soul.

For the first time in many years, he was genuinely questioning his choice to follow his passion into this line of work. What did it matter where the solar wind 'went' when it arrived at The End? What did it matter why several fundamental laws of physics lost their coherence in the final few meters of space? They did, and this was its own fundamental law. Studying the phenomenon didn't change the reality. It didn't better society or improve anyone's personal happiness. Including his own.

He still hoped to take a ship out to the deep space monitors and confirm they were operating properly. Because if they were, the anomalies meant *something*, and that something represented a true problem, whether a pompous KP priest wanted to admit it or not.

A shudder rippled through him, for it wasn't the type of problem he'd signed up to get involved in when he'd become a scientist researching esoteric physics. But in spite of himself, a corner of his brain couldn't resist noodling over how one would *fix* a breakdown in the universe's integrity. He didn't know the answer, obviously, but that vainglorious corner dared to suggest he might be able to work out a couple of possibilities.

The resources required to attempt a repair of the manifold were gargantuan, but if their very existence was at stake, surely the government would make any investment necessary. Surely even the KP would. Wouldn't they? To admit a problem existed with the manifold was to introduce the possibility that the Guardian wasn't infallible, or they hadn't created a perfect universe for the Elakri to thrive in, and he full well recognized the organization's reluctance to do this.

But if it was true, it was true, doctrine be damned. For that matter, doctrine counseled that the Guardian endowed their children with the talent to overcome any obstacle. What if the anomalies represented a test the Guardian was placing in their path—a challenge through which they'd evolve to reach ever greater heights?

Caught up in his mental gymnastics, Laurent paid little heed to where he was walking, and the next thing he knew, he'd drifted into the Tafen Bridge railing, banging his shoulder against one of the posts. He winced, stopping to rub at his shoulder with the other hand and—

A white beam flared in his peripheral vision, so close his hair singed in its wake. What was that?

He glanced behind him and saw a man in a loose emerald field suit rushing toward him, an object of some kind braced over a forearm. An object with a narrow tube and a circular opening at the end. And a hand grip. And a—

Was he being *shot at?*

Panicked, he spun and tried to run away, but promptly stumbled over his feet to land on his hands and knees the same instant a second beam sailed over his head. Dumb luck had saved him twice now, but he doubted it would save him a third time.

His pulse screamed in his ears, or possibly he was screaming. But he possessed enough of a survival instinct to realize he couldn't stay frozen, not if he wanted to live.

The bridge railing was too high to vault over into the Praska Tributary, at least quickly. If he made it to the street on the other side of the bridge, there were people. His assailant wouldn't fire into a crowd, right?

Why was he being shot at?

He crab walked forward until he reached a crouch, then a stooped-over jog.

From the opposite direction of the shooter, a man with curly black hair wearing an out-of-style, overly long coral jacket sprinted toward him. Alongside him ran a woman whose long burgundy locks fell over a casual chartreuse blazer. Why was he noticing their lack of fashion sense, of all things? He'd never cared about fashion—

The man ran past Laurent without slowing, but the woman skidded to a stop directly in front of him just as the assailant fired another shot. It impacted the woman above the waist, and a charge sparked across her chest. No hole opened up in her blazer, and no blood gushed forth from any wound. It idly occurred to him then that he might have experienced a psychotic break following his soul-crushing meeting with the priest. Full well lost his grip on reality.

"You're not the bad guy in this scenario, are you?" The woman stared at him pointedly, still not gushing blood. Her phrasing was awkward, her accent strange.

He struggled to find his voice. "No. I have no idea what's happening."

"Okay." A small, aerodynamic device appeared in one of her hands, while the other hand reached out and grabbed his; she kept her body in front of him. "Let's get out of the line of fire."

"What about your companion?"

"He'll be fine."

Laurent began backing up, but his steps faltered as, over the woman's shoulder, the black-haired man slammed into the assailant in the emerald suit. From this far away, he couldn't make out the details of the struggle, but the stranger seemed to move in an unnatural blur of motion. A bright shimmer flared between them.

"Seriously, we need to make ourselves scarce," the woman said. Her grip on his hand tightened, and she began dragging him off the bridge and onto the riverwalk.

But he couldn't resist peering back one last time. It looked as if the struggle had intensified. Punches were thrown. A weapon fell onto the bridge—then the stranger was flipping the assailant over the railing and into the tributary below. Huh. Maybe he should have tried to vault over it....

"Come *on!*"

He relented, stumbling after the woman as they cut through curious onlookers beginning to gather. People shouted things in his direction, but the words didn't penetrate his stunned brain.

The woman didn't slow down once they were through the crowd. She veered onto the first side street, then again to the left, then once more to the right. He allowed her to lead him without complaint; it took all his concentration to keep his legs steady and his feet moving.

She came to a stop under the awning of a restaurant and turned to him. "We're going to go in here. Do whatever it is you do to get a table for three, and let's take a seat."

"Um, okay." He shook his head roughly, trying to clear the fog. *Someone had shot at him!*

The woman dropped his hand once they were inside, but she stayed close at his side as he tapped '3' in the box on the vertical panel near the entry. He noted the number it displayed and walked in a daze to a table along the left wall. She sat facing the door and gestured for him to sit opposite her.

Abruptly a lopsided smile broke across her face, and her comportment visibly relaxed. "Order us basic drinks—water if you all do that sort of thing."

"Plain water?"

"As plain as they offer."

He studied the menu, as he'd never been to this restaurant before, but he couldn't manage to bring any of the items into focus. He squinted until he recognized a list of refreshments, then ordered the first one on the list.

His mind was bouncing wildly among questions he should probably be asking when her companion appeared out of nowhere to slide into the seat beside her. The man produced a tiny black object from a pocket and set it on the table. "You veiled on the way here?"

The woman nodded.

"As did I. We should be safe for a few minutes."

"What's 'veiled'?" Laurent asked, noting in a detached way that the man continued to look pristine (if unfashionable). No blood, no sweat, no rumpled hair.

"You and I were invisible after we got through the initial crowd near the bridge," the woman replied.

"What? We can do that?"

"No idea."

The things she said were almost as strange as the way she said them. "What's this?" He pointed to the object sitting on the table.

"It subtly muffles our voices, so other people can't understand what we're saying."

"I can barely understand what you're saying. You speak strangely."

"We're working on it," the man replied, leveling a kind but intense gaze at him. "I'm Caleb, and this is Alex. What's your name?"

For a split second, he blanked on his name. The odds of him having experienced a psychotic break increased notably.

"I'm, ah…Laurent. Laurent Kovalne."

"It's nice to meet you, Laurent. Now, do you know why someone tried to kill you?"

"I have no idea."

"I suspect you actually do," this Caleb person said, "even if you don't realize it. But the 'why' can wait until you're out of immediate danger. Do you have someplace safe you can go?"

Laurent took a deep breath and let it out slowly. "You're going to say my apartment isn't safe, aren't you?"

"Are random assassination attempts on total strangers a common occurrence here?"

"What? Of course not!"

"Then we have to assume you were targeted, which means the assassin or the people directing him know who you are. No, your apartment isn't safe."

"How about my office?"

The man shook his head. "Sorry."

His heart took off racing again, pulse rushing past his ears in an encore performance. None of this made any sense. "I can rent a hotel suite."

"Do you have a way to pay for it that isn't tied to your identity?"

"You mean hard currency? No hotel would accept it as payment. Also, not on my person."

"So that's a no." Caleb paused as the server deposited limone spritzers at the table, waiting until it had left to continue. "Unfortunately, we don't have nearly enough information about your situation, so I'm hesitant to recommend you go to a friend or coworker's place."

"We could take him to the *Siyane*," the woman suggested.

"Let's not get carried away just yet," Caleb replied. "Is there any place in the city you can find shelter that doesn't register your identity?"

"I don't…." He trailed off as a possibility occurred to him. It had been years since he'd interacted with that world, and he wasn't certain if the club still existed. But if it did?

He took a long sip of the spritzer to soothe his sandpaper throat. "I know of a place. It'll have people who should be able to help." He lifted his shoulders, feeling emboldened by the refreshment. Someone had tried to kill him, but he'd survived! "I can get there on my own. I owe you my life, both of you, but I can't ask you to continue risking yours for me. You don't even know me."

Alex glanced sideways at Caleb. "He has a point."

They were silent for a long minute, gazing at each other. And while they were obviously a couple, Laurent had a feeling the silence wasn't about adoration. They were likely furiously messaging each other, debating the merits of continuing to help him.

He'd offered his heroic, stalwart declaration, but his bout of bravery fled almost as soon as it had arrived, and in truth he desperately hoped they'd decide in his favor. He was frightened and way out of his depth. For unknown reasons, these strangers didn't seem to be.

Finally, Alex rolled her eyes, and Caleb bestowed another kind smile upon him. "If you have an active hit out on you, you're not safe on the streets. You don't have a weapon, and I'm not going to give you mine or hers. Something tells me you're not a great shot, anyway. We'll get you to this place and into the hands of someone who can help you."

Laurent exhaled in relief. "Thank you. In return, when I can, I'll pay you in whatever manner you'd prefer. I'm not wealthy, in funds or culture—I'm just a lowly extraplanetary physicist—but I'll find a way to offer recompense—"

"You're a *what?*" Alex interrupted.

Caleb groaned. "*Now* you care."

"Damn straight I do."

"Fine, but save the physics questions for later. We've lingered here for too long already. I'll leave first to confirm the street is clear of threats. Alex, you follow with Laurent. Head left out of the entrance, and I'll join you on the next block."

"Got it." She reached up and touched Caleb's cheek. He placed a kiss on her wrist, then stood and casually exited the restaurant.

6

Deunan offered the prospective customer a curt shake of her head. "I don't do blackmail. Or I *do*, but only if it's interesting. Bribing your boss so you can get more culture credit without jumping through the required hoops is boring." She leaned back in the booth and shrugged. "Sorry."

The man looked crestfallen. "But my brother said this was the kind of thing truvas did. That you viewed such acts as a way to disrupt the system, even if in the smallest ways."

She'd be offended at this short, dowdy desk slave daring to lecture her on what truvas did and why, but he was such a pathetic mess of a man. What must it be like, to live such a miserable, cowed life?

She perched her elbows on the table. "And this is an admirable bit of low-level rebellion on your part. You keep this fighting spirit alive, you hear me? But the job is still boring. Listen, I'm going to send you to Saji. He's starting out in this business and needs to build up a reputation. He's got skills enough. He'll take care of you."

"Okay!" The man's dull complexion lit up in renewed hope. "How do I find him?"

"Wander over to booth #8. Order a drink and relax. Saji will stop by in a few minutes."

"Thank you, Miss...?"

"Just Deunan." She waved a hand dismissively. "Off you go."

"Yes. Thank you." He wiggled out of the booth and crossed the soundproofing field into the main thoroughfare, eyes darting around in search of his destination.

Deunan typed a message to Saji on her flexpad. Then she kicked her boots up onto the table, sipped on her drink and considered heading out into the night. She didn't need work at the moment, boring or otherwise. With a quick change of clothes, she could infiltrate an art exhibition and whisper scandals in the ears of the attendees, then tag them and watch the repercussions ripple through a culture niche for weeks. Don yet different attire and deface a Guardian shrine with gauche graffiti, then leave a dot cam to capture the appalled reactions from passersby.

"Ugh...." She groaned into her drink. It was time to admit it: She was in a rut. An ennui-laden funk. The Brenfield caper had cemented her reputation as the most audacious truva in a century, which meant everything to transpire since had been a letdown. Her friend Seralaen liked to say that a chance to touch the Guardian only came around once in life (because as soon as you did, you'd die in an inferno of primordial cosmic fire). She hadn't soared quite so high, but for a few brief days, it had almost felt as if she had.

And two years later, here she was, slouching in her booth at the Sacroneti Club, taking meaningless jobs for oroun or other hard currency and momentary rushes of adrenaline as the grim reality of existence reasserted itself. She hadn't changed the world in the slightest, because the world couldn't be changed.

She rattled the ice around in the depths of her glass. Finding it empty, she started to refill it, but decided she needed some fresh air first. She locked the booth and strode toward the front door. The crowd was light tonight, and the music filling the air to augment the soundproofing had grown maudlin.

A group of people was clustered around the entrance, where a man gestured animatedly at the shift guard.

The man looked as if he'd fallen out of a saylon tree into a sponge pit filled with sugar-dosed six-year-olds. His clothes were wrinkled and knocked askew on a lean frame; one decorative pin was missing and another dangled from the workmanlike fabric of his jacket for dear life; his mahogany hair, though cut scandalously short, pointed in so many directions that she had to wonder if he'd recently taken an electric shock. Still, his emerald-to-amber eyes radiated openness, as if he held nothing in reserve—a clear mistake on his part. He was almost attractive, in a 'rumpled professor' sort of way.

The two people who flanked him were…her senses tingled to life. In a manner she couldn't define, they were *wrong*. It wasn't that the man on the professor's left gave off a predator—or even killer—vibe, or that the woman on the professor's right was strung as tautly as sail ropes in a hurricane, both of which were true. It was more that…they wore their skin like it was a set of ill-fitting clothes.

Finally, something interesting to liven up her night.

She placed a hand on the guard's shoulder. "Is there a problem?"

"These people don't have a code for entry—"

"Please," the professor interrupted. "I used to know Tamse Renishon. Her personal code is 651C2."

"And I was about to explain to the gentleman how that wasn't good enough, because—"

"Because it's an old code, of course," she cut the guard off. "It's all right. I'll take them."

"Are you certain?"

"I am." She gave the motley crew a cool smile. "Come with me."

When they reached her booth, her three guests scooted onto the long bench opposite her. The killer took the outside, his eyes assessing the contents of the booth before sweeping across the club beyond it.

"No one can see inside the booth, or hear what we say."

He stared at her for a beat, but relaxed a fraction.

Deunan slid three glasses out from the valet and distributed them to her guests, then pulled one knee up onto the cushion beside her and dropped her chin on it. She considered them speculatively, each in turn, before settling her gaze on the professor. "How did you know Tamse?"

He sipped greedily on the drink for several seconds before answering. "We, ah, kept company for about eight months a few years ago."

"You. And Tamse."

"Yes. Is it so hard to imagine?"

Tamse always had been a bleeding heart, a true softie. "Not as much as it should be. Then it will pain you to learn that she's dead."

The man spewed his drink across the table, several droplets narrowly missing Deunan's cheek. "What? When? How?"

He truly hadn't known. Okay. "She took on the wrong client."

"One of her clients killed her?"

"No, but she got caught in the crossfire when the criminals he ran afoul of killed him."

"*Malede.* I'm…sorry…to hear it. She was a good person."

"Too good. So what's your name?"

"Laurent Kovalne."

"And you two?"

"Caleb and Alex Marano," the killer replied.

"You're bonded?"

The tightly wound woman nodded.

"Lovely. Well, Laurent and Caleb and Alex, I'm Deunan. What can a truva do for you tonight?"

"Someone tried to kill Laurent this evening," Caleb answered. "He needs somewhere safe to stay, somewhere unattached to his identity. He seems to think you, or this establishment, can help him find such a place."

And the surprises just kept coming. Maybe she'd misjudged Laurent, and he wasn't remotely the professorial type? She didn't think she had. One didn't become as skilled a truva as she was without learning to size strangers up with a glance and a passing word. "Why is someone trying to kill you?"

Laurent shook his head ponderously, eyes a touch wide. "I do not know."

"And you two? What's your role here?"

"They saved my life," Laurent replied.

"We happened to be in the area when Laurent was attacked," Caleb said. "We intervened."

"Do that often?" she asked.

Caleb shrugged with a forced mildness. "When assassination attempts happen to cross our path, yes."

Killers didn't typically go around rescuing hapless innocents, so what was the man's story? Was no one here what they appeared to be? " 'Assassination' is a word with a specific meaning."

"Yes, it is. And it fits what I witnessed."

"And the assassin? Is there a body and a police investigation to complicate matters?"

Caleb shook his head. "He wasn't dead when I sent him into the river. Given the lack of information I possessed at the time, I didn't feel justified in killing him on the spot."

So definitely a killer—she hadn't fallen too far off her game—but not an indiscriminate one. Deunan idly stirred her drink. Nothing about the story or the people in her booth made sense. But if she took things at face value (which she never did), Laurent Kovalne did arguably remain in danger. And people like him were utterly unequipped to survive in the world once the trappings of civilized society were stripped away from them.

"I don't take culture credit as payment. I'll need hard currency."

"I have some oroun," Laurent offered. "In my apartment."

All three of them stared at him.

"…Which I can't go back to. *Malede.* Can I owe you?"

She chuckled lightly and dropped her feet to the floor, readying to send them on their way. "No. Look, I feel for you, I do, but I've got to make a living."

"Laurent, how far away is your apartment?" Alex asked.

"Not far. Eight blocks or so. Why?"

"We'll go get your money."

"No. I won't have you risk your lives for me *again.* This is getting out of hand."

"I'm sure you'll be able to pay us back later," Alex insisted. "Tell us how to get there."

Laurent frowned at Alex, lips drawn tight, then relented. "The address is—"

"An address won't do us any good," Caleb interrupted. "Explain how to get there from here."

Now Deunan gaped at Caleb, incredulous. "You can't access the infolace map?"

"No, we cannot."

"Where are you from? Your accents are most unusual," Deunan challenged.

"Paesaan."

"I've been to Paesaan. You're not from there."

"Sure we are." Caleb shifted toward Laurent. "Directions?"

"Ah, head left out of the entrance for four blocks, then take a left at Crichton. Two blocks, then a right at Shole. After you pass Glaskeh, my building is on the right. Fifth floor, apartment #518. The door code is D88B3. The coins are in the top left drawer of the desk in the main room."

"Thank you." Caleb fixed his penetrating yet somehow not malevolent stare on her. "Deunan, is it all right if Laurent stays here with you while we retrieve his currency?"

She sighed dramatically. In truth, she didn't intend to let this crew slip away until she'd worked out the story behind their semblance, but she also didn't want to let on how intrigued she now was. "I suppose. But if you're not back in an hour, I'm kicking him out."

"Hey!" Laurent exclaimed.

Caleb nodded as he slid out of the booth. "We'll return long before then."

7

T hey emerged from the club into a pervasive twilight glow—not from a shining moon, but rather from the ubiquitous floating globes that permeated the air with soft, diffuse light.

Alex peered up as they adopted a brisk pace. "They're rejecting full dark, and I don't blame them. A night without stars would be a goddamn tragedy."

Caleb reached over and squeezed her hand. "You practically leapt over the table in your eagerness to help our new friend."

"He's an astrophysicist. We need him."

"Technically, he's an 'extraplanetary' physicist."

"That's what they would call it here," she replied. "There are no cosmic phenomena beyond their sun. No astronomy to study."

"You think Laurent knows what's causing the tears, or how to break down the barrier keeping this universe isolated?"

"Maybe. But even if he doesn't, he's still the best lead we could hope for, and we should take care not to lose him." She glanced over at Caleb, briefly taken aback by his Elakri disguise. They'd kept as close as possible to their normal appearances, but it was nonetheless jarring. His sapphire irises were now as large as the rarest of natural gemstones, contrasted with tiny ears pressed almost flat against his skull. His cheekbones stretched out wide above a harshly angular chin, and his skin was lightened from a faint iridescence that reminded her a bit of the Novoloume. "Why are *you* so eager to help him?"

They jogged across an intersection, as the clock was ticking, and took the next turn. "It feels like the right thing to do. He doesn't strike me as someone who deserves to be murdered."

"Oh, good point." She shrugged. "That, too."

The foot traffic thinned as they transitioned into a quieter residential neighborhood, but the persistent glow warding off the black did not diminish. "And the other one? Deunan?"

"Can't be trusted, but she can be bought." Caleb's steps slowed as they reached the mid-rise building on this block. "So let's buy her."

Inside, a small lobby was modestly adorned compared to most of what they'd seen, but it was immaculately clean. Rust-colored filigree with burnt orange accents decorated cheerful beige walls, and a sculpture crafted from a malleable material shifted through a series of poses off to the left.

Dual rectangular pads of glass were the only other items in the lobby. They stepped on the left one. A column of numbers in elaborate script animated one side, and Caleb pressed the script that represented '5' in the Elakri language.

A transparent field whisked them upward off the glass and into a tube painted in soothing pastel swirls. Their progress slowed to a stop almost as soon as it had begun, and an archway led to a wide, high-ceilinged hallway.

"Stay on guard," Caleb admonished her as a gamma blade materialized in his right hand. He refused to carry an adiamene blade, though not because it was illegal. He insisted the metal's eagerness to slice through the hardest atomic shell robbed the wielder of fine control. If he was going to kill someone, it would be because he meant to do so.

Out of instinct, Alex fondled the smooth material of her spiral bracelet with a fingertip. She'd wielded the conductivity lash it manifested in active combat maybe half a dozen times in two decades, but it remained only a directed thought away.

Beside the entry to Laurent's apartment, a small pad glowed in the same script lettering of the lift, and Caleb tapped in the code. The door slid open—

A white beam of light shot between them to sear into the opposite wall.

Caleb blocked Alex's body with his as she flattened herself against the wall. An Elakri barreled out of the entry, weapon raised.

The instant the man cleared the doorway, Caleb swept his blade around to slice into the assailant's upper arm, and another shot wobbled wide of the mark.

The next second, the assailant shoved Caleb into the wall—and her. But rather than engage in close-quarters combat, the man then took off running for the lift.

"Are you okay?" Caleb asked as he pivoted to face her, feeling over her neck and chest for injuries.

"I'm fine—go! I'll get the coins."

His eyes met hers for confirmation; on finding it, he spun and gave chase.

Fucking hell. She wanted to follow. Her combat skills didn't hold a candle to her husband's, but they didn't know what manner of weapons the Elakri had at their disposal. And it had been many years since Caleb had been a black ops agent.

But for better or worse, Akeso's gentle, pacifist soul wasn't whispering in his mind right now. She'd already sensed hints of a harder, honed edge in his behavior that reminded her of the Caleb she'd once known, before he'd gained a spiritual companion. She trusted that he could handle this.

She rubbed at her nose, which stung from the forceful impact of Caleb's shoulder blade, and hurried into the apartment.

CS

The fleeing Elakri glanced over his shoulder and, on seeing Caleb pursuing, pointed a handgun around his body and fired.

Caleb instinctively dodged to the right, grazing the wall as the fire sliced past him. The aim had been off, but the shot had likely been designed to delay him more than wound him—though he doubted the man cared if the latter occurred as well.

Instead, his muscular cybernetics kicked into gear and he sprinted at full speed to reach the lift just as the Elakri leapt into the tube. He crashed into the man's chest and sent him thudding against the lift wall. As he did, his mind registered the fact that this was the same person he'd battled on the bridge earlier in the evening.

Using the remaining advantage of his momentum, he slammed a forearm into the man's wrist, but failed to dislodge the handgun. A knee landed on his stomach, but without any room to maneuver in the lift tube, the impact lacked much force. Still, his suspicion on the bridge was all but confirmed: His sparring partner was a professional. The assailant had responded to violence not with panic or flailing, but deliberate, strategic violence of his own.

Caleb brought his blade up and stabbed the man below where ribs would be on a human. He met no resistance as the blade slid smoothly through clothing and deep into the skin, and he couldn't guess whether he'd caught any vital organs or whether the wound might eventually prove fatal.

He'd made the decision to kill the man without a blink of hesitation. In the absence of an empathetic protest by Akeso, the calculus was simple. On the bridge earlier, he wasn't certain that Laurent hadn't been the initial aggressor, so he'd taken reasonable steps to not end the assailant's life. Now, though? This man had used a deadly weapon to try to kill him—to try to kill Alex. The threat must be removed.

He twisted the blade, feeling his hand grow slick with blood, and the man grunted in raw pain. But abruptly Caleb was stumbling backward and out into the open air of the rooftop, shoved off his feet by the Elakri.

The man fired point blank at his chest, and his personal shield easily dissipated the energy. A look of surprise flashed across the man's face; instead of firing again, he tossed the gun aside. Caleb used the time the act took to leap to his feet.

The man charged.

Caleb timed the coming collision and, at the last second, twisted his torso and spun to deliver a roundhouse kick to the head—it bounced off the assailant's shoulder. Dammit, he hadn't adjusted for the Elakri's exaggerated height. He was out of practice.

No stars lit the night sky, and the roof lacked the omnipresent warm glow of the streets below. As such, he almost missed the glint of a metal blade as it darted for his neck. He feinted backward, and the blade skimmed a millimeter above his skin.

He instantly lowered his head and tackled the man, seeking to neutralize the height differential. They tumbled to the rooftop's surface, perilously close to the ledge. The man's fist connected with his chin, jolting his head back in a painful snap. The blade reappeared in his peripheral vision, and he threw all his weight onto the man's arm before it made contact. They rolled again, and suddenly Caleb's head and shoulders were suspended over the ledge.

Well, this escalated quickly. The Elakri had all the advantages now: height, leverage and a solid surface beneath him.

But Caleb had a bead on the weight distribution of the assailant's frame. He braced his feet on the rooftop as best he could, snapped his hips and kicked upward, flipping the man up and over his chest. He allowed their combined weight to continue in the direction of their momentum, even as it threatened to send him fully over the side…and let go of the grapple.

The man dropped.

Caleb grabbed hold of the lip of the roof and scrambled to safety. He breathed in, then out, and crawled several meters away from the ledge before standing, lest anyone be looking up at that moment.

Adrenaline burned like fire through his veins. Time had slowed to a crawl when the man had burst out of Laurent's apartment, and it hung suspended in the air around him now. It felt as if hours had passed, when the entire encounter had lasted two minutes at most.

He'd never attempted to draw his Daemon, though not because he hadn't intended to kill. There had been a beat in the hallway when he'd considered it, but reaching the lift was more important, and he didn't want to risk the movement slowing him down. Once they'd emerged onto the roof, the Elakri had kept close, which was fine. He'd always enjoyed the rush of hand-to-hand combat.

His assailant had never drawn blood, but Caleb's life had nonetheless been in genuine danger at several points during the altercation. He wondered…did enough of Akeso remain in his blood to heal him if he were grievously wounded? If his skull had split open upon the sidewalk below? Or was this like the eighteen years he'd served as an intelligence agent, when his life was constantly in peril and there were no primordial life forms lurking around to patch him up and grant him virtual immortality?

He'd never hesitated back then. Perhaps he ought to think about whether he should now.

But what he felt right now was *alive*. He'd worn the mantle of violence as a second skin. Disconcerting? A little; if he wanted, he could tease out a thread of regret from his conscience. Without Akeso—peaceful, beautiful, wise Akeso—murmuring in his head, was he just a killer?

No, not just. Never just. But for his life, for Alex's life? Absolutely he was.

The sounds of a growing commotion on the street below snapped him back into the present. A dead body was going to draw all sorts of attention they didn't need.

He retreated from the ledge and departed the roof.

Veil and meet me at the lift.

CS

Laurent's apartment was probably spartan, as there wasn't much in the way of decor or furniture: two overstuffed lounge chairs, a side table, two bar stools at a kitchen counter, and a large L-shaped desk taking up the entirety of what looked to be a dining nook.

It was difficult to say for certain, however, because most of said furniture had been upended and kicked about. An overturned drink glass had spilt a pale green liquid on the wood floor. A long gray coat lay crumpled on the floor, and a pair of loafers peeked out from beneath one of the flipped-over chairs.

Alex ignored the mess to head straight for the desk. Crystalline cubes were strewn across the surface and floor, and two screen pads teetered half off the left edge. A knocked-over thermos leaked a bright yellow liquid onto the desktop. Three permanent wall screens were affixed above the desk, one of which displayed a series of complex equations.

In spite of herself—she needed to hurry—Alex found she was scanning the equations. Their translation program didn't include the Elakri version of scientific notation, so she didn't follow everything, but….

She reminded herself not to jump to conclusions. Besides, no way could they have gotten *this* lucky.

She forced herself to ignore several other physics-related accoutrements on the desk and opened the top left drawer.

It was empty.

"Dammit, Laurent!"

She checked for a false floor or back, in case the coins were especially valuable or contraband, but found nothing. None of the drawers were hanging open, so she didn't think the intruder had stolen them; perhaps they'd interrupted the man before he'd had a chance to finish searching the desk.

She opened the two lower drawers. One held a moving visual of a smiling Elakri woman with white hair and sparkling citron-and-gold eyes. A sister? The deceased ex-girlfriend? The bottom drawer was stuffed with more of the screen pads, and she dumped them out on the desk until she was satisfied no coins hid beneath them.

She shifted to the other side and rifled through the remaining drawers as quickly as possible. She didn't dare message Caleb and risk distracting him at a critical second, but she worried. Akeso's diminishment likely made it easier for him to lean into the violence, but it was also throwing him for a bit of a loop, whether he admitted it or not.

Her hand slipped past something cool in the bottom right drawer. Metal. She hurriedly removed a bunch of small trinkets from the drawer and tossed them on top of the pads until she spotted a pewter disk. She picked it up.

It was unexpectedly heavy for its size. Intricate white-silver ridged etchings decorated both sides of the coin, all the way out to a scalloped edge.

Physical currency seemed at odds with the Elakri's overall level of technological development, but...she rolled her eyes. The coin was art, same as the buildings and the attire.

She retrieved another dozen coins from the drawer and dropped them in an inside pocket of her ridiculous blazer—

Veil and meet me at the lift.

The worry seizing her chest eased. He sounded tense, with an urgent undercurrent to his words, but not in distress. Whatever had transpired, he'd won.

Found the coins. On the way.

She didn't clean up after herself—his words told her there wasn't time—before activating the Veil and sprinting out the door and down the hallway.

I'm here.

So am I. Get on the lift.

Done.

The field swept them downward to the lobby. His hand brushed across hers, then grasped it firmly.

We need to stay veiled until we reach the club. Just in case.

She didn't press him for details, but she was now guessing the intruder was dead.

This assumption was all but confirmed when they encountered a large crowd of people gathering to the left of the building's entrance.

Caleb turned right. It was hardly the first time he'd led her on a meandering route while they were both invisible, so she followed his lead as they gave the crowd a wide berth before retracing their steps and returning to the club.

They caught the door to the club opening to allow someone to leave and slipped inside, then skirted around the security guard and made their way down the long center aisle to Deunan's booth. The contents—table, occupants, handy drink bar—were shrouded by a milky curtain projection.

Caleb deactivated his Veil, and Alex followed suit.

"We're back," Caleb announced.

The curtain projection dissolved. Laurent sat where they'd left him, tapping his long fingers on the table in an erratic rhythm, while Deunan lounged against the rear of the booth, sipping on her drink and looking bored. She waved them in half-heartedly. "Ten more minutes, and I was booting him. If I didn't fall asleep first."

"Excuse me!" Laurent exclaimed. "You told me to stop talking, so I did."

"And thank the Guardian for that. Did you find his supposed currency?"

They slid into the booth next to Laurent. Alex retrieved the coins from her pocket and offered them to Laurent under the table, as he might not want Deunan to know how many he possessed.

"Thank you." He gazed across the booth at Deunan, chin held high. "How much to arrange me a safe place to stay for…I guess a few days?"

"Three hundred oroun."

"That's unconscionable!"

"Pay it," Caleb offered. "The man from the bridge was at your apartment when we arrived."

"What? What happened?"

"A lot, but the end result is, there's now a dead body on the street outside your building."

"What?" Laurent seemed to have gotten stuck in a loop of disbelief.

Caleb shrugged. "It was him or me. He was not there to talk. Also, he was a professional."

"Professional what?" Laurent asked weakly.

"Law enforcement. Military. Intelligence. Or more likely the criminal equivalent of one of those."

Deunan sat up straight, posture stiffening. "I hope you weren't followed back here."

"Do you have extensive public surveillance on the city streets?" Caleb asked. "Police monitoring of ordinary pedestrian movements?"

"No. Crime is fairly low in the city. But you still could have been followed."

"We weren't."

"How can you be sure?"

"They can be invisible," Laurent mumbled distractedly.

"They can be what?"

"Invisible. I don't know…what did you call it? 'Veiled'?"

Deunan's eyes widened, and for the first time, her aloof demeanor faltered. "Who *are* you people?"

"Simply bystanders in a position to help," Caleb answered. "The important thing right now is to get Laurent someplace safe—somewhere with a bed and a kitchen and a shower, where he can take a breath."

Good dodge.

She won't be put off forever, but we'll worry about it later.

"Do I really need a place to hide now, though?" Laurent asked. "You killed the man who was trying to kill me."

"He wasn't who's trying to kill you," Caleb said. "He was merely the instrument. If eliminating you is important to them, whoever's behind him will send someone else."

"I should have asked for more money…." Deunan groaned. "I'll do it, but it will take some time to arrange for somewhere as clean as it appears poor Laurent here requires. Until then, there's only one location I'm certain is safe enough. Let's go to my place."

8

Arien Colonnei nudged his way through the crowd of onlookers lining the sidewalk until he reached the field barrier erected around the crime scene—or rather, the first crime scene. He broadcast his ident, and the barrier allowed him to pass through.

An opaque shield blocked the body from public view, though congealing sprays of blood leaked out past the shield to stain the sidewalk and titillate the spectators. His eyes flicked up to the roof overhead. A ten-story fall would not create a tidy aftermath.

The scene that greeted him behind the shield confirmed his observation, sending his stomach churning in protest. Some years had passed since he'd last viewed such a grisly death in person, and the defenses against such horrors he'd erected as a frontline officer had long since atrophied.

"Director Colonnei, it's an honor to have you here."

Arien turned toward the speaker, a young man wearing the insignia of Ventise police investigations. "You're the investigator who caught the case?"

"Yes, sir. Agent Endreje Perrina, detective third grade. When I heard you were on your way, I instructed forensics to hold the body here."

"Thank you. I don't claim to be able to offer any insights above and beyond those of the forensics team. I simply want to get a feel for the scene." His gaze returned to the roof. "Witnesses say he was pushed?"

"They say another man was spotted at the edge of the roof with him, and the two were scuffling. It's not clear whether the other individual actively pushed the victim, or whether he lost his balance during the altercation and fell."

Arien nodded thoughtfully. He appreciated the man's insistence on accuracy; details mattered. "Anything else of note from the initial review of the scene?"

"Ah, yes, sir. The forensics officer who examined the body says there's a wound on one arm and a more significant one on the torso that were unlikely to have been caused by the fall. They could be stab wounds, but we'll have to wait for the autopsy results to confirm."

"Okay. You can release the body. I'm not planning on riding your investigation, Agent Perrina. You should proceed as you see fit—but do copy me on your reports."

"Yes, sir. Thank you, sir. I'm happy to do so." Perrina went over to the forensics team members who'd been waiting off to the side to start the process of clearing the body.

Officers began dispersing the crowd from the sidewalk, and Arien took in the particulars of the scene a final time. But not much stood to be learned here; the body on the sidewalk was the result of a sequence of events that ended here. The search for answers would begin upstairs.

He headed toward the entrance—

"Director Colonnei!"

He started to ignore the shout, assuming it originated from a member of the press…but the voice sounded vaguely familiar, so he glanced toward it.

A Khesa Prutet priest stood at the field barrier near the entrance to the apartment building. Over the standard black-and-gold priest's uniform, the man wore a flame-patterned shawl, marking him as a leader of the organization's upper echelon. Arien's autonetics served up a name to go with the face: Insaf Devran, science and technology chair for the Khesa Prutet. They both enjoyed seats on the Khesa Prutet's Board of Advisors, though he couldn't recall ever having spoken to the man outside of meetings.

Arien adopted a friendly but professional mien and walked over to greet the priest. "Chair Devran, this is a surprise."

"I can say the same. What brings the director of the Ventise

Bureau of Investigation out to a crime scene?"

"It's not every day that one of my agents gets thrown off a building."

Insaf gasped in horror, his eyes darting to the gurney being guided toward the forensics vehicle, then to the roof high above. "Oh, dear. How horrible. One of your agents, you say? He was murdered?"

"Yes to the first. I don't want to jump to conclusions as to the second."

"I imagine no investigator would. Regardless, most tragic."

"Indeed." Arien forced himself not to cut the conversation rudely short. His evening schedule hadn't included a visit to the crime scene, and he was already running late for a dinner appointment. "Are you just happening by?"

"Me? No, I intended to visit one of the residents of the building here, a Laurent Kovalne."

Arien's gaze sharpened, all thoughts of his overdue appointment discarded. Ground zero of the crime scene waiting for him inside was Kovalne's apartment. Many years ago, his mentor in the bureau had taught him that while coincidences did on occasion manifest, they should never, ever be trusted.

"Can I ask what business the Khesa Prutet has with Mr. Kovalne?"

"I met with him this morning about a mission request he filed with the Department of Extraplanetary Affairs. I was in the neighborhood, so I decided to come by and deliver the bad news in person that his request was denied."

"When was the last time you spoke to him?" Arien asked.

"The meeting we had this morning. Why? Has something happened to him as well?"

He chose his words carefully. Insaf was a colleague and a man of some good reputation, but this was a murder investigation, one of his agents the victim. "I'm sorry, but I'm not at liberty to say. Listen, an agent might be in touch with some questions about your interactions with Mr. Kovalne."

"There's something you're not telling me…which is under-standable, under the circumstances. Very well, I'll expect a comm."

"Thank you. Now if you'll excuse me, I need to get inside." He motioned a farewell and hurried through the doors before anyone else waylaid him.

The entire fifth floor was a second crime scene, starting at Kovalne's apartment, then trailing down the hallway to the lift and spilling out onto the roof. Scorch marks streaked jagged lines across the walls between the apartment and the lift. A spatter of blood decorated the wall past the apartment door, and additional drops had fallen every few meters in the hallway. Based on their elongation, whoever was bleeding had been running toward the lift. The trail told the story of a violent altercation leading from Kovalne's apartment up to the roof, before concluding on the sidewalk below.

The forensics people could handle the physical evidence. Arien wanted to see the apartment.

Techs cleared the way ahead of him like parting waters, and he gestured for them to stand down. "Please don't mind me. Continue your work. I merely want to have a look around."

Flustered nods followed. One by one, everyone hesitantly resumed their activities.

The apartment had been upended from one end to the other. Furniture, clothes, chrystors and flexpads littered the floor, and all the drawers at the desk that dominated the far end of the main room hung open.

Arien went up to one of the techs he'd just dismissed. "Excuse me. Has there been any blood discovered in the apartment?"

"Ah, no, Director. In the hallway, on the lift pad and up on the roof, but not in here."

"Thank you."

This suggested, though it didn't prove, that the mess here wasn't a result of the physical alteration that concluded on the roof. He took in the scene again. He'd viewed many such scenes over the years, and his instincts told him the state of the room was caused by a single individual searching its contents, not a violent tussle between multiple parties. For one, no one knocked drawers open while exchanging punches. And the remaining disarray, though extensive, felt...calculated.

But then who ransacked the apartment? It made zero sense for the answer to be his agent. Far more likely it was the person who'd been spotted on the roof with him. But Laurent Kovalne wouldn't have ransacked his own apartment, which cast some small doubt on the easy assumption that the man on the roof was Kovalne. Unless Kovalne had staged the scene, in which event this was not going to be an ordinary case.

Of course, murder was never ordinary. Under Arien's stewardship, violent crime in the Ventise region had fallen to its lowest level in almost a century. The Guardian took every wrongful death as a personal affront, and so did he.

Nothing here gave a clue as to what his agent, Seizon Pietri, had been doing in the building in the first place. But this answer, at least, would be found in the agent's active cases.

Arien had pulled the file for Laurent Kovalne on his way over, but it was rail-thin. Handsome enough man, but slight of build—from outward appearances, not the type of person who was capable of overpowering a trained Bureau of Investigation agent. The man worked in an obscure field of physics. He was an intellectual, a science-phile, possibly a *strana*, with meager culture credit to his name. A quiet man who had made no notable contributions to society, but also committed no obvious sins.

Did this make Kovalne the rebellious sort? A bitter loner? Arien didn't have to wonder, because Agent Perrina would learn the answers to those questions in the coming days. Arien buried the stirrings of excitement over a puzzle demanding to be solved, for he was not the investigator here. As head of the department, his sole role was to ensure said investigation was conducted thoroughly and to the highest standards, such that his agent's killer was brought to justice before the law and the Guardian.

An alarm rang in his interface. He was now running too far behind schedule to ignore it. He frowned at the apartment, disturbed by the way nothing fit neatly together, and departed.

9

Deunan grabbed a hat and flowing coat out of the club's communal wardrobe for Laurent to wear. This was far from the first time someone who stumbled into the club panicked and disoriented belatedly realized they needed to disguise their appearance, and the staff kept a few items on hand for such occasions. Then she signed out of availability and led the odd crew she'd collected outside.

A scolding voice in her head demanded to know why she was taking three complete strangers to her home. The potential danger didn't bother her as such, but she did work hard to keep her personal sphere firmly walled off from her professional work.

But she also prided herself on being the best truva not merely in the city, but on the planet and thus in the universe. This poor sap of a scientist was in genuine mortal danger, and stashing him in a hotel under a hastily cobbled-together fake ident wasn't going to get the job he was hiring her for done. She'd need time to professionally construct a true new ident record and historical trail for him, and until she was able to do so, her home was the one place she knew for certain was safe.

And the other two? They were inscrutably enigmatic—supremely competent in most ways, yet oddly incapable of basic tasks in others. And *pazi*, but this made them interesting. They were also dangerous, sure, but apparently not to Laurent. So long as she was aiding Laurent, therefore, not to her, either.

They spread out a little on the sidewalk so as not to draw attention to themselves. Caleb stayed at Laurent's side at the rear, while Alex bridged the gap to Deunan.

The precaution proved not to be necessary, and the trip passed without incident. They regrouped at the lift in her building, then rode it up to the thirty-fourth floor. Only four residences were accessible from the landing, and she led them to her door on the far left.

She held a hand over the panel and sent impulses to each key in her code—a secondary security measure. When the door slid open, she stepped inside and waved to the right. "Guest room is down the hallway, second door—oh." She turned to Alex. "I assume you two have a place to sleep?"

"We do. But we'd like to stay for a few minutes and talk to Laurent. See if we can figure out what's going on."

"Suit yourself. I'll fix us some drinks." Deunan made to go into the kitchen, but Laurent was blocking her path, standing in the entryway gaping at the expansive open space that comprised most of her home.

Windows spanned the left wall all the way up to the drastically elevated ceiling. Their one-way tinting provided an unvarnished view of downtown, with the towering spires of the Evanstadin Museum framed by the center window. Hand-woven rugs covered most of the floor, allowing the descanti marble to peek through here and there in the gaps, and personally curated art decorated the brick wall opposite the windows.

She nudged Laurent in the back. "Excuse me."

"How are you living here?" he asked incredulously. "No way do you have this much culture credit. Or any, for that matter."

She laughed as she elbowed him to the side and ordered up four lavender waters from the panel. "Oh, I have heaps of culture credit."

"*How?*"

"I broke into the Ventise Regional Bank and awarded myself what I felt was a fair amount of compensation for my contributions to society."

"You cheated."

"It's not cheating if the system is *dannati malede*. Besides, what's the point of being a truva if I can't enjoy a few perks of the job?"

"Tamse often said the same thing…" Laurent's expression darkened in escalating disapproval "…but she never had a residence as nice as this one."

A pang of sympathy echoed annoyingly in Deunan's chest. "Tamse was just starting out. She would've gotten here."

"I'd like to think so."

Deunan grabbed the glasses and set them on the counter. "It sounds as if you cared about her. Why'd you split?"

"All this? The truva lifestyle? The thrills and dangers that accompany it? It wasn't my world. And my world wasn't hers."

This, she believed.

Alex and Caleb took two of the glasses and sat together on the long sofa perpendicular to the windows. Deunan collapsed sideways in her favorite chair and dropped her head against the plush cushion, leaving the other chair for Laurent.

Before she could demand answers of her own, Caleb dove in with the questions. "Laurent, earlier you said you had no idea why someone was trying to kill you. So tell me what's been different about your life recently. Have you met any new people? Before us, I mean. Experienced any strange interactions? Has anything unusual happened at work?"

Laurent leaned forward and draped his forearms on his knees; though he was obviously stressed, he was frankly holding up better than Deunan had expected. "My life is dull. I don't have a lot of friends or engage in many social activities. I'm well-enough regarded at work, I think, but like me, my coworkers keep to themselves. We're a cerebral lot."

"Because you're a physicist," Alex prompted.

"Yes. An obscure and uninteresting profession, I know. My focus is on the interactions of fundamental particles in the far reaches of the universe. See, the concentration of matter begins thinning out rapidly a few hundred meters from the cosmic edge, without an obvious mechanism to cause the—"

"Oh, I understand what you mean," Alex cut him off.

"You do? What's your background in the area?"

Caleb laid a hand on Alex's knee; the motion was subtle, but Deunan noted it. "Let's focus on what might have put you in danger for now. What about your personal life? Could trouble in your family have triggered something?"

"Triggered a hit on my life, you mean? I hardly think so. My parents live in Haman. They own a restaurant and live an ordinary existence."

"Girlfriend?"

"No. I've never found anyone who can tolerate hearing about fermions and bosons for more than a few months. And no one at all lately."

Deunan listened to Laurent's responses with half an ear while she directed most of her attention to watching Caleb. His interrogation was gentle, but a simmering intensity thrummed beneath it. He wasn't law enforcement—if he was, he'd have taken Laurent into protective custody instead of hiring a truva—but he was definitely *something*. Curious.

"Okay." Caleb nodded thoughtfully. "Let's return to your work. Have you been studying anything interesting?"

"Yes!" Laurent's entire demeanor brightened...then instantly dimmed. "But this is...well, I don't want to concern you all unnecessarily."

"I'm sure you won't."

"Oh, but I might."

Caleb tilted his head. "We'll take the risk."

Laurent glanced at Deunan, and she shrugged mildly. It was adorable that he believed anything involving subatomic physics could be worthy of her concern.

"All right. A month ago, I detected an anomaly in one sector of deep space, as one approaches the cosmic edge. A band of...more of a streak, honestly, of intense radiation with no obvious source. It lasted for several minutes before dissipating. Then yesterday...it feels as if it were weeks ago, so much has happened since then. Yesterday, the phenomenon flared for the third time. Only this time, the anomaly expanded a thousandfold in size. So I escalated the matter to my boss.

"See, I'm concerned. What if the universe is...decaying somehow? What if I've picked up the first signs of the end of the world?"

The conclusion was absurd on its face, so Deunan wasn't

inclined to give it any credence. Alex, though? The woman's hands were fidgeting like mad in her lap, and she chewed viciously on her lower lip. But she didn't act frightened. Rather, she acted excited. Yet again, it wasn't the response one would expect. Nothing about these two added up.

Caleb renewed his calming hand on Alex's knee. "What did your boss say about your theory?"

"He read my report, but we haven't had an opportunity to talk in person. He took it seriously enough to get me a meeting with a Department of Extraplanetary Affairs official, a Mr. Khaleen."

"And have you had that meeting yet?"

"Yes, and no. It was yesterday…or possibly two days ago now. What time is it? It doesn't matter. But it was pointless. When I arrived at Khaleen's office, a KP priest was waiting for me instead."

Now Deunan's nerves did light fire, and she dropped both feet to the floor to learn forward in interest. "Why is the KP nosing in on obscure physics experimentation?"

"I asked the priest the same question," Laurent replied. "He gave me a speech about us sharing an appreciation of science. He said Mr. Khaleen was unavailable, and insisted on hearing my report. When I finished relaying it, he agreed to pass on my request for a mission to visit the deep space monitoring equipment and inspect it for any malfunctions, before showing me the door."

Deunan snorted. "There's your answer."

She felt her blood pressure elevating, a physical manifestation of the visceral reaction a simple mention of the KP evoked. Flip over a random rock, and you were as apt to find KP malfeasance lurking beneath it as a worm or scurrying ants. Its priests and the chairs who guided them hid behind their robes and temples and endless coffers of influence, layering an impenetrable veneer of spiritual authority atop a soulless, rotting corruption that knew no bounds, so far as she'd found.

Part of her wanted to stand up, shove her guests out the door and wash her hands of this whole affair, because she'd spent the last twenty years taking great care to ensure she and the KP never crossed paths. But another part of her—the part that usually got her into trouble—salivated at the notion of tossing a wrench into KP misdeeds. Also, if the KP was involved, then Laurent was in even more danger than she'd believed. Without her help, he'd never survive. Decisions, decisions….

Laurent gaped at her in confusion. "What do you mean? What's my answer?"

"Sorry, Laurent, darling, but the KP is trying to kill you, which means you are in deep *malede*."

"Don't be absurd. Why in the world would the KP want to kill me? Why would anyone want to kill me, for that matter, but especially the KP?"

"To silence you, of course."

He frowned, uncertainty shadowing his eyes. "I admit that if my theory is correct, and there is a problem with the integrity of deep space, the revelation could cause some uncomfortable discussions regarding the Guardian's plan for us. But I'm just the messenger. The science will be what the science is. And anyway, in the exceedingly dubious event that someone wants this kept quiet, it'll be the government, not the KP. Doctrinal issues notwithstanding, the far greater concern is public panic and unrest."

"On the contrary. Do you really not see?"

"I guess I don't."

Deunan stood and wandered over to the windows, where far below, the city gleamed in the artificial twilight of a sea of radiant globes, towering edifices fading into blackness where the light failed to reach. "If our universe is decaying, this means it's not the embodiment of absolute perfection. And if the universe is not perfect, then neither is the Guardian. And above all other considerations, the KP cannot allow anyone to begin to suspect that the Guardian is not perfect."

10

lex exhaled quietly as the door to Deunan's home closed behind them. The strain of pretending to be something she was not—Elakri, not to mention someone who'd lived her entire life on this planet when she knew fuck-all about it, such as what the KP was and why they worshipped something called a 'Guardian'—had worn her out. She'd been performing for hours upon hours, and she felt nearly as worn out as Laurent.

Their discussion of this mysterious KP and why the organization—church? shadow government?—would or wouldn't want to kill Laurent had barely started when the poor man had crashed hard, his eyelids drooping as he sank deep into the chaise cushions. He'd had a hell of a day.

So they'd ushered him off to the guest room, and Caleb had offered their excuses for making a polite departure. She suspected Caleb knew she wasn't up to fending off pointed questions from Deunan, questions they didn't dare answer. Not tonight.

They took the lift down to the lobby and exited onto the street. It was rather late now, but warm lighting cast a soft glow upon the air; were the Elakri truly afraid of the black void sky, or did they simply not want to be bothered by it?

Caleb guided them into the first alley they came across, where they retreated deep into the shadows cast by the buildings framing it. She used the tiny Caeles Prism on her bracelet to open a wormhole back to the *Siyane* and left the city behind.

"Ugh…." Alex collapsed on the couch in the main cabin, one leg dangling off, her shoe lazily grazing the floor. "How did you manage undercover work for so many years? That was exhausting!"

"Still comes fairly naturally to me. I guess some skills don't atrophy from disuse." He crouched beside her and brought a hand to her face. "Deactivate the Shroud."

"Oh, right. I forgot." She sent a command to the device.

"Hmm." His lips curled up in pleasure. "Much better."

"You as well. I mean, the Elakri aren't unattractive as such. I suspect they'd pass Marlee's 'bounds of reasonableness' test with flying colors, for instance. But it's beyond strange seeing *you* as one. Like viewing you through a funhouse mirror."

"Marlee's what?"

Oops…. She plastered on a blasé expression. Caleb had come a long way in accepting that his niece was now a grown woman with a full breadth of life experiences, including a healthy sex life, but this didn't mean he liked being *reminded* of it. "Oh, just a theory she has of how close to human an alien species needs to appear before we consider them…pleasing in appearance."

"Uh-huh."

She smiled breezily and kissed him, then sat up. "I'm going to take a shower, try to wash the Elakri off."

He didn't push the matter any further, because he *had* come a long way. "I'll check the surveillance logs to make sure no one wandered too close to the ship while we were gone, then get clean after you. Do you want something to eat?"

They'd hidden the cloaked ship in a meadow many kilometers outside the bustle of the city, since the ability to travel via wormhole meant they didn't need to hike to and from it. Finding an unobserved location to deploy a wormhole required a little effort, such as the alley tonight, but it was safer than parking the ship too close to civilization, where someone might literally bump into it.

"It's a bit late. Maybe just some cheese toast?" She removed her hidden weapons from the pockets of her ridiculous outfit and placed them on the shelf in front of the storage cabinet, then immediately started discarding said outfit as she headed downstairs and straight into the shower.

CS

Alex snuggled against Caleb's chest, fingers idly playing with the hair trailing down his abdomen. His skin was still warm from the shower, or from the spectacular sex. Presumably both. Because after getting clean, she'd found she wasn't quite so tired after all. They hadn't gotten around to eating the cheese toast, and she couldn't summon up the desire to leave his arms and go upstairs to retrieve it now.

"So. That wasn't how I expected our first day on Elakrin to go."

"Me either," Caleb replied. "We learned a lot, though."

"We did? I'm overwhelmed by how much I don't understand."

"Absolutely. We learned the local church is called the Khesa Prutet, or 'KP' to those who look upon it with disdain, and it might have turned evil—or possibly has always been evil. Also, their local deity goes by the name of 'Guardian.' We learned they don't know they're living in a pocket universe. They think this is everything that exists, which means they've forgotten whatever happened in the past to get them stuck here.

"Despite their ignorance about the larger universe, they comprehend subatomic physics. Maybe quantum physics as well, though they don't seem to utilize widespread artificial intelligence. Oh, and they are excessively focused on stylistic matters: art, architecture, music, fashion, appearances. Their society and at least a portion of their economy runs on what they call 'culture credit,' which I suspect is a measure of how much a person contributes to the overall beauty, sophistication or general wellbeing of their world."

"Granted, we did learn those things," she conceded. "We also learned that the dimensional tears are visible from this side as well—and they have no idea what's causing them. Don't actually realize they're tears in the manifold at all, merely 'anomalies.'"

"True, but we picked up possibly the one person on the planet who can help us figure out the cause."

"Damn fine luck on our part, that." She tilted her head up and kissed him along the jaw. It was scrupulously clean-shaven to help the Shroud in its transformative work, as they'd yet to see a single

Elakri with facial hair, and the smooth skin felt odd beneath her lips. "I caught a glimpse of Laurent's data on the tears when I was in his apartment. He doesn't know what he has, but he is hot on the trail. So now we need to encourage his research without revealing why. While also keeping him alive."

"That's the plan, for as long as we can manage it. We told Deunan we'd stop back by in the morning, but we'll need to be careful. The transition from protecting Laurent from assassins to partnering with him on a physics mystery will be a tricky one."

"Will it, though? What if Deunan's correct, and this KP is trying to kill him because he discovered the manifold tears? In that case, the goals are and will continue to be intertwined."

He smiled, twirling a damp strand of her hair around a finger, then using it as leverage to draw her closer for another kiss. "I adore the way your mind works. Excellent point, but we'll need to tactfully guide them to reaching the same conclusion on their own. We came within one wrong remark of exposing ourselves tonight."

"And Deunan is suspicious—of everything, I expect. She reminds me a lot of Claire Zabroi. Which is to say, I don't especially like her, but I do get her." Claire was a hacker and gray market dealer she'd known during university, and they'd crossed paths again during the OTS conflict. Claire was a Prevo as well, and spending her time elbow deep in god only knew what manner of schemes these days.

"Deunan's definitely got a story, though we might not get a chance to learn it," Caleb replied. "Our focus needs to remain on Laurent. So, tomorrow. I'd like to learn more about the Khesa Prutet before we return to Deunan's place, as that's where we're most apt to be vulnerable. We also need to work out their communication system, if we're going to continue to interact with the two of them."

"Let me set a filter running on the feeds the ship is pulling in. It'll flag anything mentioning the 'Khesa Prutet' or 'KP' and analyze it while we sleep." She closed her eyes and linked into the ship's analytical ware, a complex array of sub-Artificial algorithms adapted from Valkyrie's ever-evolving programming. It resembled inhabiting the circuitry of the ship herself, thankfully while also retaining the use of her living body and mind this time.

But she could visit whenever she wanted to now, so she didn't linger. "As for their comms, I need thirty seconds at one of the computer terminals. Think you can distract Deunan for me in the morning?"

"Easier said than done, but I'll try." Caleb sighed and sank deeper into the pillow. "I wonder what Akeso is doing right now."

She propped up on an elbow and caught his gaze. "Orbiting its star at 82,306 kilometers per hour, while rotating through its 21.3-hour day. It's a planet, *priyazn*. It's doing what it does."

"Smartass." He rolled his eyes. "I imagine it's worried about me."

"Should it be?" She dropped the levity, allowing her countenance to grow serious. Events had been moving so rapidly ever since they'd put boots on Elakrin, and they hadn't a chance to really *talk*. "Are you doing okay?"

"Other than fretting over the emotional state of a planet-sized intelligence like a nervous parent, you mean? I am."

"And the violence today? At the river…up on the roof?"

He shrugged weakly. "I don't think enough of Akeso's consciousness is present to manifest feelings one way or another about it. And as for my feelings? The violence was second nature. Neither good nor bad, but simply something I did, because it was necessary. I admit, it is nice to not be suffering any nasty aftereffects from it, the way I did on Namino."

"I imagine so." She searched his features for cues that existential turmoil raged beneath the surface. And there *was* something there, but only at the margins. "Still, the question stands."

"Persistent much?"

"When it comes to you? Yes."

He coaxed her down against him, hugging her to his chest. "Akeso's absence is taking some getting used to. We encountered a number of novel sights and events today. I kept waiting for a response to what we saw, or a bewildered query…and there was nothing. I haven't been alone in my head like this for eighteen years. *But,* I was the sole resident of these brain cells for many more years before then. I'll be fine. I already am."

"All right. You'll tell me if this changes?"

"I will. I promise."

11

L aurent stirred awake with the sunrise. Light streamed in from a window behind him that he hadn't realized was there. In fact, he'd been so exhausted the night before, he scarcely remembered lying down, never mind any details of the room.

He shifted on the floating mat, and it contoured itself to his movements. It was far nicer than his own floor-bound bed, much like every aspect of this woman's opulent residence. He didn't love the culture credit system, for mostly selfish reasons—it had doled out only scraps to him for years—but it rankled him that Deunan had stolen all of this. Truvas were supposed to be rebels, working outside the system to right perceived wrongs society inflicted on those who ran afoul of its protocols, but Deunan seemed to be using her success as a truva to take advantage of the system instead.

Still, she had allowed him to crash at her place…for compensation, and a great deal of it. He sighed, rolling his shoulders to stretch out some kinks. She was attractive and confident and bursting with an edgy magnetism that made one feel a touch more alive in her presence. He needed to steel his gaze past it, though, and remember all of this was a business transaction to her. Nothing else.

Guardian's grace, had someone truly tried to kill him? Yesterday's events felt like a surreal nightmare, soaked in adrenaline-fueled terror, with the details blurred into a gauzy haze. Had any of it been real? He lay here on a strange bed in a stranger's home, so it must have been.

Deunan believed the KP was trying to silence him because of his research on the deep space anomalies. He didn't love the KP any more than he did the culture credit system, but he found it hard to accept the notion of them being assassins. Grifters, perhaps, and as a rule more interested in wealth and influence than virtue, but murderers? A chasm stretched between everything he accepted about the way the world functioned and such an assertion being true.

It could be the government instead. What if Mr. Khaleen had skipped out on their meeting in order to deflect suspicion when Laurent later met an untimely demise? This was only slightly more believable, as the current administration had never struck him as particularly ruthless or despotic, but the fact was, *someone* had tried to kill him. Arguably, twice in one day. And before yesterday, the only thing remotely interesting to transpire in his life was his discovery of the anomalies. So whoever was behind it, the phenomenon had to be the reason, didn't it?

His data! Laurent sat bolt upright in bed, causing the mat to hurriedly stiffen to support his shifting weight. He'd kept summaries and notes at his apartment, but the detailed measurements he'd collected were stored on the office server.

Caleb would say it was too dangerous to go to the office…but if the secret of the anomalies was worth killing over, he needed that data. To stand any chance of returning to his normal life, or possibly to keep any life at all.

He'd slept in his clothes from yesterday, and he didn't have any other outfits—why would he? So he patted out the worst of the wrinkles and pulled on his shoes, then donned the hat and jacket Deunan had lent him from the club. He'd never needed to engage in subterfuge before, but he did realize he shouldn't be spotted strolling into his office building.

Cognizant he looked a wreck but lacking the means to improve his presentation, he quietly stepped out into the hallway.

No lights were on, though dawn gleamed in full glory through the enormous windows in the main room. He paused long enough to appreciate how it was quite lovely; there were worse ways for Deunan to have spent her truva spoils. A peaceful, warm silence permeated the loft. She must still be asleep.

He drafted a brief note to her on his flexpad, then affixed it to the guest room's door, stopped off in the kitchen to chug down a glass of lavender water, and departed.

CS

The trip to his office passed in a fog of pinched anxiety and fraying nerves. Laurent didn't dare take the transit paths, as doing so would register his ident. City Services kept track of such things, and too many uses in a month netted you a scolding reminder to take time to appreciate the splendor of city life. Was it paranoid of him to fear City Services would flag his location and send a new assassin after him? He suspected Caleb wouldn't think so.

He wondered if he'd ever see his saviors again. They'd already done far more than he had any right to ask of them, so he'd understand if they chose to wash their hands of the affair and get back to their regular lives, whatever those involved. He had no idea how to pay them back for saving his life, but he hoped he got the opportunity to try.

He kept his chin low as he walked, almost on his chest, and tried not to furtively glance around every five seconds. It felt as if a hundred eyes were boring into him, and not as a result of his bedraggled appearance. Was that the muzzle of a rifle sticking out of a cracked window up ahead? He increased his pace…and continued to draw breath.

Maybe he ought to have waited until Deunan awoke and asked her to accompany him. But what were the odds she'd have said yes? His oroun was a meager and dwindling resource, and he couldn't afford to pay her for every trivial task. He was petrified—his ears sang, his skin thrummed, his chest burned—but he had to look out for himself when and where he could.

But no one shot at or stabbed him on the journey across the city, and he exhaled in relief when he finally reached the unassuming lobby of the building that housed the Space Physics Institute. Luckily, the building seemed to be deserted this early. He didn't think he'd be able to pull off small talk with coworkers right now, and he shouldn't linger in any event.

He took the lift up to the third floor and hurried down the hall to his office. A renewed surge of relief washed over him when the door opened to reveal everything still in order. No overturned chair or smashed terminal. In fact, the space was exactly as he'd left it the day before when he'd departed to meet with Mr. Khaleen, which was to say, a fair bit messy and unkempt. Flush with excitement over the astounding readings from the latest anomaly, he'd been too busy running numbers and mapping out theories to do any housekeeping.

He grabbed an empty chrystor from a drawer, dropped into his chair and opened up his files.

The raw data from the deep space monitors took priority, but he should copy out the analyses he'd performed and the algorithms underlying them as well. Might as well grab his notes of crazy speculations, too, while he was here. The answer wasn't contained within them—of this he was fairly confident. But the seed that revealed a path down which waited the answer could be.

A quiet scuffing sound echoed behind him. But, caught up in scanning his notes anew while copying the plethora of files onto the chrystor, he'd momentarily forgotten how someone was trying to kill him. So he didn't bother turning around to see what the noise might be.

A lancing pain shot through his skull, and everything went black.

12

———————————

"This is worthless. It's all 'exalted Guardian' this and 'Elakri are so awesome, shining magnificently with the Guardian's light' that. 'Art party at ten and symphonies at thirteen, fifteen and eighteen.' 'Have you molded a sculpture out of bronze for the weekly Great Guardian Gala yet? Submit your entry by tomorrow and share your splendor with your fellow citizens!'" Alex groaned and closed the screen displaying the overnight scans. "And I thought the Novoloume were decadent."

"No, the Novoloume are refined. The Elakri are…decadent captures it well enough." Caleb took a sip from the coffee mug he cradled in both hands; if the Elakri drank anything akin to coffee, they hadn't encountered it yesterday, so he was making a point to enjoy it while they were on the ship. "You're right. This is all propaganda. If we want to understand what occurred to trap the Elakri here, we need to find some actual historical texts."

"Yeah. I'd love to learn how this bubble of space exists and why. But the manifold tears mean something is happening to it now, which strikes me as more important."

"Unless the answers to the secrets of the present lay in the past."

Alex narrowed her eyes at him.

"What? Without Akeso here, I've got to think up my own sage wisdom." Her expression only grew more dubious, and he dipped his chin in concession. "Why don't we go talk to Laurent about his anomalies?"

"Let's do that." She leaned in to kiss his ear on her way to the printer module in the far left corner of the cabin. "I wonder what the printer has fabbed for us to wear today…*no*. Absolutely not."

He turned to see her holding something flaming citron and velvety by the tips of two fingers. His lips pursed in an effort to not burst out laughing, which he utterly failed at.

"You didn't do any better."

The next second something hit him in the face. He grabbed it on instinct, and found he was holding bright sapphire-and-black striped pants made of a satiny material.

"Not laughing now, are we?"

"Nope." He grimaced. "But we have to fit in. This is just another disguise. Speaking of, make sure to tweak the Shroud projections, in case we were seen yesterday."

"Oh, I did." Her eyes twinkled with delight. "I grew your hair out past your shoulders. You have the most fabulous ringlets now. Don those pants, and you'll be spiffy enough for a dance ball—which, by the way, they've having at eighteen thirty downtown."

CS

Deunan held the door to her home open while she inspected them critically. "You two look different."

"Possibly not different enough," Caleb remarked.

"If you're worried about surveillance footage of you yesterday, you'll be safe. I'm good at noticing details is all. Comes with the job." She waved them inside. "I assume Laurent's still asleep, and I haven't been in a hurry to wake him. I enjoy my quiet time in the morning. But now that you're here, we might as well kick off the day." She wandered down the hall.

He watched Alex as she took in the residence in the light of day, a corner of her lips tweaking upward. He imagined she was thinking of their loft in Seattle. They didn't get there much these days, and as wonderful as their home on Akeso was, he knew she missed it at times—

"That stupid *moron*." Deunan stomped out of the hallway and headed for the kitchen. "He left a note, said he was going to his office to retrieve the data on his precious anomalies."

Alex groaned. "You've got to be fucking kidding me. What about 'assassins trying to kill him' does he not understand?"

Caleb cursed under his breath. They should have gotten back here earlier. It was stupid of him to assume Laurent would stay put, passively waiting to be instructed on how to behave when his life had been upended. "Normal people have a difficult time internalizing the reality of such an improbable event. He said he worked at the Space Physics Institute. Deunan, do you know where that is?"

Her silvery skin flushed almost white, and she pointed to a screen on the wall, where a news broadcast aired. "You mean *that* Space Physics Institute?"

The visual showed an aerial view of smoke and flames billowing out of a six-story building. Fire suppression material poured down upon the burning structure from overhead drones as red flashing lights strobed through the air.

Shit!

We can get to him in seconds.

Alex was right, of course. So much for keeping their identities secret, but there was no tricky calculus to the decision. Saving an innocent life always won out over lesser considerations.

Do it.

Alex spun to Deunan. "I need to know precisely where that building is located."

"Uh, sure." Deunan, heretofore the picture of cool nonchalance, acted a bit flustered by this turn of events. "Let me look up the address."

"No, not the address. I need to know *where* it is. On a map. And please hurry."

"On a *map?* Fine." She tapped three fingers rapidly on the wide, semi-translucent band she wore on her wrist, then held her arm out, and a holographic map materialized in the air above the band. "It's…here." One finger hovered above a cluster of buildings opposite a triangular greenspace.

"And where is the, uh, the bridge…?" Alex looked to him in question.

"He said it was called the 'Tafen Bridge.'"

"Where is the Tafen Bridge in relation to this?"

Deunan shot Alex a suspicious glance, but zoomed the map out a little, then pointed to the top left. "Here, up to the northwest."

Alex's eyelids hooded, and her posture slackened. Though he knew she could remain standing while in sidespace, he nonetheless rested a hand on the small of her back to steady her.

"What floor is his office on?" Alex murmured faintly.

"Let me check. He should be in the city register." Deunan rushed over to the desk in the corner. A holographic keyboard activated on the surface, and her fingers flowed across it. "Office number 314."

Two seconds later, Alex's eyes snapped open. "Got it."

Caleb nodded sharply. "Let's go."

Alex flicked her wrist, and a wormhole opened in front of her—thick, acrid smoke billowed out into the kitchen.

"What in the *dannat?*" Deunan exclaimed.

Caleb lifted his satin shirt up over his nose and mouth and rushed through the wormhole.

Pervasive smoke drove him to his knees, where he found only modest relief. He switched his ocular implant primary to infrared. Normally, he'd search for a heat signature, but the fire had super-heated the air so much that the humanoid form sprawled ahead of him registered cool in comparison. Worryingly so, but maybe Elakri's core temperature was lower than humans'.

He crawled forward—his hand impacted a scorching hot surface, and he yanked it away. Likely the door to Laurent's office. He braced himself for the pain, then slid his fingertips along the surface until they found an open space, as if the door had malfunctioned halfway open.

It was a tight squeeze, and embers flickered on the material of his shirt by the time he'd shimmied through the opening.

The smoke was all but impenetrable in here, the heat almost unbearable. Caleb had his cybernetics force his breathing to slow and grow shallow while suppressing the autonomous cough reflex. His eyes smarted as he crawled toward the form lying on the floor. He didn't take the time to check for a pulse or a breath or even to confirm it was Laurent before grasping the body by the upper arm and dragging it toward the door—

Alex appeared beside him, crouched low on the floor, and grabbed the other arm. The rim of the wormhole now glittered behind them.

You were taking too long. I got impatient.

When was she not impatient? *On three. One, two, three!*

They scrambled backward with their charge in tow. When the body's feet had cleared the wormhole, it shut down.

Deunan's living room had filled with smoke while he was gone, though it was a pittance compared to what had roiled inside the building.

Caleb let a coughing fit overtake him; his left hand burned on the cool marble flooring as blisters began to form.

"Are you okay?" Alex's worried voice was at his ear.

"I'll be fine." He climbed to his knees and scooted up to the victim's face. It was Laurent, and he wasn't breathing.

Without knowing Elakri internal biology, he didn't dare try to perform chest compressions. He searched around for Deunan and spotted her through the smoky haze, hurrying toward them from the hallway. "Where's a hospital? He needs urgent medical attention."

"And you can portal him directly there, huh?"

"Yes."

"No." Deunan dropped to the floor opposite him, nudging Alex out of the way. She palmed a long cylinder and jabbed it straight into Laurent's abdomen.

Laurent's body jerked, torso bowing up off the floor and neck snapping back. He hung frozen there for a beat, muscles locked...then he inhaled a shallow, wheezing breath and collapsed to the floor. A second halting breath dissolved into a full-body coughing fit.

Alex moved behind Laurent's head and held him up at the shoulders, steadying him while he hacked.

Immediate crisis averted, Caleb checked his hand. His cybernetics had dulled the pain, and nanobots were hard at work healing the blisters. If Akeso were here with him at full strength, though, they'd already be gone. So a tumble off the roof yesterday may well have been fatal after all. Duly noted.

He regarded Deunan curiously. "Have stimulants lying around for such an occasion?"

"Things happen. I'll have a truva-friendly physician stop by to check him over."

"Thank you for doing that."

"It seems like if we took him to a hospital, someone would just show up and try to kill him again."

It did in fact seem likely.

Laurent's coughing finally subsided, and his head lolled against Alex's chest. His eyes remained closed. Deunan disappeared for a minute, then returned with a pillow. Alex backed away, allowing her to slide the pillow beneath his head.

Until the physician arrived, there wasn't much more they could do for him, so Caleb considered Deunan anew. She'd responded well during the crisis, but having cardiac stimulants on hand and a black market doctor on speed dial couldn't be *typical* for Elakri. "The truva business is often dangerous, I take it?"

"I wouldn't say 'often,' exactly, but work has been known to get spicy from time to time." She planted her hands on her curvy hips and glared at him, accusation and suspicion animating her enormous fuchsia-to-silver irises. "What are you?"

He started to launch into their cover story. "As I said, we're simply—"

"No, not 'who.' 'What.' Portal technology like what you just used does not exist on Elakrin. I'd know."

Given everything they'd learned about this place, the concept of aliens shouldn't exist in their frame of reference, so he had to wonder what she imagined the possibilities were. Synthetics, maybe? They hadn't seen any evidence of artificial intelligences, but they'd only been here for a day. "I'm not so certain you would."

"I am. Explain, or I kick the two of you *and* poor Laurent here out onto the street."

He didn't believe her. She was shrewd and calculating, with

honed mercenary sensibilities, but she was not so callous as to eject an unconscious man after she'd gone to the trouble of saving him. Regardless, it didn't matter; the wormhole had called their bluff for them.

He nodded carefully. "Okay. But not until after the physician has come and left."

"I have your word? For whatever it's worth?"

"More than you know. And you do."

"We'll see. By the way, your disguises are somewhat lacking. Neither of you has a trace of soot on your face."

He'd noticed Alex didn't, but she'd only been in Laurent's office for a few seconds. If he didn't either…well, the Shroud technology was still in the prototype stage. He'd file a bug report when they returned home. Right now, they had bigger problems.

13

A rien smoothed out the lines of his dress coat before rounding the corner and striding through the ornate doors.

More ballroom than meeting room, the Executive Conclave Suite's centerpiece was a long oval table crafted of specially hewn omoska wood harvested from deep within the Cornice Mountains. Thirteen high-back chairs shared omoska wood frames but were each upholstered with hand-woven fabric featuring unique patterns designed by the finest Elakri artists.

The table was dwarfed, however, by the towering mural-adorned ceiling and wrought iron columns lining the wide marble steps that descended to the table from all sides. To complete the sensory overload, vibrant paintings thousands of years old gleamed upon the walls, each one enveloped in a halo of subtle light. It was a space designed in every respect to intimidate and humble those privileged with a coveted invitation to visit it.

But nothing about the Executive Conclave Suite, the Seat complex that housed it, or the Khesa Prutet itself intimidated Arien. His family had built the organization from scratch millennia ago, and his father had led it for decades until his untimely death. Arien respected and honored the Khesa Prutet, of course. Its storied history, its crucial role in elevating Elakri society out of ruin, the important causes it had long championed to improve the lives of all citizens. But he'd played hide-and-seek with his sister in these hallways as a child, so intimidate? No.

The resurgent memory brought a smile to his face, though it quickly faded into a pang of regret. He hadn't spoken to Magnelle in years; their last words had been hurled at one another in grief-fueled anger, and the barbs had lodged too deeply to ever heal.

Solna Paran, current high chair of the Khesa Prutet, entered the room from an archway in the back, and a dozen conversations quieted. She was draped in the elaborate vestments of her office—a high-collared, black-and-gold robe that swooshed across her calves, with brocaded princess sleeves cuffing her wrists—and carried herself with unmatched grace.

He'd known the woman since those hide-and-seek years. She'd been his father's chief deputy for almost a decade prior to his death and had ascended to high chair in the wake thereof. At the time, Arien's sister was the eldest living Prime-lineage Colonnei, but her aversion to the organization had precluded any chance of her taking up their father's mantle. If Arien had been a little older, the position may well have been his to refuse. But it was just as well. While he didn't share his sister's distaste for the Khesa Prutet, he'd never wanted the high chair throne. He was an investigator, a solver of mysteries and dispenser of justice. Not a priest.

Solna Paran, on the other hand, was brilliant, shrewd, diplomatic and quietly ruthless. In truth, she ran the Khesa Prutet better than his father had, or at least more efficiently and profitably. Dad had been a touch too soft, often giving his underlings second and even third chances when they made mistakes.

No one got a second chance under Solna.

His personal interactions with her were frosty at best. He'd done everything politeness allowed to assure her he did not intend to make a power play to usurp her. But she continued to view him as a low-grade threat to her position and influence, observing his every action with cold, evaluating precision, as a viper poised to strike the instant her prey exposed a vulnerability.

"Please, everyone…" Solna's voice rang out like a finely tuned bell "…take a seat, and let us begin."

Arien moved to his appointed chair three down from Solna, nodding greetings to the other attendees as he did. Only after the meeting began did he realize one seat was empty: the one near the far end reserved for Insaf Devran, the priest he'd encountered at Agent Pietri's murder scene yesterday. Curious.

Devran had been interviewed by one of Endreje's men. The story the priest had relayed didn't shed any light on what might have led Kovalne to kill his agent, and it struck Arien as a touch odd that Devran had involved himself in what should've been a routine bureaucratic matter. Devran had addressed the anomaly by saying he was friends with the Department of Extraplanetary Affairs official, a Mr. Khaleen, and Khaleen had asked him to cover the meeting when he'd been called away for a family emergency. Simple enough.

Still, no one missed a Board of Advisors meeting without a good reason, and Arien idly wondered what Devran's reason might be. Ever the detective.

The meeting had begun while he speculated; today's business focused on planning for the upcoming Reclamation celebration, as well as the opening of a new educational institute in Olgavi and various budgetary matters he couldn't manage to follow. He usually took care to pay attention and actively participate in board meetings, but his mind kept drifting to his agent's murder. To Laurent Kovalne, and the strange intersection of their paths.

"Director Colonnei, do you have any objections to the budgetary proposal?"

He met Solna's gaze thoughtfully. "Not at this time."

"Very well. Let us put it to a vote."

CS

As the meeting broke up an hour later, Arien was making small talk with the woman who'd sat next to him, the chair over Khesa Prutet education initiatives, when Solna materialized beside him and placed a hand on his arm. "Arien, forgive the interruption. I wanted to say how sorry I was to hear of Agent Pietri's murder. Such a tragedy."

He blinked in surprise. At her seeking him out and her non-confrontational demeanor, but most of all the reason for it. "Ah, yes, it is a tragedy. He was a talented agent. How did you hear of it,

High Chair? I've taken care that news of his death not reach the press until the investigation is further along."

Her eyes lowered in an impression of sheepishness. "I confess that Seizon Pietri worked private security for me on occasion—only when he was off duty. My advisors assured me it was a perfectly legal arrangement."

"As it is. Many agents choose to take on additional private work from time to time, as the private sector will always compensate better than the government. Did you know him well, then?"

"Oh, no. We only spoke conversationally in passing during events. He was a consummate professional, always. But I am sorry to hear he's gone to the Guardian's embrace. Do you have any suspects?"

"I hesitate to go that far, though we have identified a person of interest." Arien grimaced, already regretting volunteering this information. Solna, wrapped in the trappings of her office while standing in this sanctified space, radiated an aura of absolute entitlement, and on occasion even he fell victim to its spell.

"This is comforting news indeed. Mind if I ask who it is?"

"I'm sorry, High Chair, but I cannot share details of an ongoing investigation. Not even to one of such elevated stature as yourself."

The shift in her demeanor was so subtle, he only noticed it because he was both a trained detective and he'd been observing her for many years. The arch of her eyes elongated as the curve of her lips flattened, deepening the tenor of her response. "I understand. Rules must be followed. Best of luck bringing his murderer to justice." She pressed her palm to his in farewell and shifted the whole of her attention elsewhere.

His former conversation partner had fled for greener pastures, and Arien was left standing there, working to keep his frown from escaping to entire countenance. Why was it that everywhere he turned, the Khesa Prutet kept popping up in this investigation?

PART II

THE TRUVA

14

Deunan studied Laurent surreptitiously. He was sitting up on the sofa, though his body sagged bonelessly into the cushions. His skin was pasty, his cheeks hollow, and his already short hair had lost several centimeters due to singeing. But his eyes were open and he was talking, if in a raspy, grated voice.

The physician had checked him over and pronounced him suffering from severe smoke inhalation. She sighed quietly; what would they do without physicians? He'd injected Laurent with a pharmaceutical cocktail to stimulate lung repair, whipped up an ongoing treatment compound on the kitchen counter, and advised Laurent to take it easy for the next few days.

They weren't friends, but the doctor had once patched her up from a nasty knife wound, so Deunan paid him with an oroun coin from her stash and sent him on his way. What were the odds she'd ever get reimbursed? Yet she'd done it anyway.

Laurent had looked so helpless lying there half-dying on her floor, and as she'd stood over him scowling, the notion had crossed her mind that she should help him...and not for compensation. She'd tried to banish the thought, but it stuck around through the physician's visit and beyond. She couldn't shake it. This man, foolish though he may be, was in serious, serious trouble. He didn't stand a chance of staying alive, never mind succeeding in uncovering whatever nefarious scheme was behind the attempts on his life, without her help. And not the kind of help a palmful of oroun bought.

A few short days ago, she'd been bemoaning the lack of excitement in her life. An object lesson in being careful what one longed for, lest it come calling—wearing threadbare clothing with empty pockets.

Caleb sat on the sofa beside Laurent, talking quietly to him, while Alex paced along the windows, where an increasingly overcast day loomed outside. And then there was *them*.

They'd done nothing but act in Laurent's best interests from the start. Yet her first impression, how everything about them screamed wrongness, had borne out. They didn't know how to read coordinates or access the infolace or use a comm address or do *anything*. All of which made for considerable evidence of their wrongness long before the magic portal that bridged kilometers in a wafer-thin gap came into play.

Deunan had no answers for what might explain them or their outlandish technology. Considering they'd lied about who they were up until now, she also had no reason to believe she could trust whatever they were going to say by way of explanation. But she was going to make them say it, nonetheless.

She adopted a steely countenance and marched into the living room. "Time's up. Explain yourselves."

Caleb patted Laurent on the knee, then stood and joined Alex in the middle of the room. "It's better if we start by showing you."

Deunan blinked through what felt like a glitch in her brain. The two…beings…who occupied her living room were no longer the ones who had stood there the previous second.

It wasn't as if they'd sprouted tentacles or scales or additional limbs, but every detail about their appearance was different. Askew and wildly out of proportion. Their faces were narrow, except for their chins, which were wide and flat. Pencil-thin noses separated tiny, orb-round eyes set above straight, rigidly horizontal lips, and gigantic ears bulged out into the room. Alex's skin was a pale alabaster—hardly a color at all—while Caleb's was dull olive-brown. Their torsos had shrunk, along with their legs and overall height to thicken above squarish hips. They possessed the correct parts, at least on the outside, but none were situated in the correct manner.

On the sofa, Laurent jerked back as far as the cushion allowed, a hand coming to his mouth. "Guardian's grace! What…I don't…am I hallucinating from smoke inhalation? Am I still unconscious?"

Deunan blew out a ponderous breath and pivoted toward the kitchen. "I'm going to get a drink."

"Get me one, too," Laurent muttered shakily.

"Sorry, but you're on medication. You'll have to tough this one out sober."

Her hands trembled as she poured a straight crantole over ice. She called herself world-wise, unflappable, impossible to shock or even impress. But it turned out she hadn't seen everything.

She took a long sip from the glass, then another, then did her best to plaster on a nonchalant expression as she returned to the living room and dropped into her chair. She wasn't certain she succeeded. "My question stands: What are you?"

"We're..." Caleb hesitated "...if we were in your situation, we would call us '*aliens*,' but your language doesn't have a translation for the term. The closest it comes is *spezie*."

"*Spezie* refers to animals and plants."

"I realize it does. What I mean is, we're not Elakri. We're not from this planet."

"Well you're not from Giarnum, either. They can get a mite quirky out there near The End, but..." she waved a hand in Caleb's direction "...not like this."

"No. We're not from this solar system. Thus we're not from this universe."

She wasn't a scientist like Laurent, but she was exceedingly well educated, and she knew for a fact that 'universe' was synonymous with 'everything that exists.' "I don't understand."

Alex moved to sit next to Laurent; somewhat surprisingly, Laurent didn't flinch away. Was he not even a little afraid? "But I think maybe *you* do," Alex said. "Or at a minimum, the possibility has crossed your mind."

"No. I mean..." he shook his head roughly "...it can't be true."

"But it can. The anomalies you discovered? They're flaws in the dimensional barrier separating your universe from the real universe."

"We're not real?" Laurent asked.

"Oh, you are. You, Deunan, this planet, your sun, they all exist. But they're trapped in a sort of bubble." Alex rounded her hands in the air, as if a visual demonstration made it all crystal clear. "On the other side of the skin of the bubble lies more than you can imagine. Trillions of stars. Innumerably more planets. Thousands of intelligent species—or we think thousands. We've only made contact with a few dozen, but we've scarcely begun to look."

Laurent's throat worked, and his gaze darted to Deunan. His eyes remained bloodshot from the smoke exposure, and his pupils had elongated. He was gobsmacked, but he still didn't act afraid. "Are you sure I can't have that drink?"

"Oh, what the *pazi*. I'm not your caretaker, so why not." Deunan retreated to the kitchen, grateful to have a few seconds to regroup in between revelations. She took the opportunity to refill her glass while she made Laurent's drink. Her blasé attitude, functioning as a layer of insulating armor, was the only thing holding her together. What they said was too absurd to be believed, but for the truth of what her eyes presented her. Because they definitely were *not* Elakri. Which meant they were something else. And there was no 'something else' here, which meant they had to originate from some*where* else.

Impeccable logic, if she did say so herself.

She handed Laurent his drink—she'd made it significantly weaker than hers—then returned to her chair. "So if we're in a bubble, how did you two get here?"

"The anomalies Laurent discovered," Alex replied, turning toward the man as she spoke. "The flare you detected during the most recent incident? We caused it. We expanded the tear in the manifold barrier until it was large enough for our ship to fit through."

"You can do that? You have a ship?"

"Yeah, we can. And we do." Alex smiled; beyond the fact that it was a smile, Deunan was unable to decipher much about what it signified. Her guests looked similar to Elakri in many ways, but with their disguises stripped away, everything about their mannerisms had been knocked off-kilter, and she couldn't begin to read their body language. Or didn't trust that she could, in any event.

"Why? Why did you come?" Deunan asked. In an avalanche of questions, it seemed the most practical one.

Caleb stepped in to answer. "Several reasons, most of which aren't important right now. But one reason is: According to historical records, the Elakri—your people, these planets and the star—were once part of the true universe, which we call 'Amaranthe.' You were a thriving species among the most advanced in your region of space. Then you disappeared. You were assumed lost, despite the fact no astronomical event occurred that could have wiped out your system. Until around a month ago, when intermittent tears in the spacetime manifold began appearing in the vicinity of where your planet was once located."

"Well, technically—" Alex started to say.

"The science doesn't matter for now. They need to understand the big picture."

"Sorry. Keep going."

"So we're here to discover what's causing these tears—Laurent's anomalies—and also, we hope, to learn what transpired here millennia ago." Caleb dipped his chin toward Laurent. "We were incredibly lucky to happen upon you. To save your life, obviously, and that would be enough. But you might be the one person on Elakrin who can help us discover what's happening to your universe."

"And that is all I want to do, other than live. But what are you saying? The radiation I've been detecting is originating from—" Laurent collapsed against the sofa cushion, his hands coming to his face "—*the data*. I went to my office to get a copy of the data I've collected and analyses I've run on it. But I'd barely started saving it when…whatever rendered me unconscious. Now my office is gone. The entire building is smoldering rubble. And without the data, all I have are a few notes and crazy ideas I can't prove."

Deunan shook her head wryly, relieved not only to have a distraction from the impossibility of her other two guests, but also a way to deal herself back into whatever this game was. "You are a complete moron."

"I know I should have kept copies at my apartment, or even better, on my person. But I had no way to know someone was going to try to kill me!"

"Clearly you didn't. I mean, who would commit murder over extraplanetary physics, right? No one cares about extraplanetary physics. But you're still a moron."

Caleb shot her what she suspected was a glare. "Deunan, don't you think you're being a bit harsh?"

"Not really, no. Laurent, do you not realize that the data on the Space Physics Institute servers is backed up to the DEA archives?"

He frowned. "Why would they archive to the DEA? The Institute is a private organization, and, as you said, no one cares about the work we do there."

"Because we aren't nearly as free as morons like you think we are. The government has its fingers in everything. And the Institute isn't fully private—it receives grants from the DEA all the time. It's one way to encourage research the government favors."

"How do you know so much about obscure public-private budgetary matters?" Laurent's tone held a note of challenge; color her impressed.

"I did some poking around while you were unconscious. Given someone was willing to burn a city block to the ground in order to get at you, it seemed prudent to educate myself on your employer."

"But I thought you believed it was the KP who's trying to kill Laurent," Caleb said. "Not the government."

She shrugged. "KP, government. No real difference, if you worm your way high enough."

"But it's a reasonable assumption to make that the fire, in addition to being a fresh attempt to kill Laurent, was also designed to destroy the data stored on the servers there."

"Sure, so his boss or one of his coworkers can't get curious and pick up where Laurent left off. But they won't need to delete the data from their secret stores, on account of them being secret."

Laurent stared at her, despondency weighing down his wan

features. "But they're *secret*."

"And I'm a truva. Nothing remains a secret if I want to know it." He just kept staring at her incomprehensibly, and she cast her gaze to the ceiling. "Moron. I can break into the DEA archive server and retrieve your data for you."

15

L aurent rubbed at his eyes, then blinked several times in succession. They still stung from the smoke, but this wasn't why he rubbed them. No, he was trying to confirm he wasn't seeing things that weren't real. Or dreaming. After all, a few hours ago he'd nearly died for the second time this week, and it wasn't the strangest thing to happen to him today. Two 'aliens' were in the room with him, and they claimed to hail from a universe beyond The End. Suffering from either a waking hallucination or a slumbering dream would explain them far better than the alternative—that they were both real and what they claimed to be.

Even so, what his bleary eyes stared at now wasn't them, but rather the full collection of his anomaly data. And, incredibly, his data stared back at him, organized neatly across two screens at Deunan's terminal. The raw readings from the monitors positioned in deep space, the results from the analytical programs he'd fed the readings through, and his attempts at using mathematical equations to impose clarity upon those results.

Deunan hadn't allowed him to pay her for retrieving the data, and he honestly didn't understand why. She'd mumbled something about taking personal pleasure in breaking into the DEA archives, then tossed a flippant hand in his direction and said she was going to take a shower.

She was nothing like Tamse…had been. He had difficulty believing Tamse was dead. He'd gotten over whatever heartbreak he'd suffered from their parting long ago, but he still felt sorrow at the idea of her no longer existing in the world. Where Tamse had been funny and kind, Deunan was harsh and dismissive. Cold and condescending.

Yet Deunan had helped to save his life and opened her own home to him while she arranged a safe place for him to stay. And now she had gifted him something arguably more precious: reclaiming the most radical scientific discovery of said heretofore unremarkable life. Which meant that maybe, just maybe, she wasn't quite so callous as she proclaimed to be. He'd like it if this were true, but he'd found the world rarely bent to his will.

Alex dropped a hand on the desk and leaned in, jolting Laurent out of his meandering thoughts. "Do you mind if I peek over your shoulder and see what you've got? I'm curious as to how closely your data aligns with the readings I took from the other side."

"Uh, sure." He slid his chair back to give her a better view. "Take a look." 'The other side'...of the *universe*. The woman—despite being of another species, she did seem to be female—had come from a place outside anything he had ever conceived of, much less known. What wonders had she seen?

He felt...small, provincial. How silly his work must appear to her cosmopolitan eyes. How naïve of him, of everyone, to believe their world was the sum total of existence. He was a scientist; he should have known better. Should have relentlessly questioned all he'd been taught about the nature of space.

Hadn't he, though? Wasn't this how he'd ended up here, with his life in mortal danger but also dancing on the precipice of the greatest discovery in Elakri history? Untold knowledge waited on the other side of these anomalies, and he hadn't merely uncovered them—he'd refused to let them go.

He glanced up at Alex, trying not to stare. He didn't dare ask her to don her Elakri disguise, though it would make conversing with her so much easier. "Are you an extraplanetary physicist as well?"

"No, though I did get a degree in stellar astronomy a long time ago." On seeing his confused expression, she elaborated. "Your sun? It's what we call a 'star.' Out in Amaranthe, there are trillions of stars—no exaggeration. And they're not all the same, so studying stars is its own scientific field. But no. I guess you'd call me an explorer. Which is kind of how we ended up here."

"Oh, I see." He didn't, not really, as his brain busily worked to wrap itself around the idea of trillions of suns. "And Caleb? Is he an explorer, too?"

She laughed. "He is since he hooked up with me. Before we met, he had a slightly different career. The kind that taught him the skills he used to save your life on the bridge yesterday." Her gaze shifted back to the screens. "Interesting. This is almost exactly what you would see if you measured the emissions of uninhabited space through a narrow slit. Which is more or less what happened. Your instruments aren't broken—they're spot on. You simply didn't have a point of reference for what they measured."

"So what do these readings signify? What am I looking at?"

"Not much, in the grand scheme of things. What lies on the other side is a fairly quiet region of space." She pointed at a line of raw numbers three rows from the top. "This is ionized gas interacting with an H 1 cloud—free-floating neutral hydrogen." Her finger skipped down a few lines. "And this is the spectra of a blue giant star located half a parsec from where the most recent tear formed. Oh, a parsec is around..." her too-narrow nose scrunched up toward her beady eyes "...a million times greater than the distance from here to your sun."

Such a mind-boggling number, and she talked about it as if it were right around the corner. "A blue giant. Is that like our sun?"

"No. Your sun is an orange dwarf."

His face fell, disappointed. It was childish of him, but everything he'd spent his life believing to be true lay in tatters on Deunan's descanti marble floor. "A 'dwarf' doesn't sound impressive."

"Oh, but it is. Most stars capable of supporting habitable worlds are dwarfs. The giants are wicked cool to look at, true, but they're dying stars. Relics. All the interesting action is at the dwarfs."

"I...." He struggled to focus on the science, lest he lose his mind. After all, science had been his refuge through every other trial in his life. "How many different types of stars are there?"

Alex grinned. "How granular do you want to get?"

CS

Deunan returned from her shower, silver-tinged magenta hair gathered up in thick braids and wound into an elaborate crown atop her head. She wore a shimmering knee-length lavender tunic with a platinum band tied loosely at her hips, and white beaded sandals.

Caleb would give the Elakri this much: Even their most recalcitrant rebels exuded style.

He joined her in the kitchen, propping his elbows on the counter and adopting a casual demeanor. "Thank you for retrieving Laurent's data for him. He's practically giddy with excitement."

"He is, isn't he? The man has no sense whatsoever. Keeping him alive is going to be a challenge." She pulled a tray of food out of the refrigeration unit, then chose a hard-shelled, coffee-colored item baked into a knot and offered it to him. "Panite?"

Caleb took it from her and bit down without thinking too much about it. If the food was poisonous to him, his cybernetics would alert him as they leapt into action to neutralize the toxins. And if they failed to counteract any negative effects…he caught himself. He'd been about to muse that Akeso was more adept at fending off toxins than any living being in existence; it had once fought off a planet-wide poisoning attack from a Dzhvar-infused sibling. But even without Akeso pitching in, he should be safe from a little food poisoning.

In the end, no alarms flashed in his eVi. He wasn't surprised; the Elakri were similar to humans in most anatomical respects, so it stood to reason their digestive systems were as well. Such assumptions weren't always accurate, but in seventeen years living among numerous alien species, they'd proved to be so more often than not.

"It's good. Thank you."

"Sure." She popped one of the breaded pretzels into her mouth. "So what now?"

The revelation of their true identities had knocked Deunan on her heels for a few minutes, but she'd recovered quickly, and her aloof, dispassionate persona was now firmly back in place.

He tilted his head toward where Alex was huddled up with Laurent at the desk. "We'll see what they say. Since I no longer have to pretend I know what the score is, why don't you tell me about the KP?"

"Ugh. The end-all, be-all interpreter of the Guardian's will."

"And what is the Guardian's will? According to them."

She stood up straighter and lifted her chin. "That we, their beloved children, thrive in splendor. That we make the universe shine from the light of our greatness as expressed by the unadulterated beauty of our creations. That we in turn celebrate the Guardian's blessings upon us by continually aspiring to reach for the utmost in perfection."

This explained the architecture, art and fashion. "So it's not an especially pious religion."

"No. It encourages arrogance and selfishness, and it has made us a petty, shallow people. It has also made the KP immensely powerful, wealthy and generally insufferable."

This was, unfortunately, true of many religions. Unchecked, power tended to corrupt the purest of motives. "Is there any counterweight to their influence? The government, or another religion?"

Deunan scoffed. "The government and the KP walk hand in hand through the fields of power, where they have divvied up the spoils between them. And how could there be another religion? There is only the Guardian."

An oddly gullible thing for someone like her to say, but everyone had their blind spots. "How about a different take on what the Guardian might want from your people, at least? Say, one that celebrates kindness and generosity as virtues. Or cruelty and submission, I suppose."

"Ah." She shrugged. "Not as I've heard of. If such a group ever existed, it's been erased from history."

Without meaning to, she'd put her finger on the crux of the issue. Caleb was beginning to suspect a great deal had been erased from their history. "Still, I'm surprised you don't have any alternative faiths. Even when my people were nothing but primitive, nomadic hunter-gatherers, they practiced dozens of religions. If the KP can make up the idea of a 'Guardian,' then someone else can make up a 'Protector,' or a 'Benefactor.'"

"Much as I disparage the worship of it, the Guardian isn't made up. It's very real."

Caleb smiled kindly. "I understand how powerful mythology can be. Several of our religions imbue their central deities with physicality in the legends."

"No, you don't understand. The Guardian is *real*. Big sphere out in space, orbiting the sun every twelve days."

"The planetoid?" Alex asked as she appeared at Caleb's shoulder. "We didn't take detailed readings, but I assumed it was just a clump of rock surrounding a metallic core. You're saying that's what you worship?"

"Not me." Deunan jerked her head toward the windows. "But those lemmings out there do."

Caleb thought back to the building they'd seen on their initial stroll through Ventise, shortly before Laurent had come under attack. "The decorative orb sculpture outside of KP temples—it's supposed to represent this Guardian?"

"It is. They plaster the orb everywhere—on their robes, on the walls of all their buildings, at the end of every missive. Probably above their priests' beds and toilets."

Caleb stifled a chuckle; this woman seriously did not care for the KP. "Does the object itself actually glow, or is that propaganda? We didn't get close enough to see."

"It glows."

"Well," Alex said, "planetoids don't glow. I should have paid closer attention to it, but no time like the present. I think we need to pay a visit to this Guardian."

Deunan shook her head. "You can't. It has its own guardians:

the Anghul. They'll destroy any ship to close within a few hundred kilometers."

Laurent belatedly joined them at the kitchen counter in time to grab the last panite off the tray. "You don't get to see the Guardian's true form until you die and ascend." He blushed, the panite halfway to his mouth. "Or that's what KP doctrine says."

"Has anyone ever tried to get close, or is the religious admonition enough to keep everyone away?" Alex asked.

"Oh, plenty of people have tried over the years," Deunan replied. "The Anghul are as real as the Guardian, and they pack a deadly punch."

Caleb arched an eyebrow at Alex. "What do you think? Can the *Siyane* slip past these Anghul?"

"The *Siyane* can slip past anything. You and I need to take a ride."

16

A rien stared at the frozen visual on his screen, trying to make it make sense.

A citizen had sent the footage in to the bureau after they'd publicly designated Kovalne 'Red One,' broadcasting it across the news programs. The photographer had been recording two of their friends performing in front of the Tafen Bridge, when they inadvertently captured a portion of the altercation that had occurred there the other day.

He'd been aware of the admittedly unusual shoot-out on the bridge, as open violence of such caliber was rare in Ventise, and he was monitoring the investigation. But until this visual surfaced, there'd existed no reason to link it to Agent Pietri's murder.

In the top left quadrant of the visual, Laurent Kovalne could be identified mid-stride alongside a woman. Seen over Kovalne's shoulder, a man pointed an object resembling a handgun in their direction. The man was too far away to definitively identify, but Arien couldn't deny he bore a striking resemblance to Seizon Pietri, who later that night ended up dead outside Kovalne's apartment.

Never trust a coincidence. And the coincidences in this case were piling up at a brisk pace.

Nothing in Pietri's active case load connected to Kovalne or to anyone else who lived in the apartment building. As an experienced field agent, Pietri enjoyed a great deal of freedom in how he went about his daily work, so it was always possible a fresh lead, one not documented, had taken him to the apartment building. But if Pietri was involved in the shooting on the bridge earlier in the day, bureau procedure demanded he report the event immediately. Instead, the agent had headed straight for the apartment without checking in.

The inescapable conclusion to draw was that Pietri was hunting Kovalne, and the man believed time was of the utmost essence. This belief was borne out by the fact Kovalne was now on the run.

So what could an extraplanetary physicist with no prior marks in his record be mixed up in that would have drawn the attention of a bureau field agent? None of Pietri's cases appeared to fit the bill, and in truth, Arien was at a loss to conjure a plausible scenario that did. Drugs and low-level culture credit theft were below Pietri's pay grade. Embezzlement or workplace corruption? Nothing about Kovalne's life suggested he was getting wealthy, legally or otherwise—

The door chimed, breaking off his train of thought before it reached another dead end. "Enter."

Agent Endreje Perrina strode into Arien's office with a fair bit of fervor, and Arien chuckled to himself. It seemed he'd convinced the agent to relax a bit in his presence.

"Thank you for agreeing to see me on such short notice, sir."

Arien nodded. "Of course. You have an update on the Pietri investigation?"

"More than an update—I have a guy sitting in an interrogation room as we speak. He's a financial advisor who, it turns out, creates false personas on the side in exchange for hard currency compensation. He came to our attention after he tripped a deeply buried flag we placed on Laurent Kovalne's record, and we brought him in for questioning. He's admitting to crafting a clean persona for Kovalne. To be honest, sir, he broke fairly quickly. I think seeing Kovalne's crimes plastered on the news spooked him."

"Good, then our strategy is working." Arien smiled, relieved the high-profile case was going to break. "Has he divulged where to find Kovalne?"

"Unfortunately, Kovalne didn't hire him. His client is a truva, goes by 'Deunan.' No last name, or so Taberas claims."

"Convenient for her. How good is Taberas?"

Endreje shrugged. "He claims he's the best, but in his line of work, who doesn't? In this case it doesn't matter, because he hasn't delivered the persona yet."

"Oh." Arien leaned forward in interest. "So this is how we'll find Kovalne. Does Taberas have an address for his truva client?"

"He swears he does not—only a comm drop. They usually meet in person to exchange deliverables."

The truva fiercely guarded her identity—or perhaps she was merely paranoid to a fault. Both were common enough traits in the city's shadowy underworld, and neither would save her in the end. "So we can tag her at the meeting, then let her lead us to Kovalne."

Endreje frowned. "You don't want to arrest her and bring her in? Make her give up his location?"

"You haven't dealt with many truvas, I take it?"

"No, sir."

"Most will go to prison rather than give up their clients. Not because they gave their word to a criminal and refuse to betray them, but simply on principle. They are true believers."

"Believers in what, sir?"

Arien blew out a breath through pursed lips. "That our society is rotten and corrupted, and it is their duty to subvert it at every turn."

"A convenient excuse for criminality, if you ask me."

He decided he liked Endreje. "Also true. So while we do run a small risk of losing both the truva and Kovalne if we let her walk, we risk more by bringing her in before she's led us to our prize." He crossed his arms over his chest. "What are the odds Taberas tips her off ahead of time, and she never shows?"

"It's a possibility, sir, but I think it's unlikely. He claims they're colleagues of convenience, not friends. And he appears to be quite the self-interested type. Greedy. The kind of man who flashes his prodigious culture credit at every cocktail party in the Panaen District, yet has no contributions to justify it. My read is, he's salivating for a deal. If we make it a good one, he'll stick to the terms."

Arien contemplated it for a moment. Taberas stood to be a high-value arrest on his own. In a society run by culture credit, the ability to become someone new and flush with credit was invaluable to criminals, and the man's client list was apt to clear a healthy stack of open cases. But solving the first murder of a Bureau of Investigation agent in eight years was worth far more than an uptick in the department's clearance rate.

"Offer to wipe his slate clean if he goes through with the meeting and doesn't tip her. Impress upon him how this is a one-time-only opportunity to go straight—there will be no second chances. Behind the scenes, we'll lock him down so tight we'll know if he sneezes wrong, at which point we will add him to our list of involuntary informants."

"Yes, sir."

"And put your best on the surveillance team. Truvas know how to spot agents. It's one reason why they're so difficult to snare. If this Deunan suspects anything, she'll bolt, and we'll lose Kovalne again."

17

Alex breathed a sigh of relief the instant she set foot back on the *Siyane*. They'd only been gone for a few hours, but yet again, those hours had been busy with violence, another close brush with death (thankfully not her own) and bucketloads of interpersonal tension.

At least their secret was out now, and they no longer had to pretend to be Elakri when they were around Laurent or Deunan. Caleb might still be able to don a false identity on command, but doing so stressed her the fuck out.

As if he could read her thoughts, Caleb sidled up behind her to massage her shoulders. "We've stumbled into it this time, haven't we?"

"We didn't stumble into anything. I pried the door open, we shoved our way inside and you poked the first hornets' nest we found with a sharp stick."

"True enough. Do you want to take a shower before we head out?"

One corner of her mouth curled up. "Is that an offer?"

His lips grazed her ear. "It's *always* an offer."

"Good." She held a strand of her hair up and sniffed at it. "And I do smell a bit like smoke. For that matter, so do you. A shower is definitely called for. But…I'm kind of anxious to go check out this 'Guardian.' I shouldn't have missed it during our initial survey. It was sloppy of me to assume it was an uninteresting planetoid. Ugh, Valkyrie would be giving me an earful if she were here."

"Don't sell yourself short. You were a cosmic-mystery-solving superstar long before Valkyrie showed up. Besides, Elakrin was far and away the more obvious prize." He placed a series of lingering kisses down her neck, then stepped away. "I am going to change out of these smoke-infested clothes while you take us off the planet."

Her neck tingled along the trail his lips had left, and she toyed with taking him up on the shower offer. Their lovemaking the night before had been notably delicious.... But curiosity about how a barren rock had taken on the mantle of a god won out for the moment.

She settled into the cockpit chair and, after a quick systems check, gently lifted off to guide the cloaked ship up through sporadic clouds and into the upper atmosphere.

While activating the Caeles Prism and wormholing directly into space from the planet's surface was possible, doing so was the polar opposite of stealthy. Laurent and Deunan knew their secret, but the last thing they needed was the whole population being alerted to their presence.

Elakrin sported a number of artificial satellites and platforms, but no orbital defenses—literally zero. There was no one or thing to defend against. No wayward comets or stray asteroids and no exocolony with ambitions of greater power, as the third planet, Giarnum, was populated only with a smattering of luxury resorts. She assumed there must be disaffected domestic political groups, for they'd never encountered a society that didn't have one or two or a dozen of those. But as spaceflight wasn't a significant component of Elakri society, any such groups shouldn't have the means or imagination needed to field a fleet of attack craft from space.

And of course, there were no aliens intent on invading. Merely her and Caleb.

The last wisps of atmosphere faded away, but she continued past the structures in high orbit at impulse speed. Beyond her inherent impatience, they weren't in a hurry. No reason to set off a proximity or spatial disruption alarm on one of the satellites and give the government reason to perk its eyes and ears up.

Caleb rejoined her in the cockpit as she finally activated the Caeles Prism and shot through it to a point five megameters from the object she'd believed to be a simple planetoid.

From this distance, the object clearly did, in fact, glow—something she would've noticed had she bothered to do a brief flyby during their initial survey. Seriously, *was* Valkyrie making her sloppy? Was three years of searching for the Dzhvar with no results wearing her down? Both outcomes were unacceptable. She'd never be able to keep her promise to Mesme if she didn't stay on top of her game. Everything depended on them succeeding.

Focus, Alex. For now, try solving the mystery right in front of you.

The Guardian. To the naked eye, it resembled a miniature sun orbiting the far larger main sequence star. But the fact that the spectrum scans had led her to mistake it for a planetoid meant the object was composed of materials a great deal more solid than any star. Beneath the glow, something metallic resided.

She checked the incoming readings. "Huh."

Caleb toed his chair around to face her. "Yes?"

"It's not hot. In fact, the only heat I'm measuring can be attributed to the proximity of the star. There's no appreciable radiation bleed-off, either. The incandescence isn't coming from nuclear fusion. The object also isn't exerting any noticeable gravitational pull, which means it has very low mass. So the metallic component isn't iron or another heavy metal. Whatever the solid material at the core is, it's lightweight."

"Exotic matter?"

"Not any we know how to create. But something is making it glow."

"What about these 'Anghul'? The guardians of the Guardian."

"Let's see." She zoomed in the visual scope and set it to pan across the body in a grid pattern. After twelve seconds, it detected a tiny, solid object and locked on. She zoomed in farther.

Caleb whistled and leaned back in his chair. "Isn't that damn interesting."

The object was a rectangular frame the size of an AEGIS frigate. Arranged in a diamond pattern on the frame, currently facing outward but set on tracks, were what her trained eyes told her *had* to be weapons platforms. In fact, the entire assembly bore a striking similarity to a node on Earth's Terrestrial Defense Grid.

There was no way the Anghul could detect the *Siyane*, for the ship's stealth was so advanced they effectively occupied their own bubble of shifted manifold. She fed some additional power to the shielding anyway, then eased in for a closer look.

An alert flashed on one of the smaller screens arranged around the HUD. Sensors had identified two further objects of similar size in proximity. "These are some serious defenses."

"Wonder what they're protecting."

She smirked. "Oh, let's do find out."

The spectral analysis of the Guardian was becoming too detailed to view on the HUD, so she directed the screens to output at the data table, and they moved into the cabin to study them.

She'd always preferred to visualize data, to swap charts around and construct a story around what it meant when disparate items lined up—and discern what it might mean when they didn't. In this case, the Guardian's spectra signature didn't fit any known profile, natural or constructed. So what *did* she know?

"There's a metallic core hidden beneath the luminescence. It's not solid, though. Porous, maybe…and spinning rapidly. Several orders of magnitude more rapidly than any other body in the stellar system. My educated guess? The Guardian is as artificial as the Anghul."

Another few seconds, and she had enough data to construct a visual representation of what resided at the heart of the Guardian. The fingers of her left hand tapped out a pattern in the air, and a new image took center stage above the table.

A tight network of curving metal created an orb-shaped lattice protecting a tiny sphere at its center. The sphere bled a storm of extradimensional quantum waves that impacted the lattice and…vanished. A fallacy on its face, but her instruments couldn't detect what transpired at the boundary.

She slipped into sidespace and projected her consciousness out into space beyond the ship. From this vantage, the Guardian was bathed in a cacophony of colliding dimensions and quantum noise. Chaos made manifest. And it all fell silent at the lattice. Fascinating.

"It looks a lot like Katasketousya Rift Bubble hardware," Caleb remarked.

She shook her head roughly and opened her eyes. "Um…it does, but it's not similar enough for me to accuse the Kats of meddling here. Not yet. Mesme said the Elakri were quite technologically advanced before they disappeared."

"Advanced enough to construct something of this magnitude?"

"That depends on what it's doing."

"It's maintaining the pocket universe this stellar system resides in."

Her eyes shot to him in question.

He held up a hand. "I'll leave the scientific explanation to you—and I won't entirely understand it, anyway. But you don't need a physical object 0.2 AU from a star, glowing or otherwise, in order to found a religion. You can call the star 'the Guardian' and achieve the same end. But someone did construct this extremely sophisticated object. Then they protected it using high-powered, deadly weaponry. And no one on Elakrin knows what it does—just like they don't know they're living in a pocket universe.

"And what does a Rift Bubble do? It shifts the physical dimensions around a region of space in order to make that region inaccessible from the outside. You say this isn't a Rift Bubble, and I believe you. But I'd stake my name on this machine manipulating dimensions in some manner—"

"You don't have to," she interrupted. "It's absolutely manipulating dimensions in some manner. I simply haven't figured out what that manner is yet."

"You will. But seeing as we happen to find ourselves inside a pocket universe, I have a theory as to the end result of those manipulations."

She smiled broadly. "I love you, *priyazn*."

"And I you, baby." He shrugged. "I've picked up a few things from tagging along with you for all these years, but mostly, this is old-fashioned analysis of the facts at hand. Whoever built the Guardian did it for a reason." His expression sobered as his focus returned to the visualization. "And this analysis is telling me one more thing. If the Guardian is maintaining this pocket universe, then there's a single logical explanation for why we were able to breach the walls of it."

"Oh? What's that?"

"The Guardian is breaking down."

18

While Laurent obsessed over his equations, Deunan called herself trying to catch up on her own work. The trouble was, there wasn't much work to be done. Oh, until Laurent had wandered into her path, she'd been making a point to spend a few hours at the Sacroneti Club almost every night, advertising herself as available for hire to anyone able to pay her justifiably high rates. But then she proceeded to turn away client after client. Individually, she had a viable excuse for refusing each job, but when viewed en masse, there was no hiding from the truth.

And that truth was, ever since the Brenfield job, she couldn't generate an iota of enthusiasm for her work. Or even the slightest desire to engage in it. She'd had a taste of what it was like to make a genuine difference—not in one life, but in many—and in the aftermath, work she'd once taken immense pleasure in for its own sake no longer measured up.

She glanced over her shoulder to where Laurent sat huddled up at her desk. Incomprehensible graphs and tables spread out before him; every so often, a line shifted, and changes rippled out across the screens in its wake. Whatever he was doing, he approached it with the fervor of a true believer. And over subatomic particles! It was ridiculous, but also kind of adorable. Admirable? No need to get carried away.

He was proving to possess more grit and strength than she'd first assumed. He'd been nearly murdered twice in three days, he couldn't go home, and his office and presumably his livelihood were destroyed, but he hadn't curled up into a whimpering ball and quit. Instead, he'd rallied, diving in with renewed enthusiasm to chase after the answer of why this injustice was being inflicted on him.

In the mental space one labeled a 'soul,' for lack of a better way to describe the whispering sensations that haunted her mind, a spark of the long-absent fire stirred to life. Physicists weren't commonly marked for execution, and the resources someone was throwing at ensuring Laurent died—and his research with him—suggested something of seminal importance was transpiring here.

It didn't seem possible, but his discovery had brought *aliens* to her living room. And those aliens had in turn brought wild tales of a vast, teeming universe hiding just over the horizon.

Now a storm raged in every direction she turned, with Laurent at its center.

Deunan nodded minutely to herself, and to all the oblivious citizens walking the streets beneath her windows. So she was all in. She'd ride this adventure to whatever end—while keeping her own self-interests front and center, of course. The scars she bore from foolishly doing otherwise, once upon an ancient time, would never leave her. She'd heeded their lessons well.

She glanced over her shoulder again. She'd nonetheless do everything she could to keep Laurent alive. One, because she didn't enjoy failing. And two…she found she didn't want to see him die. Not in a high-minded, 'innocent people shouldn't be murdered' way, but in a more personal one.

A message arrived then, saving her from more dangerous introspection.

> *Deunan,*
> *The gold-plated persona you ordered is ready to go. It was a doozy to pull off, so bring a tip. Meet me at Elagatee at 1820.*
> *—Taberas*

Good. She was going stir-crazy in here. "Hey, Laurent."

"Hmm?" he mumbled distractedly.

"I need to head out for a little while. Don't run off on some new damn fool stunt, okay?"

He shifted around in the chair and offered her a sheepish smile.

"I won't. I'm all out of foolish stunts for today."

"And don't trash the place while I'm gone, either."

His brow furrowed. "I wouldn't dream of—"

"It was a joke. But also, don't."

"Right…." He stared at her strangely for a beat before shaking his head and returning to his data.

She grabbed a jacket and headed out.

CS

Elagatee was located in the Panaen District, all the way across the city, so Deunan skipped up to the top-level transit path and let the streets speed by below her. The ID she fed the system belonged to her tertiary false persona, one unconnected to the persona listed as the owner of her residence.

As the path raced above Granholm, the buildings on both sides lit up in a dancing pattern synced to a multi-tonal harmonic originating from somewhere beneath her. A crowd was surely gathered below, soaking in the sensory experience—and she was past it and crossing briefly through the Capitol District before reaching Panaen.

She descended the paths until she reached street level and strolled the final two blocks to Elagatee. It was pretentious and overpriced, like Taberas; also like him, it filled a necessary niche in society.

The restaurant wasn't crowded, it being an hour earlier than any civilized person would consider eating dinner, but Deunan chose an immersive booth near the rear anyway. The neighborhood was higher class than she preferred, but Taberas fancied himself a culture climber. His supposed 'friends' were apt to toss him into the Praska Tributary if they ever discovered what he actually did for a living. He played a dangerous game, but it was his choice. He was the best persona forger in Ventise—his own culture standing was proof of that—and he appreciated the value of keeping his mouth shut when it came to business. She'd known him for almost ten years, and not liked him for a day of them, but he'd proved his worth numerous times.

Five minutes after she arrived, Taberas slid into the booth across from her wearing a frown. "We look as if we're hiding back here."

She triggered her portable surveillance shield and activated the booth's mountainscape ambiance. "No, we're simply enjoying the full sensorial experience the establishment offers."

"Fine." But his frown only deepened, and he shifted in the booth, as if he couldn't get comfortable. "You look like baked *malede*. You stepped foot in the Panaen District wearing that?"

She peered down at her clothes. Flakes of soot decorated her shoulder, and a gray smudge marred the filigree decorating the left panel. "Had a rough morning. Forgot to change. What is some street officer going to do, dock me five culture credits?"

"It's your life," he scoffed. "But about that. I've never known you to represent murderers before."

"What are you talking about?"

"Your client—the one you requested the new persona for? There's a manhunt on for him. He's wanted for murdering a Ventise Bureau of Investigation agent outside his apartment building."

She kept her expression scrupulously neutral. "He's innocent."

"Then…and I can't believe I'm saying this…he should spend the currency he must possess to pay for this persona and hire a skilled attorney, then turn himself in and prove his innocence. The goods are tight—" Taberas tapped his jacket pocket "—but if he touches a single aspect of his old life, he's toast. My contact in the Ventise Bureau of Investigation says they've designated him Red One."

Dannat, how high did this scandal go? For all the KP's power and influence, they couldn't designate someone Red One; only top bureau officials enjoyed that authority. She ignored the pang of sorrow that tolled like a bell in her chest. "I'll pass your advice along to him. On the assumption he'll decline to take it…." She held a hand out.

He removed a small chrystor from his jacket pocket and placed it on the table, keeping one fingertip on it. "Payment?"

She considered insisting on reviewing the persona first, but he'd never cheated her. So she sent a command through her autonetics and transferred the funds to his private account. People who did this sort of thing professionally didn't traffic in coins when doing business with one another, as they were loud, heavy and unwieldy. Instead, they used markers secured by a private bank vault. "Done."

A few seconds passed while he confirmed receipt. Then he slid the chrystor over to her. "Be careful with this one, Deunan. He's hot. Damn hot. I'd hate to see you go down with him. Our little community of troublemakers would be lesser for your absence."

"Aww, thanks. You say the nicest things. Or you said the nicest thing this one time, anyway." She rang up a hundred credits in the booth's system. "Have a nice meal on me." She stood and left the restaurant.

Outside, the evening pedestrian traffic had grown brisk, and two people bumped into her before she reached the transit path entry and glided upward, grateful to leave the aureate rabble behind.

CS

Deunan returned home to find Laurent weaving an erratic path around the living room. A tethered screen trailed along beside him, struggling to keep up.

He glanced her way as the door closed behind her, flashing her a distracted smile. "Welcome back."

It struck her as odd, someone welcoming her into her own home. She so rarely brought guests here, and almost never left one unattended. "Uh, thank you." She arched an eyebrow at the screen as she slid her coat off and tossed it on the kitchen counter. "Make any progress?"

"Two steps forward, one step back. I thought I'd identified a burst of energy in the vicinity of one of the anomalies before it formed, which could have pointed toward a cause, but it was only the remnants of a solar—never mind. You don't care about any of the science."

"That's not…precisely true." She sat on the sofa; she didn't usually sit here, preferring her chair, and the cushion struck her as oddly stiff. Not used enough to be broken in. "Listen, I need you to take a break from your work. We need to talk."

He closed the screen and perched on the edge of the sofa beside her. "What's happened?"

"First, the good news." She removed the chrystor from her pocket and held it out to him. "Your new ident. It comes with the works. Family history dating back a century, previous residences, schooling, job history, and a healthy deposit of culture credit."

He regarded the cube as if it were a hideous insect. "I thought you were just finding me a safe place to stay for a while."

True, that was what he'd originally hired her for, but their original deal was already long ago and far away. It was impossible to survive in their society without a culture-credit-backed ident, and he was going to require a resilient one if he expected to evade assassins while unraveling his subatomic mystery. At least, that was the logic she'd talked herself into when she'd ordered the persona. Regardless, it hardly mattered now.

"The bad news is, you're going to need a bit more than a temporary bed. The man Caleb tossed off your roof? He was a Ventise Bureau of Investigation agent. And they've pinned his murder on you. The bureau is scouring the city—probably the planet—hunting for you."

All the shimmer drained from his face. "But…but…it was the same man who was on the bridge, wasn't it? He tried to kill *me!*"

"And the fact that it appears the KP and Bureau of Investigation are working together to try to kill you is something we'll all want to discuss at some length." A twinge of doubt twisted in her gut. What if the bureau was the only bad actor, and the KP wasn't involved? In some ways, this possibility was worse—and also incorrect. If the Guardian was in play, so was the KP. "But at a minimum, this means you won't be able to return to your old life. Not anytime soon. They've designated you 'Red One.'"

"I…" his shoulders sagged "…you know what? Fine. It's not as if I had a lot going on outside of my work. And it appears my work is the reason I'm in this mess. I mean, I don't know what I'll do for a job or…."

"Right now, you need to focus on surviving."

"Yeah, I'm not certain I'm any good at that." His gaze rose to meet hers, emerald inner irises shining so brilliantly they drowned the amber ringing them. "I don't know how much all of this is costing, but I can guarantee I don't have the hard currency to pay for it. I'll give you everything I do have, then maybe we can work out a payment plan for the rest. It might take me a decade, but I'll find some way to reimburse you."

He started to stand, but she reached out and took his wrist, halting his progress. "Don't worry about it."

"What?"

Ugh, what was wrong with her? "Giving me an opportunity to ruin the nefarious schemes of both the Bureau of Investigation and the KP at the same time? It's payment enough."

"Oh." He stared at where her fingers encircled his wrist. "I appreciate the sentiment, but you don't owe me anything. No matter what surprises follow, I guarantee I'll still be owing you. And I don't want to leave my debts unpaid."

Why did he have to be so earnest, so *good*? She let go of his wrist. "Let's just see how things play out, okay? If it turns out—"

In the middle of the room, a ring of light tore a hole through the air. She leapt up, one hand going to the blade she kept sheathed inside her belt while she stepped in front of Laurent.

The ring revealed a window to another location. She caught a glimpse of a curved wall beyond a navy fabric couch before Alex leaned into frame and motioned for them to come through the ring. "The two of you need to see something."

19

Laurent had only been aboard a spaceship twice in his life, both times to visit Tillanti Station. Neither of those ships had looked anything like this one.

The walls—or was it the 'hull' on the inside, too?—were a bright, pleasant pearl color too textured to be metal. The furniture, though efficiently distributed and a touch sparse due to limited space, looked comfortable; livable. To his right, two chairs populated a sleek cockpit busy with holographic displays. To his left, near what he took to be a kitchen space, a spiral staircase wound to a lower deck.

"Welcome to the *Siyane*," Alex said.

Deunan nodded slowly. "Not bad. You live here?"

"Sometimes," Caleb replied. "Listen, I'm going to be honest with you. We debated about whether it was a good idea to bring you here. What you're about to see is going to change the way you perceive your world—"

"More than the last few days already have?" Laurent blurted out. His voice sounded off pitch and taut, even to him, but in fairness it had been a rough five minutes. He was a wanted man, a fugitive from the law, a discoverer of a secret his government, or possibly his church, or possibly both, were willing to kill to keep. And now he was on board an alien spaceship. Surely no girders remained standing to knock out from beneath him.

Caleb chuckled softly. "Fair point. But maybe. Nevertheless, your life is at stake, Laurent, and you deserve to know why. And Deunan, you need to understand why his life is at stake as well…then decide what that means for you."

Deunan rolled her eyes. "The suspense is killing me. Can we hurry up with the reveal?"

"Of course." Caleb motioned them toward the cockpit, where beyond a heavily filtered viewport, the Guardian's light bled into the overwhelming brilliance of the sun.

Deunan shrugged. "The Guardian. We grow up watching KP vid specials on it. Granted, I've never been nearly so close, but it looks pretty much the same as it did in the vids."

Laurent was rather enjoying seeing it up close and personal, but he didn't disagree with her overall point. No surprises so far.

"I imagine it does," Alex said. "Now come with me back here, to the data center."

The long, rectangular table had been situated behind Laurent when he'd walked onto the ship, and it hadn't registered in his mind what it must be. The surface was constructed of a perfectly smooth metal he couldn't identify…he blinked and peered at it more closely. Thousands of minuscule dots glittered subtly not on, but within the surface. Or were they fibers?

Three large virtual screens hovered above the table. Two were currently blank, while the leftmost one displayed the same scene as the viewport.

"I'm pulling in a variety of readings from the ship's sensors," Alex explained. "Here is the visible light feed of the Guardian. Now I'm going to strip away the noisy emissions to remove the obscuring glow."

All semblance of a heavenly object evaporated, leaving behind a spinning orb—neither a lattice framework nor a solid sphere, but somewhere in between. An immense network of curving alabaster rods wove together in an intricate pattern. The image provided nothing for scale reference, but Laurent couldn't shake the impression that it was much smaller than he'd expected, as if the visible light the Guardian emitted increased its apparent size by orders of magnitude.

He'd never been a particularly devout man, and he felt oddly calm at this new information. So, the fact the Guardian was not what it was advertised to be, but instead metal beneath the luminance? Not a girder fortifying his sanity. What a relief!

"What is it made of?" he asked.

"A complex carbon-based metamaterial," Alex said. "The spectral analysis is picking up traces of lonsdaleite, amodiamond and a graphene analogue, as well as several signatures I've yet to identify."

"Fascinating. Have you determined what's driving the spin?"

"There's a mechanism inside the frame that most likely serves as an engine, among other functions."

Deunan wandered around the edge of the table and disappeared behind the screen. "Huh. So the Guardian's a machine?"

"It is," Caleb replied. "And so are the Anghul." He tilted his head at Alex, and the center screen flared to life with a hyper-zoomed-in section of the Guardian. Against the lattice network, a much smaller object orbited at a comparatively languid pace.

Deunan hurried around to squeeze in beside Laurent and lean in close to the screen. "What am I seeing?"

"It's a weapons platform," Caleb said. "There are four more identical platforms orbiting the Guardian. Each platform fields four discrete weapons. We can't determine how powerful each one is without triggering a strike, but given their size, we can assume they wield substantial firepower."

"And they shoot down any ship that approaches." Deunan groaned. "*Dannat.* The Guardian isn't smiting down anyone who dares to gaze upon their face—someone at the KP is controlling these weapons to snipe out anyone who draws close enough to spy the machinery behind the glow. Okay, so the KP is evil. Already knew this. But what does any of this have to do with Laurent's anomalies? They're appearing way out there at The End, aren't they? Not here at the Guardian."

It was an excellent question. Laurent felt as though the threads of an answer were hiding deep beneath an avalanche of revelations, but he wasn't able to grasp any of them as they slid through his mind. Too much had transpired too fast.

"We have a theory," Alex said. "Without knowing more about the machine at the heart of the Guardian, it's only a theory, but it's consistent with what we've learned."

Deunan shot the screens a glare, then went over and plopped herself down on the couch. "Enlighten us."

Laurent couldn't bring himself to tear his attention away from the spinning orb. *The Guardian, a machine.* "Please, do."

"All right," Alex replied. "We believe the—" A chime rang out from a panel on the wall behind the table, and Alex cut herself off. Her eyes unfocused for a second; she flicked a finger, and an additional screen materialized at one corner of the table. "A new anomaly has just formed. Shall we go see it?"

"Yes!" Laurent didn't try to contain his enthusiasm. He was never going to get approval to take a government ship out to The End—the understatement of this week—but now he didn't have to.

"I thought so." Alex moved into the cockpit, and the Guardian was soon receding from the viewport and spinning away. "These events don't tend to last long, so I'm going to pinpoint jump to the area." She glanced over her shoulder. "You all might want to see this as well."

Laurent searched for Caleb, to find the man had sunk onto the couch as Deunan vacated it. He sat leaning forward, elbows on his knees and his chin resting on his chest, face hidden.

Laurent moved into the cockpit and, after a moment's hesitation, lowered himself into the seat next to Alex.

In most objective respects, what materialized off the bow of the ship wasn't so different from the portal Alex had created in Deunan's home a few minutes earlier—except for all the ways it clearly was.

For one, it was a fair bit bigger. The ring stretched out beyond the breadth of the ship and then some. For another, it was in space. Obviously. The scene on the other side, being empty space as well, meant he was able to focus on the ring itself.

No physical mechanism held it open; it hovered untethered in the black. Framed by so much darkness, it glowed the purest gold, sparkling and crackling like a fire drunk on oxygen.

"Are you creating this one, too?"

"No, the *Siyane* is," Alex said.

"But it seems as if you're mentally wired into the ship's systems."

"True. One day, I'll have to tell you about the time I died, and my consciousness lived in the circuitry of the ship until Caleb could revive my body."

"It what now?"

She laughed as she eased the ship forward. "As I said, some other time, preferably over drinks."

The ring slipped past the viewport on both sides and out of sight, and they were presumably somewhere else now.

Alex sighed. "The complete lack of stars really is disconcerting. Don't you find this utter void suffocating?"

"Yes," Deunan remarked dryly, which was when Laurent realized she'd come to stand behind them. Caleb remained on the couch.

Laurent lifted a shoulder. "It's difficult to conceive of anything else. What do stars in space look like?"

"We get a few minutes of downtime, and I'll show you. But for now…" Alex's fingertips danced across a flat panel "…let's catch this anomaly before it's gone."

After about ten seconds, the faintest haze of amber-tinged gray splotched across the blackness in a long, narrow strip, like a fog bank receding into the night.

Alex brought the ship closer until the anomaly filled the viewport.

Laurent frowned. "I'm not going to lie. It's a little anticlimactic. I mean, incredible that it's here at all, but it doesn't seem so impressive."

Alex tapped a small lighted circle, and a screen materialized in an overlay of a corner of the cockpit, then divided into six quadrants.

No longer a faint haze, the anomaly was now a jagged bolt of lightning, a hairline crack of dazzling light. In each screen quadrant, it shone in a unique color. She'd split it out into different spectrum segments, all but visible light.

"We can study these readings in greater detail later at the data center table, but this gives you an idea of what's going on through the tear."

"Your universe is truly so loud? So bright?" he asked.

"Compared to here, yes. The tear accesses a fairly empty region, too. You should see a galactic core. It's deafening." She leaned back in the chair and closed her eyes. "Give me a minute. Need to have a quick conversation before the tear closes."

The feeling of smallness, of shame Laurent had experienced earlier renewed itself now. He'd believed his people to be technologically advanced. In fact, the entire ethos of Elakri society was built around the conceit that they were the pinnacle of evolution. Of technology. Of culture. Of achievement. On the cusp of perfection.

But they were nothing. Primitives using a torch to light the walls of their cave and believing it to be the universe.

"Ha!" Alex chuckled as she opened her eyes. "Sorry...." She pointed at her head. "So we're running at twenty-six minutes and counting now. Laurent, what's the longest you've registered one of these?"

"Twenty-four minutes, nine seconds." The anomalies were lasting longer each time.

"Okay. We'll stick around until the end." Her brow furrowed. "The tear is measuring almost six nanometers, which is a good bit wider than the one we came through—until we forced it open, anyway. Does this comport with your data?"

Laurent shook his head. "The equipment I used wasn't designed to capture such level of detail."

"It's fine. Another data point."

Deunan moved up to stand directly beside the chair he was seated in. "So it's real, huh?"

He peered up at her. "Did you think we were all lying?"

"No. But I assumed it was just math. Measurements not matching with equations or something. But this is a real phenomenon. And on the other side is..." she glanced at Alex "...everything you said."

"And a whole lot more," Alex replied.

"Noted." Deunan spun and went into the main cabin.

Laurent watched her for a few seconds before dragging his focus to the anomaly, in all its many forms splashed across the overlay. In the back of his mind, a kernel of a dream took hold, one of studying the universe that existed beyond the crack in his world. Oh, the endless wonders it must hold! Wait, was it endless? "Does your universe have an End?"

"It does," Alex said.

"Is it like this?"

"Um, more or less. It's expanding, though."

"Into what?"

"Isn't that the question? How can the universe be 'everything,' yet have a defined border? A border with what? Many physicists posit that Amaranthe is still one of many—"

Caleb dropped a hand on her shoulder; at some point, he'd quietly joined them in the cockpit. "Now you've done it, Laurent. She and Valkyrie will debate this stuff for hours on end if you can't find a way to derail them."

"Who's Valkyrie?" he asked.

"My, ah, artificial intelligence companion," Alex replied as she peered up at Caleb. "You good?"

Caleb nodded, a slight smile briefly lifting his features.

Alex squeezed Caleb's hand, then returned her attention to Laurent. "Hey, which reminds me. Do the Elakri have artificial intelligence?"

He shook his head. "Creating a life form more intelligent than ourselves would be blasphemy against the Guardian." Blasphemy against a machine.

"*Slaboumnyye tupitsy.*"

"Alex, that wasn't polite," Caleb chided.

"True, but Laurent doesn't know Russian." She rolled her eyes. "Sorry—I wasn't being rude to you. You all can build it, though? You have the technological capability?"

"In theory? But any research that even begins to creep toward the line is shut down hard."

"Well, if it makes you feel any better, you're not the first species to try to keep a lid on artificial intelligence. But no one ever succeeds forever. It always gets out. Always—oh, hey. Twenty-nine minutes and eighteen seconds. This is now the longest-lasting anomaly either of us has measured." She glanced up at Caleb. "More evidence for our theory."

He nodded soberly.

"What is your theory? You got interrupted by the anomaly," Laurent remarked.

"We'll talk about it once we're back at Deunan's," Caleb answered. "For now, let's collect as much data as we can."

The anomaly lasted for another two minutes and six seconds before fading away, leaving only an impenetrable blackness behind. The End…and on the other side, a beginning.

20

As soon as Deunan and Laurent returned home through the wormhole, Alex closed it and crossed the distance to Caleb. Her hands rose to cup his cheeks, and her eyes searched his face in obvious concern. "How's Akeso?"

He pressed a palm into her hand, enjoying her warmth. "Even more worried about me than I have been about it."

"But okay?"

"Perfectly fine. Like you said, it's a planet, with no natural predators. What's going to happen to it? The answer is, unless or until the Dzhvar show up in its stellar system, absolutely nothing."

"True. And how are you?"

"Hmm." It wasn't as if he could conceal his state of mind from her, should he want to. "To be suddenly flush with Akeso's spirit, then have it all but vanish again a few minutes later? I admit, I'm experiencing a bit of whiplash here."

It went beyond whiplash, though. He'd been growing rather used to existing alone in his head—to feeling like a younger, simpler version of himself. Enough so that he'd toyed with guilt over not thinking of Akeso more often, though he recognized this was a vicious cycle in the making. Then the tear had opened, unleashing a deluge of consciousness too overwhelming for his body to contain. His breath stolen, his mind submerged beneath its waves. And about the time Akeso's thoughts had settled into coherence and they'd remembered how to coexist, the tear sealed and Akeso was again gone. And now he felt empty. Hollowed out inside.

Did he dare engage in uncomfortable self-analysis to determine which he preferred? To what end? His preference didn't matter, for he and Akeso were forever intertwined. It was the price of living, which was something he quite enjoyed doing. He'd made peace with this reality a long time ago, and their temporary separation didn't alter the calculus.

He breathed out. Better.

Alex was scrutinizing every minute twitch in his expression, her eyes narrowed and brow knitted tight, and he leaned close to rest the tip of his nose on hers. "I'm a little discombobulated, I admit, but I'll be fine. Akeso now understands what happened to cut us off from one another, and that it's a short-term imposition."

"Can Akeso talk to Valkyrie? Because she was about ready to call in the Concord fleet to blast a new manifold tear into existence and send in a squad of marines to extract us."

"Valkyrie has never been one to sit on the sidelines."

"No." Alex rolled her eyes. "Like Akeso, I think I did calm her down. She absorbed everything we've learned so far and will run with it. I wish I could've given her more details on how the Guardian actually operates. I doubt the visuals are going to do much to help her or Mesme deconstruct it."

"So you'll figure it out yourself." He smiled a touch wistfully. "Remember when it was just the two of us, diving into cosmic mysteries with nothing but our wits and our all-too-mortal bodies?"

"I do. And we did all right for ourselves."

"We did at that."

CS

They returned to Deunan's place to find Laurent buried in his files with renewed vigor, and Deunan lounging in her chair, mixed drink in hand, staring at the back of Laurent's head while wearing a perplexed look on her face.

Deunan glanced their way as Alex closed the wormhole. "So, is it science time?"

He and Alex sat on the sofa, leaving the second chair for Laurent. "Not yet. As much as I'm sure Alex is itching to fly the *Siyane* directly into the center of the Guardian and go at the mechanism with a crescent wrench—" Alex arched a hopeful eyebrow "—I think we need to understand a few important details before we decide on our next steps."

Laurent belatedly joined them, but chose to pace along the windows instead of claiming the free chair, nervous energy animating his steps.

"If you say so," Deunan offered. "What information do you need?"

"Your history—Elakrin's history. Has the Guardian always been here?"

"We don't know."

"Obviously." He rephrased. "What I mean is, has the Guardian been here since the Elakri started recording history?"

Deunan shrugged. "We don't know."

The woman had a strong tendency to be difficult for difficulty's sake. He didn't want to treat this like a hostile interrogation, but he would if she persisted. "Then how long *are* you certain the Guardian's been present?"

"For 8,928 years."

"That's a highly specific number."

"That was when The Fall happened," Laurent volunteered. "Which...you don't know about. Sorry. It's easy to forget you're...new."

"No, we don't. What's 'The Fall'?" Caleb asked.

Rather than let Laurent explain, Deunan jumped back in. "We don't know—I'm not being snarky. We genuinely don't. Exactly 8,928 years ago, our world suffered a devastating event. Some believe it was a natural disaster—a shift in the planet's core or something—"

"It wasn't."

"Thank you, Laurent. Some believe it was a violent civil war. KP zealots insist the Guardian grew displeased with us and determined to teach us a lesson. Regardless, the effects were cataclysmic. Cities burned to the ground. Millions died. Much of the technology that ran our society failed and was lost." Deunan frowned. "But this can't be precisely true, can it? In the aftermath, people stood amid the ruined machines, and they understood what those machines did. Some must have understood how they functioned, how they were built. But for whatever reason, the knowledge was, in time, lost as well. Not all of it—we didn't start again from scratch, rubbing two sticks together to make a fire. But a great deal of it."

Explains the mismatch in the level of technology from before they disappeared, Alex pulsed.

It does.

For once, Deunan seemed to be playing it straight. She'd lost the biting sarcasm, the feigned disinterest and annoyance. He'd suspected it was all an act, and here was his proof. The question was, why now? Why had the mention of 'The Fall' triggered a change in attitude?

"And all the historical records?" Caleb asked gently.

"Gone," Deunan replied. "Or perhaps we forgot how to use the tech that read them, so we threw the hardware in the trash bins. Regardless, for all intents and purposes, our history as a people began anew the day we began cleaning up after The Fall."

"What about the KP? Did they arise in the aftermath?"

"According to their propaganda, yes. They claim they executed on the Guardian's will to help us rise above the disaster that befell us and strive to achieve greatness once more."

He idly ran a fingertip along Alex's hand.

I wonder if The Fall is what created this pocket universe?

The event itself shouldn't have been so violent. The Displacement only rattled some windows and knocked people out for a few minutes, and it was a far more disruptive affair, cosmically speaking.

True.

"Private conversation?" Deunan asked.

"Sorry. Talking about parallels in our own history." He shifted his attention. "Laurent, does the KP ever interfere in scientific research? Are some subjects taboo?"

"The KP is extremely supportive of scientific endeavors. My experience is somewhat narrow, I admit, but I've never heard of them shutting down an avenue of inquiry—other than artificial intelligence. Not until this week." His face blanched. "Guardian's grace, what if they kill everyone who asks the wrong questions?"

Deunan snorted. "I wouldn't put it past them."

"It probably doesn't matter." Caleb steered them away from the tangent before it took hold. The KP may well be behind the attempts on Laurent's life, but they wouldn't prove it sitting here. "What about evolution? The Fall didn't destroy Elakrin's geological record."

"True," Laurent replied. "It's commonly accepted that the Elakri, as well as other life forms, evolved over billions of years from single-celled organisms."

"All part of the Guardian's grand plan," Deunan remarked wryly.

"Understood. So if…." The instincts that had once made Caleb a top-tier intelligence agent flared a warning. He'd heard something without knowing he'd heard it—in part because his aural cybernetics were state of the art and in part because decades of experience had taught him what to always be listening for.

A sound reverberated beyond the entrance: too heavy to be a neighbor arriving home alone, and too deliberately quiet to be a neighbor arriving home with a bunch of friends.

He held up a hand to ward off anyone speaking and honed every sense….

The sound repeated. And outside the windows, a light that hadn't been present before flickered unnaturally.

"Get down!" Even as he said it, he was shoving Alex to the floor and shielding her body with his.

The rush of adrenaline in his veins, driven to heightened purpose by a flood of nanobot regulators, focused his thoughts and stretched time to his advantage. In the instant it took to blink, he evaluated their situation and chose a course of action.

The guest bedroom would provide a defensible choke point and buy them time, but the hallway leading to it was too close to the front door—they'd never make it. They needed to get clear of the line of fire for long enough to effect an escape.

"Stay low and get to Deunan's bedroom!" He shifted off Alex's back and urged her forward, keeping himself between her and the door.

Nothing had yet transpired to prove his intuition was well-founded, but everyone obeyed the command. The ability to project authority had its advantages.

As such, they were already halfway across the main room when the front door exploded.

Engineered chaos descended upon the residence. Shouts overlapped with a dull roar he couldn't identify. Smoke billowed through the door, cut by laser tracers.

Snap judgment. Alex had a defensive shield as strong as his, but to his knowledge, neither Laurent nor Deunan wore any such protection. So he ignored his every gut instinct and desire.

Forget staying low. Shield up and run. Wormhole as soon as you get through the bedroom door.

Got it.

Alex vaulted to her feet and took off. He moved behind Laurent and Deunan, snatched them each up by the arms and shoved them forward, doing his damnedest to keep his body between them and the door.

His shield sizzled from the impact of laser fire; the intruders were shooting to kill. His ears rang from the concussive effects of something like a stun grenade, and in front of him, Laurent stumbled to his knees. Caleb hefted the man up and half-carried him forward. He was barely able to make out the doorway to Deunan's bedroom through the smoke, but he zeroed in on the opening in the wall.

When he reached it, he hung back, shielding Deunan until she made it into the bedroom and keeping Laurent positioned in front of his chest as his shield crackled and hissed anew. Sounds thudded close behind him. Not much time left.

He shoved Laurent through the doorway ahead of him. It wasn't as smoky in here, and a wormhole gleamed against the walls. Alex was on the other side, motioning Deunan onward.

He basically tossed Laurent through the wormhole, then dove after the man as the walls and floor shook and laser fire shot past the doorway.

"Close it!"

The wormhole faded away, and the quiet calm of the *Siyane's* cabin welcomed them.

He completed his rolling tumble and rose to his feet, immediately spinning toward Alex. "Did you get hit?"

She shook her head, but his eyes automatically scanned her body for blood. Finding none, he knelt beside Laurent, who was sitting on the floor, legs splayed out in front of him, holding his head. "Laurent?"

"I'm…I think I'm okay. My head hurts, and my ears are ringing. But there's no horrifying pain originating from anywhere in particular."

He didn't see any open wounds or pooling blood. "Good. Sit and find your bearings."

"*Dannati pazi malede*," Deunan muttered colorfully. She was still on her feet and seemed to be in one piece.

Caleb exhaled and worked to dial down the combat mode. They were now many kilometers away from the scene, ensconced in a hidden, well-protected and heavily armed ship sporting an indestructible hull. *Breathe in, breathe out. Let time resume its natural march forward. Refocus.*

He touched Deunan on the arm as she stormed by. "How did they find you?"

"That weaselly, conniving snake Taberas must have sold me out. It's the only explanation. But…" she frowned "…he doesn't know where I live."

"He knows your name, though?"

"Only my first name. And the residence is registered under a different name, anyway." She cut a ragged path through the cabin. "I must have been followed from our meeting. But, no, I'm confident I wasn't. I always take precautions. My home is my sanctuary. *Was* my sanctuary. *Dannat!*"

"What about a tracker of some kind?" he asked.

"I don't see how…oh, *malede*. Two people bumped into me as I was leaving the café. One of them grabbed my arm to steady themselves."

"Then they can track you here—"

"No. I took my jacket off when I got home." She rubbed at her bare arms, as if to confirm nothing was stuck to her skin.

"Did they touch your neck? Your hair?"

Her hands went to her neck. "No. It was my jacket sleeve both times." She jerked her chin downward. "I'm certain."

"All the same." Caleb went over to one of the cabinets and retrieved their handheld scanner. He set it to wideband, then ran it over each of them in turn, just in case…but nothing was attempting to broadcast a signal out beyond the walls of the ship. "We're okay."

"Okay?" Deunan exclaimed. "We are most definitely not okay. My home just got raided by paramilitary troops. I can never go back there."

"Welcome to the club," Laurent murmured shakily.

"Never say never, but we won't be returning until we get things sorted." He turned to Alex, who'd taken up a position resting against the data table, acting nonchalant even as tension exuded from every pore. "The outer sensors are active, just in case?"

"Already checked."

"Good." He retrieved several bottles of water from the kitchen unit and passed them out.

Laurent sucked his down so greedily that drops of water spilled onto his shirt. Then he gingerly climbed the short distance from the floor to the sofa. "What do we do now?"

Caleb gazed around the cabin and its limited space. "I'm not convinced the *Siyane* makes a great hideout for all of us. It'll get cramped, and we'll be forced to rely on wormhole travel far too much. We'll risk the wormholes being spotted."

"It's a terrible hideout," Deunan snapped. "I need access to the infolace, for one. There are things I need to do. Transfer funds, protect assets."

"All right." He kept his tone of voice calm and steady, working to bring the temperature in the cabin down. "This is your world. Where else can we go?"

Deunan's posture sagged as she sank against the wall. For the first time since he'd met her, she seemed…defeated. "I know a place. It's outside the city, so travel might still get inconvenient, but there'll be plenty of room for all of us. It's secure enough, with a full-featured infolace terminal, and it isn't tied to any of my current identities. The authorities won't connect it to me."

"Help Alex locate it on the map, and we'll take a look."

21

They stepped out from Alex's wormhole onto a well-manicured lawn of semi-wild sage grass. A frigid evening breeze bit into Laurent's skin; he shivered, though it could be from a mild case of shock as much as the cool air. The jacket Deunan had lent him when they first met was still at her place, so he rubbed his hands over his forearms. His head throbbed, and he found he wasn't certain precisely what had transpired in the last ten minutes or so.

They stood in front of a white, two-story clapboard house. Tall, narrow windows decorated the edifice, framed in a charcoal metal that matched the awning and sloping roof. Three steps lead up to a wide porch bound by chiseled columns. Beyond the house, the horizon of a large body of water peeked over what might be a cliff. Based on the geography, angle of the sun and chill in the air, he suspected it was the Ruchin Sea.

Deunan strode up to the front door and entered an elaborate pattern on the lock pad. The door slid open, and without looking back at them, she walked inside.

Caleb rotated in a slow three-sixty, taking in the scene. "Alex, stay with Laurent on the porch while I check out the interior. If someone, anyone, approaches, land or sky, evacuate. Don't wait for me."

"I don't like it."

Caleb shot her an easy smile. "You can come back for me after you get Laurent to safety. In fact, you had better come back for me."

She rolled her eyes, but ran her fingertips along his palm as he strode past them and followed Deunan into the house.

"Come on." Alex waved him forward, and they climbed the wide steps onto the porch.

Laurent leaned wearily against one of the columns. The throbbing in his skull left behind a sour taste of guilt. Everyone was repeatedly risking their lives in order to protect him. Deunan had lost her home because of him, joining him as a fugitive from the law.

He felt helpless and weak…and terrified of what would happen if they abandoned him to his fate. He was a scientist, a numbers guy. Less politely, a *strana*. His life was predictable and dull, and nothing he'd done had ever mattered to anyone but him. He wasn't equipped for assassination plots or paramilitary raids. He wasn't equipped for *any* of this.

Laurent glanced at Alex, who steadily shifted her gaze among the open door, the long, curving driveway, and the skies overhead. Of course, she was a scientist as well, and she seemed to be able to handle herself in dangerous situations without difficulty.

She offered him an encouraging smile before peering upward again, one hand absently stroking the onyx bracelet that wound like a serpent around her wrist and forearm. "The adrenaline dump after the kind of scene we just experienced is a bitch and a half. You'll be shaky for a while. When we go inside, eat a little something that has carbohydrates—but not too much—and drink some tea. Then sit down and give your body a chance to settle."

"Thank you."

"Sure."

"No, I mean *thank you*. For all of this. For saving my life for the…I've lost count of how many times."

She shrugged. "I've been where you are. We both have."

"You've had assassins—had your own government—try to kill you multiple times?"

Her eyes fixated on a point in the distant shadows up the drive for a second before moving on. "Yep."

"Wow. Seriously?"

"No lie. It's sort of how Caleb and I met, in fact. Then someone almost killed us again, later. And…also later." She chuckled. "I guess it really has happened a few times. In fairness, we tend to ask for it.

But not the first time. No, the first time, we simply stumbled onto an enormous secret that incredibly powerful people didn't want known. So yes, we've been exactly where you are."

"How did you survive it?"

"I don't know if you've noticed or not, but Caleb's *extremely* good in a fight."

"I had, actually."

"Yeah. And I'm…well, I'm relentlessly stubborn, which shouldn't be as effective at keeping me alive as it is. We kept running, and digging, until we pieced together the whole truth. Then we told the world."

"How did it go?" he asked.

"I won't deny it was rough for a while. I used to believe the truth should always be told to everyone, that keeping secrets from the public is always wrong. I've recently come to appreciate how it's…" a shadow swept like a storm cloud across her sparkling diamond-like eyes "…not always so simple. There are times when secrets are the only way. *But,* our government shouldn't have tried to kill us to protect its secrets, and yours shouldn't be trying to kill you, either."

"I agree. I just wish I understood why. Killing me won't stop the anomalies from manifesting. And if they continue to grow stronger, others are going to notice."

"We'll figure it out." Her expression brightened perceptibly as Caleb stuck his head outside.

"The coast is clear. Come on inside."

All the lights were on, illuminating a cheerful, airy interior, with textured, pale gray plaster walls and a weathered, paint-stripped wood ceiling. Stairs rose from the entry, and beyond them a wide hallway opened up to a living room on the left. On the right sat a kitchen with white ceiling-height cabinets and a long marble island. The fixtures presented clean lines and minimalistic interfaces in a way that conveyed 'tastefully expensive.'

The house was beautiful, though it lacked the ornamentation and frills one typically encountered in city residences. Less 'industrial chic,' more 'cozy place to relax and get away from it all.' It felt comforting, like a home one could be happy in.

They found Deunan flicking through menus on the hub screen outside the kitchen. "I know it's cool in here, but it'll warm up in a few minutes. There's plenty of bedrooms upstairs. Pick any of them."

"Whose house is this?" Laurent asked.

"It belongs to someone I know. Don't worry, they won't be visiting anytime soon." She tapped an icon on the screen, then walked up to him and held out her hand. "Give me the persona chrystor."

He fished it out of his pants pocket and handed it to her. She promptly walked over to the kitchen trash chute and chucked the cube inside, then turned back to him. "I'm sorry. I'll work you up a new persona while we're here. It won't have all the little flourishes, but it'll get the job done."

"You got me a persona with all the little flourishes?"

Her eyes cut away to scowl at the kitchen stovetop. "Don't make a thing of it. I took pity on you, nothing more."

The flutter that had leapt into his chest evaporated. "Now this, I believe."

"I...." She scowled at him then spun away. "Make yourselves comfortable. I need to see to some things outside. I'll be back in a bit."

CS

A gentle drizzle mixed with a steady ocean spray thrown up over the rocks by the crashing waves, and in seconds Deunan was soaked in a fine mist.

Not that it mattered; her clothes were already a mess from the chaos at her place. And also from the fire at Laurent's office before then. Needless to say, she would not be welcome at any of Ventise's evening galas wearing her current attire.

She didn't mind the dampness, though. It reminded her of her childhood, when she'd gleefully played in the ocean spray for hours on end, oblivious to the cold or the ruin she was making of her clothes.

Funny how, the instant her home was lost to her, she'd run straight back to the *other* home that was lost to her.

Not technically lost—for here it was, and here she was. But the person she'd been when she lived here was gone forever. Evanesced alongside a time of innocence, when her parents were alive and she was too young and naïve to understand the corrosive darkness strangling the world her family inhabited.

Eh, but she'd donned a colossal set of rose-hued glasses minutes after her return, hadn't she? In truth, things had grown sour sometime before her parents were murdered. Months, maybe a year or two, as her relationship with her father steadily deteriorated, his frustrated disappointment feeding her spiraling animosity toward him, toward *everything.*

Then one day, fire had consumed them all—her parents' bodies, and her soul.

She glanced back at the house, with its shining white boards cast defiantly against a leaden gray sky. It remained in pristine condition, which didn't surprise her. It was a trivial matter for the trust to pay to maintain it, and she supposed those who controlled the trust couldn't bring themselves to sell it. The property had been in her family's hands for centuries. No one could bear to live here now, but it felt like an unforgivable betrayal to allow anyone else to do so.

So here it sat, empty and unloved, except in memory.

Why had she chosen to bring them here? Why, when she enjoyed trustworthy contacts capable of hiding them in half a dozen locations across the continent?

It felt as if her present was on a collision course with her past. Was she powerless to veer off course, or steering hard into the turn? She'd long avoided dangerous introspection, so who could say?

While she'd spent decades nurturing her hatred of the KP like a prized napali vine, she'd long since given up on fighting to change the state of affairs. Bitter and resentful, somewhere along the way she'd thrown in that towel and decided to just live for herself, to take what she could wrest from this life without guilt or obligation. Living outside the system while flinging poison darts back inside its walls was the smallest victory she was able to exact, and she'd spun it into everything.

Now everywhere she looked, the KP and its resurgent sins leered out at her. Daring her to challenge it once more. Mocking her with its absolute confidence in how it was sure to win again, and again forevermore.

Inside the house, Laurent moved across a window, his face up-turned as he inspected his new surroundings. She smiled in spite of herself. The events of the last several days should have leveled him flat, but though he was definitely reeling a bit, he hadn't lost his sense of endless curiosity and wonder toward a world that kept trying to beat him into submission. How terribly foolish of him. Heartening, even worthy of respect, but foolish. She'd once thought the way he did, and her reward had been to lose everything she held dear. She wished she could save him from the same fate, but the world would have its due.

Guardian, she was bleak! She knelt down and picked out a pebble, worn smooth by the wind, then flung it off the cliff and into the water. The seabed below was littered with pebbles tossed from this cliff....

Ugh, she should not have come here. This place drowned her in the failures of the past, when Deunan the truva could do anything she wished. It was her mantra, the armor that held her identity together.

Could she do this?

Last time, she'd found herself alone in the fight. Abandoned by a family who, whether out of fear or something darker, refused to open their eyes and see what had always been hiding in plain sight, right in front of them all.

But this time, she had allies. People too stupid or ignorant to recognize this was a fight they had no chance of winning. She wondered…might it change anything, not being alone?

She shook her head roughly, flinging water droplets off her hair to chase the pebble into the sea below. An invisible hand squeezed her chest, and she had to beat back the overwhelming urge to keep running. Run until she ran out of road. Those events had shattered her family and nearly destroyed her. She'd slammed the door shut on her past in order to survive. It had made for a hollow facsimile of a life, but a life nonetheless.

Now here she stood, the road forking like lightning bolts in front of her. Run away, start over for a second time, pretend none of this mattered. Set Laurent up with a fresh name and culture credits and wish him well, knowing sooner or later, the assassins would catch up to him again.

Or turn into the pain and throw in with her companions for an impossible chance to make a difference. For Laurent and for their world—she was far too jaded to ever believe she could make a difference for herself.

Did she dare take a chance? Would anything remain of her if she did and failed? Was anything of her worth preserving if she didn't?

22

The penthouse loft-style residence resembled a war zone. Scorch marks blackened the brick walls like art graffiti gone wrong. Most of the seating had been shredded by those same lasers, when it wasn't overturned and lying askew. An acrid odor permeated the air from where several of the kitchen appliances had shorted out, and a haze lingered within it, the residue from multiple smoke grenades.

A forensics team pored over the scene, collecting evidence Arien hoped would definitively tie Laurent Kovalne to the location and identify the truva who was helping him. A drone cam had spotted a man who resembled Kovalne standing at the windows; combined with the tracker they'd placed on the truva, it was enough to green-light the raid on the residence. But now they needed more.

Arien glanced at the visual an agent had snapped of the truva in the restaurant where she'd met with Taberas Marziale. She was an attractive woman, exuding an air of elegance and composure not completely obscured beneath a veneer of caustic indifference. Especially her eyes. The visual had caught her as she reacted to something Taberas was saying, and the so-called windows to her soul suggested hidden depths. Which made her choice of career all the more reprehensible. He'd met people like her before—selfish, narcissistic individuals who rejected the social compact in favor of acting only for themselves.

According to the heat map the raid team captured before entering, two other people were present in the residence as well. And now, he had a much greater mystery to solve. Because despite the fact that both exits were covered—the front door and a fire escape leading to the roof and the street below—and the block cordoned off; despite the fact that the raid team identified four persons moving through the living space toward the rear bedroom during the raid…there was no one here.

Endreje saw him from across the room. The agent in charge of the Kovalne case squared his shoulders and walked deliberately up to Arien. "Sir, allow me to tender my resignation, effective immediately, or as soon as I've had the opportunity to brief my replacement."

"Denied." Arien waved off the offer. "As far as I can tell, the raid was executed properly. Movements of the people inside suggest they had at most a few seconds of warning. Whatever happened here, it's outside the bounds of what even the most skilled investigator could expect or plan for."

"Yes, sir. Thank you, sir."

"So what did happen here? What do we know?"

"Not nearly as much as I'd prefer, sir. The person the residence is registered to, Bria Salnese, doesn't appear to exist. Presumably a truva-generated false persona. The rent is paid from a culture credit account belong to a Sheria Kaitori, who also does not appear to exist."

Arien frowned. "So 'Deunan' is merely one of several aliases, and our truva suspect remains unidentified."

"Yes, sir. I've activated our undercover agents who move within the truva community and other criminal circles to quietly make inquiries. Truvas' greatest currency is often their reputation."

"But Kovalne couldn't afford to hire a truva of good reputation, could he?"

"Not so far as we're aware," Endreje said. "But many truvas also only take payment in hard currency. We didn't find any in his apartment, but this doesn't mean he didn't possess any."

"Consider me schooled. What else?"

"Forensics was able to collect hair samples from the master bedroom and bath. I'm optimistic we'll be able to obtain good DNA from the samples, but it will take a little time."

"I'll authorize the funds to prioritize the analysis." Arien wanted the case solved, for a rapidly expanding list of reasons.

"Have you spoken to the agents posted on the ground and on the roof? Is there no way someone got past them?"

"I have, and they confirm full coverage of the exits. We don't need to accept their word for it, however, since we have drone footage of the fire escape. No one came out the window at all."

"And there isn't some sort of hidden passage in the walls?" He sounded addled asking the question, but....

Endreje pointed to a man walking slowly down the hall while holding a small device out in front of him. "We're doing acoustic tests now. So far, nothing, but we'll rip open the walls if we need to."

"I try never to encourage speculation in the absence of evidence, but if you have a theory that makes this make sense, I'd love to hear it."

"Ah...some type of stealth technology, perhaps? I've heard rumors of elite research labs developing advanced concealment wraps."

"The footage from outside—did it show the window being opened?"

"No, sir. Good point."

"So based on the heat maps, four individuals were here one second, scrambling toward the bedroom in the rear. Then they were gone."

Endreje nodded tightly. "I've reviewed the recordings myself. I, uh, don't suppose we've secretly developed some manner of...teleportation device?"

"Not as I'm aware of, no. Honestly, though, I might need to ask the question." He noted one of the forensics agents heading their way and clapped Endreje on the shoulder. "Keep me informed."

Arien exhaled carefully, studying the scene for nonexistent clues before turning to leave. Where in the name of the Guardian had they gone, and how?

CS

Arien had scarcely stepped into his office when he received a priority message from the chancellor's chief of staff. Chancellor Levintis had extended an invitation to join him for afternoon kovfé. In less than an hour.

He reversed course. He supposed when you were the head of state, the world moved according to your schedule.

He'd met Levintis multiple times, both in an official capacity and simply due to the social circles he traveled in. The man had always struck him as well-meaning and sincere for a politician, but a touch weak of personality. Lacking strong convictions of his own, Levintis seemed prone to influence by those with credit and power. But in practical terms, he'd proved to be a better executive than the last chancellor, which was what mattered.

Arien took his personal skycar to the Capitol. While it was generally considered bad form to zip past the many cultural wonders of the city, such rudeness was overlooked for officials in positions such as his. They were hard at work protecting the people and thus had to make sacrifices.

As he landed at the small port inside the Capitol grounds, he noticed three people striding across the pad and climbing into a skycar emblazoned with the fiery orb of the Khesa Prutet. He only caught a glimpse, but he was fairly certain one of them was Solna Paran. Then the doors closed, and a few seconds later the skycar departed.

He imagined it wasn't unusual for high-ranking Khesa Prutet functionaries to visit the Capitol, or even the high chair herself. The government and the church worked together closely on many initiatives.

It took him fifteen minutes to clear security and be escorted upstairs to the chancellor's office.

"Arien, come in, come in." Levintis clasped him at the elbow then gestured over to the informal meeting table, where a kovfé setting already waited, steam wafting up from ornate, oversized porcelain. "When did we last see one another?"

"At the Trenae Porteau Exhibition, I believe, sir. How have you been?"

"Do you want the real answer, or the political one?" Levintis asked as he took a seat, signaling for Arien to follow suit.

"The political one seems safer, sir."

"Quite. I'd ask how the family is, but I understand you persist in remaining a bachelor. This is a statement against interest considering why I asked you here today, but you should keep in mind that work is not your life. Find love, start a family."

Wouldn't want the Colonnei Prime line to die out. But because Levintis was a skilled politician, the implication went unsaid.

"Easier said than done, sir. But I will try to remember to make the effort." Arien took a polite sip of the kovfé. "You have something in particular you want to discuss, then?"

"I do. Minister Sairento has informed me he wants to retire soon. His daughter has asked him to help her start a new learning center in Paesaan. It doesn't strike me as his wheelhouse, but anything for our children, yes?"

He gazed blithely at the chancellor.

"Ah, right. As we covered, you don't have any children yet. Regardless, Sairento has been at this job for a while. It wears you down. It wears all of us down." For an instant, a shadow darkened the chancellor's eyes, but it swiftly disappeared behind a politician's poise. "I've known you since you were a boy, Arien, so I'll come straight to the point. You were the first person who came to mind for his replacement. Your tenure as director of the Ventise Bureau of Investigation has been exemplary. Under your watch, the city has never been safer."

"Thank you, sir. I'm honored you'd consider me."

"Forget 'consider.' If it were up to me, I'd name you to the position today. You're young, though—in fact, you would be the youngest Elakrin Security Minister in six hundred years, or so my chief of staff tells me. As such, the parliament might need some convincing." The chancellor sipped on his kovfé with a nonchalance that must be feigned. "If you were to score a big, public win...say, bringing Laurent Kovalne to justice, for instance? Public opinion will steamroll you through confirmation. Especially as a Colonnei, of course."

"Of course." The response came out rote. "You're aware of the Kovalne case, sir?"

"Who isn't? It's all over the news. And yes, I do watch the news, at least whenever my wife forces me to. The murder of a bureau agent is bad enough, but then arson at the Space Physics Institute? Now, I'm sure this Kovalne fellow is just a troubled young man who's had some kind of psychotic break, but we can't have someone so dangerous running around on our streets, throwing people off roofs and torching architectural landmarks."

"No, sir. I assure you, I have deployed every resource under my command in the investigation. Mr. Kovalne is, unfortunately, proving elusive." *Because apparently, he can vanish from a room with no exits.* "But we will locate him, sir. We're closing in."

"I am glad to hear it. I've got every faith in you. Bring this one home, and I guarantee the Security Minister position is yours." Levintis stood and patted him on the shoulder. "Terrific to see you, Arien. Now, I'm afraid, duty calls, and I must run. Please, enjoy the rest of your kovfé."

Arien watched the chancellor stride out of the office, leaving a guard—one of his own men, in fact—behind to watch him.

He sipped on the kovfé and worked to assess what had just transpired. Levintis had never asked him if he *wanted* to be Elakrin Security Minister. At this level, it was assumed no one would refuse such a promotion. And he wouldn't either. While in a perfect world, he'd prefer nothing more than to still be an agent like Endreje, puzzling out mysteries and solving crimes using his wits and knowledge of the streets, this wasn't a perfect world. He was a Colonnei, and if he wasn't going to lead the Khesa Prutet, he was certainly expected to lead something.

Still, this was an odd ask. The Kovalne case had attracted media attention, yes, but it was hardly a matter of planetary concern. Though he could imagine a scenario where, if it weren't solved by the time he went before the parliament for a confirmation hearing, senators jockeying for points might use it as evidence he didn't deserve the promotion.

The kovfé wasn't to his taste, so he stood, nodded at the guard, and departed the chancellor's office. He didn't need the added incentive to solve the case, regardless. Up until now, he'd been making a concerted effort not to step on Endreje's toes and interfere unduly with the investigation. But after today's inexplicable events, he couldn't afford not to get more involved.

Somehow, all of this revolved around Laurent Kovalne. The Tafen Bridge shooting and Agent Pietri's presence in Kovalne's apartment prior to his plummet from the rooftop. An entire building burning to the ground from a fire started in Kovalne's office. The truva with the disconcerting eyes and their impossible escape from a sealed residence.

Until three days ago, the man had lived an utterly ordinary existence. No fines, no exemplars, no impact on society at all. So what recently changed in his life? What was the spark that ignited this storm?

On his way back to his skycar, he sent a message to Endreje.

I want to interview Insaf Devran, the Khesa Prutet priest who was at Kovalne's apartment, again. Personally this time.

23

Alex flopped down sideways across the bed in the room they'd chosen. The mattress instantly molded around her body, cradling it in a pillowy embrace; she adjusted her shoulders then considered the weathered wood ceiling. Given the continued escalation in violence, Caleb thought it best they stay at Laurent's side for now, instead of returning to the *Siyane* at night, and she didn't disagree.

Once upon a time, she'd have shrugged, muttered a Russian curse and walked away from a clusterfain like the one on Elakrin. Boarded her ship and cleared town before the blood started flowing in earnest. But that was before Caleb had made her care about the world she lived in. Before Valkyrie and her family and Mesme had given her reasons to fight for its survival. It was kind of addicting, honestly, saving the world. First her world, then the Khokteh's world, then Concord's. Hopefully now the Elakri's world. Next, everyone's worlds.

Besides, the voice normally content to quietly occupy the recesses of her mind that spoke up when something was capital 'I' Important was starting to whisper to her.

In a distant past, the Elakri had manipulated cosmic dimensions with a degree of skill only the Kats could match. Yet for all the Kats' tremendous intelligence and rarefied talents—honed over a million years then a million before that—they remained unable to ferret out the Dzhvar. What if the Elakri's technology could do so? Or if not find them now, could help defeat them when they roared back onto the manifold and resumed their universe-destroying ways?

No one alive understood how the Guardian functioned—but function it did. The answer to how must exist somewhere. Granted, if they were unable to locate it, she just *might* fly the *Siyane* directly into the center of the Guardian and go at the machine with a crescent wrench. Caleb would fuss, but he'd back her play; he always did. Her mind drifted into a memory…on the planet Ireltse, almost twenty years ago, when she'd taken it upon herself to confront the Kat—they'd still called them 'Metigens' back then—who masqueraded as a god to the local residents.

"Alex, what the bloody hell were you thinking? It could have hurt you—it could have taken you!"

Her gaze roved around the temple grounds, still hoping it would return for another go. "I was thinking I wanted some damn answers, and this might be my best or even only chance to get them." She steeled herself and reluctantly looked at him. "I didn't wake you because you wouldn't have wanted me to come here."

"Because it was a stupid thing to do. And now you've exposed us."

"Oh, come on—they knew we were traversing their portals. Remember when they chased us through a bunch of them? They have alarms on every damn one."

"Well, now they know we're doing a bit more than surveying the scenery."

"Good."

"Good?" He ran a hand through his hair. "Dammit, Alex, do you have the first care for your safety? Are you trying to get yourself killed?"

"No, of course not. I'm starting to think the Metigens can't hurt us, at least not directly."

"Why not? They can manipulate their environment—Mesme built a house. They can transport us."

"I know. But when it comes to violence, they act through others or via machines. I don't have an explanation, but the evidence speaks for itself."

"The evidence is a little thin. Too thin to act so recklessly. Not without a damn good reason—something I believe I rather clearly said we didn't have."

"You think a chance to get answers isn't a good enough reason? Why are we here then?"

He leveled a deeply scathing scowl at her. "To find the answers ourselves. To fit the puzzle pieces together one at a time instead of trusting aliens who have plainly ulterior motives to give us the truth. Otherwise, we would've simply gone to Mesme, right?"

She sank against the table to stare at the ground instead of him. "Yeah. They—the Metigens—drive me mad. They play with people, with whole species, like they were toys, to be tossed aside when they no longer amuse. I wish they had throats so I could strangle them."

He eased back beside her, and his voice softened a touch. "But not to death."

"That depends...." She risked a glance at him. "I'm sorry I snuck out on you."

His eyes remained hard though. "No, you're not."

She chewed on her lower lip and tried again. "Okay, I'm...sorry you wouldn't have agreed to come. I'd have preferred it if you were here with me."

He gazed up at the high, curved ceiling of the temple, once more tinted an ominous crimson now that the Metigen had departed. "Look. We've both spent a long time going our own way and not asking permission before we did. I'm not your keeper, nor are you mine. I just wish like hell you'd told me what you planned to do."

"Then we would've argued."

"As opposed to what we're doing now?"

She huffed a weak, resigned laugh. "Valid point."

"Alex, I can handle being angry with you—I don't like it, I don't want to be, but I'll deal. Already have some experience at it. But I have to be able to count on you. I have to know you won't go behind my back when you don't care for the answer I give."

She met his distressingly harsh gaze and nodded. "All right. I promise I won't go behind your back again, and will instead face the wrath of your expressions of pained patience and exasperated frustration."

He tried and failed to stifle a laugh. "There's no wrath to my expressions."

"Oh, yes, there is. And so many, varied kinds." She took his hands in hers, grateful he didn't jerk them away. "I realize I still occasionally revert to old habits. I'll try to do better. I will do better." Her forehead rested on his. "Out of curiosity, would you have come with me if I had asked?"

"Depends on how determined you were."

"So yes, then."

He sighed, but wrapped his arms around her and drew her closer. "Eventually, yes."

She was smiling to herself when Caleb returned from the lavatory and stretched out beside her. "What a day, huh?"

"Eh, not the best, not the worst."

He chuckled lightly. "Don't tempt fate. It's not over yet."

"About that. Fate, I mean." She propped up on an elbow to gaze down at him. "I'm increasingly worried you're one hundred percent correct. The Guardian is malfunctioning, and when it breaks down, there's a good chance it's going to obliterate the entire stellar system."

"You don't think this region of space will pop back out into Amaranthe?"

"If the machine undergoes a controlled shutdown, maybe. But if it blows a gasket? The shockwave will rip this bubble apart at a subatomic level."

He nodded thoughtfully. "Can you prevent the machine from self-destructing?"

"Once I understand how it functions? I mean, I'd kill for an assist from Mesme, or even from Valkyrie. Dashiel would likely have a few brilliant ideas, too. But…" she quirked a grin "…you're correct about this, too. Yeah, I can do it."

He leaned in and kissed her full on the mouth. "That's my girl. Let's get started, then."

CS

Caleb settled next to Alex on a sofa adorned with plush, soft cushions. It faced a wide stone fireplace, flanked by wood-shuttered windows offering peeks at a turbulent sea beyond. Despite the somewhat rustic setting, replica logs populated the fireplace; gas-lit flames danced behind the glass, and the warmth it generated was real enough.

Laurent sprawled in a deep lounge chair off to the side, looking utterly exhausted. Deunan didn't sit, instead leaning against one of the windows with her arms clasped tightly over her chest. Though the house exuded a comfortable, almost serene vibe, the woman wasn't relaxing.

Caleb took the lead in steering the conversation, as he knew all too well how Alex would quickly dive off into the scientific weeds. There would be a time for that, but this wasn't it. "Now that we've all caught our breaths, we need to try to bring all these threads together and come up with a plan to move forward."

"What kind of plan?" Laurent asked.

"Ultimately, one which results in people no longer trying to kill you."

"That sounds terrific."

"I imagine so. But also, a plan that saves all of your people from extinction."

Laurent blinked, but didn't look shocked by the laden statement. Either he was too worn down to summon enough energy for surprise, or the possibility had already occurred to him.

By the window, Deunan merely arched an eyebrow; then again, she was far more skilled at masking her true thoughts. "Explain."

"Laurent's anomalies—the tear in the manifold that allowed us to come here? We think they're occurring because the Guardian is malfunctioning."

"I don't understand," Deunan said. "Malfunctioning how?"

"We think the Guardian created this pocket of space your stellar system inhabits. Created it, and is maintaining it now. In effect, it's holding up the walls of the pocket—"

"The anomalies are cracks in those walls."

Alex nodded at Laurent. "Correct."

"And they're getting more frequent. And longer."

"Yes. There's no easy way to say this, but you both deserve to know. We're worried that if they continue to do so, eventually this pocket will collapse."

"But how can a machine be powerful enough to warp the manifold of space?" Laurent asked, too fixated on the science for the troubling implications to sink in yet.

Alex sighed and curled her legs up beneath her on the couch. "There's no simple way to explain it, but I believe the Guardian is itself a dimensional engine. Which is to say, it draws energy and…let's call it 'physics' from the non-spatial dimensions in order to manipulate the spatial ones. In this case, to create a hidden pocket of real space inside the non-spatial dimensions of the larger universe."

"What you call 'Amaranthe.'"

"Someone named it that long before we came around, but yes."

"Who would have the skill to construct such a machine?" Laurent leaned forward intently, showing signs of rallying past his exhaustion. "Can your people do so?"

Alex shook her head; she'd swiftly wrested control of the conversation away from Caleb, and he'd been foolish to expect anything less. "Humans? No. The Kats can, however. And a long time ago, the Elakri could as well."

"We've fallen rather far from the Guardian's grace, haven't we?" Deunan laughed darkly. "Our own creation is going to destroy us."

"Is this truly what the anomalies mean?" Laurent asked. "Is Elakrin going to be destroyed?"

"Not if we can help it," Caleb replied.

"So, heroes," Deunan remarked, challenge dripping from her voice. "Have a plan to save us all from extinction?"

"It is kind of what we do," Caleb muttered under his breath.

Three years after he, Alex and Nika Kirumase had committed genocide upon the Rasu in order to save trillions of lives, his feelings on the topic remained…complicated. He'd never regret saving a single one of those lives—and most of all the life of the woman sitting beside him. But it had marked the second time he'd extinguished a mind-boggling number of adversaries in order to save everyone else, and he'd as soon never be forced to do so again. Luckily, everyone here deserved to be saved, possibly excepting Laurent's would-be killers.

"Hmm? Didn't catch that," Deunan said.

"Nothing." Alex squeezed his hand, and he shot her an easy smile. Any genuine crisis of conscience over those events resided long in the past, having left behind only a vague uneasiness in the crevices of his soul.

His meandering thoughts left too wide an opening, and Alex dove into it with growing fervor. "We need to learn more about how the machine functions before we can determine how to move forward. I'm concerned about what will happen if we simply shut it off. If it were a Rift Bubble—a device some flighty, capricious, ethereal aliens back home engineered—then the dimensional shift would fade away, revealing what was hidden inside.

"But the Guardian operates differently. It's not shifting the curve of the physical dimensions around you to conceal your presence. It's holding up a real space—and there's no release valve, no portal to connect this bubble to anywhere else. So we need to either fix the machine before it goes critical, or ensure we can safely power it down. But to do either, we need to understand how it works."

Caleb stepped back in, as the weeds were starting to get a bit high. "Based on everything that's happened, I believe the KP knows how the Guardian works. In fact, I believe they know it's failing."

Alex's gaze snapped over to him, a question in her eyes. He hadn't had a chance to share the picture coming together in his head with her, but the pieces all fit. The Guardian was causing the anomalies, and the discovery of those anomalies had pitched Laurent's life into danger. The government was now involved on some level—the raid on Deunan's residence proved this—but the KP was the face of the Guardian. And if the Guardian was not remotely what the organization presented it to be, then neither was the KP.

"It stands to reason they want to keep news of its malfunctioning a secret," Caleb said. "That's why they're trying to kill you, Laurent. Now, maybe they know how to fix the Guardian themselves, and their attempt to silence you is a bid to buy time until they can do so. This is good for your people, but not for Laurent personally, because they'll always want him dead so the world never discovers the truth. Or maybe they're panicking, scrambling to figure out what to do and, again, trying to buy time.

"But either way, the KP is the one holding the secrets—secrets we need to learn if we're going to clear Laurent's name, keep him safe and save this world from annihilation."

"I was afraid you were going to say that," Deunan remarked from the position she'd staked out by the window. "*Dannati malede.*"

Caleb scrutinized her in interest. He'd suspected for some time now that there was more to her hatred of the KP than a simple antiestablishment bent, and possibly a great deal more. "Is this something you can help us with?"

Deunan pushed off the window and launched into furious pacing in front of the fireplace. "Most people think the government works in open partnership with storied corporations and research institutes to maintain our historical knowledge. Vast libraries are scattered across the planet, in orbit and on Giarnum to prevent something like The Fall from ever happening again. To ensure everything we know, everything we've learned, will be protected from any future calamity—short of our literal universe being ripped apart, I guess. I expect no one realized we'd need to hedge our bets for that eventuality. Anyway. Laurent, you believe the ultimate repository of scientific knowledge is housed at the Ventise Central Foundation, I assume?"

"Well, yes. Obviously."

Deunan snorted. "Think again. The Foundation's collection represents a small fraction of historical scientific knowledge. It's all smoke and mirrors, a performative façade for the public. Just like the KP Seat is a shiny, disgustingly overwrought campus that is little more than a tourist attraction.

"The true KP headquarters is a place referred to by those in the know as the Scenza. It's located two hundred kilometers outside of Ventise, on a ranch the official records say is privately owned by a wealthy family. But inside its walls—mostly beneath them, actually—are not only copies of every file of any value generated by every government agency, corporation and research institute, but the *only* copy of vastly greater knowledge. Records dating back to the first months after The Fall. Nine thousand years of history.

"So if the KP knows how the Guardian works, that's where the information will be found."

Deunan's entire demeanor had transformed when she'd started speaking, revealing a woman they hadn't seen before this moment: knowledgeable, serious, *invested.*

"Okay," Caleb said. "I have a lot of questions, but for now I'll take what you're saying at face value. Alex can use sidespace to scout the facility and give us an idea of what to expect. We'll use the intel to plan our infiltration. Then, she can open a wormhole to drop us inside. Once there, we can—"

"You'll be killed in seconds," Deunan said.

"We'll be stealthed. Invisible."

"Won't matter. The security measures they have in place at the Scenza are too sophisticated. In order to get beyond the first floor, you have to pass a genetic scan. Anyone for whom the system doesn't grant access will be shot by automated defenses if they attempt to infiltrate the lower levels. If the environment isn't conducive to lasers flying around—there's some valuable heirlooms stored in the depths—the doors will seal and the room will be flooded with poison gas."

Alex looked dubious. "You must be exaggerating."

"I am not. They are deadly serious about their security. And their secrets."

"I've never heard even a rumor of anything such as this," Laurent said. "How do you know so much about it?"

"Because I've been to the Scenza. And...." She paused to stare pointedly out the window, as if she were seeing something beyond it they did not. "I can get us in. More relevantly, I can ensure we're not all murdered in gruesome fashion once we're there."

It wasn't quite the dramatic reveal Caleb had been expecting. "Deunan, you are skilled at what you do. I mean it. But if what you say is true, how do you imagine you can circumvent a DNA-based security system?"

"By not circumventing it at all."

Now was not the time for her to be difficult for difficulty's sake. "What does that mean?" he asked thinly.

"It means...it means my last name is Colonnei."

"Oh," Laurent said. "*Ohhhhh....*" His eyes widened precipitously, and he gaped at Deunan in evident confusion. "Wait, no. There aren't any Colonneis named 'Deunan'—not in the Prime lineage."

"I changed my name, moron. It wouldn't have been much of a disappearing act if I still went around calling myself 'Magnelle.'"

"Oh! You're telling me *you're* Magnelle Colonnei?"

But Deunan's focus was locked out the window once more, and she didn't respond.

Alex glanced at Caleb, brow furrowed; he shrugged. "We're confused. What does your last name have to do with anything? Or your first name, for that matter?"

"Her family founded the KP," Laurent offered. "Her father was the previous high chair, before he...Deunan, I don't know what to say."

Caleb sank deeper into the couch. He'd assumed there was a story lurking in the woman's past, but he hadn't expected *this*.

"They didn't merely found the KP." Deunan shifted back to face them, and Caleb amended his earlier observation. Her demeanor hadn't transformed earlier so much as he'd thought, but it sure as hell had now. "In the nine thousand years since the KP began, a member of the Colonnei Prime lineage has always either been high chair or served on the Board of Advisors. *Always.* It's in the charter. And even when a Colonnei isn't sitting in the chair, the ranking member of the family has unfettered access to every aspect of KP business."

"Any chance you're the ranking member?" Caleb asked.

"Ah, no. I renounced my family years ago, after my parents were murdered. Walked away from the cursed Colonnei name and never looked back. Until today, it turns out."

"So who is the ranking member?"

"That would be my younger brother, Arien. He's the director of the Ventise Bureau of Investigation. Laurent, he's probably the person who put the Red One designation on you. For what it's worth, I'm sorry. If I had any influence with him—or any contact at all—I'd clear this up, but I don't.

"While I assume the KP leadership revoked whatever official access I'd otherwise have had, they can't change my blood. My DNA will get us past the initial security checks and prevent us from being killed by the automated defenses. But if we want to gain access to the most protected information vaults, we're going to need my brother's passkey."

She offered up a haunted, melancholy smile. "Care to help me steal it?"

PART III

THE KHESA PRUTET

24

Laurent found Deunan at the house's workstation, which was tucked into an alcove off the living room. She hadn't sat down, instead bending over the desk as she scrolled through a series of menus. Her body language screamed that she didn't want to be bothered, but this had been true nearly every minute since he'd met her.

He dropped a shoulder on the archway beside the desk. "Hi."

Her eyes cut over to him, then back to the screen. "Don't."

"Don't what?"

"Whatever it is you're going to say. That you've never known a celebrity before. That you're sorry about my parents. That you liked me better when I was just a truva—or liked me less. Don't."

"Actually, I was going to ask if you mind if I raid the kitchen and cook us all a proper meal." It was a lie, but she'd blown his planned opening.

"Are you a decent cook?"

"It's the only thing other than physics I'm any good at."

Her lips twitched, softening her expression a touch. "I'm sure that's not true. I mean, it can't be true, right?"

"It absolutely can be." He smiled gently. "Do you miss your brother?"

"I'm not...why would you ask me this, of all things?"

"I'm not trying to pry. It's merely...I had a sister. She was three years older than me, and I idolized her growing up. She died in the freak tornado storm on Amalee Island a few years ago, and I still miss her every day."

"Oh. I'm sorry. I, um...sometimes, yeah. I do. He was all right. My father's favorite, but he never used it against me. Stupid *cugna*, though. I tried to convince him—" She cut herself off. "Never mind."

"You can tell me, if you want to."

"And why should I want to?" She shoved off the desk and stormed upstairs.

He thudded his forehead slowly on the wall. Why had he bothered trying? She was utterly impenetrable. A brick wall. Stone cold. Or maybe she simply didn't like him. Obviously she didn't *like him* like him, but maybe she didn't care for him in the slightest, and was going to cheer with relief when this crisis was over and she never had to speak to him again. The persona with 'all the little flourishes' had given him a flash of hope, but the notion that her taking extra care in creating it meant anything personal was foolish. She took pride in being skilled at her job, nothing more.

Alex came around the corner and saw him standing there. "You ought to get some rest while you can."

"Eh, I thought I'd make everyone dinner. Hungry?"

"Famished. I won't be much help—Caleb's the cook—but I'll keep you company."

"Sounds good." He went into the kitchen and opened the refrigeration unit. It was well stocked, which struck him as odd. Deunan had insisted no one would be coming to the house, but it looked as if the kitchen had been supplied with enough groceries to feed multiple residents.

He backed away and considered everything he'd seen here with fresh eyes…and the realization hit him. This house didn't belong to a friend, client or colleague. This was *her parents'* house—which meant it had been her house when she was young. Or at a minimum, a family vacation place, as he needed to allow for how a family as wealthy as the Colonneis maintained multiple residences. But why keep the kitchen supplied if no one was using it?

Unless it was a perfectly preserved tomb, kept forever intact for the day a rightful resident would return to its hallowed halls. A place frozen in time by tragedy.

He shuddered; however coldly she treated him, his heart ached for her. It must be so difficult for her to be here now. He wanted to go upstairs and try to offer some manner of comfort, but the sting of her last rejection was fresh enough to stay him. He'd concede he was slow to learn, but he could be taught.

So instead he pulled out a frozen fowl and a container of vegetables. "Alex, what do you want?"

"Still don't know much about what you guys eat. But our digestive systems are robust. Whatever you make will be fine."

"Hopefully so." He put the fowl in the oven to thaw, spread some cucurbi and toma out on the counter and started slicing.

"So, this 'Colonnei' thing. It's a pretty big deal here?" Alex asked.

"It's a huge deal. Her ancestors who formed the KP, Lirin and Jenova Colonnei? They're practically revered as saints. The entire family took on mythological proportions thousands of years ago, and esteem for them has never waned. When her parents died, it was the top news story on the planet for weeks on end."

"How did her parents die? She said they were murdered."

"Yeah, I'm not sure what she meant. I only know they died in a skycar crash. Out over this very sea, in fact…and it just occurred to me that they must have been traveling to or from here when it happened."

"Are you saying this was their home?"

Laurent found a bowl for the vegetables, then grabbed several seasonings from the pantry. "Puts a new spin on things, doesn't it?"

"It explains why she believes we'll be safe here. What happened with the crash?"

"Single-vehicle incident—it fell out of the sky. It was blamed on faulty equipment. As I think about it, there were some initial questions about possible foul play, but authorities eventually ruled it out."

Alex glanced over her shoulder, checking for Deunan. "Do you have any idea why she renounced her family?"

"No. I intended to ask her a few minutes ago. But our conversations rarely last for long before she dismisses me, and this one was no exception. But the way she feels about the KP…it's got to be tied up in what happened to her parents."

"Why do you say so?"

"Her father was high chair when he died. Had been for forty

years or so. Her grandmother was before him. In fact, our current high chair, Solna Paran, is the first non-Colonnei to hold the seat in several hundred years."

"Is that unusual?" Alex asked.

"For someone other than a Colonnei to lead the KP? It happens. There's not a strict line of succession—at least, not officially. Unofficially, who knows?" He tried to recall the facts from his schooling. "I think there's only been three outside the family in the last five centuries. Possibly four."

"Yet her brother didn't take the position when their father died?"

"He was too young for it, if I remember correctly. Solna was Gandrin Colonnei's—her father's—chief deputy, and her ascension was billed as one of stability and continuity of leadership."

"And has it been?"

He shrugged as he turned his attention to the fowl. "Can't say. I kind of tuned out on KP politics once I finished my schooling requirements. Buried my nose in my research and have kept it there ever since."

Alex sighed. "I know something about the weight of family legacy and expectations, and refusing to participate in those games. Not on this scale, but I can empathize with her running away from it all. I kind of ran away, too. I didn't publicly renounce my family or anything so dramatic, but I did take the *Siyane* and abscond into the stars for almost a decade."

"Not any longer, though?"

"No. My mom and I...I guess you could say we found our way back to each other. And my dad...well, he's a much more complicated story. But I am living proof that no matter how fucked up family dynamics get, it doesn't have to be too late to mend the wounds."

"If she's a truva and her brother's the director of the Ventise Bureau of Investigation, I suspect the option isn't on the table." He looked around the kitchen, struck again by his initial impression of a home one could be happy in. Instead, there was only tragedy. "I can't imagine what growing up must have been like for her. Then to lose her parents, with the whole world watching her as she grieved. I suppose this explains a great deal about why she's so private. Closed off." Laurent frowned at the vegetables, absently tossing them with the seasoning. "Trouble is...."

"Trouble is what?"

"I don't think knowing what she's been through is apt to make her any easier to talk to."

Alex studied him, eyes sparkling, her oddly flat lips curling up on one side. "You have feelings for her."

"I'm not that much of a glutton for punishment. Or maybe I am—I did become an extraplanetary physicist, after all. But it doesn't matter."

"Well, let's get through this little crisis and see what happens."

25

Deunan flipped the small object over in her hand, then over again. It was a matte black oval four centimeters long and two wide, with a flush clip on one side. "And this little gadget is going to make me invisible?"

"Try it," Caleb said. "Feel the depression on one side? Hold your finger on it for two seconds."

She moved the tip of her finger until it rested where the object grew concave and pressed, then glanced down. "I can still see myself."

"Hold your arm out."

She complied and— "Oh!" A few centimeters beyond her elbow, her arm disappeared. She kicked a leg out in front of her and watched it disappear. "Wild."

"The Veil doesn't truly make you invisible, but rather alters the air around you to mask your form with a copy of your immediate environment," Caleb explained. "There was some early experimentation with pulling the field in against clothing, but it turns out body awareness is critical for enabling us to move around smoothly in the world. If you can't perceive your body, you get dizzy, bump into things, fall down." Caleb glanced at Alex, who was sitting on the sofa, eyes closed and hands flat on her thighs, doing something they'd called 'sidespace.' "Some people can get used to it, but the developers decided it was safer to have a small buffer of space before the field kicked in."

Deunan placed her arm in front of a painting on the wall and moved it rapidly in all directions. The details of the painting never blurred or faded. Given the range of feats the Humans had proved capable of performing, she shouldn't be impressed, but she was.

"Walk around for a few minutes and get acclimated to it," Caleb suggested. "Even with the buffer, it's a strange sensation to interact with the world while invisible. Our brains aren't wired to process it. Well, ours aren't, and it's a reasonable bet yours aren't either."

"I've got excellent situational awareness. Comes with the job. Or the risks of the job."

"I had noticed that. Nonetheless."

She didn't care for the patronizing tone humming beneath his words, but she relented and walked down the hall and into the kitchen—and clipped the island with her hip. Luckly, Caleb didn't see it. She wound through the space between the island and refrigeration unit, then between the breakfast table and the windows, deliberately squeezing through the smallest spaces she could find.

Thirty seconds later, she returned to where Caleb waited, shut off the device and handed it to him. "Got it."

"Okay." He didn't challenge her assertion, so perhaps she'd imagined the patronizing tone. "The field extends out for a meter and a half, so a bit past your leg-span, but be aware of the distance if you're carrying something large or interacting with something outside its range."

"Someone sees a floating vase, and they're going to either question their sanity or start believing in ghosts." She nodded. "Understood. On that note. As we've talked about, Arien's security at his home will be top-notch. Despite this, I can bypass his door. But he'll likely have a security cam in the hallway, and it'll pick up the door opening."

"That's what Alex is working on." He turned toward his wife, an almost-smile lifting his lips. "What's the word?"

"One more minute."

Caleb tilted his head toward the living room, then went over and sat next to Alex to wait.

Alex opened her eyes; with the act, it was as if life flooded in to animate her body. "There's a pantry off the kitchen large enough for entry. It's near the center of the apartment, with no other ingress or egress, so I can't imagine it's covered by a cam."

"Is the door to it closed?" Caleb asked.

"Right now, yes. If it's open when we go, there is also a closet attached to the bedroom. It struck me as a place an intruder might hide if they wanted to ambush someone, so it's conceivable it's covered by surveillance. I doubt it, though."

Caleb nodded. "We'll keep the closet as our fallback."

Deunan stared at the two of them in turn. "What did she—Alex, how do you know this?"

"I went to your brother's apartment with my mind."

"Excuse me?"

"It's something where…honestly, you all have remained so strangely ignorant of quantum dimensions, I don't think even Laurent will understand it, so I'm not going to try to explain the mechanics. It's something I can do."

"Project your consciousness to random locations?"

Alex shook her head. "Not random—I need to visualize where I'm going, which was why I asked for you to point out the apartment building on a map."

Deunan peered around for Laurent, curious what he thought of this nonsense, but he was nowhere to be seen. He'd been making himself scarce for a while now, and it occurred to her she might have hurt his feelings during their last conversation. It hadn't been her intent, but she wasn't ready to talk about Arien or her parents or *anything*. Didn't expect she'd ever be.

"But if you know where you're going, you can go…anywhere?" she asked.

"Normally, yes. But I can't get past the barrier enclosing your pocket universe, which is a testament to the power of the Guardian machine. It has locked you up in here tight."

Caleb placed a hand on Alex's knee, and she grimaced. "Sorry. That was unartfully put."

"No, it seems a fair assessment. But you two are very strange."

Caleb shook his head. "She's the strange one. I can't do it."

"Trust me, you *two* are very strange."

CS

Arien's pantry smelled of a recently baked panite and apple cinnamon scones, and Deunan had to stifle a chuckle. Her brother always had loved warm, breaded treats.

The glow from the wormhole lit the pantry like a spotlight, and they waited until Alex closed it before moving. Deunan placed a hand in front of the door…nothing happened. Because it was motion activated, and she was invisible.

Caleb: "Back up against the side. Let me."

She and Alex had rigged up a cross-compatible comm channel so they could all speak silently to one another, in case the security system included aural listeners. Most didn't, but her brother was the director of the Ventise Bureau of Investigation, and she'd expect him to employ nothing but the best.

Deunan: "Done."

Caleb de-stealthed, flattened himself against the narrow span of wall beside the door, and waved his hand at it. The instant it began opening, he vanished.

Caleb: "Go now."

She rushed out of the pantry, assuming he would follow.

The kitchen felt cold and impersonal. Did Arien employ a chef? He'd never been much of a cook growing up. Their mother had been such an excellent one, and neither of them had been pushed into developing the skill. As of today, Arien remained unbonded and childless, which must be a topic of some consternation among the extended family, and glee within Solna Paran's inner circle. So long as no Colonnei Primes stepped up to claim the Seat, the usurpers could cement their power on a long-term basis. The thought rankled her more than it should; she didn't care who ran the KP.

Deunan moved through a high, wide archway into the living room. Impeccably decorated, with an enormous Etrusian woven rug that complemented the upholstered seating. A large permanent screen hung dark above a marble fireplace. The far wall featured two atrocious paintings, but on either side of them….

She wandered closer, then swallowed heavily to quell a flutter in her stomach.

Photos of their family, spanning the years when they'd been together, framed the paintings. A trip to the Grand Falls when Arien was just a little boy—surely he didn't actually remember the vacation? The four of them all dressed up in finery for some cousin's or other's arrival gala, posing in front of the water fountain at La Palaigna. A zoomed-in photo of their parents embracing, mutual affection brightening their expressions. She and Arien had climbed out on the roof at the house and sneaked around to the cliff-facing-side to spy on them—

Caleb: "Have you found his terminal yet?"

She jumped, startled out of her reverie.

Deunan: "Not yet."

Caleb: "Keep me apprised. I'm watching the entrance and the windows."

Right. Terminal, terminal, terminal. Important man like Arien, he'd have a proper office.

She located the office on the left off the hallway leading to the entrance. An intricately carved and polished wood desk dominated the room, with a chrystor cabinet on the left and a reading chair on the right. The walls were decorated with visuals of her brother alongside a parade of impeccably dressed companions. The few she recognized were wealthy corporate magnates, famous artists or politicians.

She wanted to spend hours here, wandering the lonely rooms of her brother's home, searching for more insights into his life. Was it a good one? Was he happy? She'd spent the last twenty years studiously *not* pondering such questions, yet now they threatened to consume her.

But the clock raced onward, and she could not afford to grow sentimental now.

Deunan: "Found it. Getting to work."

If there was heightened security anywhere in the residence, it would be in this room. But this wasn't her first infiltration, and she'd brought a few toys of her own.

Still invisible, she placed a projector on the edge of the desk. The device captured the desk and surroundings as they appeared, then rebroadcast the image for the benefit of any security cams in the room. Once she confirmed the projector was doing its job, she reached under the desk's surface and activated the terminal. A screen and the outline of a keyboard flickered to life on the desk.

She nudged the chair out of the way, slid a spike into the terminal's input slot, and typed a command.

The most recently accessed file surfaced first, and she did a doubletake. The raid on her residence.

She'd internalized the likelihood that Arien was involved in the search for Laurent, at least at a supervisory level, but—as with everything else about her brother—she'd forced herself to not spend any time contemplating what this meant. And what it meant was that while he didn't know it, her brother was now hunting her.

The notion made her nauseated. Not because she was worried about him ever realizing that she was who he hunted. They'd collect her DNA from the residence, but she'd long ago swapped out the records so her profile pointed to a long-deceased person, for precisely this reason. Assuming they didn't think to check for the Colonnei genetic marker—and why would they—it should be another dead end.

But for all their disagreements, for how much he'd broken her heart so many years ago, she'd never hated Arien.

She tapped past voluminous directories and portals related to his work, until she finally located the portal for the KP. It gladdened her heart to see it was so low on his priority list. Maybe he hadn't turned completely evil after all. It didn't matter for their purposes, but she'd like to believe some part of the boy she'd loved endured in the man.

Caleb: "Checking in."

Deunan: "Promise I'll tell you when I'm done."

Caleb: "I think I'll keep checking in."

The fact that she wouldn't be here without his help stayed her tongue, but only just. She activated the KP portal.

TRUSTED SOURCE CONFIRMED.
PASSKEY:

The thing was, his passkey wasn't going to be stored on any media. He would simply know it; knowing it, he'd have no reason to record it somewhere and create a security vulnerability. He did have to enter it every time he wanted to access private KP data, though the system, being a fairly secure one, would not cache the information. But there were always traces left behind. Routes that were followed again and again.

She minimized the directory and entered another command for the spike program. It surfaced the keys activated in the first ten seconds after the KP login window was accessed: REGIA MTOB

She waited while, in her head, her autonetics worked out the possible combinations, accounting for duplicate presses. Technically, the passkey could be any of the many combinations. But no one ever chose a meaningless jumble of letters. For one, it made the passkey far more difficult to remember; after all, brains were pattern-recognition programs. For another, people were sentimental in the dumbest ways, and often defaulted to a personal—

MAGGIE BATORE

She stumbled back into the chair, sending it bumping into the wall. Her heart leapt into her throat, and for several seconds, she couldn't breathe.

Caleb: "Deunan, status? I heard something."

As she stared at the arrangement of letters in her mind, a tear welled up in the corner of her eye then fell unbidden down her cheek. A thousand regrets she never gave the oxygen necessary to breathe burst free to burden her conscience, and a great sorrow for all she'd lost settled heavily onto her soul.

Caleb: "Deunan? Answer me."

Assumptions she'd made over the years flashed through her

mind, so many of them branching out from vindictive words they'd hurled at one another that night while thunder rattled the windows of the beach house.

Uncertainty wasn't a sensation she brokered, and the terror of it now seized her chest. Was everything she believed wrong?

Caleb: "I can't find any intruders. Are you in the office? What's happened?"

Deunan: "Sorry. I was distracted. I, uh...I've got the passkey. We can go."

Caleb: "That's it? You were distracted?"

Deunan: "This is my brother's apartment. No surprise something caught my interest. That's it."

Caleb: "Fine. Meet me at the pantry."

Her breath felt stuck in her lungs, as if she'd fallen from a great height and had the wind knocked out of her. The terminal screen wavered and blurred, until she was barely able to make out the words.

Dannat! She hurriedly wiped at her eyes and worked to tamp down the turbulent emotions, shoving them far away, back behind a door in her mind that would no longer close.

She fished a film out of the sleeve in her pocket and grabbed Arien's fingerprints from the keyboard overlay, then returned the chair to its proper location. Lastly, she removed the projector and hurried out of the office.

26

T he body lay crumpled on the sidewalk a few meters from a transit path entry. Rumpled black robes concealed most of the copious blood spilt from the neck wound. A stain would be left behind once the body was moved, but city maintenance was standing by to sweep in and erase all evidence of such a heinous crime here in the Capitol District.

Arien paced deliberately along the perimeter of the scene, arms clasped across his chest, while he waited for Endreje to finish conferring with a forensics officer. He shook his head clear to combat the sensation of déjà vu overtaking him. A few short days had passed since he'd done much the same outside of Laurent Kovalne's apartment building. Moments later, he'd been flagged down by the man who now lay bled out on the sidewalk.

Endreje nodded to the officer then strode over to Arien. "Sir."

"What do we know?"

"Witnesses say a man accosted Mr. Devran on the sidewalk, demanding his priest medallion and any other items of jewelry on his person. When Devran hesitated, the man stabbed him in the neck and took off running. Witnesses describe the man as looking disheveled, wearing stained yellow pants and a long burgundy sweater. A vagrant, possibly."

"Here in the Capitol District? There's an officer on every street corner. Why did none of them gently escort this man to a more appropriate neighborhood?"

"The officer on duty for this block was called away to deal with a medical emergency in Querin Park a few minutes before the attack." Endreje gestured toward the greenspace in the distance. "As for how the attacker made it this far, I've ordered the street cam footage for the entire district pulled for review. Whatever happened, we'll see it."

Arien scowled at the body; he was still having trouble accepting the who, how, and most of all, the why. "He was on the way to the interview we'd scheduled."

"A safe assumption, sir. He confirmed the appointment time with the office a little over two hours ago."

"Is there any hint in the scene or the witness reports suggesting this was anything more than a robbery gone wrong?"

"Other than the presence of a vagrant in this neighborhood in the first place, which you've already identified? Not so far."

"I don't like it, Endreje. I don't like it at all."

"Sir..." the agent's lips drew tight, and he stepped closer "...are you insinuating someone wanted to silence Mr. Devran before he spoke to us?"

"Khesa Prutet priests do not get murdered in the middle of the Capitol District during dinner rush. I daresay it's never happened, not in the nine thousand years since The Fall. The prospect that he was killed to ensure his silence is unthinkable, but any alternative is...impossible."

"Yes, sir. We'll investigate his personal life. Business dealings. But even if there is another motive, why here?" Endreje cleared his throat. "The, ah, description of the suspect doesn't match Laurent Kovalne. Lighter, longer hair. Taller, bulkier build."

"I don't—" Arien cut himself off. He'd started to say, 'I don't think Kovalne did this.' But why? What insight had his brain worked out, yet neglected to divulge to him?

"Sir?"

"Kovalne is facing execution if he's caught and convicted of Agent Pietri's murder. I'm skeptical whether anything Mr. Devran could have divulged to us would have worsened the man's situation."

"Unless the man on the roof wasn't Kovalne. We don't have a good description of him from witnesses."

"No, we do not." Arien sighed. "Let me know what the street cam footage shows. I have a charity gala I can't skip tonight, after which I plan to sit in a quiet room and determine how to proceed.

I wouldn't want the next person we decide to interview meeting Mr. Devran's fate as well."

CS

"I understand the records of the Department of Extraplanetary Affairs are subject to the usual privacy protection regulations." Arien shrugged off his coat and tossed it on the entry table, then headed to the kitchen for a drink. "But I'm not a private citizen. I'm director of the Ventise Bureau of Investigation…yes, I absolutely intend to seek a documentary warrant, and we both know the judge will grant it. Therefore, I'm hoping we can speed things along here."

He retrieved a lime spritzer from the valet, then reversed course to his office. "Yes, as a personal favor…" his steps slowed, and he cringed "…for the Colonnei family." He tried not to pull such strings unless necessary, but sometimes the family name was the only thing that could slice through knots of government bureaucracy. "Thank you. I'll look for the documents in my system shortly."

He set his glass on the desk and went to sit down—and almost missed his chair. He glanced back, frowning. It was in the wrong place, sitting slightly off to the left.

Hmm. Maybe the cleaning bot had knocked it askew during its normal routine. He scooted it over and sat, opening up the new report from Endreje.

The street cams were a dead end, except to the extent they recorded the crime itself; though the angle wasn't ideal, the footage confirmed the witnesses' accounts. The suspect appeared on a cam at the corner of Sailon and Dreen six minutes before the attack on Insaf Devran, and nowhere else. The intersection was near the edge of the Capitol District proper, making it likely the man had entered from that direction. Surveillance coverage was far from comprehensive in the other districts, so it wasn't unusual that no other cams captured him. Of course, if the attack was premeditated, the man could have slipped in a building and discarded a coat, hat or otherwise altered his appearance as well. He may well be present on a dozen videos, but unrecognizable.

Premeditated.... What was he getting at here? He suspected he'd spooked Endreje with his conspiratorial musings at the crime scene. While the case had raised red flags from the beginning, and every new crime it spawned added to the mystery, until tonight, he hadn't seriously considered a genuine conspiracy might be to blame for the violence. But here he was.

So, a conspiracy to commit malfeasance (beyond the public crimes), or to conceal it? With Devran's murder, perhaps both.

27

C aleb settled onto the sofa next to Alex. "Find anything dire in the anomaly data we collected on the *Siyane?*"

"Only what we already knew—it's getting worse. Laurent and I went over his historical data, though, and the good news is, the decay seems to be close to linear for now. Well, it's not that great of news, because I can't predict what the tipping point will be. There's a threshold beyond which the tear will be too large for the brane enclosing this space to maintain its integrity. We likely have some time, but...."

"But we shouldn't count on much."

"No." She tilted her head toward where Laurent sat at the workstation, attention locked upon a complex table of data. "He's really pretty brilliant. The only thing holding back his genius is that he doesn't know what he doesn't know. His understanding of physics is limited in these random ways, a consequence of this universe's isolation.

"No one here ever thought to ask the questions that would've led to the discovery—or I guess *re*discovery—of exotic matter, or learning how supernovae seeded the universe with the heavy metals needed for new stellar formation, or a hundred other questions that demanded answers in our universe. So he has zero frame of reference for the type of cosmic phenomena that could cause the readings his equipment was measuring."

"It's good you're here." He squeezed her hand affectionately, then sought Deunan out with his eyes. The woman stood in front of a visual on the far wall, to the left of the dining table. If he recalled correctly, it was a visual of two young Elakri standing arm in arm in the shadow of a typically ornate building façade. It didn't take ace detective skills to deduce it was an image of her and her brother. The girl didn't closely resemble Deunan, but given her family's fame, she'd presumably altered her appearance along with her name when she became a truva.

She'd been standing there staring at the image for quite some time. Something she'd discovered in her brother's apartment had knocked her off-kilter, but he recognized the futility of asking her about it. And unfortunately, time was not their friend, so he cleared his throat. "Deunan? We need to discuss our next steps."

She nodded vaguely, but it took another few seconds for her to turn around and come over to prop on the arm of one of the chairs. "As I said, we need to access the KP's secure archive at the Scenza. If information on the true nature of the Guardian is anywhere, it's there."

Laurent left the workstation to join them as well; he considered the chair Deunan propped on for a minute as if he wanted to sit there, then moved to the other empty chair instead. "I always thought the Scenza was nothing but a library for KP priests to go study up on ancient proverbs and such."

"You thought wrong. Oh, it has a library in the front, and there are always a few *strana* priests wandering around, their heads buried in portable screens. But most of the structure is actually underground."

Limited entry points hadn't posed an impediment for him or Alex in years. "As with Arien's apartment, Alex can scout ahead in sidespace and locate the access point for the archives' central server. She can find a private location where we can wormhole in and—"

Deunan was already shaking her head. "I tried to tell you before—your fancy tricks won't work this time. Oh, Alex should do her mind travel magic to map the layout for us, but we won't get away with teleporting anywhere inside the building. We won't be able to hide the entry portal, as security cams cover every square centimeter of the interior. Using your 'Veils' won't do us much good, either, because I'll need to interact with multiple access points. And even if we were somehow able to reach the vault undetected, the security system will trip the instant I start accessing restricted records and sound the alarm."

"I understand that your family enjoys special access to the facility, but am I correct in assuming you never served the KP in any official capacity? How do you know so much about the security there?"

Deunan finally eased down into the chair, throwing one leg over the arm and dropping her head into the corner of the high back. "When I was sixteen, my father took my brother and me to the Scenza. The purpose of the visit was to impress upon us how terribly solemn a responsibility it was to lead the KP. To convey the weight of history imbued in the institution, our family's long relationship with it and other such nonsense.

"He took us through the security screening to reach the lower levels and into the archives, where he regaled us with facts about the kinds of information the shelves upon shelves of chrystors held. Thousands of years of KP history, and thus the history of our people. It was a painfully dull tour. But while we were there, he received a comm from one of his functionaries at the Seat. Based on his reaction, it must have been important. He instructed us to stay where we were and went to another area of the archives.

"I never did as I was told, even back then. So I followed him. My brother begged me not to, and was too much of a coward to come with me. I stealthily sneaked along behind my father, using the rows of shelves as cover, and watched as he traversed another security checkpoint to enter a circular room enclosed in glass. I don't know what he did in there, as the room was soundproof. But when he finished, I scurried away ahead of him and warned Arien I'd tell our father about his pornography collection if he tattled on me."

She smiled. "As far as I know, he never did."

Caleb worked out the variables, idly drawing patterns on Alex's leg with a fingertip as he did. "You said your DNA will get you into the archives?"

"I was being overly general for simplicity's sake. It's not my DNA as a whole, but rather a genetic marker that identifies me as a member of the Colonnei Prime lineage."

"What's special about the 'Prime' lineage?"

"It's all so prosaic and overwrought. A tradition indicative of the bloated, self-important institution the KP has always been." Deunan sighed dramatically. "Elakri don't have large families—we live for hundreds of years and only have one habitable planet, so we need to carefully control our population. Nonetheless, over the course of millennia, the Colonnei bloodline has spawned many branches. There are thousands of people alive right now who can claim measurable Colonnei blood in their veins. So fairly early on, maybe a thousand years after The Fall, a single lineage was designated as *the* lineage: Colonnei Prime. It's kept intact by periodic genetic refinement. A sort of re-injection of 'pure' Colonnei DNA every so often. Ugh, it makes me ill to think of the machinations they go through."

Laurent was nodding along as she explained, suggesting this was common knowledge to Elakri.

"But the fact remains, those are the rules," Deunan continued. "Anyone who isn't descended through this lineage must append a modifier to their surname: Colonnei-iraj, Colonnei-tepin, and so on. My brother and I are currently the only two people alive who are allowed to call ourselves 'Colonnei,' no qualifiers. Should both of us die without children, our two cousins—my father's nephews—will be permitted to have their future children 'adjusted' into the lineage."

"Why don't they simply clone a Prime member when the branch ends?" Alex asked.

"Cloning is considered blasphemy against the Guardian and is highly illegal. Which is not to say the KP wouldn't do it on the sly. They may have a couple of times in the past. And if they try to clone me, I will burn the Seat to the ground."

"Okay." Caleb absorbed the details he needed. They offered fascinating insights into the history of the KP and the Colonnei family, not to mention the insular pressures being trapped in this bubble created in their society. "Can you just provide a blood sample and walk into the archives, then?"

"I doubt it. Security includes visual scans as well. I don't look much like Magnelle Colonnei any longer—and if I did, they'd still call security on me, as I am persona non grata, Prime lineage or not."

He'd expected that answer, and turned to Alex. "Can you modify one of the Shroud programs?"

"In what way?"

"Ideally, to make Deunan appear to be her brother."

"Never show the wreckage I make of the code to Devon, because it will be a mess of a hack job, but…probably?"

"Which means yes," Caleb said. "Deunan, will this plan work if you impersonate your brother? I can act as an aide or security guard, if that would be expected of him, and we'll walk right in the front door."

"Audacious. I like it. But with a disguise, the genetic marker and Arien's passkey, I can access the vault, find what we're hunting for and walk back out said front door. Why do you need to come at all?"

He smiled wryly. "For when the plan falls apart and somebody shows up and starts shooting at us."

28

Deunan stared at herself in the lavatory mirror, but her brother stared back at her.

A sensation of visceral unease crept through her chest. This wasn't natural, wasn't right.

She'd tried not to think about Arien much at all for the last twenty years, but she couldn't escape him in the mirror. Oh, he—she—looked much older now. Adult and serious and a touch worn at the edges from the strain of a high-stress profession, as Alex had based the appearance off recent images of him from the news. But it was every centimeter her brother. The brother she'd played chase with on the cliffs outside during long, dull summer evenings and watched adventure films with while poking fun at the overdramatic heroes. The brother who'd come to her, tears streaming down his face, the first time a girl had broken his heart (she'd located the girl the next day and put the fear of the Guardian in her, possibly for life).

The brother who, when she'd in turn gone to him and begged him for help in proving their parents were murdered by the very KP they'd dedicated their lives to serving, had shook his head sadly and told her she needed to get past her wild conspiracy theories and accept reality, then walked away.

Ah, there. Sentimentality overcome. She checked her appearance in profile, then tried out the voice modulator.

"Arien Colonnei. I have authorization. Arien Colonnei. I'll be in the vault archives—I'm not to be disturbed."

She sounded passably like the most recent recording she'd been able to locate of him, from when he spoke at a symposium six months earlier. The voice was far from identical, but so long as she didn't bump into someone who knew him well, she ought to be safe. She had occasion to use a voice modulator in her work from time to time and knew that less was more when employing it.

She strode across the bedroom a few times to get used to the shoe lifts Alex had printed on her ship to bring her height close to Arien's. Again, they should suffice.

Satisfied, she left the bedroom to go pack her gear—and almost bumped into Laurent in the hallway.

"Sorry—oh!" His face screwed up at her. "This is weird."

"You should be the one wear—" she shut off the voice modulator "—wearing the disguise."

"I imagine it is odd to look in the mirror and see your brother."

"That's not what I meant—I mean, it doesn't matter who I look like, only that I look different." How did he always manage to leap straight to the crux of the matter? It was as if he'd implanted a listening bug in her head. "I don't care that it's my brother."

"Don't you, though? At least a little?"

"I haven't seen or spoken to Arien in twenty years. And we weren't close, anyway."

"Fine." His expression crumbled. "I was obviously mistaken. Forget I said anything." His shoulders drooped, and he started walking away.

"Laurent, wait." She sighed. "I wasn't trying to be rude."

He half-turned back toward her. "Your personal life is your own business. I shouldn't have pried."

"You were just being..." she fumbled for the button on the Shroud device clipped inside her waistband and pressed it "...polite, or something."

"The word's 'empathetic,' actually. But thank you for saying so. Also, better. The disguise really is unsettling."

"Yeah. The truth is, when we were young, we *were* close. But he grew up to take too much after our father, and he didn't support me when I needed him most. So if I feel anything at all about looking like him, it's annoyance that I need to do so." Even as she professed her party line, however, his passkey danced pirouettes in her mind. *Maggie Batore.*

"On the bright side, he's going to help us solve this mystery, whether he wants to or not."

"True." She smiled. "Good perspective."

"I'm not going to be much help in your mission, but I can be your cheerleader from the far seats."

"If we succeed, I'll bring you back voluminous scientific files for you to obsess over. You'll never be bored again."

"Bored?" He regarded her strangely. "You think I'm bored?"

"Um…no. I don't." Why was she always saying the wrong thing to him? "I think you're probably reeling from having your entire life turned upside down. I would be—oh wait, mine has been, too. But my life has long teetered one mistake away from being turned upside down, so I'm used to the feeling. You're not. Listen, I don't know if I can get your life back for you or not. But I will get answers for why you lost it. I promise."

"You, uh…" his throat worked "…thank you. I appreciate…everything." He tilted his head toward the stairs. "You should get to it. I think Caleb's itching to leave."

CS

There wasn't a tram stop at the Scenza—Deunan assumed it would have brought far too many people to the complex's vicinity—and they decided it might raise questions if 'Arien' appeared at the front door without any apparent means of transportation. So Alex opened one of her portals to a secluded corner of Entaise Park in Ventise, near a skycar rental store.

Alex gave Caleb a stern glare before he walked through. "I'll be monitoring everything through sidespace. Say the word, and I can evacuate you both in less than five seconds."

"I'm counting on it, baby." He kissed Alex, long and fulsomely enough for Deunan to roll her eyes. Yay for them that they loved one another deeply and passionately, but she wanted to get this whole affair over with. The sooner the mission was done, the faster she'd lock away these resurgent ghosts of her past where they'd trouble her no more.

When he finally followed Deunan through the portal, she set a brisk pace out of the park and toward the rental agency.

"You're walking like a woman," Caleb murmured beside her, sporting a variation on the Elakri disguise he'd worn when they met. "Stop swaying your hips, widen your stance and lift your shoulders back."

"You're highly observant."

"We need to blend in, and not give anyone a reason to linger over us."

"Is this something you do often?" she asked. "Impersonate aliens and walk among them?"

"No. But once upon a time, my job did depend in no small part on how perceptive my observations of others were."

"You were a spy, weren't you? Or an assassin, even?"

"I was not an assassin." The edge roughing his voice was impossible to miss.

"But you did kill people as part of your job."

"When absolutely necessary, yes. But solely to protect others." The words, while voiced as an emphatic declaration, held a hint of a question this time. Was he lying to her, or to himself?

"And now, you do what, exactly?"

"Recently? Try to help Alex save the universe."

"No, I don't mean right now, here. I mean in general."

"So do I."

She looked at him sharply. "The big universe? This 'Amaranthe' you hail from?"

"Yes—and that's a much longer story for another time."

"All right, but I won't forget."

"I am sure you won't."

They took the next left and entered the rental agency, and she rented the skycar under one of her many disposable identities. Five minutes later, the two of them were rising into the sky.

"How long will it take us to reach the Scenza?" Caleb asked.

"About forty minutes."

"Then let's go over the plan and our contingency options one more time."

29

Caleb activated his Veil before they landed, as Deunan doubted she'd be allowed to bring a security escort into the private depths of the complex. He swore no surveillance system in existence was capable of detecting his stealthed presence and, after the wonders the Humans' technology had thus far performed, she believed him.

A security officer met Deunan as she exited the skycar. "Mr. Colonnei? This vehicle isn't registered to you, or I would've cleared your entry."

"I'm having some upgrades installed on my vehicle, so I needed to use a rental today."

"Ah. I see. Don't let me hold you up, then."

"Thank you." She nodded politely, because Arien had always been a polite boy, and strode off toward the entrance of the Scenza.

A bronze arch with the KP emblem periodically etched upon it framed heavy wooden doors with elaborate bronze handles. The ornamentation sported all the expected flash and flair, but it was subdued for what it represented. Another example of the subtle pains the KP took to not draw too much attention to the Scenza.

The receptionist wore a shiny cream suit with a frilled high collar trimmed in gold. "Mr. Colonnei, how good to see you again. It's been a while."

"It's nice to see you as well." As she suspected, her brother rarely visited this place. When they were young, he'd displayed as little interest in the KP as she had, in his own way. More an 'indifferent' way than a 'white-hot hatred' way.

She kept walking, past the counter and inside. The initial area was officially open to the public, though few people other than priests ever visited. Replicas of KP tomes sat on pedestals of honor; in chambers beneath them, chrystors holding the actual contents could be checked out and taken to tables for study.

A few priests sat at the scattered tables, taking notes for whatever meaningless purposes, but the main library was quiet this time of the evening.

Caleb: "Interesting."

Deunan: "How's that?"

Caleb: "It reminds me of a place I visited on Earth once, the Vatican Library. A religious institution—over a thousand years old—situated in the center of an ancient city, with another entire ancient city enveloping it. The library felt so reverential I worried God would strike me down upon entry as punishment for my copious sins."

Deunan: "I don't know what most of those words mean."

Caleb: "Fair enough."

She walked down the left aisle, reminding herself not to try to be stealthy. She belonged here. Or rather, Arien did.

In the rear of the library, they encountered the first security checkpoint. She provided Arien's fingerprints—affixed over her own—and was subjected to a facial scan...which she passed.

Deunan: "This is some technology you have here."

Caleb: "I'll pass along your compliments to the creators."

The lift on the other side took them down to the restricted library, which housed the documents reserved for the eyes of higher-ranking priests and administrators. What sort of scandalous secrets did the documents hold? Details of outré-bonding affairs? Genetic enhancements gone wrong, resulting in some bastardized stub of a Prime bloodline? Nah, more apt to be financial misdeeds. Graft, bribery, corruption. Those, the KP trafficked in like fine wine.

The truva part of her lusted over the sort of juicy material she could abscond with from the files here, but her heart wasn't in it.

In the Brenfield job, she'd exposed the many transgressions of the corrupt owner of Brenfield Pharmaceuticals to the world. The resulting blowback had taken down three storied financial firms and two of the chancellor's cabinet members and resulted in the reimbursement of hundreds of millions of culture credits to the over five hundred employees he'd spent years defrauding. 'The Scandal of the Century,' the news programs had called it. And though her identity had remained safely hidden from the authorities and the public, the other truvas knew who'd pulled it off, and her reputation had soared.

It had been a moment.

Yet after all she'd learned in the last several days, the notion of exposing the malfeasance of KP or government officials for fun and profit felt achingly pedestrian. Small. *Petty.* Whatever may happen in the coming days and weeks, she was playing for larger stakes now.

At the end of the hallway, she turned left into a dimly lit, unadorned corridor. All the trappings of KP pageantry died out. Unmarked doors were spaced every so often, with only numbers above the doors differentiating them.

The corridor twisted right, then left again, before dead-ending at a force field. In front of it, a pedestal presented a depression for a hand. She knew from experience that a nasty little needle waited beneath the surface of the cradle for the center finger.

She braced herself and placed her hand in the cradle. The needle barely bit; either they'd improved the process, or sixteen-year-old her had been a crybaby.

It took ten seconds, but the reinforced door slid open. Her genes marked her as worthy of entry.

She stepped onto the lift, and the door slammed shut behind her so hard she jumped in surprise.

Deunan: "Didn't crush you, did it?"

Caleb: "No, but only because I move fast."

The lift descended both swiftly and for some distance. By the time it slowed to a stop, she estimated they were a minimum of fifty meters underground.

Another, equally formidable door slid open to reveal a hulk of a man wearing a crisp business suit, hands clasped together in front of him. He towered over even her artificially elevated height and sported arms as thick as her thighs. To either side of him, shelves stacked neatly with chrystors stretched until they curved out of view. Her father had intoned at length about the storied histories contained here that day, before being called away. Secret, arcane knowledge all, but not so secret as whatever was locked inside the central Vault.

Traversing the Scenza was akin to peeling a veritable onion of secrets and lies. Or terrible truths.

"Mr. Colonnei. Welcome to the archives."

"Thank you. I need to check some records in the vault. I might be here for a while."

"The time is yours, sir." The guard gestured to a small panel behind him. "Your credentials have been confirmed, so now the system requires only your passkey."

Deunan nodded tightly and stepped up to the panel. Her chest fluttered in angst and conflicting emotions with every letter she typed in. Arien's choice of passkey had opened up all sorts of questions she'd believed long foreclosed, and she didn't have time for any of it.

A crimson light turned green above the panel, and a glass door parted.

"I'll be here if you have any questions, Mr. Colonnei."

"Understood." She took a measured breath and walked into the chamber.

CS

Caleb: "I'll stay out here with Conan."
Deunan: "Your translation needs work."
Caleb: "Nah, it doesn't."

Between the first row of curving shelves and the frosted glass-walled room Deunan had entered was a narrow span of open space three meters wide. Caleb could see her (technically 'him') through the glass wall as a smudged, amorphous shape. He assumed the opacity was a security measure, so no one outside the vault was able to read whatever appeared on the large screen at the center of the room.

But he'd confirmed the vault was empty as she'd entered, which meant any threats would originate from this side of the wall. Starting with the beefy security guard.

The guard projected a mien of alert disinterest. The man's gaze was directed at the lift door, though he clearly received advance notice whenever the lift activated on the upper levels. He stood with one hand lightly grasping the other, a stance that allowed for swift movement of both hands, such as to alternately draw the holstered weapon at his side or respond to a physical attack.

Caleb had fought men like this one before, and though he typically won, he never walked away unscathed. He was quick and agile; when coupled with smart decisions, this counted for more than brute power, but brute power was never to be trifled with. This was only one reason why he'd brought a gamma blade and his custom Daemon. He had an adiamene blade stored on the *Siyane*, but its use was reserved for certain highly specific scenarios, ninety percent of which were never going to occur now that the Rasu were extinct. In his opinion, the weapon was not merely too dangerous to use, it was too dangerous to carry.

And this guy? He was big, but he was simply flesh and blood. He'd cut easily enough.

So Caleb adopted a ready stance to the right of the lift door and watched the guard silently, while keeping Deunan in his peripheral vision.

CS

Shelves built into the wall displayed twenty-one ultra-high-density chrystor units, which meant the amount of data stored here must be upwards of ten exabytes. Nine thousand years' worth of dastardly secrets too sacrilegious for anyone but the high chair or a single Colonnei each generation to know. To the left of the shelves, a permanent screen hovered at eye-height, with a glass tray beneath it for key entry.

As she stepped up to the tray, the screen and the keypad lit up, and an orderly file directory greeted her. She explored the controls, confirming the file system provided her with full access. She could navigate to any folder or file, enter a natural language or expression search, or request an entry by designation.

For a moment she was overwhelmed. How could so much information be so tightly guarded by the KP? She'd always believed the organization was hiding things, but was it hiding *everything*?

She scanned the folder titles, but soon realized everything was cross-referenced. Information was organized by date, by KP high chair, and by topic at a minimum.

She was here for information on the Guardian. Most specifically, how it operated. She started with a natural language search.

The top results were old. *Really* old. From…before The Fall. This wasn't supposed to be possible, was it? It was an article of faith, taught to children in bedtime stories, that all historical records predating The Fall were lost.

Yet here they were.

The results all had the same alphanumeric code after them: 4E. Her attention darted to the shelves of chrystors, noting the codes etched on them. Got it.

She didn't want to copy out the wrong information, or leave something crucial behind, which was why she'd brought three blank chrystors of her own. She retrieved one from her bag and…didn't see an obvious I/O port.

Cognizant of the guard on the other side of the frosted glass, she casually tilted her head to scan the frame of the screen. Nothing. A photal fiber line ran from the terminal to the shelving, then split off to each chrystor cradle, but there were no access points in the hardware.

She tried requesting a copy of a folder from the system.

Copying of vault data is not possible.

Not 'not authorized.' 'Not possible.'

Her eyes returned to the shelving. A front panel of glass twelve millimeters thick separated her from the contents. Further, she could make out tiny sensors beneath every chrystor. If one was removed, security would know. Or maybe only Solna Paran would know. Didn't matter.

So much for this being a clean in and out.

Deunan: "Are you capable of taking the guard out?"

Caleb: "Without killing him, you mean? It will be difficult, but I think so."

Deunan: "Start working on how you'll do it."

Caleb: "I already know how I'll do it. I'm just not one hundred percent certain it'll work. Why am I going to need to disable him?"

Deunan: "Because it doesn't appear I can copy off any of this data. I think we're going to have to steal the chrystors. But give me another minute."

If this was how things were going to go down, she might as well get her hard currency's worth. She longed to take all the chrystors—because leaving the KP's cupboard bare would be a delight—but her bag wasn't roomy enough to hold them all. So she ran a series of searches to ensure she identified the chrystors containing any and all information related to the Guardian—not the worship and exaltation of it, but the object itself. Then she ran one additional search. The combined results meant she'd be taking five chrystors with her; they'd be snug in the bag, but they should fit.

Her right hand went to the inside of her jacket. As the director of the Ventise Bureau of Investigation, Arien wasn't only authorized to carry a handgun on his person at all times—he was expected to do so. Oh, she imagined that with the elevated nature of his position, he'd long since left behind the days of gunfights in the streets or any real violence whatsoever. At this point, the weapon was a status symbol. But it was a status symbol that had enabled her to bring a gun into this room.

Deunan: "If you're not able to disable him, I'll kill him."
Caleb: "Why?"
Deunan: "If you were to kill him, it wouldn't be in self-defense. I won't ask you to murder a man in cold blood for a cause not your own. But the information we're about to take out of here is going to change

the world, and I'm willing to stain my hands crimson for that to happen."

Caleb: "Careful, Deunan. I might start to suspect your cold, unfeeling, acerbic demeanor is just an act."

Deunan: "Blasphemy. I'm going to walk to the door like I'm leaving. It will distract him and give you an opening. Be ready."

Caleb: "I always am."

CS

Every alien species had a unique physiology. One evening over dinner not too long after The Displacement, Richard Navick had filled him and Alex in on the new course material the intelligence agencies were developing to educate agents on relevant physical differences among the humanoid species of Concord. 'Relevant' meaning as it related to killing or disabling members of each species. The information Richard shared had been most enlightening.

Caleb didn't have the benefit of such briefing materials for the Elakri. The good news, to the extent there was any, was that at a macro level, the similarities still outweighed the differences. If a species spoke through a mouth positioned above a throat, they had some form of windpipe that was vulnerable to blunt force trauma. If they had a brain encased in a skull atop a torso, some manner of spinal column connected the two and was subject to being traumatized or severed. If they used eyeballs to see, those eyeballs were usually (but not always) vulnerable. And so on.

Lacking useful information on the location of Elakri internal organs, however, he'd have to focus on the most obvious weaknesses. Caleb positioned himself to the left of where he expected the guard to move when stepping out of the way of the opening door.

Alex, we'll be needing a hasty exit route shortly.

Eyes on you. Say the word.

Deunan's hazy form approached the door, and it slid open. The guard stepped back and turned to face where Deunan would emerge when she walked through.

In one fluid motion, Caleb stabbed the guard's arm in a manner that should render the man unable to hold or fire a weapon with any accuracy. At the same time, his free hand formed a rigid knife and jabbed the guard in the throat.

He ducked in anticipation of the swing from the guard's other arm, then leapt upward and delivered his boot toe to the side of the guard's head, at the soft spot above the Elakri's diminutive ear.

The guard crumpled to the floor, stunned—but not unconscious. The weapon he'd been in the process of drawing skidded across the floor.

Caleb: *"Whatever you need to do, do it now."*

Deunan's gaze ricocheted between the guard on the floor and where she guessed Caleb was standing. "Right." She hurried back into the vault, where she drew her handgun and fired it at the glass barrier protecting three shelves of crystal storage cubes. Glass shards rained down to scatter across the floor in a shrill cacophony of *clinking* sounds.

Caleb backed into the room as well, most of his attention on the guard, who writhed on the floor, gasping for air. Meanwhile, Deunan clambered over the shattered glass to the shelves and grabbed three, four, five cubes—

An alarm pealed through the air as red strobing lights flashed overhead. The guard struggled to his knees.

Alex, now, please.

You got it.

Caleb: *"Hurry."*

She stuffed the cubes into her bag and closed it up, then pivoted toward the door. On seeing the guard rise to a knee, she brought her handgun up.

Beside them, the air ripped apart in a golden oval, and Caleb placed a hand on her arm. "Not necessary. Go."

Rather than retreat, however, Deunan rushed to the shelves and started tossing storage cubes through the wormhole.

The guard stumbled to his feet, eyes searching for his weapon.

Caleb drew his Daemon. "Now!"

"I know." She abandoned the remaining cubes and, weapon pointed at the guard, backed through the wormhole.

Caleb leapt through after her. "Close it!"

As the shimmering glow began to fade, a laser streak passed twenty centimeters from Deunan's head and sliced a hole through the window behind her.

Then the Scenza was gone, and the familiar environs of the beach house welcomed them.

30

Deunan glared at the jagged hole in the window as a damp wind whistled through it to whip around the living room. "I definitely should have shot the guard."

"Or, alternatively, moved faster," Caleb remarked dryly. Alex's hands ran over Caleb's chest, surreptitiously checking him over for wounds even as he did the same for Alex. Their concern for one another wasn't necessary; the only person the stray fire had come close to hitting was her.

Laurent stood in the middle of the room, frozen in place by the brief frenzy of activity and gunplay. She waved a hand in front of his face. "Laurent?"

He blinked hard, and his focus landed on her. "Sorry. Are you hurt?"

"No."

"Good." His gaze dropped to the floor, where half a dozen chrystors lay scattered across the rug. "Do these hold the information we need?"

"No, those are bonus material." She fished four of the chrystors out of her bag and offered them up to him. "If the Guardian information we need isn't stored on one of these, it doesn't exist."

"Thank you." He brandished a lovely smile, full of exuberance and an aspect of sincerity she rarely saw in people, as he took the chrystors from her and carried them over to the workstation.

Apparently satisfied no one was bleeding, Caleb gestured to the broken window. "Where can I find something to patch that up?"

"Uh, the supply room is behind the kitchen. Check there."

Alex joined Laurent at the workstation, so Deunan retrieved the extra chrystors from the floor and stacked them neatly on the dining table, then sat on the sofa.

Adrenaline still flooded her veins, and her ears rang with the echoes of the glass shattering in the vault. She withdrew the fifth chrystor from her bag and idly rotated it end-over-end in her hand.

Lately it felt as if she was falling freely into her past, when she'd never meant to do any such thing. If she'd known this was where agreeing to help Laurent find a safe place to stay was going to lead.... She glanced over at him, his shoulders tense and chin lifted as he leaned in close to a screen populated with files. She would've run away from him, from all of this…and it would've been a mistake.

Yet the prospect of what she'd find on the chrystor she held in her hand gave her heart palpitations, pushing her nerves, already on edge from the infiltration, toward the brink of panic. The truth at last, or the exposure of her most jealously guarded beliefs as a lie? No, she knew the truth. This was only evidence, if it was anything.

She stuck the chrystor in her jacket pocket as Caleb came over, a thick roll of tape for the window in hand. "Your stunt there at the end was stupid."

"No, it wasn't. I had time. I'm not a heist virgin."

"I did not expect you were, and it was still stupid."

"We need the information on those chrystors. To fix the Guardian, to save Laurent's life, to save everyone's life. To expose the KP for the liars and traitors they are."

"Is the last reason why you snatched the rest?"

"That depends on what we learn from the files."

He arched an eyebrow. "Well played. I will thank you for not killing the guard when you could have."

"No need. He thinks I was Arien…" her heart skidded to a halt "…oh, *malede*. He thinks I was Arien. So do the security cams."

"And what was a routine visit to the vault by your brother became a serious crime when you broke the glass and stole all these cubes?"

"Yes. Um, excuse me for a minute." She stood, yanked the Shroud device off her pants and tossed it to him, then hurried upstairs to her bedroom.

Once there, she paced erratically between the bed and the door. It wasn't merely how her actions, committed while wearing Arien's skin, were a crime. They were a crime *against the KP*. Arguably the most serious crime imaginable against the KP—the theft of its most zealously guarded secrets.

The same KP that had spent the last week trying to kill Laurent for far less serious transgressions.

She had to warn Arien. She readied a message…and stopped. If she exposed herself to him now, the ruse she'd spent decades maintaining would collapse in an instant. He might be her brother, but he was also the most powerful cop in Ventise. Besides, he hadn't believed her twenty years ago when she'd insisted the KP had killed their parents. Why should he believe her if she insisted the KP was going to try to kill him now?

But it was true all the same, and she had to do something. The tattered remnants of her conscience, shriveled from years of disuse, would never survive her brother dying when she could have saved him.

So she set the message up to originate from an anonymous source, then routed it through three dead-end nodes on its way to him.

Director Colonnei,
Your life may be in danger. Trust no one. No one.

She told herself it was enough. Arien was a highly trained law enforcement agent. Properly warned, he could take care of himself.

Her fingers brushed across the crystalline cube in her pocket. She'd been fondling it without meaning to. She removed it and considered it for a minute before depositing it on top of the dresser. It didn't have any bearing on their current predicament; she'd read it later, or possibly not.

"Deunan?" Laurent's voice was muffled through the closed door.

"Come in."

The door slid open, and he hovered in the entry, as if hesitant to breach the threshold. His gaze took in the room.

"What?"

"It's smaller than I expected. I assumed you'd claimed the master."

"Sleep in my parents' bed? That would be creepy." Her chin lowered. "This was my room when I was growing up."

"I see." He huffed a breath. "Sorry. I guess I've been so caught up in my own problems, plus this insane science I'm trying to wrap my mind around. I sometimes forget how difficult it must be for you, being back here."

"It's not, actually. I mean, it is, in some ways. But..." she shrugged weakly "...this feels like home. Which is ridiculous, because it hasn't been home in a lifetime. Did you need something?"

"Hmm? Oh, yes. We found an item I thought you'd be interested in." He offered her a tiny chrystor. "I copied it for you."

"What is it?"

"It appears to be a journal from around the time of The Fall. It's written by Lirin Tafen Colonnei."

She scowled at the cube. "Why would I care what that *cugna* has to say about his power play to control our world?"

"Look, I just scanned it until I realized what it was, but I believe it might cast the KP in a new light." He held up a hand to forestall her tirade. "Not the KP of today, but what it tried to be in those early days. I'm not sure. Regardless, he's your ancestor, so I thought you should be the first one to read it."

She stared at the chrystor warily, then sighed and took it from him. She'd gone to the trouble of retrieving these vast stores of information; it was ridiculous for her to be frightened of *all* of them. "You guys are going to be obsessing over physics for hours on end, so I might as well pass the time somehow."

"Okay. I'll get back to it, then. You know, the volume of data you acquired is mind-blowing. It's going to change our—"

"Laurent."

"Right. I'll be downstairs." He backed out the door and let it close behind him.

Deunan rolled the tiny chrystor between her fingertips four or five times. The revelations were coming fast and furious now. What was one more to add to the top of the pile?

She grabbed the mobile reader from the bedside drawer, sat cross-legged on the bed and, after a moment's hesitation, inserted the chrystor into the slot.

31

The camera's vantage showed a varnished wood table in front of a beige plaster wall. It might have been a dining table or office desk—nothing on the surface or the wall behind it gave any clues as to its purpose or location. The utter lack of ornamentation anywhere in the frame made Deunan doubt the setting was Elakrin, as no room on the planet was so bleakly plain.

The man who sat at the table, however, was instantly known to her, for a painting of him had hung on the wall in her father's office at the Seat. Lirin Tafen Colonnei. Co-founder of the KP, alongside his bonded spouse, Jenova Colonnei, in the aftermath of The Fall. Together they'd led the organization for nearly a century, inspiring all Elakri with the light of the Guardian in their darkest time while picking up the pieces of a ruined civilization—or so the bedtime stories went.

A chill passed through her as she gazed into this ghost's eyes; the family resemblance was *so strong*. But it would be, because KP scientists had made certain her father, brother and herself retained a suitable percentage of Lirin's DNA in their cells. Though he'd been dead for nine thousand years, genetically, the man could be her grandfather.

The sensation of falling freely into her past surged forth to overwhelm her…she hit 'play.'

"I leave this record now in case I don't survive the battle that is already underway, in the hope someone does. Someone who can ensure what happened isn't forgotten." Lirin glanced down, a shadow passing across his face. "No, not 'what' happened, but why it did. No matter what transpires in the coming days, I fear history will not be kind to us. But if we succeed in holding off the rebellion, then perhaps one day our descendants will understand.

"It's been two hundred twelve years since we deployed the Piega Strai *to hide ourselves away within the unseen dimensions of space—to flee from an enemy we didn't know how to defeat."*

Lirin's voice reminded Deunan of her father's. Lyrical and pleasant, carrying an aura of trustworthiness alongside an undercurrent of gravitas.

"In running, we left behind hundreds of millions of Elakri to fend for themselves. We'll likely never learn what became of our brethren, though it counts as a fool's hope to imagine they survived in any but the smallest numbers. But when the Rasu bore down upon Elakrin—an enemy that could only be slowed, never killed—we had no other choice. Much like today, we found ourselves quite abruptly out of time, and acting with utmost haste was the only option to prevent our own genocide."

A flash of light off camera drew his attention for a few seconds; when his gaze returned to the camera, Lirin's demeanor had grown yet darker, almost haunted. "And now, two centuries later, we may ourselves finish the job the Rasu started. The rebels have declared all-out war on the government and the Khesa Prutet, and they are far stronger and better armed than any of us credited them with being. They have launched simultaneous assaults on dozens of strategic locations across the planet.

We no longer maintain a military to speak of—whom would we war against? There is no one here in this light-forsaken prison but us. Shortsighted in retrospect to disarm ourselves, but we didn't foresee that our next enemy would rise up from within. And I fear our police forces lack the numbers or resources to beat the rebels back.

"We should have moved faster, planned better. Should have formed the Khesa Prutet and built the weapons platforms to protect the Piega Strai *far sooner. I tried to warn those in power several years ago of the growing threat the rebels posed. To her credit, Jen believed me and tried as well. But the government is...as the*

government has always been. Arrogant, insular, bureaucratic, hemmed in by its own hubris. The chancellor and his advisors believed they had the situation under control, right up until the moment when they did not."

Lirin laughed hollowly. *"I helped in the only way I'm qualified to do so—I killed the man in charge of the rebellion last week. But this time, cutting the head off the monster wasn't enough to stop the conflagration from spreading. This malignant movement is far larger than one man, its rallying cry far more insidious. For it takes advantage of the longing in each of us to sate the aching emptiness we all feel in our hearts.*

"The irony is, I understand where the rebels are coming from. Losing the stars cost us so much more than we realized it would. My heart shatters every time I look up at our oppressive black sky, devoid of the celestial wonders I so loved. All the life and beauty they represented...gone. In fact, I never look up anymore. I can't bear it.

"And I'm not alone in struggling with a broken soul. As a people, we despair, we stagnate, we regress. The rebels lash out against this slow decline, and I understand. But we are still alive, and in their rash passions, they have forgotten that the choice thrust upon us was this haunted half-life, or eternal death."

Lirin's focus blurred, and his thoughts seemed to drift away to a far-off place for a minute. Finally he shook his head roughly, blinking and reengaging with the camera. *"Dr. Kenzu is not convinced his proposed method of reversing the process by which the Piega Strai sealed us here in this bubble of space will work. He puts the odds of success at sixty-two percent, which, when we are—or were—doing well by any objective measure, are simply not high enough odds to risk attempting a return to normal space. Especially when the odds are easily as great that the enemy lies in wait for us on the other side of the dimensional barrier.*

"We tracked the Rasu for over eighty years as they conquered their way across our little neighborhood of the cosmos, drawing ever closer to Elakrin. Why should we believe that, a scant two centuries later, they are somehow gone? No longer a threat? In our galaxy

cluster, no other species existed half so advanced as us. There is no one else who could have defeated this enemy.

"No, the truth is, the Rasu are surely continuing their campaign of annihilation unhindered. I don't know when it will be safe to return to normal space. I don't know if it will ever be. But I do know today is not that day.

"But the rebels? They know only their desperation. They pine for what was lost and are willing to risk everything for the chance to regain it. Worse, they are now killing for the chance. And this, I cannot forgive—"

Movement off camera drew his attention once more, and a second later Jenova Colonnei appeared in the frame to rest a hip on the edge of the table. "Lirin, the chancellor has called an emergency meeting of his cabinet."

"I'm not a member of his cabinet."

"Only because you refuse the official title. You know he needs you there." She reached out and placed a hand on his. "I need you there. Please."

Lirin nodded tightly, then faced the camera once again as Jenova walked away. "Matters will draw to a head soon, to whatever end. If you can find it in your heart to do so, wish us well."

The recording ended there, and Deunan hurriedly backed out to the file list. There was but one way the story could end—for she was sitting here in the same bubble of space, alive to view the journal—yet her heart pounded in her chest, tense with anticipation.

The journal contained one additional entry.

The setting was different—a smaller table, with the edge of a bed in the right corner and a window in the left one. Heavy clouds drifted past outside the window, obscuring any other geography that might provide a clue to the location.

Lirin again sat at the table, his hands clasped loosely upon it. He looked as if he'd aged a decade; his cheeks were gaunt, his eyes burdened by dark shadows.

"We have...I can't bring myself to say we have 'won.' We have survived, I hope. Our cities smolder, many of them little more than ruins. The electrical grid has failed, and unfortunately, we have lost not merely the ability to transmit power but, in many cases, the ability to generate it as well. We're using a portable solar generator to power this building, but with most of our factories destroyed, we lack any means to scale such power.

"The good news is, the majority of our emergency food stores and field vats were untouched, so our people will not starve. Not for a while. But tens of millions are dead, as are the chancellor and most of his cabinet. Jen would be dead as well, if I hadn't abandoned a pointless mission the chancellor tasked me with and took it upon myself to kidnap her from the Capitol minutes before the rebels stormed the complex.

"She hated me for it, for a while. It's not the first time, and likely won't be the last. But yesterday we walked the decimated Capitol grounds, just the two of us, and I think perhaps she forgave me." Lirin tried to lift a smile, but mostly failed.

"Most importantly, the Khesa Prutet succeeded in its mission. The weapons platforms defeated a sustained assault by the rebel space fleet. How the rebels managed to construct such a fleet without the government's knowledge..." he exhaled harshly *"...it no longer matters. The bureaucrats who failed in their jobs are all dead, having paid the ultimate price for their incompetence. Thankfully, Jen saw to it that I received the funds and staff needed to construct weapons platforms powerful enough to prevent the attacking fleet from reaching the machine. It was our sole success, and possibly the only one that truly matters.*

"And so the Piega Strai *continues to churn on, maintaining this bleak bubble of space to shield us.*

"I fear our people's hearts are broken in ways they were not before. Now we've lost not only the stars, but countless loved ones and so much of the technology and infrastructure that made this gilded cage almost bearable, so long as we remembered not to look up too often.

"But no matter the devastation, we must soldier on, mustn't we? Jen says we must, and she's always had a terrific sense of the room.

"And so, though I feel old deep in my bones, I will work to ensure the Khesa Prutet continues to protect the Piega Strai, *for that infernal machine is our guardian against monsters more terrifying than even ourselves. We have no funds, no materials and no capability to manufacture what we need, but I will find a way to strengthen the organization. It was created in desperate haste, but its mission is more vital than that of any government. It was our last line of defense, and the line held. Stars forbid, it may one day need to do so again.*

"As for the rest? I'm no politician, nor giver of rousing speeches. I'm just an old spy who's too stubborn to concede when it's time to give up. So I will support Jen however I can, as she ventures out into the ruins and tries to rebuild our world. For today, tomorrow and the uncertain future that looms ahead of us, Elakrin remains all we have."

32

The reader tumbled from Deunan's grasp to roll across the bedcover. She stared at her empty hands where it had sat, her thoughts jumbled and confused.

Everything she'd been taught growing up *and* everything she'd chosen to believe in defiance of those teachings were wrong. If both could be the case, was anything about her life, her family, her world, true?

Lirin's words. His testimonial, flung across the millennia to reach her, at this moment, felt true—achingly true. But he'd told a story she didn't know how to accept. She held no frame of reference in which to place the true events of The Fall that made sense.

She glanced toward the door. It wasn't as if she'd thought Caleb and Alex were lying about where they'd come from, exactly. More that their world was part of a fairy tale, a legend rooted in truth but bearing little connection to reality today. But Lirin had belonged to their world as well. All of her people once had.

Whatever the KP was today (presumably as evil as she'd long believed), the organization started out noble. Her despised ancestors had been the *heroes.* In a past erased from historical knowledge, the Elakri had nearly wiped themselves out in desperate longing for something she didn't comprehend—for a universe she'd never seen, until a few days ago had never known existed. And her family ensured they didn't succeed. They'd saved everyone. The *Khesa Prutet* had saved everyone.

What would Lirin think of Elakrin today? Would he be proud of the society that arose out of those smoldering ruins? Would he tip his palm in appreciation of their magnificent art and music, sculptures and architecture? At the way every centimeter of this planet glittered and gleamed in the light?

Jenova might, for she seemed to be imminently pragmatic. But Lirin? No, she suspected he'd be distraught over how they didn't remember who they had once been.

Deunan belatedly realized tears were streaming down her face, and she wiped clumsily at her cheeks. If Laurent showed back up and caught her like this, she'd be mortified. Weeping over an ancient journal!

This couldn't stand, so she went to the lavatory and splashed water on her face, then patted it dry. Caught her reflection in the mirror and paused. It almost felt as if she didn't recognize herself. Oh, she looked the same as she had since her reinvention twenty years ago, if a mite unkempt at present on account of the evening's adventure.

But she had Jenova's eyes. No longer the same colors after she'd changed them, but the patterning was identical, and they sloped and curved in the same way. No one had ever told her this—likely because she'd have taken their head off if they did. She'd seen plenty of paintings of the woman, but no motion visuals survived from those desperate decades after The Fall.

Except it turned out some did, and the KP had locked them away. Sealed off the truth for its own ends. Lirin might be sad over how the Elakri had forgotten their legacy, but he would be utterly heartbroken to learn how the KP had twisted its original mission. The organization still guarded the Guardian, but it did so in pursuit of power rather than security.

As she studied her features anew in the mirror, a smile tugged at her lips, and something she hadn't felt since she was a small child stirred in her heart: pride.

Lirin and Jenova's DNA wound through every cell of her body, and for the first time she could *feel* the truth of it. Her family legacy was so much more valuable than she'd ever understood, even if it wasn't at all what she'd believed. And now, against all the odds, she stood here today with a chance to maybe, just maybe, save everyone. Same as Lirin and Jenova had done millennia ago.

And once she accomplished that? The KP had always belonged to the Colonneis, and it was past time to do a little housecleaning.

Satisfied she looked presentable, she headed downstairs, where she found everyone hard at work. Laurent had passed around reference materials, and while he continued to study data at the workstation, Alex and Caleb pored over entries using mobile chrystor readers on the sofa.

She cleared her throat as she stopped in the center of the living room. "You were right, all of you. About the universe outside of this one, about the Guardian's true purpose." She nodded at Laurent. "About the origins of the KP. Thank you for Lirin's journal."

"Of course." His features lit up. "What did you learn?"

"Where to begin? A few hundred years before The Fall, we built the Guardian to hide us away in the folds of space from an enemy called the Rasu. The machine—"

"Say that again?" Caleb exclaimed.

CS

"Elakrin was threatened by an alien species called the 'Rasu,'" Deunan continued, having misunderstood the reason for his interruption. "The Guardian—its original name was the *Piega Strai*—engineered this protective bubble of space for us. We always intended to return to the proper universe once it was safe to do so—though it wasn't clear when the time might come. But then The Fall happened, and…we forgot. Everything."

Alex leaned in close to Caleb, until their foreheads almost touched. "What are the odds?"

Maybe it wasn't as unlikely of a coincidence as he'd first taken it to be. "I mean, the Rasu *were* in the neighborhood."

"The Rasu controlled the entire galaxy cluster—by the end, they were in every neighborhood. But the Kats don't have a good grasp on the timeline in this region. I guess I'd assumed the Rasu moved through here more recently—a millennium or two ago—

but their factional expansion was kind of uneven." Alex shrugged. "It's plausible."

"Excuse me," Deunan raised her voice. "Care to enlighten us?"

Caleb leaned forward and dropped his elbows on his knees. "Your people were right to hide. The Rasu were a monstrous, nigh-unstoppable enemy that slaughtered thousands of civilizations across countless galaxies."

"Were?"

"The Rasu are gone now."

"How can you be certain?"

Air whistled through his pursed lips. He hadn't expected those events to follow him here, to this isolated, snowglobe world. "Because I killed them. Every last one of them."

Deunan snorted. "You, personally?"

"In point of fact, yes."

"They couldn't have been that formidable, then. No offense meant—I respect your combat skills. But you're just a man."

Painful memories rose up to darken his thoughts, and he willfully shoved them back into the shadows, where they belonged. "I am, and formidable doesn't begin to describe what they were. Nonetheless, they are dead by my hand."

Deunan stared at him for several long seconds, and since he'd gotten to know her fairly well, he saw the instant it dawned on her that he was telling the truth. "Well. You'll have to tell me that story one day."

"Probably won't."

"Suit yourself. So the Guardian's reason for being no longer exists. We don't need to stay trapped here, alone."

She nodded thoughtfully, and her gaze drifted, as it so often did since arriving at the beach house, to the windows overlooking the cliffs. "Then what do you all say? Shall we return the Elakri to where we belong? To these wonders you call 'stars'?"

33

Arien rubbed at his eyes and glanced at the time. Somehow two hours had passed, and it was now quite late in the evening. Technically quite early in the morning.

The documents sent over from the Department of Extraplanetary Affairs led straight into another dead end. Kovalne's meeting with Mr. Khaleen—the meeting that Insaf Devran inserted himself into—had involved a routine maintenance request on a set of scientific instruments floating in the black out beyond Giarnum. Only a handful of people knew the instruments existed, and a search revealed zero mainstream news articles written about them—upon their deployment or since. According to the DEA file, the instruments took measurements of the regular flow of particles in the region of space bordering The End; a few scientists, such as Kovalne, then studied those measurements, for no discernable purpose.

To Arien's knowledge, no one had ever murdered anyone over a physics experiment.

A scouring of Devran's final hours had come up empty as well. He'd agreed to visit the Ventise Bureau of Investigation Headquarters for a follow-up interview, rearranged an appointment to allow for it, stopped for a small meal at a café near his office, then departed for the Capitol District. Still, Arien had shifted Endreje's focus to Devran's murder and taken the related investigations onto himself.

His efforts were now focused on a singular goal: Find Laurent Kovalne. Then he'd be able to ask the man what in the Guardian's name was causing this obscene explosion of violence across *his* city.

Reports from the failed raid on the truva's residence littered Arien's desk. The DNA test of the hair sample had come back a dead end, much like everything else today, for it belonged to a woman from Haman who'd been dead for thirty years. He'd give her this much: the truva was good. She lived and worked behind a veritable maze of false identities and accounts, as if she were her first and most important client.

Exhaustive forensics reports provided no further clues beyond confirming that Laurent Kovalne had been present in the residence; the guest bedroom showed signs of recent use, and DNA testing of a hair left on a pillow matched Kovalne's records. Several additional samples collected from the living room had somehow become tainted and were unable to yield usable results. The lab was launching an inquiry into what had gone wrong with the samples, but the evidence was lost either way.

Recordings of the raid, though, were infuriating. They unambiguously showed four people in the residence seconds before the raid. Who were the other two? Was one of them the man on the roof with Agent Pietri? Nothing else had been recovered from the scene that might identify them.

Then there was the greatest mystery of all: one second all four individuals were running for the master bedroom. The next, they were gone. Heat maps revealed they didn't dart into a secret passage in the wall or out the window or anywhere else. They simply vanished.

In desperation, he'd actually sent a private query to several research institutes and to his higher-ups in the Security Ministry asking if anyone, anywhere, was working on teleportation technology. It seemed ridiculous to contemplate the notion, but how else did four people disappear in a blink? Even invisibility-grade stealth didn't explain it, for the residence was locked down and saturated with his people for hours after the raid.

His door chimed, and Arien jumped in surprise. It was far too late—or too early—for visitors.

The cam video showed it was Solna Paran. Alone.

He frowned. Had she ever deigned to visit him at his home? Had he ever seen her without a minimum of two escorts? Not since she'd ascended to the high chair, in any event.

Whatever she wanted, it was bound to be a pain in his ass. With a sigh he stood and went to the door.

"Solna, this is a surprise." He was possibly the only person alive, other than her spouse, who could call her by her first name and get away with it. He was certain she hated it.

"It shouldn't be." She brushed past him and strode inside. "You had to expect I would come the instant I learned what you'd done." She tilted her head toward the open door to his office. "Are they in there?"

"Are what in there? What do you believe I did? What are you talking about?"

"Do you take me for an idiot, Arien? I realize you don't care for me, but I'd have hoped you'd grant me a modicum of respect." Her eyes searched the living room; on landing upon the bar, she walked over to it. "Let's have a drink and discuss the matter as colleagues. Please."

He rubbed at his temples as the headache that had been his companion for hours worsened. "I'm happy to discuss any matter as colleagues, but I have no idea to what you're referring. If you're concerned about Insaf Devran's murder, I assure you my people are working around the clock to solve it."

"What? Oh, yes. I'm told it was likely a random mugging. Don't deflect, Arien." She kept her back to him while she poured the drinks. "I don't understand what you hope to achieve by these blunt denials. I admit, I am curious why you developed a need to read the entirety of the vault's contents out of the blue, as you've never shown the slightest interest in them before now. But as a Colonnei Prime, it was always your right."

She turned and offered him a glass, which he took but promptly set on the shelf behind him. "But why steal them? Why commit violence upon treasured heirlooms—and injure a guard as well? Have you been overtaken by a sudden madness and are trying to burn your own life and your family's heritage to the ground?"

He blinked in growing confusion. "What happened at the vault?"

"You know precisely what happened. You were there."

"I assure you, I was not. I've been here at home working for the last three hours. Before then, I was chairing a far-too-lengthy staff meeting at the office."

She regarded him oddly. "All evening?"

"Yes."

"And you can prove this?"

"Uh, my residence security system should show that I never left after arriving home. Because I haven't. There isn't a recording of the staff meeting, but the attendees will vouch for my presence at it."

"Then…." She shook her head roughly, abruptly snatched the glass she'd just given him off the shelf and drained both glasses empty into the bar's sink. "Come with me to the Seat. There's something you need to see right away."

CS

Arien stared at the surveillance footage in utter disbelief, watching as 'he' entered the vault, went to the interface and began typing. Several minutes later, 'he' returned to the door. At this point, the latest inexplicable event of the week occurred, as the guard was stabbed in the arm and leveled by thin air. 'He' shot out the glass protecting the storage chrystors, grabbed five of them and stuffed them in a bag. A shimmering oval materialized to hover in the chamber, and 'he' tossed several more of the chrystors through the oval. Then 'he' trained a gun on the guard and backed through the strange oval, after which it melted away, leaving the vault empty save for the guard.

Solna dipped her chin in reproach. "You now see the reason for my skepticism."

"It's not me."

"So you say."

"So I know." He checked the time stamp. "I was in the staff meeting when this occurred. I can prove it."

"Well. You're the investigator. What's your theory?"

His *theory*? Mythical magic, long the province of children's fables, had been set loose to wreak havoc upon the lands of Elakrin. "Someone obviously altered their appearance to look like me."

"An insufficient explanation. This person was able to gain access to the vault, which means they possess the Colonnei Prime genetic marker. Your sister?"

He shook his head. "My sister is—" *squandering her life wallowing in bitterness* "—currently working at a little tech shop way over in Olgavi."

"Still keeping an eye on her?"

"She's my sister."

"Be that as it may, she could have absconded to the Scenza for a few hours, no?"

"I'll of course look into it, but I don't believe she did, no. Besides, she's markedly shorter and slighter of build than me. She'd never be able to pull off such a disguise." He didn't volunteer how he kept a rather tight surveillance net around Magnelle. If she ever needed help, or if tragedy befell her, she'd never reach out for his assistance, so it was up to him to ensure he knew.

"If she was not involved—if *you* were not involved—then what other explanation do you have?" Solna asked.

"An extremely sophisticated genetic manipulation. It's not impossible."

"Oh? Please do inquire, because if it is possible, we need to revise our security measures. And your passkey? The individual knew it."

He swallowed. The chair out of place in his home office…. "I'll have a digital forensics sweep run on my home and workplace as soon as I leave here. My security is tight, but no system is impervious." He gestured to the screen. "Clearly."

Solna nodded slowly, then lifted a graceful arm to point at the glowing ring. "And that?"

And that, indeed. Teleportation, invisible forces inflicting physical trauma, and now portals? Unless the first and last were the same thing…. Absurd notions flickered to life in his mind, sending his thoughts racing to circle back on themselves. "I don't know. But I will find out."

"See that you do, Arien. Such a heinous crime against the Khesa Prutet cannot go unpunished."

"And it won't." He stared at the security footage, which was running on a loop, as 'he' began grabbing chrystors. Not random ones, either. The thief was choosing them with precision. "You know, the answers to some of our questions could lie in the information on those five chrystors—the ones the thief took care to acquire. Perhaps it *is* time I reviewed the contents of the vault, or at least the relevant portions."

Solna regarded him with such icy enmity, a shiver raced toward his toes. "I doubt it. The truth is, those chrystors contain historical curiosities that would fascinate only the most devout priest. Personal journals of high chairs long deceased and speculative treatises on the possible nature of The Fall, among other errata. It's not what was stolen, but the fact that it was."

Your life may be in danger. Trust no one. No one.

The strange, blunt message had arrived earlier in the evening while he was traveling home after the staff meeting. Unsigned and untraceable. It had given him a minute's pause, but nothing more. Between his family name and the breadth of cases he'd worked over the years, his life was always in some small degree of danger. He'd internalized the reality years ago; he was highly trained in self-defense, always armed and prepared to defend himself. Without more specifics, there was nothing else to do, so he'd put it out of his mind.

So why had he thought of the message now, of all times? Solna could be cold and calculating, even ruthless, on her best days—of which this was not one—but she'd never cause him physical harm.

Nonetheless, the violence in her orbit was mounting, as she'd known both Agent Pietri and Insaf Devran personally. And now this incident at the vault. He readily admitted he did not have a handle on what was behind recent events. Thus he needed to keep every possibility open to consideration.

He plastered on a blasé expression. "If you say so. But if you don't mind reviewing the contents and letting me know if anything jumps out to you?"

"Of course." Her thin smile didn't reach her eyes. "It's the least I can do to aid the investigation. I personally vow to do everything in my power to see the culprit brought to justice and those chrystors returned. Can I assume the same of you?"

"You can indeed."

34

"T he functionality underlying the Guardian is some of the most complex dimensional manipulation I've ever seen, and I've seen a lot. It's also ingenious. It has to be robust and *physical* in a way a Rift Bubble doesn't." Alex cut off the lengthy explanation she longed to launch into; oh, how she wished Valkyrie was here to share in her enthusiasm over this incredible piece of machinery.

"You keep saying that phrase, 'Rift Bubble,' but you've never explained what it is," Laurent commented.

The workstation had become a wholly inadequate space to analyze the information contained on the stolen chrystors, so they'd converted the dining room table into a makeshift command center. Deunan had moved the terminal over, then gathered all the chrystor readers in the house on the table. Alex had transferred anything relevant to the Guardian's technical operation into her cybernetics so she could dynamically generate aurals as well. It was chaotic, but everyone was able to see the information at once.

"It's a collection of related technologies—and also doesn't really matter," Alex replied. "The Kats are going to be embarrassed to learn your people outdid them, though."

"Not 'our people,'" Laurent said. "One man: Dr. Evaim Kenzu. Alex, while you've been studying the engineering files, I've been reading up on the Guardian itself, and its deployment. A number of scientists came together to try to develop a machine capable of folding space around itself, but it never would've seen fruition without Dr. Kenzu. Even then, it almost didn't. There was a great deal of intrigue in the final days—terrorist plots and kidnappings and assassinations—but it's not relevant to our problem now. Sorry, Alex. You were about to explain how the Guardian functions."

"Or try, anyway. It works by sort of 'teasing apart' not merely the three physical dimensions, but six quantum dimensions as well, which it uses to erect an orb of brane scaffolding around itself, 1.3 AU out from the machine. Then a new layer of physical dimensions settles onto the scaffolding and forms a solid shell. I can't say if this Dr. Kenzu intended it or not, but the robust nature of the scaffolding is what makes this space impenetrable on a supradimensional level. It can't be reached by sidespace or by any creature or technology capable of traversing quantum-based dimensions."

"Not even *diati*? Or kyoseil?" Caleb asked.

"Your inability to sense Akeso here suggests the answer is no for kyoseil. We don't have a way to test whether *diati* can penetrate it, but I'm not aware of any phenomenon that *diati* can traverse that kyoseil can't."

"I'm not either. Dzhvar?"

Alex prevaricated. "I don't know enough about how the Dzhvar travel to say for sure. But it's possible they could gobble up the entirety of Amaranthe, and this little bubble of space would remain intact. The sole physical space to exist."

She and Caleb shared a weighty glance, and she sighed. "Now's when I ask if you're certain you want to return to Amaranthe. Because there's a decent chance sometime in the next hour, year or century, the Dzhvar are going to pop back out into the universe proper and resume doing their damnedest to feast on the spacetime manifold."

"Well that sounds unpleasant," Deunan remarked. "What are the Dzhvar?"

"Pop back out of where?" Laurent asked.

Right. Still so damn much they didn't know. "The Dzhvar are a species, and we honestly have no idea if there's such a thing as 'a' Dzhvar, or only 'the' Dzhvar. Regardless, they are the third and nastiest primordial life form originating in the dawn of the universe. As for where, I imagine from somewhere not unlike this bubble here—a space where dimensions twist and warp in ways they shouldn't."

Two perplexed stares blinked back at her, and she grimaced. "Caleb, want to handle this one?"

"I do have somewhat specialized knowledge. As far as we've been able to deduce, the early universe was dominated by three entities: *diati*, kyoseil and Dzhvar. To simplify matters, *diati* represents energy, kyoseil information and Dzhvar…they destroy. A million years ago, the Dzhvar experienced a resurgence in which they began devouring the spacetime manifold.

"In order to halt the disintegration of the universe, the *diati* joined with a humanoid species called Anaden—technically, with one Anaden in particular—and together, they defeated the Dzhvar. Or they thought they did. It has recently come to our attention that in truth, the Dzhvar have spent the last million years…slumbering."

"Hiding," Alex interjected.

"Hiding implies volition, and we don't know that they have a choice."

She held up her hands in concession. "Fair point."

"Regardless, the Dzhvar exist in the spaces between the physical dimensions the rest of us live in."

Laurent nodded vaguely. "Makes as much sense as anything else has this past week. Why do you believe they're going to return?"

Alex opened her mouth to reply, but Caleb waylaid her. "It's not important right now."

He was correct. If they dove off that cliff, they'd never climb back up, and more pressing issues demanded their attention. "Just realize it's a risk, so the question stands. It kind of sucks for you in this bubble, but you are safe. Or at least safer than anyone else in Amaranthe."

"This is what you meant when you said you were trying to help Alex save the universe, isn't it?" Deunan asked.

Caleb nodded.

"Good to know. But…" Deunan gestured vaguely at the air "…look what nine thousand years of being safe have gotten us. It sounds as if you all are on top of the problem, and you've already beaten these Dzhvar once. If it's up to me, I say we take our chances."

"Is it, though?" Laurent asked.

"Is it what?"

"Up to you. Listen, I agree—I want to see this Amaranthe place so bad I can taste it. But this isn't like choosing the year's Vanadam champion. Rejoining the larger universe will change everything for our people. Don't they deserve to make the choice for themselves?" Laurent's expression grew increasingly pained as he spoke, as if it made him physically ill to challenge Deunan so directly. But he did it anyway. Good on him.

Somewhat to Alex's surprise, Deunan didn't bite his head off; she even took a minute to consider the question before responding. Everyone was full of surprises tonight.

"The people didn't get to choose to retreat into isolation. The government decided for them, judging it was the best way to save the most people. And don't you dare say the government should therefore decide now. Chancellor Levintis and the parliament are bought and paid for by the KP, and the KP will never willingly allow us to break free of this prison."

Deunan shook her head roughly. "Everyone hated needing to flee to this space. Lirin, the government, the people. *Malede*, the people hated it so much they nearly committed civilizational suicide trying to reverse it. And they all knew something you and I don't—what it was like on the other side. So I'm inclined to trust their judgment."

Laurent's expression had morphed from pain to admiration as she spoke. "Okay."

"That's all? 'Okay'?"

"You convinced me. Okay." A smile lifted his features as he shifted toward Alex. "Dr. Kenzu had a plan for how to reverse the manifold architecture the Guardian—the *Piega Strai*—implemented. But work on the plan petered out after he died. I'm not certain why."

"I know why," Deunan replied. "They almost tried his plan. But there was no reason to believe the threat from these Rasu had abated—"

"It hadn't," Caleb offered. "The Rasu ruled your region of space until three years ago."

"Lirin assumed they remained a threat at the time. But a rebellion formed to force the government to turn the Guardian off anyway, or however reversing it worked. Most of the government was killed in the fighting that erupted. Lirin and a newly formed KP successfully protected the Guardian from an assault, and the rebellion failed. But the consequences were catastrophic."

"The Fall," Laurent said, his voice tinged with sorrow.

"Yes."

"Then sometime after The Fall, everyone forgot?" Laurent asked. "Forgot how to alter the Guardian's operation? Forgot it could be altered at all?"

Caleb stepped in then. "Not everyone. I left the science to the scientists, and I perused the historical records. The KP started out as a literal protector of the Guardian—Deunan, I think this is something you've discovered as well. But over the centuries and millennia, the organization grew corrupt in the same manner all such organizations do. Power and greed. It became in their best interests for the Elakri to remain locked away, because this meant the KP was the ultimate power in your universe. It's why they hid these records deep underground, accessible to only a very few people. I doubt the KP rank and file know any of this. They're indoctrinated into the religion same as everyone else."

"But this means…as high chair, my father must have known. All of this!" Deunan let out a disgusted growl. "*Dannat* his name."

While the others were talking, Alex had opened the files containing Dr. Kenzu's notes on how to undo the Guardian's effect.

Her eyes raced through the notes and equations, absorbing them in a manner more Artificial than human, letting the vestiges of Valkyrie always residing within her analyze them alongside her own skills as a dimension whisperer. Lost in the science, Deunan's bitter exclamation barely penetrated her awareness.

"It wouldn't have worked," she murmured.

"What was that, baby?" Caleb asked.

She looked up, surprised to discover she remained in the living room with everyone else. "Dr. Kenzu's plan for how to return Elakrin to Amaranthe. It wouldn't have worked. Or rather, it would have succeeded in dissolving this space, but everything inside would've been crushed into a singularity."

Laurent scooted over beside her to frown at the screen. "How can you determine that from these notes?"

"I can't explain it in words. His equations are facially valid, and the math to disprove them doesn't exist. But I understand how the manifold interacts with its quantum dimensions, how everything interlinks together, and I'm telling you, it wouldn't have worked. So it's good they never implemented it."

Laurent's frown deepened. "But what does this mean for us now? Dr. Kenzu's plan is the only idea we've got."

Alex smiled confidently and patted his hand. "Only because I haven't come up with a new one yet. Give me a few hours."

"A few *hours*? To eclipse what it took our brightest mind two centuries to develop? What are you?"

"Extraordinary. That's what she is." Caleb winked at her, and damn if it didn't send her pulse racing. More than twenty years together, and she still flushed with pride beneath the glow of his praise.

"*Bol'shoye spasibo, priyazn.*"

"We don't have much cause to doubt you, I suppose." Deunan rubbed at her temples, weariness seeming to take the edge off her earlier enthusiasm. "Alex, why don't you take those few hours and see what you can come up with? Laurent and Caleb, keep poking around in the rest of the files for information we need to know. About the Guardian, the KP, the government. Anything to help us maneuver our way out of this mess."

35

After retracing his mental steps three times, Laurent decided he'd exhausted his ability to extract useful information from the vault records. Everything remaining was either politics, which bored him, or math and engineering beyond his capacity to comprehend. Which bothered him, because in his narrow field, which happened to be *this* field, he'd always been the smartest person in the room.

Alex said the Elakri's understanding of extraplanetary physics had been stunted due to the closed environment they found themselves in. For her people, the quest to discover the true nature of the stars hovering overhead in the night sky had driven them to develop entirely new scientific disciplines, and each subsequent discovery had pushed those disciplines further against the boundaries of the unknown. Here, though? No mysteries existed to inspire people to challenge conventional wisdom or push back the darkness of ignorance, and as a result, vast swaths of fundamental physics principles remained undiscovered for the want of anyone asking the question.

As a justification, it made logical sense, but it still shamed him. He comforted himself by remembering that this was exactly what he'd been doing in his research into The End—asking questions targeted at the point where physics began to break down. Of course, doing so had resulted in him losing his job, his home and very nearly his life. But it had also resulted in him meeting aliens, which was pretty special. And Deunan, which might be yet more so.

He'd taken a risk in giving her Lirin's journal. Her scars ran wide and deep, and the contents of the journal could have opened them up to bleed all over again. He didn't want to cause her pain, but to his mind, the truth only ever healed. She believed she'd been lied to—by her family, the KP, society. If he could help her peel away the curtain on those lies, he had no choice but to do so, no matter if it cost him personally.

But the expression on her face when she'd come downstairs, the tenor in her voice when she'd proclaimed they were going back to the stars? It made every risk worthwhile.

He suddenly realized he hadn't seen or heard her in some time…and just as suddenly realized he knew this because over the last several days, he'd become attuned to her presence, and thus her absence. She was akin to a low-level hum animating his perception of the world around him.

So he went to the kitchen and poured two crantoles, made the way she liked it, then ventured off in search of her.

He got no answer when he called out at her bedroom door. He searched the rest of the house and came up empty. This left outside. A steady rainfall had petered out in the last few minutes, and droplets tumbled lazily from the porch awning.

"Deunan?"

"Over here." Her answer was muffled by a frigid wind, but it had come from the direction of the sea.

He found her sitting barely a meter from the cliff's edge, her knees tucked up under her chin, a woolen sweater draped over her shoulders. He was already shivering, but no way was he returning inside to get a coat now.

He settled to the ground beside her and handed her one of the glasses. "I thought you might need one."

"Need, want, whichever." She smiled at him before taking a long sip. "Thank you."

"Sure." He tore his gaze away from her before it graduated to staring and considered the waves crashing into the rocks below. "I'd ask you what's on your mind, but…."

"I was wrong. About so many things. Granted, I was also right about virtually everything, but I nonetheless feel as if my entire world has turned inside out tonight. The origin of my hatred of the KP resided in my certainty that Lirin and Jenova Colonnei were selfish and amoral, even evil—and thus every generation after them, triply so.

"But while the KP ultimately became all those things, *they* were not. They suffered and struggled over and over again to protect us. To save us. For the first time in my life, I'm proud of my name. And I'm furious that their descendants—my ancestors—sullied it."

Delight lifted his lips as he watched her down a fulsome sip of her drink.

Which earned him a scowl. "What?"

"You gave me a straight answer. An honest answer. No snark, no sarcasm, no insults. I have to say, I know this has been a difficult few days, but I like the new you."

"The Colonnei me, you mean?"

His delight faltered. The bite in her voice was mild, but it *was* there. Did she imagine he was so shallow as to care about her celebrity? But he was too far out on the limb to retreat. "The *real* you, whatever your last name is. Someone who fights to save her people, even from themselves. Someone who's willing to alter her perspective when lies are replaced with truth, even if it hurts to do so."

So far out on that limb now, he sensed it threatening to splinter apart and send him crashing face-first into the sea below. She stared at him with such intensity, it took every ounce of his courage to keep from scrambling away in search of shelter. But he held his ground, and her gaze.

"Laurent Kovalne, you continue to surprise me."

"In a good way?"

"Eh, I haven't decided. Check with me later."

It was something. "Hey, you know what? You should take it back. Your family name. We get through this, and you should tell the world what heroes Lirin and Jenova truly were."

"Hmm." Her eyes narrowed at him, but the usual stinging retort never came. "Maybe I will. Probably not, mind you. I'm not much for public speaking or politicking...much like Lirin, it turns out...but maybe." She took another sip of her drink, then rested her head on his shoulder. "What about you? What's on your mind?"

His heart leapt up to lodge in his throat, all his senses set ablaze by the weight of her against him. He didn't dare answer her question truthfully, so in desperation he reached for what he'd been pondering earlier. "Ah, something Alex said to me, about how looking up at the stars drove her people to understand the universe and how it worked, then to go out and explore it."

He pointed up using his free hand, careful not to jostle her, lest she realize what she was doing and withdraw. "We never look up. We've never had a reason to. There's nothing but endless blackness up there. Can you imagine what it must be like to sit under a sky glutted with stars? With galaxies of stars? With clusters of galaxies of stars?"

"Woah, there. Calm down." She chuckled lightly, and he felt its resonance in his chest. "What if it's similar to a fireworks performance? Say, the one they perform at Lake Onasi on Festine Eve?"

"Could be. That's an impressive show. Or the one that closes out the inauguration?"

"Too overwrought. They always...." Deunan sat up straight, and he mourned the loss of her touch. "What's that?"

He followed where her finger pointed. "I don't see anything."

"Give it a second."

Just then, a narrow streak of light bolted across the inky sky. "Lightning?"

"Doesn't resemble any lightning I've ever seen."

He waited for it to appear again. High in the sky, dark clouds swept by, mottled gray superimposed over void black; when they at last departed, the streak of light remained. It fuzzed at the edges, but was clearly defined in the center.

"Oh, no," he muttered.

"What?"

"I think it's a new anomaly. But to be visible through the atmosphere, it would need to have grown in size by a factor of...at least a million? More?"

"What does this mean?"

"It means the Guardian's breakdown is getting much, much worse." He stood and offered her a hand. "Come on. We need to tell Alex and Caleb."

CS

Alex studied the aural screen in front of her, elbows on her knees and hands clasped at her chin.

The technical information in the files Deunan had stolen was woefully sparse, but in truth, she was lucky it contained as many details as it did. Without these files, she'd be forced to physically crack open the Guardian's control center, tap into the operational code as it ran, map its flow out, *then* figure out how to alter it to their needs.

She didn't feel especially lucky, though. Dr. Kenzu had been a certified genius, and her head throbbed from the effort of comprehending his multidimensional math. For the fifth or thousandth time since they'd arrived, she lamented Valkyrie's absence.

But absent Valkyrie was, so she squinted and leaned in closer—and the screen moved equidistant away, because her ocular implant was generating it. Damn, she was weary. She exhaled, blinked and began anew.

The lattice surrounding the Guardian's solid core ran a program on its embedded photal fibers that had the effect of performing a dipyramid function transformation on the quantum waves the core generated—a necessity if one wanted to shift dimensions around. But once the waves hit the lattice, they...vanished? Or did they instead...?

Ah! Was this how it worked? Brilliant. Utterly, brain-meltingly brilliant.

Weariness forgotten, she tore through the code with renewed fervor, and the pieces settled neatly into place. The machine was monstrously complex, as it should be, but now that she'd unlocked the cipher behind it, each step in the process flowed logically from the last. There was only one way such a machine could function. Well, there were two ways, but they represented branching pathways that, once separated, never met again.

"So? Do you understand how it operates?"

Startled, she glanced over to see Caleb sitting on the sofa next to her. He handed her a kovfé, which bore a passing resemblance to coffee.

"Hmm. Thanks. I needed this, which I expect you deduced." She sipped carefully on the steaming cup. "I do understand it. Despite the superficial similarities, it's unlike a Rift Bubble in all but the most general of ways. Where a Rift Bubble sort of drapes a dimensional cloak over what it wants to hide, this device builds a concrete bunker around it. I mean, the analogy isn't perfect, but it suffices." She frowned. "Honestly, this is a cautionary tale I ought to heed."

"Oh?"

She set the kovfé on the side table and curled her legs up beneath her, facing him. "Our technology—humanity's technology— has advanced by leaps and bounds since the Metigen War. Arguably singularity-scale advancement. The unshackling of Artificials has definitely played a significant role in this evolution. But the outsized factor, at least in the realms of physics and the weapons that utilize the new physics, has been us adapting Kat tech. Klepping it, then making it our own to suit our needs. And no one has been more guilty of this than me."

He laid a hand over hers. "You've saved countless lives by doing so. Billions, at a minimum."

"I know, and I'm not ashamed of what I've done. Any means necessary, right? But it's so easy to get in a rut, especially when everything is working. To develop blinders and no longer notice alternative ways of approaching a puzzle. The Guardian? I wouldn't have come up with it. I intuitively understand dimensional manipulation better than anyone—I'm sure there are some scientists who'd disagree, but it's true—and I would never have devised this solution. Not because it's beyond my comprehension, but because it's not the way the Kats do things. And that's a problem."

"Was." He smiled, rich sapphire eyes twinkling. "Was a problem. Now you see it, so those blinders are crumbling away."

"I hope so."

"They are, and I can't wait to see what you unleash as a result.

But speaking of the Kats." Caleb took a sip of his own kovfé, letting the silence linger until he had her attention. "Mesme *has* to have known it was the Rasu who drove the Elakri to disappear."

"Why?" she asked.

"Because we're here now, and we know."

"It might not have gone this way before."

"Come on, Alex. What are the odds? Which begs the question, as always, of why it didn't tell us."

She bit her tongue, forcibly reining in her gut inclination to defend Mesme. Once upon a time, she hadn't harbored such a strong predisposition, but everything about her and Mesme's relationship was different these days.

Instead, she conceded the point. "When we get home, I'll ask—"

An avalanche of messages cascaded into her eVi in concert with an enthusiastic greeting from Valkyrie. Information flowed between them more rapidly than she could give words to. The brightest minds in Concord were having little success at predicting or controlling the manifold tears, which made perfect sense given how the Guardian operated—Valkyrie agreed—and also there were problems back home because—

Oh, crap.

Her attention darted to Caleb just as a storm began transforming those sapphire irises to a turbulent indigo.

"Marlee's missing," he said. "She was kidnapped during a Consulate mission to a newly discovered alien world. Some kind of quantum block is preventing anyone from tracking her or even communicating with her."

"I know." Alex stood. "Let's get to the *Siyane*. We don't have time to traverse the atmosphere, so I'll wormhole directly out into space as soon as we lift off. We risk being seen, but it is what it is. I'll widen the manifold tear like before, and we'll slip out."

He stood as well, taking her hands in his. His lips parted, but it took a few seconds for words to make it out. "All of these people will die if you don't repair the Guardian."

They really would. If there was one thing she knew for certain, it was that no one on Elakrin was going to be able to either fix the machine or shut it down safely. They had once counted among their number scientists as talented as any in Amaranthe, but the Elakri had lost the type of knowledge required to comprehend the Guardian long ago.

"I'll come back alone. As soon as we're on the other side, I'll open a wormhole for you to Concord HQ. I should have time to get back through before the tear closes. Probably."

Caleb's brow drew into a straight line, his jaw rigid as glass. He stared at her, but he wasn't seeing her. His mind was megaparsecs away, working out the variables of how to infiltrate another unfamiliar alien world and rescue his niece. But the clock was ticking…for everyone.

She squeezed his hands to draw him back to her. "If we're going, we have to go right now."

His gaze focused in on her, and she saw something in it she hadn't expected. Not raging determination, but a sadness-laden clarity. He shook his head. "No. We'll stay."

She should take him at his word. But if things went poorly for Marlee, he'd have to live with this decision. "*Priyazn…*are you sure?"

"I am. Marlee's a remarkably capable woman. I taught her how to survive in the most difficult of circumstances, and she's learned those lessons well. And this isn't like Namino, where I had a map and friendlies waiting on the ground. I'd be going in blind, and she could be anywhere on an entire planet. Also, Concord's best are actively searching for her. They have intel and surveillance and tools I don't."

"Dad will go to war to get her back, if it comes to that."

"I know he will." He inhaled deeply, let it out slowly. "I trust David. I trust Miriam. I trust Concord to do everything in its power to reclaim one of its own. Most of all, though? I trust Marlee. She doesn't need me to save her. She will save herself. But these people…" his jaw twitched, one last rebellion against a choice he hated being forced to make "…they desperately need our help. I can't abandon them."

"I love you. You're the best soul I've ever known—"

The rear door slid open and Deunan poked her head in. "Outside. Now."

Alex nodded. "We know about the anomaly."

"I don't think you do."

What did that mean? She shrugged at Caleb, and they headed outside.

Deunan had jogged on ahead to rejoin Laurent, who stood near the cliff peering up at the depressingly empty night.…

Oh, *sukin syn.* It was as if the sky itself had cracked open. On the other side, an entire universe was trying to claw its way in.

She rushed to Laurent's side. "How long has it been there?"

"We noticed it around two minutes ago. It could've been there for longer, though. We were talking…not looking up."

She did the math in her head. "This is bad."

"That's what I said," Laurent offered distractedly. "And it might be worse than we realize. It sort of 'stuttered' twice before it solidified, as if it was glitching. The anomalies have never done this before. Alex, what do you think it means?"

"Nothing good, I'm afraid."

"People are going to notice this," Deunan remarked. "And the government won't be able to provide any answers. I wonder…did anyone see in the files? Does the KP know what's actually happening with the Guardian?"

Caleb shook his head. "There aren't any files more recent than several decades ago. Not in what you were able to grab."

"No matter. Even if they do know, they'll never tell the public the truth," Deunan replied. "What's the word, Alex? Can you fix it?"

"Given enough time, I think I can. But the Guardian is an incredibly complex piece of machinery. I worry it'll take me months to find the specific component that is breaking down, never mind devising a way to fix it using existing materials. And I don't think you have months. You might not have weeks."

She blew out a breath and considered the ominous fissure in the sky. "I'm sorry, but I'm afraid the question of whether the Elakri *want* to return to Amaranthe is now moot. You don't have a choice. We're going to have to shut the Guardian down, and in such a way that doing so doesn't crush everyone and everything here into a cosmic singularity."

PART IV

THE GUARDIAN

36

A rien popped a stim and closed his office door, then sank into the desk chair. He'd never gone to sleep the night before, and he couldn't see his way to a restful slumber anytime soon.

Your life may be in danger. Trust no one. No one.

A cryptic warning from an untraceable source. And now someone was impersonating him to infiltrate the Scenza and steal the Khesa Prutet's most prized archival data. A case that had started with the murder of one of his agents and escalated to a manhunt for a physicist had now swept his own life into its clutches as well.

Interesting. He was assuming it was all the same case. Why?

He fixated on the ceiling of his office—a blank canvas for him to try out answers. Because though the Khesa Prutet had taken center stage with this most recent crime, its tendrils wound through every event:

- Insaf Devran, a high-ranking priest, intervenes in a routine scientific petition filed by Laurent Kovalne.
- Hours later, Agent Pietri tries to kill Kovalne on the Tafen Bridge, then shortly thereafter ends up dead outside Kovalne's apartment. It turns out Pietri has been working private security for Solna Paran.
- Minutes after Solna meets with Chancellor Levintis, the chancellor offers Arien the brass ring if he can capture Kovalne.
- When he asks Devran to come in for a more fulsome interview, the priest is murdered.
- Someone breaks into Arien's home, learns his Khesa Prutet passkey, and uses it to steal the organization's most secret and treasured archives.

- Finally, rather than act like a victim of a shocking crime should, Solna insinuates and obfuscates with one hand while making scarcely veiled threats with the other.

Solna's unsettling behavior toward him might have kept him awake all on its own, but he couldn't afford to devote much worry to what it meant right now. Their relationship had always been fraught on multiple levels, and he'd spent years doing his best to ignore the simmering conflict. He feared he'd about run out of rope on that strategy, but…later. Once this case was solved.

And if the mysterious warning related to her?

The answer remained the same. Solve the case. If she was involved, there was his answer for her escalating eccentricity. If she wasn't, then he'd make an effort to resolve the interpersonal drama.

He'd escalated his earlier casual inquiry about teleportation research into an official demand for any information on cutting-edge technologies being pursued by even the most clandestine government departments and private corporations. When he'd hit resistance from the bureaucracy, he'd requested assistance from the chancellor, insisting the intel was of critical importance in finding Laurent Kovalne. He still didn't understand why this case was so important to the chancellor, but it clearly was, because the play had worked; Levintis had ordered all departments to comply with the request and put his weight of influence behind the appeal to the corporations. Arien had thus far received negatives in response, but it had only been a few hours.

He called up the surveillance footage from the Scenza vault and watched it for the fifth time, this time at quarter speed.

The guard was definitely hit by *something* multiple times. The man's statement said he'd felt the impact of a sharp weapon on his forearm, followed by a blunt force strike to his throat. On a list of outlandish options, stealth so advanced it equated to invisibility was the *most* plausible answer. Which meant Arien's doppelganger had an accomplice, a theory further bolstered by the fact that their subsequent actions seemed timed perfectly with the attack on the guard.

Solna had hedged away from a definitive answer when he'd asked whether there was anything special about the data stored on those five chrystors in particular. 'Ancient histories' and 'high chair personal records' and 'various other Khesa Prutet data.' Which told him nothing. So he'd asked the question of the records chair, flexing his Colonnei muscle. He'd been referred through three different departments with no answers before being sent back to Solna's office.

How was he supposed to determine a motive if he didn't know what the thief had stolen?

He stared at the screen, where the playback had frozen at the manifestation of the…portal, for lack of a better word. There was no way to tell when the stealthed person traversed it, but the portal evaporated three seconds after the thief went through it. Long enough for an additional person to follow, if barely.

He advanced the video frame by frame, watching the thief draw down on the guard when the man struggled to regain his feet. As the thief reached the portal, he discerned movement of some kind on the other side. A clothed arm, maybe. The thief stepped one foot through the opening, and the arm moved out of view.

Arien's finger hovered over the 'advance' control…and shifted over to 'zoom' instead. He expanded the image until it started to pixelate, then enhanced it to the limits of the software.

In the upper quadrant of the view through the portal, opposite where the thief was busy making their escape, a painting hung on a wall. A painting he hadn't seen in two years, and then only in a perfunctory glance during a dutiful property inspection.

But it didn't matter. The painting was indelibly imprinted on his mind from many years of walking past it. And it couldn't be hanging in some other location, for the painting was one of a kind, the artist a close personal friend of his deceased mother.

He sank back in his chair with a slow exhale as a number of impossible possibilities jockeyed for attention in his mind—then he exploded to his feet, grabbed his jacket, and headed out the door.

37

"No. Absolutely not," Caleb protested, shooting her a resolute glare to emphasize his objection. He was going to take a bit of convincing, then.

They'd gathered around the dining room table with a basket of panite and fresh kovfé. The anomaly had finally disappeared after thirty-eight minutes. There was no telling how soon another one would emerge, but it was irrelevant now. They'd move as quickly as possible toward ending the danger, or run out of time.

Alex shrugged. "It's no different from sticking my hand inside a Rift Bubble generator. Safer, honestly, as I'll be wearing an environment suit."

"A Rift Bubble generator is less than three meters in diameter. The Guardian is the size of a planetoid."

"Size isn't a factor. I could walk into the sizzling heart of a Rift Bubble generator—" she grinned teasingly "—in fact, I ought to do that next time."

"Alex."

Right. Not the time for humor. Caleb was plagued with worry over Marlee's safety; she ought not to crack jokes about her own. "My point is, the danger involved is all or nothing, with a Rift Bubble generator and the Guardian. If I can touch it, I can enter it. And I've already proved I can touch it."

Across the table, Laurent's expression grew troubled. "Listen, if it's that dangerous, we can't ask you to do it. This isn't your fight."

"Trust me, 'this isn't our fight' has never once stopped us before. Probably should have, but it hasn't."

"On this, we agree," Caleb replied. "We won't let millions of people die when we could've prevented it. But, Alex, surely there's a safer way."

"There isn't—or rather, there isn't in the short term, and the long term is no longer available to us. I scoured the files, and the KP does not appear to have remote access to the Guardian's controls. Maybe they once did, and the interconnectivity was lost in The Fall, or maybe they destroyed the hardware to ensure no one ever tried to turn it off. Regardless, I need to access the controls at the source."

"You can't use the *Siyane* to send a directed signal? A jury-rigged shutdown command?" Caleb asked.

"I considered the option, but I haven't been able to come up with something that will work. At its core, deep inside the storm of energy and massively intricate programming, is physical machinery, and that machinery needs to be turned off the old-fashioned way. And no, sending a missile in to destroy the core won't work either. If we simply blow the Guardian up, it will take this whole bubble of space out with it."

He nodded tightly. He recognized when she'd done the work and wasn't being reckless. "Okay, I believe you. Acceptable risk. What are you planning to do when you get in there?"

"I am going to—"

Deunan abruptly leapt up and hurried out of the dining room. Caleb motioned for silence, tilting his head as his eyes searched the windows. "I don't hear anything."

After another few seconds of silence, he raised his voice. "Deunan, what's wrong?"

She rushed back into the room before he'd finished asking the question. "Perimeter security alert. You have to vacate to the *Siyane* right now."

Caleb shook his head. "Not without you. Who's arriving?"

"Someone who isn't going to hurt me. I'll be fine. But you all are…a lot, and I need to do this alone."

"I'll stay—I'll use the Veil and keep hidden, but I should be nearby in case you need me."

"No, Caleb. This is private. Family business. Now go, all of you. Now!" Deunan waved a hand at the ceiling…then winced in Alex's direction. "It *is* possible he'll try to arrest me, though. Alex, can you be ready to open a portal so I can escape?"

"You bet." Alex stood and positioned herself in a span of empty space near the living room. When Caleb didn't protest further, she opened a wormhole to the *Siyane.*

Still, no one moved. And she got it. Caleb didn't want to leave because his default mode was always that of protector, and Laurent didn't want to leave for more personal reasons.

She sighed. "Guys, I think Deunan has proved herself to be quite capable of taking care of herself. Why don't we leave her to her business?"

Caleb nudged Laurent toward the wormhole while leveling a warning glare at Deunan. "I'll keep our comm channel open. The first sign of trouble, you shout."

"I will."

He didn't look remotely mollified, but after a beat, he motioned for Alex to go through the wormhole, then followed her.

CS

Deunan watched the security cam feed as the skycar landed outside. The front lights illuminated on its arrival, bathing the lawn in harsh artificial light.

Arien stepped out of the vehicle…and when no one else emerged, she breathed a sigh of relief. He hadn't brought a raid team with him; he hadn't even brought backup. The discovery of her brother's passkey had ignited an ember of hope in her heart that he didn't harbor such hatred of her as she'd long imagined, but she was definitely a criminal and he was definitely law enforcement.

Though from the beginning she'd done everything practical to cover her tracks, this reunion was guaranteed to arrive sooner or later, if only because of the genetic marker. To her knowledge, which she conceded was not absolute, there was no way to fake it. So she'd accepted this inevitability the instant she'd stepped foot on the Scenza grounds. Didn't mean she was in any way prepared for it.

But hey, it was a day for revelations. Might as well squeeze one more in before dawn.

Arien approached the house cautiously, right hand drawing his sidearm as his eyes swept the grounds. He stayed out of the frame of the door as it activated, then leapt inside and flattened himself against the wall.

Deunan positioned herself on a counter stool in the kitchen and waited. She'd be lying if she proclaimed her heart wasn't lodged firmly in her throat, but she did her best to ignore it. The next several minutes were apt to determine the course of the rest of her life. Admittedly, 'the rest of her life' might be a few short weeks, if Alex didn't succeed in wrangling the Guardian into submission. All the more reason for this reunion to matter far, far too much.

Arien activated the lights as he moved through the house, and finally the lights above her switched on when he broached the archway into the kitchen.

In a flash his gun was leveled at her chest. "Stay where you are. Hands where I can see them."

She lifted her hands, palms up, as a tiny smile animated her lips. "Hello, little brother."

The muscles in his left cheek twitched, but he didn't otherwise flinch. "You are not Magnelle. Who are you, and why are you trespassing in my house?"

"Ugh, please never use that name again. And technically, it's *our* house. I know I don't look like your sister—it wouldn't have been much of a disappearing act if I did. But I do sound like her, don't I?"

Now his composure did break a touch, consternation drawing his features in toward his nose. "Magnelle is currently in Olgavi. I checked before I came here."

"A useful double I hired years ago. She's done a fantastic job of portraying a lazy, selfish dropout with impulse control issues, hasn't she?"

The gun wavered, lowering by a couple of centimeters until it aimed at her stomach. "I don't believe you. But I do recognize you. You're the truva who's been sheltering Laurent Kovalne."

So Taberas had sold her out. Assuming she survived all this, she'd see to it that no truva ever worked with the traitorous *cugna* again.

"Laurent's innocent, you know. Innocent of everything except uncovering a truth that is going to rock every Elakri's world—but his tale can wait for a bit." She shifted on the stool, and the gun rose once more. "You want me to prove to you who I am. I can do so.

"When I was nine years old and you were six, we were playing ball out on the lawn here one day. You were batting, and you connected with the ball—honestly, the strongest hit you'd ever made. A penueva bird happened to swoop in at the same moment, and the ball whacked it in the head. The bird tumbled out of the air and over the cliff. We raced over and peered down to see the bird lying on that rock shelf I was always threatening to climb onto. One of its wings was broken from the fall.

"You convinced me to hold your ankles while you hung down over the cliff and tried to reach the bird. But when your fingertips brushed across its body, it rolled off the shelf and into the sea below. I hauled you back up, and you sat there and cried for half an hour while I hugged you against me. Then you made me promise not to tell Dad how you'd cried over a bird. And I kept my promise." She smiled sadly. "I imagine life has long since beat that tender heart out of you."

He shook his head roughly and his locked countenance flickered, but only for a second. "Magnelle could have told someone about the bird."

Ugh, he was vexingly stubborn. "Why would I? And I just said I *kept my promise.*" She tipped a hand down to expose a wrist. "Blood test? No, wait, it won't work. I switched my records with a deceased woman from Haman in the government database years ago. But you already know I possess the genetic marker."

"No, someone who disguised themselves to look like me faked the genetic marker."

"It was a fabulous disguise, wasn't it? You are not going to *believe* how I did it. Oh, Arien, there's so much I want to tell you! But first we have to get past this pesky mistrust of yours." She sighed in resignation. "Nothing left to do but bare my soul. Fine. You were the only one I ever trusted with my secrets, anyway.

"For the last twenty years, I've believed you hated me. We ended things so badly that day. Here, outside, on the edge of the cliff—not far from where the bird fell—when you refused to help me burn our family to the ground in an attempt to prove the KP murdered Mom and Dad. I raged at you, called you horrible names, but none of it made a difference. You simply walked away. Heartbroken, and now truly an orphan." She blinked back nascent tears. "I'm sorry. Sorry for the things I said. Sorry for leaving you alone in the world. For giving you no choice but to leave me alone in it."

Whew. How long had she wanted to say those words? Far longer than she'd ever admitted. "It made it easier all these years, I think, for me to believe you hated me for it. But then, a few days ago, I broke into your home and stole your KP passkey in order to use it to access the Scenza vault.

"*Maggie Batore.* Magnelle the Troublemaker. I'll be honest, I could scarcely breathe when I discovered it. My heart, which I'd believed irredeemably shriveled and pruned, burst to life with all these ridiculous *feelings.* And ever since then, I haven't been able to escape the notion that maybe, just maybe, you don't hate me after all. Maybe you still love me, if only a little bit." A tear broke free, and she hastily wiped it from her cheek. "And it's ruining my whole deportment. How can I be caustic and uncaring and flippant, if my little brother loves me?"

The gun had lowered to his side somewhere during her speech, and it hung loosely from his fingers. His countenance melted, guarded cop eyes bursting to life with roiling emotions. "Magnelle? Can it possibly be you?"

"I am begging you, please, *please* don't use that name. I've been 'Deunan' for eighteen years now. And you know I always hated it, even when it was my name. What was Mom thinking, naming me after that horrid great-grandma of ours?"

"I remember." He made to set the gun down, but paused with

it hovering above the counter as he stared at her, one last shred of doubt persisting in his countenance.

Then the gun fell to the counter and he closed the distance between them, taking one of her still outstretched hands in his. Her chest flooded with warmth; his touch was like coming home. For real this time.

"I don't understand. Anything, really."

"I know you don't." She squeezed his hand, to keep it close for a moment longer. "I'll explain everything, but I have to warn you. It's a doozy of a story."

38

Caleb rolled the hilt of his blade across a palm while he watched Alex as she watched Deunan from sidespace. Her eyes were closed, her hands resting lightly on her knees, her posture displaying the artificial tension of a somewhat absent owner.

He'd damn near activated the Veil and stayed behind at the beach house, despite Deunan's insistence for him to leave. People had been trying to kill them almost nonstop for almost a week, and now the woman was inviting the person in charge of hunting Laurent into their safehouse.

He recognized it was far more complicated; family always was. But love of her brother would slow her reaction time and her will to act in ways it would not his. So why hadn't he stayed behind, hidden?

Why hadn't he gone after Marlee?

Too much second-guessing, when he'd never lacked for certitude. He'd meant every word he'd said to Alex about Marlee, though his muscles screamed even now to find a way to wrench open the barrier, race to the newly discovered world of Belarria and tear the planet apart searching for her. If he didn't stand behind his professed beliefs, they were just empty words. He had to trust her.

And as for Deunan? She had agency, and she'd made her wishes crystal clear. Also, Laurent was apt to rat him out after the fact, and he felt as if he'd only recently gained Deunan's full confidence. Besides, Alex could have him back in the house in two seconds.

So he watched Alex and waited for his cue.

What arrived instead was a smile. "And the gun is out of play. They're not quite hugging, but tentative affection is being expressed. I think we're out of the woods."

"Whew," Laurent exclaimed. "This was reckless of her."

"I don't disagree," Caleb replied. He started to add that reckless-
ness was Deunan's *modus operandi*, but it wasn't exactly true. The
woman took great care to protect her identity and personal safety.
But her world had been thrown askew easily as much as Laurent's
had been, and being knocked out of one's comfort zone didn't lend
itself to cautious, rational behavior. "Continue to keep an eye on
them. Sentiments can still turn sour."

"What about her privacy?" Laurent asked.

He shrugged. "Don't care about it. Not in this scenario."

"That's…fine." He took up pacing through the cabin.

Caleb suspected they might be waiting a while, as Deunan and
her brother had twenty years of air to clear. "Hey, Laurent. Would
you be interested in learning some specifics about Amaranthe? The
way space works, how galaxies form and such?"

"Yes! I mean, it'd be interesting, sure."

He went to the data center control panel and pulled up a begin-
ner primer on astronomy. It was made for students, though he
didn't mention this. Physicist or no, when it came to the real universe, the man was a babe lost in the proverbial woods.

He passed the virtual screen over to the kitchen table and motioned for Laurent to sit. "Have at it."

"Thank you." Laurent sat down and, seconds later, was utterly
absorbed.

Caleb joined Alex on the couch, reaching up to play with a stray
lock of hair that had loosed itself from her forever messy knot. "Any
new developments?" He kept his voice soft so as not to draw Laurent's attention to their conversation.

"She's started explaining to her brother what all has happened
since we arrived. He looks dubious."

"I would be, too." He leaned in and kissed her ear. "Keep an eye
out for signs of escalating tension, but it sounds as if there won't be
any violence tonight. So I was pondering something. Is it possible
that, when we pried open the tear to fit the *Siyane* through it and
come here, we somehow accelerated the failure of the barrier?"

"Mmm-hmm," she replied, equally quietly. "I've had the same concern. And now that I understand how the Guardian operates, I'd say it's a virtual certainty. It's also given me an idea for how to dissolve the barrier safely, but we can talk it over later, as a group.

"Don't misunderstand: The Guardian was already breaking down. It was always going to break down eventually, as it wasn't built to last for so many thousands of years. There are notes in the files about how they had to cut corners in the final days because the Rasu were advancing faster than anticipated. But as for our maneuver…it's kind of like picking at a scab, right? We hastened the inevitable, and made everything messier in the process."

"But the end result would've been the same without our intervention? Complete implosion of this bubble of space?"

"Yep." She reached over and squeezed his knee. "Which means without us here to help, the Guardian's failure would have killed everyone. So don't feel guilty. Our presence is still a net good, and it's not a close case."

"Excellent. I try to always be a net good." He said it in a lighthearted manner, but it was the story of his life. Kill in cold blood to preserve an innocent life. Cause the death of a billion to rescue billions more. Commit genocide of a species to save trillions.

> *"Caleb, the fact is, when everything is on the line, someone has to be the one to make the agonizing, impossible decisions for the sake of everyone else."*
>
> *"Funny, I've always believed that was me."*

Nika's words had echoed back to him in his mind more than once over the last three years, for more than one reason. It complicated his feelings toward the woman—toward what he now knew she truly was—the notion of her being *like* him in some ways. Ways that mattered.

"Caleb? Are you okay?" Alex had dipped out of sidespace to gaze at him in searching concern.

"I am." He flashed her an easy smile. "It's good we came. Nonetheless, the fact we've cut their time short means we have to make things right."

CS

"Other suns. Other planets. Other intelligent beings?"

Deunan nodded as she sipped on her crantole. The urge to turn the glass up then instantly refill it was overwhelming. Not to run from the real world, but out of a joyous relief terrifying in its power. She wanted to celebrate—to dance on the rooftop while crooning a party hymn—because it appeared that in the most improbable of events to emerge from this surreal crisis, she had her little brother back. *Family*, when she'd believed herself alone forever.

But celebrating was a touch premature, seeing as the world was literally ending. So instead she calmly sipped her drink and tried not to smile too much.

"And we...." Arien gestured to the screen, where the final words of Lirin's journal hovered in silver text against a black backdrop. "This is our family's legacy? The Khesa Prutet's legacy?"

"This is what the KP was *meant* to stand for. But its mission became polluted, twisted along the way. A thousand small corruptions over thousands of years, until the rot took hold."

She reached into her pocket, then offered him the chrystor she'd retrieved from the dresser in her bedroom. "This contains the private journals of every high chair for the last five millennia, up through Dad. There's nothing on there from Paran. I expect the journals don't go into the vault until the author is deceased.

"I assume Dad knew all of this: the true nature of the Guardian, the reason for its existence, the events of The Fall, everything. It was his right as high chair to know, and arguably his responsibility. But I find I don't have the stomach to learn the particulars of his deception, or the myriad ways he lied to the people. As much as he and I clashed while I was growing up, I harbored a childlike worship of him, and I want to hold on to as much of it as I can. I mean, he's gone, so tearing him down won't do any good. But if I read all the nasty minutiae, I'll never get that nostalgic version of him back. You're welcome to read it, though."

Arien took the cube from her, but set it on the table. "He did know."

"Why are you so certain?"

"He said something to me once. I hadn't thought about it in years, but now? One night, he'd been drinking a bit more than usual, and I was slouched in the burgundy upholstered chair in his home office, whining about some perceived slight I'd received in my schooling."

"The one Grandma Kela foisted off on him before she died? It was hideous."

"True, but it was also well-suited for slouching. Anyway, when I eventually ran out of steam, he said, 'Arien, the universe is so much larger and holds so much more wonder and terror than you can possibly imagine. One misguided decision by one instructor in one course? It's of no greater consequence than the passing bite of a gnat on the rump of a canine in a village on Plethez a thousand years ago.'"

She huffed a laugh. "Sounds like him."

"He did enjoy his poetic pronouncements. I said I didn't understand what he meant, and he replied, 'One day, when you succeed me, you will.' Considering the rest of us believed we had a firm grasp of the precise size, scope and contents of the universe, I think he must have been talking about all of this."

"It makes sense. When *you* succeeded him, huh?"

"Hey, by that point in time, you had made your opinion on the Prutet perfectly clear to the family." Arien's expression flickered, his brow bunching up at the center.

"What?"

"You sound like yourself, but you look so different. My brain keeps glitching over the incongruity." He drew back to peer at her intently. "Oh."

"Oh, *what?*"

"Your eyes. When I saw the visual of the truva—you—something about her eyes bugged me. With nothing else pointing toward you, I didn't make the connection. But now it's obvious they belonged to you."

"They're not remotely similar to how they used to be. I changed both colors."

"Eh, they're still the same shape, but this isn't what I mean. The *look* in your eyes is the same. Windows to the same soul." He frowned. "I do prefer the original colors, though."

"Sorry. I did what I had to."

"Had to for what?"

"To be free."

"I admit, I'm a little jealous. It might be nice, to live free of the weight of expectations. Of this blasted last name."

Funny how he would say such a thing, just when she was finding her way to being proud of the Colonnei name. But his journey through their complex heritage was always going to be different from hers. "On the other hand, you're on a *first*-name basis with Chancellor Levintis. And I imagine dozens of the greatest artists of our generation, whoever they may be. I don't keep up."

"True. Most of them are quite vapid." He fondled the cube on the table, but made no move to breach its contents. "So, do I ever get to meet these 'aliens'? And the elusive Mr. Kovalne?"

"First, you have to promise not to arrest Laurent."

"Magn—Deunan, he did kill one of my agents."

"Actually, he didn't. Caleb, one of the aliens, did. But only because your agent was trying to kill him. And had gone to the apartment to kill Laurent, because he'd failed to kill Laurent on the Tafen Bridge. Sorry, Arien, but your agent was an assassin working on the sly for the KP."

"The Prutet doesn't take out hits on innocent civilians," he protested.

She detected traces of doubt in his voice, though. He'd already begun to suspect the truth. "Yes, they do. Or perhaps only Solna Paran does. It wouldn't be the first time."

"Don't tell me you still—"

She held up a hand. "I don't want to dredge up those events right now. We have more immediate concerns to focus on at present. But this—" she pointed at Lirin's journal on the screen "—is the KP's greatest secret. Laurent's discovery of the anomalies threatened to expose the truth about the Guardian, and they have been trying to kill him for it ever since. You know it's the sole scenario to fit all the facts."

"Since when are you an investigator?"

"Hey, I played 'detective' with you all the time when we were young, didn't I?"

"Only because I followed you around begging until you did. Okay, I concede your assertion explains a lot of the facts. I'm not ready to convict the entire organization or High Chair Paran in particular, but I'll for certain turn the investigation in the Prutet's direction. Now, your guests?"

"You didn't promise not to arrest Laurent."

Arien sighed. "I promise. You're protective of him."

"He's…worthy of protecting." It occurred to her then that her feelings might involve something greater than a protective instinct, but she set the notion aside. She could only handle so many revelations in one day. Her well was dry.

"And the aliens? You're not worried I'll try to arrest them?"

She shrugged mildly. "Wouldn't do any good. They'd simply portal out of wherever you stashed them."

"That's a sobering thought. But you trust them?"

"I don't trust anyone. But they're risking their lives to save all of ours. And even if they weren't…you know what? I think I *do* trust them. Eighteen years as a truva means I've developed a keen judgment for character or lack thereof, and they're good souls."

She sent a message to Caleb, then stood and finally allowed herself to refill her drink.

39

Alex rested against the kitchen island and watched in interest as Caleb and Deunan's brother felt each other out. There wasn't time for them to develop any meaningful level of trust, so they were each going to have to take it on faith that they wanted the same things here. And that neither was going to try to kill the other—always a risk with the sort of men they were.

She suspected it would work out okay, though, if only because Arien reminded her a bit of Richard Navick. While Deunan's brother presumably needed to inflict violence from time to time in his profession, he didn't strike her as a violent man. More the quiet, observant, reasoning type who excelled at their job by understanding far more about the way the world worked, the good and the bad, than anyone appreciated.

For instance, Arien was taking the whole 'aliens' surprise in impressive stride. After some initial consternation and awkward gawking, his demeanor had undergone a definable shift, and he'd begun to treat them like…people. Which was sure to make this *so* much easier.

Laurent came downstairs and walked over to join her in the kitchen, though his focus never left Arien while he made the journey. He sat on one of the stools, twice glancing over at where Caleb and Arien were talking in the living room before clasping his hands on the counter. "Not getting arrested is nice."

"Deunan wouldn't have let you come back here unless she knew you'd be safe."

"You think so?"

"I do. She projects a cold, indifferent exterior, but she'll protect you."

"Because I hired her to do so."

"At first, yes, but we've moved well past those motivations now. And also no. She likes you."

Laurent looked over his shoulder again, this time searching for Deunan. When he located her sitting at the workstation pretending to read through some of the Scenza files, he sighed. "Pities me, maybe."

"Don't do that. Don't sell yourself short. I realize you've been thrown for a tremendous loop here. I know how everyone trying to kill you can fuck with your head. But you're a brilliant scientist, Laurent. This started because you bucked the conventional wisdom. You questioned things, and you refused to stop until you found answers."

"Which almost got me killed, repeatedly."

"It does tend to put one's life in danger. I hope it won't cow you, though. Maybe you didn't know you were brave until all this happened. But you're still standing, and you're going to help save your world."

His shoulders lifted perceptibly. "Thanks for the pep talk. You're skilled at giving one."

"Nah, I'm really not, as a rule. But you, I understand." She smiled as Caleb left Arien in the living room and came over to join them. "All good?"

He nodded. "Arien has some serious malfeasance within his organization—both of them—to investigate, but we agree it needs to wait until the problem with the Guardian is resolved."

"In that case, let's gather around and talk about how we're going to resolve it."

CS

Alex had never been much of a formal speechmaker, so instead of taking center stage, she plopped down in her usual spot on the sofa and rested her elbows on her knees. Caleb sat beside her, Deunan and Laurent in the chairs, and Arien dragged an extra chair in from the dining room.

"Dr. Kenzu never intended for the Guardian—or the *Piega Strai*, as they called it—to be a permanent solution. The intent was always for the Elakri to return to Amaranthe once the threat had passed or they devised a way to defeat the Rasu. Unfortunately, he didn't have time to develop a method to reverse the dimensional folding process before the Rasu advanced on Elakrin, and your ancestors were forced to activate the machine ahead of schedule. So he did the only thing he could concoct to preserve a chance of returning one day.

"A tether runs from the Guardian all the way to the barrier wall of this space. It's nothing more than a chain of elementary particles strung together like a string of pearls. It's so narrow—barely a femtometer in diameter in physical space—that the *Siyane's* sensors never picked it up. Since I know what to look for, I'll be able to detect it now, but I would've had to trip over it with an electron microscope to notice it.

"I think it's so minuscule because were it any larger, the Rasu might have detected the 'dimple' the connection point creates in the manifold on the other side." She grimaced as a parade of atrocities they'd committed circled through her mind. "The Rasu are—or rather were—very thorough, and they didn't care for it one bit when their prey escaped. They hunted the remnants of a species called the Ourankeli across the stars down to their last refuge in a hollowed-out asteroid, and likely did the same to anyone else who tried to slip from their grasp. So Dr. Kenzu was wise to be cautious.

"Tiny as it is, however, the tether keeps this bubble of space anchored to Amaranthe's manifold. Caleb, it's why from our perspective on the other side, the tears are occurring in the same region this star occupied before it disappeared. Accounting for the expansion of space over time, galactic rotation and so on, the anchor is located approximately where Elakrin's stellar system should be situated.

"Unfortunately, the tether is also the origin of the cracks in the barrier. In what is otherwise a solid, impervious wall, the spot where the tether connects to it is a weak point. And while I haven't had a chance to go inspect it, I suspect the tether is starting to fray, which is causing unpredictable quantum fluctuations and exacerbating the situation. This is the cause of the problem, but also the key to solving it."

She paused and took a sip of her water, trying to parse out how to explain the next part in a way any of them would comprehend. "I'll be accessing the Guardian's core. Specifically, the machinery generating the tether. From there, I intend to carefully, gently increase the size of the tether from the 'inside' out." From the quantum space within the dimensions weaving through it, technically, but it didn't matter for their purposes.

"When a new anomaly manifests, I'll incorporate it into the expanding field and allow the tether—it'll now be more of a funnel, I guess—to consume the barrier in a controlled manner. And since space here is functionally equivalent to space on the other side, the two should reach an equilibrium. Hopefully."

"*Hopefully?*" Deunan exclaimed.

"There will be some momentary disruptions in this space, such as when your stellar wind impacts the interstellar medium. I don't expect it to be too destabilizing to Elakrin's orbit, atmosphere or magnetic field, though it is a risk. But so long as the planet holds together in the short term, once we're back in Amaranthe, the Kats can help fix any issues that do arise."

"Kats?" Arien asked, because of course he knew nothing about the universe outside these artificial walls.

"Katasketousya. A species of ethereal beings who are uniquely skilled at manipulating all things universe-related."

Arien blinked, but didn't inquire further. He'd likely reached his quota of new information he could absorb several conversations ago.

"If you say so." Deunan shrugged. "So what do we do while you're...?" She waved her fingers in the air. "Watch the show from the cliff outside?"

"No such luck. See, there's a potential complication. Dimensions get weird inside the Guardian's lattice perimeter. They waver and blend and blink in and out of existence. I could sense it from sidespace when I ventured there earlier. The three physical dimensions hold together, but the others, not so much. This means the technology Caleb and I use to disguise and protect ourselves is at risk of failing. Our personal Veils, the ship's stealth, the Dimensional Rifter that diverts incoming fire from the *Siyane*, and so on? They're all based on extradimensional tech. Now, the *Siyane's* adiamene hull can withstand any conventional firepower…" she winced at Caleb "…but I can't."

A storm passed through his eyes, and she knew his thoughts had pitched back to those terrible moments on Rasu Prime.

Deunan nodded understanding. "You need us to disable the Anghul."

"Correct," Alex replied. "The files indicate the controls for the weapons are located at the KP Seat. Can you get inside and access them in the same way you did the vault at the Scenza?"

"Where are these controls?" Arien asked.

"Somewhere called 'Special Controls,' if you can believe it," Caleb offered.

"Right. That's under Executive Operation, which means the high chair and the KP security chief. The Colonnei, ah, 'privileges' will get us close, but I doubt they'll allow us to actually control the Anghul. There will be an additional passkey security layer."

"I'm guessing the Anghul are automated defenses? Software runs them?" Deunan asked.

"That's what the files say," Caleb replied.

"Then there's got to be an override function, doesn't there? For when a KP vessel goes to check on something with the Guardian and doesn't want to get shot up? No need to answer. I'm certain there is. Every piece of software we write contains an override function." Deunan eyed her brother speculatively. "Do you think you can trick Solna Paran into entering her passkey in her terminal?"

"How will this…?" Arien's gaze sharpened. "Oh. You'll stealth, or veil, or whatever it's called, and use one of your truva tools to swipe her passkey. But you didn't need me to type mine in order to steal it."

"No, but I don't know how extensive the KP security system is, or how many layers Paran has passkeys for." Deunan smiled tenderly at her brother; it was the first time Alex had seen Deunan do anything 'tenderly.' "Also, there was only one combination of frequently used letters that made sense in your case. I don't think Paran has a nickname for me that she's using as her passkey."

"She might have one for me, though I doubt it would be repeatable in polite company. But I take your point." Arien frowned. "We'll have to give her a reason to access the system."

Alex sighed. "If my Veil fails, she'll have one—me. My presence inside the Guardian's perimeter will set off the Anghul."

Caleb squeezed Alex's hand. "And here I was beginning to think my role was going to be limited to holding on to you so you don't tumble into the dimensional maelstrom."

"That's *always* your role, *priyazn*." She smiled. "But no, not this time. I need you on the *Siyane*."

"Painting a neon bullseye on its broadside."

Alex winced in abject pain at the notion of inviting weapons fire onto her ship, but nodded. "The *Siyane* can perform basic flight maneuvers on its own, but there's not enough of Valkyrie residing in its circuitry for me to feel confident it can handle combat, never mind while navigating through a dimensional maelstrom, as you so colorfully put it."

"So you need me to fly your ship for you." He smirked as he said it.

She laughed; it was an old joke between them, from a time when she'd first dared to place her life, her heart *and* her ship in his capable hands. "I absolutely do—and that's not all. I may need you to come rescue me, something else you're damn good at. Or rather, rescue me and Laurent."

"What?" Laurent sat up straighter.

"You heard me. At some point in the process, we're going to have to shut the Guardian's engine down at the source, or else it'll just continue churning out new particles for the barrier to replace the ones the tether is consuming. But I can't shut the engine down while I'm also expanding the tether. Now, Caleb could handle this part, but as I covered, I need him to fly the ship and draw the Anghul's fire.

"Laurent, I know you've been poring over the technical files from the vault. You understand how the Guardian functions, if not the deep magic of *why* it functions. So…have you ever gone on a spacewalk before?"

40

Laurent paced along the railing of the cliffside patio. The weather had finally cleared, and a gentle breeze buffeted the ocean waters, serving up breakers to brighten the night. A scent of mountain clover, sprung free by the rains, tickled his nose and reminded him of a cabin a few hours from here where he and his sister had vacationed several years ago, not long before she died.

It wasn't that he was a coward, because it turned out—somewhat to his surprise—he wasn't. It was merely that such monumental acts as this had never been asked of him before. The only true demands ever placed on him were intellectual in nature—and, once he went to work for the Cosmic Sciences Division, budgetary. When vague societal expectations of cultural contribution had nipped at the edges of his awareness, he'd assured himself scientific research fulfilled the obligation and put it out of his mind. But this?

The door behind him opened, and he looked back as Deunan stepped out on the porch, then paused. "Oh. I didn't realize you were out here. If you want to be alone, I can—"

"No. In fact, please distract me from my thoughts."

"All right." She propped on the railing to face him. "What thoughts?"

"A *spacewalk*? Have you ever heard of such a thing? Automated drones venture out into space to work on equipment like the deep space monitors. Not people. Even the residents of Giarnum don't go frolicking around in space. They live in domed arcologies where there's atmosphere and heat and light, as is right and proper. Alex and Caleb? They truly are mad."

"No question about it. But don't you find the notion exciting? I mean, you're a physicist. Doesn't this mean you love space?"

"I love *studying* space. The notion of floating around out there in the nothingness, though? Mad, I tell you."

The corners of her lips twitched in amusement. "You're having the time of your life, aren't you?"

"What? No. Absolutely not. I've been shot at, knocked unconscious, set on fire, bombed, shot at again. And now those lunatics want me to go traipsing about in space wearing nothing but a flimsy piece of fabric between me and the void. *Inside the Guardian.* How can you possibly suggest I'm enjoying any of this?"

She started laughing. "Makes you feel alive, doesn't it?"

"I…." He blew out a breath, dropping his chin to his chest so she couldn't see him smiling. "Is it obvious?"

"A little bit, yeah."

"Maybe I'm the one who's mad."

"It's okay. Mad is good. Or interesting, anyway."

It took too long for her words to penetrate his skull, but when they did, his pulse quickened. He worked to keep his voice casual; probably failed. "You think I'm interesting? No one thinks I'm interesting."

She set her gaze on the sea. "Tamse must have found you interesting."

He flinched at the mention of his ex-girlfriend. He'd hardly thought about her death these last few days, which wasn't right. She deserved better, deserved for someone to remember her. "For a while. Then I proved her wrong."

"What do you mean?"

"I balked. She was getting invested in the truva life, and it was exciting and rebellious and a bit dangerous, and I balked. I refused to follow her down the path. So she left, taking all the excitement with her, and I retreated to my staid, boring life of science."

"Which, it turns out, isn't so boring after all."

He chuckled wryly. "Yeah. Didn't see that coming."

They stared out at the surf in silence for a minute. He should be obsessing over the terrifying prospect of a *spacewalk*, but he found he couldn't get past the buzzy warmth of Deunan so close beside him. Their arms were touching, and while two pairs of shirts and sweaters were in the way, it might as well be bare skin. She'd taken a shower, and the heady scent of her floral shampoo complemented the clover after the rain.

"Do you regret it? Balking?" she asked, breaking the comfortable silence.

"Do I regret not staying with Tamse? No. She was fun and sweet, but the spark never quite lit. Do I regret the choice to eschew the life of rebellion being with a truva brought, though? Not at the time, I didn't. But now? I think I'd follow you down that path."

"You'd…what?"

He shook his head roughly. How had such an admission tumbled off his lips? The madness must have taken root. "Oh. I just mean the, uh, excitement. You're right. I admit it. All this danger and adventure does make me feel alive. It's exhilarating."

"Oh. I see." Her features, animated in what he'd taken to be teasing a minute ago, slackened, and he swore she looked disappointed in his answer.

Why was he still balking? Had everything changed for him, or hadn't it? He was going to go on a *spacewalk* in a few hours! And if he survived it, he was going to find himself in a new universe, one filled with stars and galaxies of stars and clusters of galaxies of stars. He could run back to his math and his algorithms like the coward he'd believed himself to be, or he could seize this moment for everything it was worth.

"Deunan?"

"Yes?"

"I lied. That's not what I meant at all." In a fit of sleep-deprived insanity, he turned to her, cradled her lovely face in his hands, and kissed her full on the mouth.

The buzzing in his head quieted, until the only thing in his world, in this little bubble of space belonging to them alone, was the delicious warmth of her lips on his. The softness of her skin beneath his palms. The taste of kovfé on her tongue and scent of hyacinth in her hair.

Until she wrenched away, shoving him back into the porch railing. "What was that?"

He grinned, his head swimming. "It's commonly called a kiss."

"Don't. Laurent, you're kind and earnest and sheltered and it's rather endearing, possibly even sexy, but you don't know what you're doing."

"No, I don't. No *dannati* idea. In fact, I believe I have definitely been driven mad. But you said mad was good."

"I only…" she winced, rubbing at her temples while avoiding meeting his gaze "…you don't want this. You're riding high on adrenaline and excitement, but trust me, you don't want this. You don't want me."

"What if I do?"

"Have you seen my life? Even before all this happened, I was…I was…."

"You were what? Lonely? Sad? Desperate to find meaning in a meaningless world?"

Her expression hardened, shutting him out. "Don't presume you know anything about my life. Whatever you imagine you feel for me, dial it down."

But he was tumbling off the limb and into the sea now, and there was no going back. "Are you saying you don't feel the same? Because that kiss? It kind of felt like you did."

"You're mistaken. *Malede*, you are such a moron!" She marched past him, knocking his shoulder as she did, and disappeared into the house.

He closed his eyes and hugged his chest, shivering in the frigid breeze from the absence of her warmth.

Great show, Laurent. Bloody brilliant.

CS

Deunan stormed inside, tearing through the living room and blindly heading upstairs to her bedroom. Halfway up the stairs, though, she heard Alex and Caleb talking in the hall, so she reversed course. Where else could she be alone for two seconds?

Without deciding to, she headed for her parents' old bedroom. She hadn't cracked the door to it once since arriving, but it should be empty.

Except it wasn't.

A low light emanated from the bedside table, casting Arien in shadow as he perched on the edge of the bed.

"Sorry, I didn't mean to intrude. I'll go."

"Please stay."

Ugh, she just needed a minute of solitude to clear her head of all the confusing, contradictory and deeply uncomfortable emotions swirling through it. "It's fine. I need to—"

"*Please*." His voice was soft and achingly morose.

"Okay," she found herself saying. Her hand waved over the wall to turn on the overhead light.

It was like stepping back in time. Distressed white planks brightened the room in warm vibes the light couldn't match. Her mother's gray cabinet with birds carved on the doors stood in the far corner next to a vertical mirror, and a burgundy-and-silver spread covered the bed. A cleaning service must keep the spread clean, but it had grown threadbare and faded.

Arien was holding the photo frame that had always hung above the headboard, fingers drifting over the surface.

He held it up for her to see. "Remember this one?"

It was a picture of the four of them standing on the lawn of their uncle's estate outside Paesaan, clad in that season's finery.

She scowled in response. "Eliane's arrival gala. I never understood why Mom chose this photo to display. It was a miserable weekend, and not a one of us had any fun. I thought Uncle Jaren was a pompous, insufferable *cugna*."

"Me, too. But I was too much of a dutiful son to say so." He set the frame on the bed. "I read through Dad's journal entries. He—"

"I told you, I don't want to know."

"I think you want to hear this. He knew about the true nature of our universe and the Guardian's purpose, yes, but he hated it. He felt it was wrong to keep everyone ignorant of our past, of who we were before The Fall. Though he was worried about the old enemy, the Rasu, he hoped nine thousand years was enough time for the threat to have passed. He'd tasked a Khesa Prutet scientist with studying options for turning the Guardian off."

She frowned and sat beside him on the side of the bed. "But that would've been more than twenty years ago. Did nothing come of it?"

"I've never seen mention of any such project, and I attend the Board of Advisors meetings. The thing is, I used my flexpad to run a bureau database search for the scientist, a Corin Maltais. He died in a botched street robbery a month after our parents' crash. I didn't want to risk using the terminal to log into the Khesa Prutet server from here, but I suspect the project died with him."

Her chest felt strung tighter than a newly tuned violin. "They were *murdered*, Arien. Mom and Dad, and I bet this Maltais, too. I've always suspected Solna murdered them in order to take power before you came of age, but maybe she actually did it to keep the truth about the Guardian a secret."

"Or for both reasons."

"Yeah. Probably both." The tightness rose into her throat. "So you believe me now?"

"I'm an investigator, Maggie. Sorry, *Deunan*."

She sighed. "I can live with 'Maggie.' For now."

"Good, since it's who you'll always be to me. Listen, I can't convict someone, even in my own mind, absent conclusive evidence. But this? This is evidence. All the more so because a few days ago, a priest connected to the Kovalne investigation—"

"You can call him 'Laurent,' you know." *Laurent.* She shoved those troubling thoughts away yet again. Avoidance and denial were stellar coping mechanisms when utilized correctly.

"Right, *Laurent*. A priest tied up in the investigation was murdered on his way to a follow-up interview. Botched street robbery. Now, twenty years separate the events, but it does suggest a pattern. And can point the way toward how I might prove our parents were murdered."

"Oh, Arien, I'm so glad to hear you say this." Dizzying joy buoyed her. She'd only ever wanted him to be on her side. "Now, we just have to save the world first."

"Yes, about that." He lifted his shoulders, possibly as grateful as she was to move on to a less sensitive topic. "Have you seen the images of space on the other side?"

"A few of them. It's a mind-boggling premise."

"It is. Here's the thing. If all this works? If the Guardian is deactivated safely and we all live through our return to the 'real' universe? Our night sky is going to light up brighter than a fireworks show. It'll be glutted with stars."

He sounded like Laurent…a pang echoed in her chest, which was taking quite a beating tonight. "It should be amazing."

"You don't understand. People are going to panic when they see it. They won't know what's happened, and they'll assume…well, all sorts of crazy stuff. There could be civil unrest. Violence, suicides, rioting."

She smiled in teasing. "Always thinking like a cop."

"That's because I am one."

"Fair enough. I confess, I hadn't even considered the possibility. Worrying about societal unrest hasn't exactly been my focus, ever."

"Comes with the job." He nodded thoughtfully. "We can't risk triggering another Fall. I need to speak to the chancellor and come up with a plan for how to keep people calm in the aftermath. How to carefully broach the truth—"

"No."

"Excuse me?"

"I mean, yes, it's a good idea, but not now. Arien, we can't tip anyone off as to what we're planning to do. If those in the KP or the government who have been trying to kill Laurent get any inkling we're coming, the plan will fail before it begins."

"But we're talking about the *chancellor*."

"Are you telling me Paran doesn't have him wrapped around her ornamented pinky?"

"I don't…." He faded off, a troubled shadow descending over his features.

"What is it?"

"A week ago, the chancellor called me to his office. He dangled the prospect of a promotion to Security Minister in front of me, then suggested my chances would be greatly improved if I located Laurent and brought the case to a close quickly. It struck me as odd even then. Why would the chancellor care about a murder investigation?"

"Paran whispered in his ear. Or they could be in league together." If there was anything she knew after years of working as a truva, it was that the KP's and the government's corruption fed off each other like a serpent eating its tail.

"I don't want to believe it. The chancellor's a political animal, but he strikes me as an ethical man. But I will concede Solna holds tremendous sway over him, if only because high chairs always hold sway over chancellors. A seemingly idle comment in passing might have been all it took. *Dannat!*"

He sighed heavily. "All right. I agree, we can't tell him ahead of time. I'll plan to contact him the instant we leave the Seat. Assuming we do."

"We will."

"You have a lot of faith in your alien friends."

"They've earned it. Their ship? It's incredible. And the things I've seen them do. To think, we used to be as advanced as them! Oh, Arien, we've lost so much of who we were. We have to get it back."

He studied the photo on the bedspread, eyes pinched. "I didn't think you cared about our people. Society. Culture."

"Don't mistake disappointment for disinterest. It's more that I didn't hold out any hope for a different future for us. Maybe now I do. Besides...Lirin cared. It's silly, but I feel as if I owe it to him to try to save us."

"I've missed you, Maggie." He reached out and squeezed her hand. "And I'm glad we're in this together."

She curled her other hand over his, holding on to this simple connection for dear life. "So am I."

41

A rien glanced over at the empty skycar seat next to him. "Unbelievable technology. You're half a meter away, and I can't see you."

"Hence its usefulness," Deunan replied. "But I get it. Caleb ran this stealth when we went to the Scenza. It took some getting used to."

"When you impersonated me, you mean."

"That's the one."

"I can sense you smirking, invisible or not."

"Good."

Arien rolled his eyes at the sky. He'd wondered many times over the years what it would be like to talk to his sister again, but what he hadn't anticipated was how...comforting it would be to do so.

Their entire universe could implode at any minute. He was about to infiltrate the Khesa Prutet Seat under false pretenses. Once there, he planned to aid and abet the criminal bypassing of the Prutet's security system so some 'aliens' could shut down the Guardian, which wasn't a god at all but instead a dimension-shifting machine, and pitch his planet into a universe overflowing with trillions more aliens. After these events wrapped up, he would in all likelihood arrest High Chair Paran for treason, if not conspiracy to commit murder.

And what he felt most of all at this moment was *comforted*. As if there was nothing he and Maggie couldn't accomplish together, and no matter what, everything was going to work out for the best in the end. It was as if he was five years old again, his big sister protecting him from the angry thunderstorm lashing the sea against the cliffs.

Instead he was the director of the Ventise Bureau of Investigation, next in line to be Elakrin Security Minister, but the feeling persisted.

Her current invisibility might be overkill, since they were alone in the vehicle, but he understood how extensive security here was. At some point soon, they'd cross a perimeter line within which his skycar would be scanned, then monitored continuously until he emerged from it. Since he didn't know precisely where that line lay, best to play it safe.

The skycar's comm activated a few seconds later.

Seat Security: "Director Colonnei, we do not have a visit from you on the schedule."

Wherever the line had been, they were inside it now.

Arien Colonnei: "I'm here to update High Chair Paran on the recent theft at the Scenza. She indicated she wanted to receive important information as soon as it came to my attention, so there was no time to make an appointment. Please inform her of my impending arrival."

Seat Security: "Understood. Land at pad three."

CS

Alex double-checked the seals on Laurent's environment suit while he fidgeted inside it. "How does it feel?"

"Surprisingly cool. Are you sure there isn't a tear? Some kind of leak?"

"I'm sure. If there is, this pad will flash red." She tapped the pad affixed to the suit's arm. "It's not about getting too hot or too cold out there, because the suit can counter both, but about temperature regulation. And nobody wants to start out a spacewalk sweating. Hence the coolness."

"Oh."

She attached a blocky module to the suit's belt. "This is your radiation shield. The best shielding money can't buy. It'll protect you from anything short of a massive gamma ray blast or sustained exposure—longer than a few hours—to anything else."

"Is the Guardian putting off intense radiation? It never occurred to me to check."

"It's definitely throwing some stray waves around when dimensions oscillate. But the greater risk is your sun. We're pretty damn close to it, and stars don't much respect organic flesh."

"No, I suppose not."

She paused to clasp him on the shoulder. "Are you going to be all right?"

"Yes." He nodded forcefully. "I am all in. This is the chance of a lifetime. Plus, you know, helping to save my people. I'm a little nervous is all. Never done a spacewalk before."

"Completely understandable. If your nerves start to get the better of you, focus on getting back to Deunan."

His chin dropped, sending his gaze to his mag boots. "Uh…no."

"Oh?"

"Doesn't look as if that's going to happen."

"I'm sorry." She couldn't say as she was surprised. Deunan might have softened a touch since her brother showed up, but she was a prickly bird in the best of circumstances. Laurent was smart and honest and good-hearted, and frankly, he deserved someone who properly appreciated those traits.

"Yeah, I am, too."

But the heart wanted what the heart wanted. "Well, we pull this off, and you'll be a hero. Women will be beating down your door."

"No woman has ever beaten down my door. Or even knocked with moderate force, for that matter."

"Science has never been sexy on your world before, either. Things change."

"Huh." He smiled gamely. "Okay. Pep talk received. Again."

She walked him through how to use the standard tools attached to his belt, then showed him how to activate and collapse the helmet and control the air flow. "Have a seat. Drink some water, but not too much. It's my turn to get ready."

Caleb had already donned his environment suit; he shouldn't need it, but nothing about this mission was guaranteed. She checked him over, a protocol he'd insisted on since their first days together, then climbed into her own suit.

Once she'd closed the seals, his hands ran gently over the connections as he checked her in turn. "Don't die out there, okay?" His voice was a low murmur, meant only for her. "Without Akeso here, I can't bring you back this time."

"I can still—"

"And if the Guardian malfunctions in new and unexpected ways, we risk being trapped here for the foreseeable future, which means no regenesis." He dropped his forehead to hers. "I'll never ask you not to be wild and fearless, but I will ask you to do your damnedest not to die."

"I won't if you won't."

"It's a deal." He kissed her softly. "Love you. Go be remarkable."

"Love you, *priyazn*. Fly like they'll never catch you."

He retreated to the cockpit, and she motioned to Laurent. "Ready to do this?"

Laurent stood, his chest heaving from a series of long, deep breaths. "I am."

CS

The outer airlock opened to reveal a tableau of primal fire. The star took up over half of their field of view, a raging behemoth of untamed energy billions of years in the making. As Alex watched, a flare licked out through the corona like a flame off an old-fashioned bonfire.

Much closer to them, the Guardian gleamed in silvery incandescence. In contrast to the star, though, the glow was uniform, so much so that its speedy rotation was barely detectable to the eye.

Alex (Mission 1): "Disembarking."

Caleb (Mission 1): "Shielding is off."

Technically, they could pass through the ship's defensive shields, but doing so would wreak havoc with their own shielding and basically ionize everything. They absolutely could not pass through the barrier of the Dimensional Rifter, but Caleb wouldn't activate it unless he came under fire.

She pushed off the *Siyane's* hull and drifted out several meters before firing her thrusters. She and Laurent were connected by a cord, but he followed her lead and fired his thrusters as well. She waited until he drew up beside her before continuing on.

"Controls feel good?" she asked on the vicinity comm.

Laurent (vicinity): "I won't be running a race with them, but I think I can keep from shooting myself off into the sun."

Alex (vicinity): "Good enough. I can handle any fine course corrections if needed. Go ahead and activate your visual filter."

She did the same. The filter transformed the star's photosphere to a mottled copper and the Guardian a ghostly gray-white. They were on the clock now, so she wasted no time adopting a course for the center of the machine.

Alex (Mission 1): "We're beyond the ship's perimeter now."

Caleb (Mission 1): "Shields up and eyes on you. Or rather, trackers on you. The Veils are holding for now."

It was always possible she'd overestimated the degree of dimensional shenanigans at play inside the machine, in which case, the only hurdle they'd face was transitioning this bubble of space back into Amaranthe without squashing it into a singularity. Still a fairly significant hurdle, but at least they wouldn't be getting shot at while they attempted it.

In the absence of the light show, the Guardian looked positively sedate. Nothing more than a wispy mist drifting around a spinning, cold metal lattice. She slipped briefly into sidespace—

A tsunami raged inside the frame as angry streams of quantum particles constantly fought to escape an unseen cage. Winking into and out of existence as scattershot fire struggled to invade the surrounding void.

Alex (vicinity): "Wow."

Laurent (vicinity): "What is it?"

Alex (vicinity): "Sorry, nothing I can show you. Just know that the Guardian is beautiful. Majestic, even."

Laurent (vicinity): "That's what the KP says."

Alex (vicinity): "In this instance, the KP is correct."

It was also powerfully dangerous, but she didn't want to fray Laurent's nerves any further.

Damn, she wished Valkyrie were here to see this. The Artificial should be able to replay the scene from her mind once they reconnected, but it was a poor substitute for experiencing this together in the moment.

She reluctantly returned her perception to normal space.

She told herself that she couldn't feel the lash of particle streams against her skin, and maybe she couldn't. But the environment suit, advanced though it was, was unable to block what didn't exist in physicality. Yes, quantum particles were 'real,' in the technical sense of the word, for they existed partially in the real world. But partially not and—

Ugh, it didn't matter. She was here, and she had a job to do. Besides, the 'unreal' was her playground, wasn't it? She'd enjoyed a special relationship with space her entire life, and the hidden dimensions girding it for twenty years now. She might be rationally cautious, but she wasn't afraid.

The gray mist began to envelop them as they neared the lattice. If she deactivated the filter, the light would blind her now, so she didn't do that. A glance at her suit's readout confirmed it was working at eighty-two percent capacity to keep the radiation out and her temperature regulated, but everything was in the green.

Alex (vicinity): "Check your suit readout."

Laurent (vicinity): "Oh. Ah...green."

Alex (vicinity): "Excellent."

Alex (Mission 1): "We're about to cross inside the lattice. Readouts are nominal."

Caleb (Mission 1): "All is quiet here."

Her gloved hand drifted along the metal of the lattice as they passed between interwoven beams, although she wasn't able to detect its temperature or texture. Nor did she have time to scrape off a sample and learn what manner of exotic material Dr. Kenzu had used to harness the dimensional energies. If all went well today, the lattice should survive to be studied at their leisure.

As soon as they crossed the threshold, things started getting…weird. Space seemed to lose some of its cohesion, and her vision undulated like heat waves off scorching concrete. It was as if she had one foot in sidespace, despite the fact she hadn't switched over.

Alex (vicinity): "Are you feeling okay, Laurent?"

Laurent (vicinity): "Other than terrified and exhilarated? I think so."

So it was just her and her 'special relationship' with hidden dimensions, then. Good. She ignored the disconcerting sensations and accelerated toward the sphere at the center of the lattice.

CS

Caleb's fingertips rested lightly on the *Siyane's* flight controls. A display on the right side of the HUD waited for any of the sensors they'd dropped near the Anghul weapons platforms to detect movement or a power surge. Closer to the center of his field of vision, two dots blinked. Alex and Laurent had nearly reached the core of the Guardian.

He and Alex had spent more time traveling in the *Siyane* the last three years than in the fifteen years before then combined. Chasing cosmic anomalies. Hunting for signs of the Dzhvar in every sensor blip and Rasu ruin. Nonetheless, his piloting skills felt rusty. After all, nothing had shot at the *Siyane* since the Rasu. Most of the time, the ship flew itself, unless Alex took the controls for a while just to enjoy the feel of it. When pinpoint maneuvering was required, if Alex and Valkyrie were busy studying readings, he'd take an active hand. But it hardly compared to what he was about to do.

But a long time ago, he hadn't been half bad at combat flying. Granted, Alex had shot him down in a dogfight in their first meeting, but still, not half bad. It was easier to remember what those times had felt like now, without Akeso in his head whispering planet-sized reveries on the interconnectedness of all life and the synchronicity of a hummingbird's wings. It wasn't a value judgment, simply a factual statement—

An alert rang out. Alex and Laurent now registered on scans.

Caleb (Mission 1): "Veils have failed, and radar says you two are visible. Time for me to work."

Alex (Mission 1): "Roger that."

He didn't know how sensitive the proximity detectors on the Anghul were, but he did know the *Siyane* made for a much larger target than two humanoid-sized bodies. He deactivated the ship's stealth.

The closest two platforms lit up immediately. He initiated a strafing maneuver, and two more distant platforms came online as well.

His hand hovered over one of the controls…then retreated. He wasn't going to activate the Dimensional Rifter. With the short distances involved, he didn't dare risk it dumping out the weapons fire it swallowed in the vicinity of the Guardian. The *Siyane's* adiamene hull—kyoseil-infused adiamene, no less—could take the abuse.

A wide, burnt orange beam missed the ship by thirty meters and continued on, and his heart leapt in panic at the realization he'd made a crucial miscalculation.

With the Guardian's core, and thus Alex and Laurent, located at the center of the lattice structure, there was no way for him to stay off their plane. This meant any weapons fire to miss the ship was in danger of striking them. He'd love to bet on the designers of the Anghul building in safeguards to prevent the weapons from hitting the Guardian's hardware, but he couldn't take the chance.

It wasn't going to matter how good of a combat pilot he had or hadn't ever been. Today, he needed to let the weapons find their mark.

He eased off on his maneuvering, not ceasing all movement but adopting a more leisurely, sluggish response.

Caleb (Mission 2): "Deunan, the Anghul are active."

Deunan (Mission 2): "Yeah, working on it."

The next beam slammed into the hull, and a violent shudder jolted him in his seat. Basic defensive shielding remained active, but it wasn't strong enough to buffer the ship from repeated powerful weapons fire; it hadn't needed to be for a long time. Impact alarms rang through the cabin.

Piloting an adiamene-hulled vessel required nerves of steel. No matter how much one half of your brain insisted the exotic metal was indestructible against anything but the most elemental of cosmic forces, the other half insisted the hull was going to crack open like a pinata and you were going to die. Any second now.

It was, in many respects, an act of faith.

42

Solna Paran pushed back from her desk and stood as he entered her office. "Arien. What a surprise to see you here."

"Forgive the short notice, but I'm glad I caught you still working as well."

"In the wake of the Scenza incident, many procedures find themselves in need of overhaul. You're here about the theft?"

"I am." Arien gestured to the small meeting table on the far side of her spacious office. "I have some files to go over with you, if we can sit together?"

"Certainly." She walked out from behind her desk and joined him at the table.

Deunan (vicinity): "Thanks for clearing the way for me."

Arien (vicinity): "Work fast."

He clasped his hands atop the table, not opening any files. "The investigation has uncovered two corporations working on advanced personal projection technology. Pure scientific research, they both say."

"I hope you don't believe them."

He shrugged mildly. "We're looking into it. One of the corporations, Ventise Specialty Systems, disclosed a potential theft by a disgruntled former employee who worked on the project. My investigators are tracking him down now." A lie crafted out of whole cloth; sometimes interrogations called for noble lies in order to ferret out deception.

"You believe this technology can transform a person's appearance to match that of someone else?"

"The demo they presented is fairly convincing."

"I see." She stared at him, her expression a perfectly cool mask. "And the genetic marker?"

Arien worked to look chagrined. The best lies, however, were always grounded in truth. "It is possible that my sister was bribed to provide a blood sample to a criminal organization in Paesaan."

"You're not certain?"

"She's gone to ground. We obtained this information by interrogating a member of the organization who was captured on an unrelated matter. I have my best team running down every lead."

"I trust you do. If those leads bear fruit, this would seem to explain the fiction of your apparent involvement, which I'm sure relieves you."

"No need." He smiled. "I already know I wasn't involved."

"Of course. What about the other irregularities? The unseen attacker and the portal through which the thief or thieves escaped, to name a few?"

"Those answers are proving to be more challenging. It's only been a few days."

"Hmm. I hope you—"

An alert beeped from Solna's desk, and she leapt up to hurry over. Once there, she leaned into her monitor, fingers of her left hand gliding over the input.

Caleb (Mission 2): "Deunan, the Anghul are active."

Deunan (Mission 2): "Yeah, working on it."

"What's happened?" he asked.

"It appears a spacecraft has breached Guardian space. The Anghul are responding."

"Seriously? I thought the consequences of doing so had been made explicitly clear to everyone."

"Someone always believes they have devised a way around the defenses. They are, as ever, incorrect." She glanced over at him. "The Anghul will handle it."

"It is why they exist." He indicated the seat opposite him. "Given that, perhaps we should continue? There is more I wish to discuss."

Solna frowned. "I should keep a watch on matters, in case the situation escalates."

"I know who killed Seizon Pietri, and why."

"What?" She looked at him sharply. He'd hoped to provoke fear in her eyes, but she was too poised to betray her true emotions.

"As I said. Now, the trail is a bit complex, but it's important for you to understand it, I think."

She came halfway around the desk, checked her screen again, then moved hesitantly toward him. "Is it? As I told you, my interest is merely personal."

"I beg to differ, High Chair."

Deunan (vicinity): "Got the passkey. Now to deactivate those platforms. Keep her talking."

"I don't understand."

Arien kept his tone measured and even, as he crossed the point of no return. "I think you do. See, Seizon Pietri wasn't only your personal bodyguard. He was also your hired hitman."

Solna stopped in the center of the room and considered him wearing an inscrutable expression—then pivoted and went over to the wet bar. "I'm sure I don't know what you mean. Drink?" She asked as she poured two. "You take it with lime, yes?"

He watched her as she produced a fresh lime without waiting for a response from him, then shielded the glasses using her shoulder. Though he couldn't see her actions in detail, the motion of her arm suggested she added something to one of the glasses...and it occurred to him that he might be the worst detective in all of Ventise. She'd intended to kill him that night at his home, and she intended to do so again now.

Deunan (vicinity): "Dannat! I can't override the Anghul's functions from here. It has to be done from the Special Controls Room."

Arien (vicinity): "Go. I've got this under control."

Deunan (vicinity): "You should know she's about to poison you. I was going to knock the glass out of your hand if you started to take it from her. Give her the fright of her life."

Arien (vicinity): "I'm aware. I've got it."

Deunan (vicinity): "Okay. Watch yourself, little brother."

He'd left the door to the office open on entering, so there was no clue to indicate Deunan's departure.

"Thank you." He accepted the glass from Solna with a close-mouthed smile, but made no move to sip from it.

"Now, what makes you think I would ever have need to employ a hitman?"

"To ensure the truth about the Guardian and our existence in this closed universe remains secret, of course."

CS

Alex forced herself not to glance over her shoulder in search of incoming Anghul fire. Caleb was the best at a great many things, and he'd protect them until Deunan was able to shut down the defenses.

She braced her hands in front of her and bent her elbows as she impacted the solid surface of the core. A few seconds later, Laurent landed beside her.

Alex (vicinity): "Follow me to the control panel."

The interior sphere was around thirty meters in diameter. The surface was faintly magnetic, and they slid along its curvature without the need for thrusters until they reached the control panel. Built to survive not merely the vagaries of space but the hellscape the machine generated, it consisted almost entirely of an enormous lever set into a grooved row with six notches. The metal was different from that which comprised the lattice, dark and roughhewn—or perhaps the bumps and ridges were wear and tear. For all its imposing bulk, it was nothing but a power switch with a series of graduated settings.

She had to believe this was a failsafe, for it had the look of an engineer's 'in case the whole shebang is fucked and you've got to elbow-grease it' solution. The primary method of controlling the machine must reside back on Elakrin—or had once done so. Whether it had been lost, hidden or destroyed in the millennia after The Fall didn't much matter, though. She was here now—

In the corner of her vision, orange light sliced through the mist enveloping the orb, and her heartbeat skipped in surprise.

Laurent (vicinity): "Ah! What was that?"

She worked to project confidence for his benefit, though she worried that Deunan and Arien might be having a difficult time of things.

Alex (vicinity): "Anghul fire. It wasn't too close."

Laurent (vicinity): "It looked close."

Alex (vicinity): "Let's just focus on our job. Now, this lever is self-explanatory. Stay here and wait for my signal to begin powering down."

Laurent (vicinity): "I understand. How long?"

Alex (vicinity): "No idea."

She palmed her way 'up' the orb until she came upon a pinprick hole rimmed in a semi-translucent material. On the visual spectrum, it wasn't doing anything at all.

She dove fully into sidespace.

Forces whipped around and through her. No, not forces: dimensions themselves. The reasons why they didn't spaghettify her body involved the fundamental structure of the spacetime manifold and the manner in which organic beings—who were still mostly empty space at the atomic level—existed upon it, but the realization left her shaken in a way she rarely was. *Focus!*

From the nozzle, a tether wove its way through the dimensional storm, so impossibly tiny it took the special magnification she'd wired into her helmet to detect it. It resembled a rainbow stretched out to infinity. A single thread of hope placed here by Dr. Kenzu more than nine thousand years ago.

For a time after she and the other Noetica Prevos had discovered the existence of sidespace, they'd believed one could not interact with the physical world from within it. Devon Reynolds had accidentally learned that wasn't precisely true, and this had ultimately led to her discovery of how to create wormholes: entries and exits in physical space, traveling through sidespace.

They weren't easy to create; in fact, before engineers had designed Caeles Prisms to automate the process, doing so had been rather difficult, requiring an intense degree of focus and the harnessing of tremendous energies. Energies similar to those whipping through her now.

Sidespace wasn't bothered by the material shell of the orb, and she cast her mind inside the structure. A lot was going on in there, but she concentrated on the source of the tether.

When she found its origin point, she dove in.

All the air left her lungs. They were in space, and out of space. Sliding between the physical layers of space as if none were truly there.

Her mind reeled as dormant, damaged pathways lit up and tried to fire, and the sensation of Caleb's arms holding her faded away. The scenes whirling around them looked like, felt like, inhabiting the ship—dancing through the dimensions, freed of any link to her physical body.

She recoiled from it and reached for it, hating it and wanting it at the same time. Her eyes, if she still possessed control of them, would not close.

She could not turn away.

Lights flashed. Not real ones but spectral luminescence, strings surfing quantum waves.

Darkness consumed her. Tendrils clawed for her, blocked only by the tenuous field Mesme's presence created.

Stars blurred, then snapped into sharp clarity, over and over.

She was falling.

Alex shook her head, in her mind anyway, to clear the disorientation of the memory. Years ago, Mesme had physically transported her and Caleb across gigaparsecs of space in a matter of seconds, taking the mother of all shortcuts by traversing hidden dimensions without the need of anything so pedestrian as a wormhole. Though she hadn't understood it at the time, Mesme was able to perform such a feat due to enjoying the most special of special relationships with kyoseil.

Alex couldn't quite pull off such a trick using her physical body; she was only human, with a side of Prevo. But she *could*, with tremendous concentration, nudge the manifold around a bit with her mind. She activated the Caeles Prism attached to the wrist of her environment suit, and it began churning the power she would need.

Lacking formal words to describe what she was attempting to do, she imagined herself creating a channel similar to the one Mesme had generated on that trip. A funnel through the manifold. At its center, the tether. And ensconced within it, her mind.

Then she gathered some of the Caeles Prism's energy and *pulsed.*

The funnel grew. Nanoscopically, but it grew, in a wave that shot out from the orb across space until it slammed into the barrier.

Caleb (Mission 1): "Alex, are you good?"

Alex (Mission 1): "Still here. I'm making progress."

His mental voice strained with tension. She suspected the Anghul continued to fire on them, but she couldn't afford to reorient herself in her body, open her eyes and check.

Alex (vicinity): "Laurent, how are you doing?"

Laurent (vicinity): "Trying to make myself a small enough target to not get shot."

Alex (vicinity): "Hang in there."

They'd timed their visit to coincide with when they believed a new anomaly was due to appear, but they needn't have bothered. The force of the shockwave's impact had splintered the barrier, sending a tear racing out in multiple directions.

Spooked by the ferocity of the response, she worked to dial in the energy on her end, but such fine control was beyond her capabilities. Perhaps impossible for any being.

Alex! You are here!

Not now, Valkyrie. A little busy.

Oh, my. Yes. Allow me to assist.

Back at her body, she was vaguely aware of the borderline power overload in her cybernetics easing up as Valkyrie took some of it onto herself.

Emboldened by the fact she now had backup, she followed the tether through space all the way out to the barrier and sort of shimmied the funnel over until it intersected the tear at its widest, then *pulsed* once more.

The funnel expanded again, more gently this time but over a greater distance.

Particles from Amaranthe washed in, and she did her best to keep the flood at bay. *Easy...easy....*

Carefully, she let the energy driving the funnel dissipate into the surrounding space a touch. The funnel grew porous where it met the barrier, and a fraction of the particles maintaining it floated free.

A bridge between the two universes now existed. Fragile as fuck, but it existed.

Her body, flush against the machine, hummed with the energy it directed. She was neither there within it, nor here at the edge of the bubble, but in both locations at once. The Caeles Prism drew power from the same infinite dimensions that the Guardian did—

A flash in the corner of her perception distracted her. Not a pseudo-visual hallmark of those dimensions, but something fundamentally *other*. A true void amongst the sparking energy. The formless intruder left eddies in the tether as it writhed, always at the edge of her vision no matter where she looked.

She reached out as if to touch it, but of course her hands weren't really here, and it slithered into shadows of its own creation—

Then it was gone. In the aftermath, she questioned whether she'd imagined the encounter.

The funnel was wavering without her undivided attention, so she of necessity put the odd experience out of her mind to refocus on controlling the funnel. She expanded it farther, letting its edges chase the tear in all directions. But the tear kept pace with the funnel's growth, expanding in turn.

This whole system genuinely was on the verge of failing. Without their intervention, the Elakri might have had only days to live, a few weeks at the outside.

She couldn't pat herself on the back yet, though. She was not remotely done.

The wall of the funnel bulged outward as the increasing pressure from Amaranthe fought to escape its bounds. A reminder that compared to this isolated system, even relatively empty space in the real universe was busy with energetic particles. She encouraged the funnel to grow more porous at the end, then jerked in surprise as a shockwave reverberated through the surrounding space.

Alex?

I'm fine, Valkyrie. This is all…just…fine.

Do take care to not explode.

Yep.

In Dr. Kenzu's notes, he'd mused that if his idea for reversing the process worked, this bubble of space would 'unfold like the petals of a flower in spring.' Her attempt wasn't proving to be nearly so elegant, but no one was here to award points for style.

She worked faster now, increasing the funnel's size and letting ever more of Amaranthe bleed out into this space. Still the tear grew, and she began to worry that the barrier was going to blow a gasket anyway.

Alex (vicinity): "Laurent, it's time to start dialing down the Guardian—slowly. One notch at a time, and pause for a minute after each one. And keep your hands and feet flush against the orb, as the ride might get a little bumpy."

Laurent (vicinity): "Bumpy, right. Decreasing the power twenty percent. Malede, *this switch is heavy…done."*

Nothing visible changed for several seconds. Then the tear grew…fuzzy. No longer a jagged streak of lightning, but more akin to a frayed edge of cloth.

She redoubled her efforts, teasing out the funnel to consume more of the tear, until particles leaked freely from its mouth.

Alex (vicinity): "Take it down to sixty percent."

43

Deunan raced through two long hallways then diverted to the broad, curving staircase so she wouldn't have to figure out how to operate the lift while invisible, then wove through another maze of hallways. The KP was a bloated, overwrought organization, lugging around the dead weight of nine thousand years of lies, and the Seat was not a small or orderly place.

Menacing security doors greeted her after the last turn.

She'd kill for a portal to drop her on the other side right about now, but Alex was otherwise engaged. So she pulled out the film she'd used to capture Paran's input and placed it on the fingerprint reader. When one light turned green, she entered the passkey she'd swiped.

The doors slid open.

Two officers in uniforms that looked more military than security staffed stations near the center of the room. Thankfully, they were fully occupied, and neither glanced back to see who walked in—or rather didn't. In front of them, a board tracked the Anghul's activity and the target they chased. To her untrained eye, it appeared all five platforms were currently firing on the *Siyane*, and hitting their mark more often than not. How was the ship still in one piece?

But she supposed their artificially stunted technology didn't stand a chance against a Human spacecraft, or whatever sort of 'super-Humans' these two were.

Caleb had drilled into her how the real threat wasn't to the *Siyane* but to Laurent and Alex. Judging from the board, she couldn't disagree. There were a *lot* of high-powered lasers bouncing around in a too-small space.

She didn't want Laurent to get blasted. She didn't want Alex to get blasted either, but she *really* didn't want Laurent to get blasted.

Bonta bae.... Was she falling in love with him? No. Surely not. That was...she didn't do that sort of thing. She had no room for such terrifying vulnerability in her world. Fine, was she falling in sexually attracted affection for him? Almost certainly.

Ugh, he never should have kissed her.

She shut off the train of thought before she got lost in a far too delicious memory and failed in her mission because she'd been swooning. How was she going to prevent Laurent (or Alex) from getting blasted? The officers occupied the only two stations equipped to direct the Anghul's operation.

Hand-to-hand combat wasn't her strong suit. She'd trained up decent defensive skills, but as a rule, she used subterfuge, gadgets and general know-how to perform her job.

Caleb (Mission 2): "Deunan, what's the word? It's getting dicey out here."

Deunan (Mission 2): "Small complication. Hold tight."

CS

Hold tight.... Caleb flinched as renewed fire impacted the ship, but kept his hands steady on the flight controls.

He danced the *Siyane* in every direction, not to try to evade the fire, but instead to try to catch as much of it as possible. The ship rattled and jerked from multiple hits; red lights flashed in the cabin as the defensive shielding fell to zero and weapons fire burnt un-impeded into the hull.

But the adiamene held; it always did. The inertial dampers struggled a bit more, though, and his neck wrenched from the violent lurches as separate beams from opposite directions slammed into the ship less than two seconds apart. The nose of the ship spun around, and he yanked it up into an arc to avoid flying directly into the Guardian itself.

Two additional beams fired in rapid succession and missed.

Caleb (Mission 1): "Alex, are you good?"

Alex (Mission 1): "Still here. I'm making progress."

God, this was a ridiculous plan. There was no way—

His senses expanded by orders of magnitude, his body filling up until it verged on bursting from such zealous life. Relief washed over and through him, but not from him.

How had he ever believed he might not want this? Nothing could compare.

Welcome back, Akeso. For good this time, I expect.

Akeso is experiencing great peace at this event. You, however, are most tense.

Yeah. Let me concentrate.

He willed himself to not search his incoming messages for news of Marlee. Her fate was, for the moment, out of his hands, but Alex's was not. He braced himself for the next jarring impact…then realized Akeso had quietly healed the aches and pains he'd suffered from the violent gyrations of the ship. So he threw the *Siyane* into a roll and let weapons fire splash across its belly.

DANGER

He jerked to attention, every muscle frozen in anticipation. The hairs on his arms stood up as if electrified. In his mind and his blood, Akeso screamed in alarm.

What danger?

DREAD

He searched the sensor readings and proximity alerts, but there was nothing. Only the weapons platforms, the Guardian, and the two tiny forms at its center. A sun in the distance.

Akeso?

I do not know. I cannot find the words.

He peered out the viewport, but the filters were of necessity dialed up so high they were likely blocking anything unusual, especially if it was energetic in nature. So instead he closed his eyes.

A shiver of malevolence crept over him. Not from within, for it was wholly separate from Akeso's disquiet. And malevolence wasn't quite correct. He didn't feel the presence of evil, exactly, but of.…

Hunger
Need
Yearn

Where did this—

And the sensation was gone. He opened his eyes, and the cabin seemed unaccountably brighter. He searched again for anything to have registered on the sensors, but nothing had so much as blipped.

Akeso, are you all right?

I am shaken, but I do not comprehend why.

Neither did he. He'd never felt anything like it before. Yet…it did remind him a little of something he *had* once felt. On a dark, forbidding planet covered in living metal.

But the Rasu were dead, by his own hand. And it wasn't the same, anyway. More akin to a harmonic resonance of what he'd experienced there.

Another beam missed the hull, and he cursed his inattention. With a grunt he dragged his hands across the controls and accelerated into the weapons fire.

CS

Deunan palmed the small device she'd brought with her as she moved to the far side of the room, out of sight of the guards, then affixed it to the side of the server rack. She didn't intend for it to disable the servers, because disabling them was unlikely to stop the Anghul from firing. If it would, she'd shoot the servers until they shorted. Problem solved. Unfortunately, if divorced from remote operational control, the Anghul would probably keep firing indefinitely—in which case she would've made the situation worse. No, this was merely a diversion.

She activated the device and hurried back to lurk beside the leftmost workstation.

3…2…1….

The device blew up, causing a delightful racket as it sent sparks shooting into the air.

"What was that? Korok, go check it out!"

The officer staffing the rightmost workstation jogged over to the server rack.

As soon as his back was turned, she shot the other officer with a stun gun Arien had lent her. He'd made her promise not to mortally wound anyone unless she had no other option. It had been an easy enough promise to make, for these men weren't her enemy—they were simply in her way.

The officer collapsed to the floor, but the noise was masked by the continuing pops over at the server rack.

She stepped over his unconscious form and scanned the readouts at the station in search of the override controls.

A hand fumbled past her ankle, then reached for whatever it had felt. Fingers curled around her leg and yanked.

She stumbled toward him, barely keeping her balance, and kicked the officer in the face with her other foot. His grip loosened with a yelp, and she leapt away. Then she pointed the stun gun down, toggled the strength dial up a notch, and shot him again.

Malede. She returned her attention to the screen while trying to give the man on the floor a wider berth.

> **PASSKEY: AD1XX24G**
> **PASSKEY ACCEPTED.**
> **COMMAND: Deactivate all Anghul.**
> **CONFIRM: Yes.**
> **CONFIRM CONFIRMATION: Yes.**
> **ARE YOU CERTAIN:**

The other officer reappeared from behind the server rack. "Thomasi! *Dannat!*"

She shot him as well.

> **ARE YOU CERTAIN: Yes.**

The information on the board shifted. Less flashing, more warnings.

Deunan (Mission 2): "Did they shut down?"

Caleb (Mission 2): "They did. And none too soon."

Deunan (Mission 2): "Sorry about that. Had to do it the hard way. Are Laurent and Alex all right?"

Caleb (Mission 2): "So far."

She breathed out—and jumped as fingers snaked around her ankle with renewed strength. While she'd been celebrating, the officer had crawled toward the workstation until he'd located her invisible form again.

She shot him a third time at the same instant as he pulled hard on her ankle. Her balance gave way, and the back of her head slammed into the floor.

"Ow...."

With a groan she slid back out of his grasp and climbed to her feet. Enough of this. She removed the restraints from her bag that her brother had also lent her. Next, she knelt down and fastened them on the man's ankles and wrists—pausing to shoot the other officer again when he began climbing to his feet—then dragged the first one to the far wall. Then she moved to the second officer and repeated the process.

This should keep their hands off the workstations, where they might have reactivated the Anghul. But they remained able to call for assistance using internal comms....

She rubbed gingerly at the back of her head, then checked her palm, relieved it didn't come away bloodstained. She was going to have to stand here and continue stunning them every time they roused until this was all over, wasn't she?

She desperately wanted to return to Arien. What if he needed her help?

But he didn't. He was strong and smart and capable, and Solna Paran was no match for him. So she'd stay here and keep Laurent (and Alex) safe.

CS

"You've read the vault archives. Which means you've recovered the stolen chrystors. Which means you've been lying to me, Arien."

Solna's stare bore into him like twin daggers; he didn't think she'd blinked in almost a minute. So he half-shifted away, as if in shame, and mocked taking a long sip from his glass. When he shifted back toward her, her posture had relaxed noticeably, and the recognition that she wasn't merely ruthless and cold, but an amoral killer, finally took root in his mind.

He should have believed Maggie all those years ago. The fact he hadn't would persevere as one of the greatest regrets of his life.

Without identifying what substance she'd poisoned his drink with, he didn't know how long he had before she realized he'd deceived her, so he needed to work quickly. "Or maybe my father kept personal copies of some of the information, and I dug those up."

"The Vault isn't designed to allow copies to be made."

"A private journal, then? Where he shared his personal misgivings about various Khesa Prutet policies?" Arien huffed a breath. "Ah, forget it. You're not buying this. Yes, I've read the information stolen from the vault. Fascinating material. You know what I think? I think Dad wanted to go public with the truth about why the Guardian exists and what it does. About what caused The Fall. About who we were as a people before we came here. He tasked a scientist to work on devising a way to safely shut the Guardian down, but the scientist died before he was able to complete the project."

He slammed his glass down on her bookcase and took two menacing steps forward. "*They all died.* Why, Solna? Why did you do it? Dad cared for you like a daughter."

"Did he? Alas, he was always far too sentimental for this job. He couldn't make the difficult, necessary decisions when troublesome shades of gray started creeping in." She watched Arien carefully, searching for signs of his impending demise. "Gandrin confided in me about his intentions. I did my best to persuade him to keep silent, but it was too late. His mind was made up. Arien, if he had gone public, it would've resulted in disaster. The Khesa Prutet's credibility would have been ruined by the revelation that we'd lied to everyone for thousands of years, at the precise moment we needed to mobilize across the planet to prevent another Fall. We would have lost everything."

"You mean you'd have lost power. Wealth, influence."

"And with the loss, our society would have crumbled into chaos. Oh, Arien, don't you see? We are the glue that holds our world together. We always have been. It gave me no pleasure to kill your father, but in doing so, I saved us all, for generations to come." Her gaze drifted to the bookcase. "Please. Finish your drink, and let's talk about how we can move forward in a way that preserves peace and security for the people we serve."

But he had everything he needed. Hours of grueling interrogation gained him nothing further, for he'd never comprehend her twisted logic.

He offered her a rough, bitter laugh and drew his service weapon. "Finish my drink? I don't think so. Solna Paran, you are under arrest for the murder of Gandrin and Iriadne Colonnei and Corin Maltais, the attempted murder of Laurent Kovalne, and treason against the citizens of Elakrin."

CS

Laurent (vicinity): "Sixty percent. Continue decreasing?"
Alex (vicinity): "Yes."
Laurent (vicinity): "Forty percent incoming."

The distinction between the various pieces and parts—the mouth of the funnel, the tear, the barrier—began to fade precipitously, what remained of their edges blending and morphing into one another.

Then it was as though someone snapped a rubber band, and the manifold convulsed. Alex's ears popped.

Alex (vicinity): "Shut it down."

Laurent (vicinity): "All the way?"

Alex (vicinity): "Yes, NOW."

The funnel dissolved in her illusory hands, like ash caught on a fresh wind.

Fully occupied in sidespace, she couldn't say whether anything changed in the physical world. If she had to guess, she imagined a sky full of stars blinked into existence.

Valkyrie, are we okay?

A significant shockwave perpetuated out into space, but it originated at the barrier, not the Guardian. Elakrin and the other astronomical bodies appear to be undamaged. As, astonishingly, do you.

Caleb (Mission 1): "Alex, are you there?"

Alex (Mission 1): "I am. As are you. Laurent, are you all right?"

Laurent (Mission 1): "I, uh, think so. Everything got dark and quiet here."

She spun down her Caeles Prism, letting the excess energy diffuse into space. When nothing else exploded after a few more seconds, she returned her mind to her body.

Laurent was right. With her visual filter reducing the star to a brooding copper, the Guardian's orb and lattice were cast in shadow. No vibrations emanated from the orb. It was, for all intents and purposes, a dead ball of metal.

They'd done it.

She breathed out, long and slow. It wasn't as if she'd doubted the plan would work, exactly—it was just she'd never done anything quite like this before.

Not the first time for that, though, Valkyrie mused.

No, I suppose not.

She maneuvered around to where Laurent remained planted in front of the control panel.

Laurent (vicinity): "Alex, I'm glad to see you. Did it work?"

Alex (vicinity): "It did indeed." She took his hand, then pushed off the surface of the orb. "*Let's go see those stars.*"

Alex (Mission 1): "Caleb, we are headed your way and ready for a pickup."

Caleb (Mission 1): "Meet you halfway. Good job, baby."

CS

Deunan sprinted back upstairs the instant Caleb gave the 'all clear.' The officers could comm for help all they wanted to now.

The door to Paran's office was closed when she arrived. She hesitated.

Deunan (vicinity): "Arien, can I come in?"

Arien (vicinity): "Yes, it's safe. One second."

The door slid open to reveal her brother wearing a weary, almost sad smile. "Good work with the Anghul."

Deunan reached around to the small of her back and deactivated the Veil. "Security will be alerted to my handiwork any minute."

"Understood."

She peeked around him to see Paran's body slumped on the floor in the middle of a florid rug. A thin trail of blood leaked out from beneath the woman's chest until it met a small handgun lying askance on the rug as well. "Looks as though I missed some excitement."

"It turns out Solna had a backup plan for if the poison didn't work." He moved out of the way, allowing her entry, and the door closed behind her. "Luckily, I was prepared for that, too."

"What happened?"

"We had a nice little talk while she waited for the poison she believed I'd drank to take effect. About power, and the welfare of our people. About Dad. It was most illuminating."

Her gaze darted to her brother, an old question in her eyes. "So she did kill them."

"For the greater good, of course. The justification of megalomaniacs throughout history." He grasped her by the shoulders. "I'll tell you everything, but for now, you need to go. I have a lot of work to do here."

She frowned. To her mind, it was over. They'd *won*. "Such as?"

"I need to comm in the police, so I can explain to them how Solna attacked me in a fit of jealous rage, certain I was here to usurp her and take her place as high chair." An odd, almost haunted expression flitted across his eyes. "Funny, that. Anyway, this needs to be handled by the book. I'm not like you, Maggie. I don't get to walk away from the bodies."

He reminded her a disturbing amount of their father in that moment. All grown up and lugging around a host of burdens she'd eschewed. Guilt gnawed at her; she should've been at his side to share the weight over the years.

The air in Solna's office wrent apart as one of Alex's portals formed, the warm light of the *Siyane's* cabin leaking out from the other side. Alex stuck her head through. "Anyone want a ride?"

Deunan motioned for her to hold on as she searched Arien's features for hesitancy or doubt. All she found was resolve.

"Deunan's coming with you," Arien replied.

"After you've handled the body, then you'll come join us?" she asked.

"No. Then I'll go see the chancellor and hopefully assist him in calming the people. Then there's..." he gestured at the room "...the Prutet to consider."

"Arien, it's not your—"

"Don't worry. Everything will be fine. Make sure the others are safe, then have a drink or three for me. You deserve to celebrate. I'll touch base with you soon, okay?"

"Very soon. Say, in a couple of hours?"

"A couple of hours." He reached out and squeezed her hands, offering her a confident smile. "Now go. Security will be here any second."

She eyed him suspiciously for another beat, but conceded he had a point. Her presence here would only complicate the crime scene and make his job much more difficult. And the rest...well, they'd figure it out. They had each other now.

She turned and walked through the portal.

44

Deunan's first, all-but-unconscious act upon stepping into the *Siyane's* cabin was to search for Laurent.

She located him perched on the edge of the couch, environment suit still on but half unfastened, elbows balanced on his knees as he stared out at nothing. He looked simultaneously exhausted, shell-shocked and utterly exhilarated.

She started to approach him, but he caught sight of her and glanced pointedly away.

Right. Things were weird between them now, perhaps irreparably so. She ought to ponder what, if anything, to do about this, but she needed to catch her breath first.

Alex and Caleb were gathered at the long table that dominated the cabin, studying a row of charts hovering above it. Caleb had a vibrant flush to his olive skin, which seemed odd.

She peered into the cockpit and found it empty. Were they moving? She couldn't tell. "Who's flying the ship?"

"I am."

She almost leapt clear out of her boots as a holographic Human form materialized in front of her. The hologram extended a hand, palm up in an Elakri greeting. "You must be Deunan Colonnei. I've heard a great deal about you."

Deunan had long prided herself on never getting flustered from even the most absurd or shocking turn of events, but she barely managed to stutter out a, "Ah-h, h-hello." After returning her jaw to its rightful location, she hesitantly placed her palm atop the hologram's, and met notable resistance. It wasn't solid, but it was close. "And, uh, you are...?"

"Valkyrie. An artificial intelligence."

"Oh! Alex mentioned she...yep, got it. But if you're standing here talking to me, then you're not the one flying the ship."

"But I am. It only takes a fraction of my processes to manifest in physical form."

Alex glanced back at them and laughed. "Deunan, your game face is slipping. You're going to need to get used to encountering a lot of new and unfamiliar sights."

"Because you did it. The barrier's gone? We're in the real universe now? In Amaranthe?"

"We sure are. Welcome home."

CS

A few minutes later, with the ship safely in orbit above Elakrin and Valkyrie tending to it, another portal deposited them at the beach house. Or rather, to the cliffside lawn, where full dark blanketed the scene…except not.

As the glow of the portal faded away, Deunan peered up, and a gasp fell unbidden from her lips. She'd work on strengthening her game face soon—but not just yet.

It wasn't remotely similar to the fireworks performance at Lake Onasi on Festine Eve, but something altogether different and ineffably better. Nothing in her life had prepared her for this spectacle.

A blanket of silver pinpricks enveloped the night. Each one twinkled in time to its own beat, millions of individual symphonies playing out across an unfathomable scale. Here and there, hints of blue and yellow…oh, red and green, too, wove color into the tapestry of light.

Planets encircling nearly all of them, life rising and falling upon their firmaments.

She understood now. Understood Lirin's heartbreaking sorrow at being forced to give this up. Understood how her ancestors were driven to madness in a desperate need to have the universe at their fingertips once again.

We made it back, Lirin. I'm sorry it took so long, but we made it. Thank you for pointing the way.

"It's something else, isn't it?" Alex asked.

"Guardian's grace, it's incredible!" Laurent exclaimed. "The visuals you shared did not begin to do this justice. There are no words...." He walked slowly forward, face upturned, and Deunan was a heartbeat away from leaping out to grab him to stop him from toppling over the edge of the cliff when he finally came to a halt. "And all of these are stars? Like our sun?"

"Oh, goodness, no," Alex replied. "Many of them are galaxies. A few are probably clusters of galaxies that are extremely far away. We'll get you a telescope and a primer on measuring distances."

Laurent nodded distractedly. "Terrific."

And though the sky was putting on a stunning light show the likes of which Deunan had never before seen, much less imagined, she found she was watching Laurent instead. His smile lit up his features in profile as brilliantly as the stars overhead, and his voice sang with unfettered joy.

He was so stupidly naïve about this messed-up world, but maybe he'd been right. Or maybe he was right now. Because from here, the future looked almost rosy. Oh, she was certain the politicians and priests and power brokers would do their best to mess this gift up, but they weren't the only players on the board any longer. There was a gigantic universe out there, full of endless opportunities and wonder.

Or so Laurent would proclaim.

"We're going to head inside and pack up our things," Caleb said. "You two enjoy the view."

"Sure...wait, us two?" Laurent spun around to see her standing there. "Oh." He cleared his throat, and his voice lost some of its delight. "It's, uh, beautiful, isn't it?"

"It is." She busied herself with studying the sky once more, not trusting herself to meet his gaze until she'd committed to one path or the other. "I think I'm starting to get an inkling of why Lirin loved space so much. Or at least the possibility that I might find my way to an inkling of what he felt. It's not empty and black at all up there—it's alive."

"That's exactly what I was thinking." She sensed his eyes boring into her, tempting her with the promise of…she didn't know. Somewhat to her surprise, she wasn't overcome by an urge to flee in response. In this new universe they found themselves in, maybe it was okay to take a chance on terrifying vulnerability? To venture out to the cliff's edge and risk a fall into the unknown?

"Deunan, you've done your family's name proud. Lirin worked so hard to try to save our people, and now you've accomplished it."

"Not alone. But I guess he wasn't alone, either." *I think I don't want to be alone any longer.* She had Arien again, of course. This was simply wonderful, and also not at all what she meant.

She stepped up beside Laurent, a little grin tugging her features up. "You know, I was thinking about everything we've been through since we met. And I came to a conclusion about something."

"What's that?"

"You're not so much of a moron, after all."

"I'm not—" he spun to face her, eyes wide "—what?"

She wrapped her arms around his neck and kissed him as the stars danced in symphonies of light overhead.

45

rien studied the newest reports from his office on the way to the Capitol. Violent outbursts were fairly rare so far—mostly alcohol-induced brawls as people turned to mind-altering substances to deal with the shock of looking up in the night and seeing an ocean of stars. A few outbreaks of looting, though they seemed to be opportunistic in nature.

But panicked calls into local police stations were through the roof; hundreds of thousands in the first hours since the event. And across the region, people were gathering in large groups at every available location: parks, Guardian temples, even in the middle of random streets. Civil unrest hadn't broken out immediately upon the event, but with great numbers of people jammed into confined spaces while they clamored for answers, it was only a matter of time. The pressure was building.

He put out the order for Khesa Prutet priests to provide gentle assurances to anxious parishioners, but not to offer any detailed explanations, with the promise that he would handle it, and soon.

Responsibility for over two billion people weighed heavily upon his shoulders, in a way surely his father had never experienced. He didn't feel prepared for the burden, but fate had other plans. So be it.

Arien abruptly realized he'd reached the chancellor's office, and the next second, the chief of staff was ushering him inside with due speed.

Members of the cabinet had gathered around the meeting table, while aides rushed in every direction. Chancellor Levintis stood and waved him over. "Arien, good. I'm glad you're here. I hope you have some answers for us."

"I do, sir. But first, I need a minute of your time. Alone."

"These are my most trusted advisors."

"Alone, sir."

A shadow flickered across Levintis' features. "I see. Everyone, take five minutes. Run down the hall and grab something to eat, as who knows when you'll have another opportunity."

Levintis studied a screen situated in front of him until the room had emptied. When Arien remained standing, the chancellor stood as well. "What's going on, Arien? Why are you wearing the lapel pin of the Khesa Prutet high chair?"

"Because as of an hour ago, I *am* the Khesa Prutet high chair."

"What's happened to Solna Paran?"

"She's dead, sir. She attempted to murder me, and I was forced to defend myself."

Shock animated Levintis' expression. Genuine, or feigned? "Murder you? Whyever would she do such a thing?"

"Several reasons, but the most relevant one for this conversation is that I was planning to arrest her for the attempted assassination of Laurent Kovalne, as well as for high crimes against the people of Elakrin."

"I don't understand."

Arien held his ground. "I think you do. I think you've done Solna's bidding for quite some time now—even when her requests took an unsavory turn. I won't go so far as to suggest you knew about the hit she ordered on Dr. Kovalne. So long as she didn't say the words, you were able to maintain plausible deniability, yes? But the pressure you placed on me to find him came directly from her, didn't it?"

"The Khesa Prutet occupies a valued and influential position in our society. Of course I take the high chair's advice into consideration. On a variety of matters."

"You do a lot more than heed counsel, sir. Honestly, I've half a mind to dig up the receipts and investigate you for corruption. Bribery, blackmail, possibly more troubling crimes. But everything about the world has transformed tonight, and I need to put the wellbeing of our people above other considerations. The question is, can you do the same?"

Levintis walked over to his desk, set the screen he'd been holding down and stared at it for a minute. Finally he lifted his gaze to meet Arien's, not as the chancellor, but as a man. "What is it you want me to do?"

CS

Press cams zipped to and fro in the air around the dais, sending beams of early morning sunlight bouncing off their lenses. A tremendous crowd had gathered in the Capitol Gardens, despite the fact that only a few minutes' notice of the speech had been provided. The entire world—their entire planet, that was—was watching.

Arien had given his fair share of press conferences as part of his job, though nothing close to this scale. But he'd been raised a Colonnei, son of a high chair, and he appreciated what it meant to be in the public eye.

The chancellor took the podium first. "Welcome, my fellow citizens. I come to you on this most momentous of days. Let me thank you all for your calm and poise in what has been a deeply unsettling time. If you haven't seen the night sky for yourself, you've seen the visuals on the news by now. And you wonder if something in our world has changed. Yes, my friends, it has. But rather than try to explain it myself, I'm going to defer to an expert on the matter.

"First, however, I bring sad tidings. Our beloved Khesa Prutet high chair, Solna Paran, suffered an unexpected medical emergency last night. Physicians did everything in their power to save her, but she did not survive. Please join me in lifting up our prayers for her eternal soul as it journeys to the Guardian's embrace.

"Fortunately, the Khesa Prutet finds itself in most capable hands. Your new high chair is someone known to us all, from the time he was a small boy. I give you the director of the Ventise Bureau of Investigation and son of the late Gandrin Colonnei, Arien Colonnei."

Onlookers actually cheered him as he stepped up and accepted the chancellor's formal greeting. This part, he was never going to get used to.

He cleared his throat and gazed out at the crowd. "Thank you, everyone. Let me echo the chancellor's condolences for Solna Paran's family. She was a wonderful steward of the Colonnei legacy, and she will be missed.

"But this is a day for joy and exultation. A new dawn for our people is upon us, for the Guardian has deemed us worthy at last. The sacred texts foretold this moment would arrive if we held true to the Guardian's teachings and strived to fulfill them. Today, it has.

"They have decreed us no longer children who need to be cleaved to their bosom for shelter. Like a parent sending their firstborn off into the world to thrive on their own, the Guardian has realized they cannot keep us to themselves. And so they have opened a larger universe to us, that we may explore its wonders and share our accomplishments and wisdom with its inhabitants."

CS

"What was that *dannati malede?*"

Maggie was waiting for him inside the skycar when he climbed in, and the glare she greeted him with held the taint of disgusted betrayal. He didn't like seeing her response, not when they were still getting used to being in one another's lives, but he'd prepared himself for it.

"What that was, was necessary."

"No, that was the worst sort of pompous, narcissistic tripe I've ever heard out of the KP. Only it came from you."

He laid a hand on hers. To his tremendous relief, she didn't yank it away. She was angry, but it appeared she wasn't going to storm back out of his life before giving him an opportunity to explain.

"You're right, it was all of those things. But the people are terrified. This is a fraught time for us, Maggie. You've had, what, over a week to get accustomed to the idea of stars and aliens and a massive universe? I've had a bit less time, and I'm reeling. Everyone else? They don't understand anything of what's happening. All they know is the Guardian is no longer shining in the sky, and a host of other objects are. And they have *no* idea what else is about to barge in to disrupt their lives.

"They need something familiar to hold on to. And the one thing they've always had is faith. Like it or not, the Khesa Prutet has provided structure to our world for a long time. Comfort, guidance, purpose. Pride. They'll need those crutches in the coming days."

"But it's a lie."

"Yes, it is. But only for a while. I'm merely trying to ease the transition for us. Keep things peaceful, orderly and safe, lest the fabric of society crumble into another Fall."

She groaned, but the anger seeped out of her expression. "This isn't you, Arien. You never wanted this job any more than I did."

"No, I didn't. But it's not solely obligation. This feels right. In a sense, I'm honoring Dad, and the generations of Colonneis before him. And as I said, it's not forever. I expect I'll be the last high chair to hold the title. In time, once we're used to living in a universe teeming with intelligent life that isn't us, the Khesa Prutet won't be needed. The Guardian will fade into history. And believe me, I hope that time arrives soon."

"So do I. The robe is lame. You look ridiculous in it."

"Thank you, sister. Good to know I can still count on you for brutal honesty." He allowed a measure of his own tension to melt away. He'd have hated to do this alone. "What about you? You don't have to hide now. You can reclaim your life or—" he stopped himself "—sorry. That's not true. You've created a full life for yourself. I guess what I'm asking is, what do you think you'll do now?"

"So, Laurent's planning to go exploring." She pointed at the roof of the skycar. "Out there. He decided a telescope wasn't nearly good enough, so Alex told him she'd hook him up with a proper spaceship. And some flying lessons."

"That sounds perfect for him. The case against him should be cleared within a week or so, then he'll be free to roam. Though I guess, if he's learned anything from you, he might take off tonight. Elakrin doesn't have a hold on him any longer."

"On any of us, little brother. Not even you."

"It's not a hold, Maggie. I want to do this."

"I don't understand it, but okay." She picked a piece of lint off her jacket lapel. "He's asked me to go with him. Laurent has."

"Oh." He hadn't expected that. He'd noticed Laurent looking favorably upon his sister, but the man didn't seem to be her type. Granted, until last week he hadn't spoken to her for twenty years, so he supposed he didn't rightly know her type. "Ah, what did you say?"

"I haven't given him an answer yet. But I was thinking of saying 'yes.'"

"I see."

"I'm not like you, Arien. I'm not a public speaker. There's never been a diplomatic bone in my body. If I reemerge into the public eye, I'll only mess things up for you."

"You won't—"

"I will, and you know it. You can get far more done without me complicating your efforts. But it's also true that my purpose...no longer is one. I've gotten everything I wanted and then some. I've exposed the corruption in the KP, avenged our parents' murder..." she beamed "...and I got my little brother back. The truth is, the truva life doesn't hold the appeal it once did. But if I'm not a truva, what am I?"

"A Colonnei."

"Yes. And Lirin Colonnei explored the stars—when he wasn't hunting wrongdoers. We're practically the same person. The point is, you and I can both follow in the family tradition, each in our own way." She reached out to touch his hand. "And it's not as if I'll be gone all the time. The ship is going to have one of their portal drives on it, so I can stop by for dinner whenever I want...or whenever you can spare a few minutes."

"For you, Maggie? Say the word, and my schedule is wiped clean." He sighed in a measure of acceptance. He'd never won any arguments with her when they were young, either. "So long as you're not just running away."

"I'm not. Not this time. Though I might be running toward something."

"Laurent?"

She shrugged, visibly holding back a smile. "Time will tell."

46

They said their goodbyes in the living room of the beach house. Elakri-style arm grasps and awkward hugs abounded, but in truth it wasn't much of a farewell.

Alex would be delivering a new ship to Laurent soon. Nothing fancy, but she'd ensure it came equipped with a speedy Zero Engine drive and a Caeles Prism so he'd be able to zip around Amaranthe, drinking from the firehose of the universe. She envied him the chance to discover the wonders of space for the first time.

Since space also took no pity on the uninitiated, the ship would include a full-featured sub-Artificial operating system so he'd stay safe despite his inexperience. Nonetheless, she planned to put Laurent in touch with a pilot friend who'd take him through the paces and teach him how to care for the ship. She'd teach him herself, but she and Caleb had important tasks waiting on them.

And in a few weeks, she'd bring Laurent—and Deunan, interestingly enough—to Concord HQ for a tour and to hook them up with some 'authorized visitor' credentials. She also needed to arrange a diplomatic meeting between Arien and Marlee in the coming weeks—because Marlee had managed to rescue herself from her captivity and return home with her own story to tell, much to Caleb's absolute delight. She'd never seen him prouder of his niece.

Not-really-farewells concluded, it was time to go home.

CS

Alex nestled against Caleb's chest, letting her head rest in the crook of his neck as they lounged on the couch in the *Siyane's* cabin. Just for a few minutes. A quiet pause to relax and revel in a job well done and a people saved. Also in being alone—or as alone as they ever were with Valkyrie and Akeso back in the mix.

Did she welcome the subtle shift in Caleb's demeanor that accompanied Akeso's return, or rue it? In many ways, it was two sides of the same coin, different brush strokes upon the same tableau. She'd loved this deeply complex man madly long before Akeso came into their lives, and just as madly after.

Regardless, it didn't matter. They were a package deal, and one she'd happily accept every day, because it meant she got to have him.

"Thoughts?"

"Many." She snuggled in closer, enjoying his warmth. "Having lived through a similar shock ourselves, I daresay the Elakri have some challenging months and years ahead of them. It's not easy to come to terms with the reality that you're not the center of the universe any longer."

"We weathered the blow pretty well, though," Caleb murmured. "Humanity, I mean."

"True. Better than I expected, to be honest. Of course, it helped that we took advantage of the power vacuum our victory in the Directorate War created to more or less put ourselves in charge straightaway. The Elakri aren't going to be able to pull off such a maneuver."

"No. But while the Elakri are prideful and a bit imperious, they're also enormously talented. If they can get past the narcissism foisted upon them by their circumstances, they'll be okay. An asset, even."

"I think so. Any people who can create technology on the scale of the Guardian by definition show a lot of promise. I think a drive to achieve is etched into their DNA, no matter the goal. Hopefully they'll learn to reach those heights again."

"Mmm-hmm." He nuzzled her ear lazily. "I wanted to mention something that transpired during the mission, though I'm not sure exactly how to explain it. I...sensed something, is the best way to put it. Or rather Akeso did. It happened right after the tear manifested, while you were still working your magic to bridge the two universes. The sensation only lasted for a few seconds, and after it was gone, it didn't return.

"Akeso can't describe in words what it experienced. Granted, words aren't Akeso's strong suit to begin with. From my perspective, it felt like a *presence*. Not in space, not physically, but as if this presence was lurking in the shadows. In every shadow. And it felt…ravenous."

She sat up and twisted around to look at him. "Strange you say that, because I *saw* something around the same time: a filament of void cutting through all the dimensions swirling in the Guardian's field, almost like a wound. I had the same impression as you: shadows in the corner of my eye. But my hands were full at the time, to say the least, so I'd about decided I imagined it."

"I don't think you did."

She stared at him in silence that dragged on for too long. "Until we say it aloud, it isn't real."

"But it is. This…phenomenon existed out there before we encountered it. Which means it's still out there now." His eyes flicked over her shoulder, as if searching the shadows in the cabin.

"It's what we've been hunting, isn't it?"

"We can't know for certain."

"I think we can." Her voice dropped to a whisper. "Dzhvar."

He uttered the name in unison with her, then exhaled ponderously, as if a new weight had settled upon his chest. "Akeso sensed its presence instantly. Doesn't understand what it sensed, because it's never come across Dzhvar before. But the kyoseil at the heart of its consciousness has."

"It tracks. The primordial life forms inherently recognize one another."

"It reminded me of what I felt when touching a Rasu—and the Dzhvar birthed the Rasu. Combined with what you saw, it all fits together." He cradled her against his shoulder. "You don't suppose…we didn't let it out, did we? When we shut down the Guardian?"

It was so tempting to flee from the uncomfortable possibility...but, much as it would be for the Elakri, reality had a tenacious way of persisting whether one acknowledged it or not. Best to meet it head-on, so she tried to give the question its due. Unfortunately, she didn't have any satisfying answers.

"We don't have any way to know. Quantum dimensions don't work the way the physical manifold does. And since the tear had already opened, I can't say whether those dimensions originated from within the bubble or outside of it. If they manifested from Amaranthe, then the tendril I caught a glimpse of could be located gigaparsecs away in terms of normal space, assuming it was 'located' anywhere at all. More likely, we simply caught a peek at the...Dzhvar's sleeping chamber as ethereal dimensions sped past one another."

"There's only one problem with your theory."

Struck by the ominous undercurrent in his voice, she lifted her gaze to meet his. "Oh, what's that?"

"What I sensed? It wasn't sleeping."

LIMINAL SPACE

SHADOWS & LIGHT BOOK ONE

A war has been waged for endless aeons. Our greatest champions fight it again and again across millions of years, in a tireless endeavor to save not merely innumerable lives but existence itself.

It is a war that has never been won. But there has never been a timeline like this one before.

When the Dzhvar, an ancient enemy that once brought the universe to the brink of annihilation, rise from their long slumber to resume feasting on the fabric of space, the battle is again joined.

If Alex Solovy has anything to say about it, for the last time.

AVAILABLE NOW

GSJENNSEN.COM/LIMINAL-SPACE

***

Twenty years ago, before Concord and the larger universe it revealed, humanity teetered on the brink of war with itself even as an unimaginable threat loomed in the void. Experience the epic, galaxy-spanning adventure from the beginning:

STARSHINE

AURORA RISING BOOK ONE

GSJENNSEN.COM/STARSHINE

READ ON FOR AN EXCERPT:

SENECA

CAVARE, CAPITAL OF THE SENECAN FEDERATION

The kinetic blade slid into the man's throat like a knife through butter. Caleb held him securely from behind as the blood began to flow and the man jerked and spasmed.

He generally preferred clean, painless deaths. But he wanted to watch this man die, and die slowly.

When the man had lost all motor function, Caleb dumped him onto the desk and flipped him over. Eyes wide with fear, confusion and outrage met his. The man's lips contorted in a caricature of speech, though no words came out.

He had a good idea of the intended utterance. Why. It was a question easily answered. Vengeance.

"Justice."

As the pool of blood spread across the desk and formed waterfalls to the floor below, the eyes belonging to the leader of the Humans Against Artificials terrorist organization glazed over. The last spark of life within them dimmed, then went out.

One down.

⁊ℛ

Caleb Marano stepped out of the spaceport into the cyan-tinged glow of a late afternoon sun reflecting off the polished marble tiles of the plaza. The chill breeze caressing his skin felt like a welcome home. Cavare was always cool and often cold; Krysk had been a veritable oven by comparison.

He descended the first set of stairs and angled toward the corner to get clear of the bustling thoroughfare, then relaxed beside the ledge to wait for his companions.

Isabela exited the spaceport a moment later. She held a bag in one arm and a fidgeting bundle of arms, legs and long, dark curls in the other. She looked disturbingly 'momish' as she struggled to brush out Marlee's tangled hair—but he could remember when she had *been* that little girl with long, dark curls…and it wasn't so long ago.

With a groan she gave up the futile endeavor and allowed her daughter to escape her grasp and make a beeline for Caleb.

He crouched to meet Marlee at eye level. She plowed into him with almost enough force to knock him over backwards. He would've laughed but for the forlorn look in her pale turquoise eyes.

"Do you have to go away now, Uncle Caleb?"

He tousled her curls into further disarray. "Yeah, I'm afraid I have to go back to work. But it sure was great spending my vacation with you. I learned a *lot*."

She wore her best serious face as she nodded sagely. "You had a lot to learn."

He grinned and leaned in to whisper to his co-conspirator. "You remember what all we talked about, right?"

Her eyes were wide and honest. "Uh-huh."

"Good. Want one more ride before I go?"

Her head bobbed up and down with gusto, instantly that of a carefree child again.

"Okay." He scooped her up in his arms and stood, made certain he had a solid grasp of her tiny waist, and began to spin around with accelerating speed. Her arms and legs dangled free to swing through the air while she cackled in delight.

After another few spins he slowed—he had learned her limits during the last few weeks—letting her limbs fall against him before he came to a stop. He gave her a final squeeze and gently set her to the ground as her mother reached them.

Isabela wore a half-amused, half-exhausted expression as Marlee started running in dizzy circles around her legs. "Sorry about the hold up. They let us back on the transport and we found Mr. Freckles under the seat." She patted her bag in confirmation of the stuffed animal's now secure location. "Are you sure you don't want to have a quick dinner with us?"

He responded with a dubious smirk. "You can be polite if you like, but the truth is you are sick to death of me and counting the minutes until you are at last rid of me."

"Well, *yes*. But I never know when I'll get to see you again...." The twinkle faded from her eyes, replaced by something darker and heavier.

She knew he didn't work for a shuttle manufacturing company, and he knew that she knew. But they never, *ever*, talked about it. Partly for her safety and his, but partly because he preferred to continue being in her mind the strong, stalwart older brother with the easygoing demeanor and wicked sense of humor, without introducing any moral grayness to the relationship dynamic.

Because he never wanted her to look at him with caution, disillusionment...or worst of all, fear.

He merely nodded in response. "I'll come visit again soon. Promise."

She reached down to pause the cyclone at her legs. "I'll hold you to it. I'm going to take Marlee to see Mom, then we'll head back home."

He leaned over the struggling cyclone to embrace her. "Thank you for the extended hospitality. I'm glad I was able to spend so much time with you."

"Anytime, I mean it," she whispered in his ear. "Stay safe."

He kept his shrug mild as he stepped away. "Of course." Not likely.

Two insistent and tearful hugs from Marlee later, they parted ways. He watched them disappear into the throng of travelers, then headed in the direction of the parking complex.

Caleb stepped in the adjoining lavatory and washed the blood off his hands and forearms. Then he returned to the office, reached under the corner of the desk and triggered the 'Alert' panic signal—the one he had never allowed the dead man to reach. There was a surveillance cam hidden in the ceiling, and he looked up at it and smiled. He had a number of smiles in his repertoire; this was not one of the more pleasant ones.

The commotion began as he exited the building. He quickened his stride to his bike, jumped on and fired the engine. Three men bolted out the door, two Daemons and a TSG swinging in his direction.

It wouldn't do to get shot. A flick of his thumb and the bike burst out of the parking slot. He laid it down as laser fire sliced barely a meter overhead, his leg hovering centimeters above the ground while he slid around the corner and onto the cross-street.

He heard them giving chase almost immediately. So late in the night the street and air traffic was sparse, which was one reason he had begun the op when he did. It reduced the chances of his pursuers taking out innocent bystanders—and gave them a clearer line of sight to him. He wanted to make certain they knew where he was going before he left them behind.

Their surface vehicles didn't stand a chance of matching his speed and it would look suspicious if he slowed...but as anticipated, they had grabbed a skycar. He kept an eye on it via the rearcam, making sure it succeeded in following him through two major direction shifts.

Satisfied, he kicked the bike into its actual highest gear and accelerated right then left, fishtailing around two street corners in rapid succession. He activated the concealment shield. It didn't render him or the bike invisible, but it did make them blend into the surroundings and virtually impossible to track from the air at night.

Then he sped toward the Bahia Mar spaceport. After all, he did need to get there ahead of them.

ᴙ

Tiny flecks of light sparkled in the night-darkened waters of the Fuori River as Caleb pulled in the small surface lot. It was nearly empty, as most people took the levtrams to the entertainment district and had no need of parking.

Once the engine had purred into silence he swung a leg off the bike and glanced up. A smile ghosted across his face at the dozens of meteors streaking against the silhouette of the giant moon which dominated Seneca's sky.

He noted the time. He had a few minutes to enjoy a little stargazing, though the conditions were far from ideal here in the heart of downtown. An exanet query confirmed the meteor shower continued for eleven days. Maybe he'd have a chance to get up to the mountains before it ended.

Committed to this plan, he secured the bike in its slot. A last glance at the sky and he crossed the street and took the wide steps to the river-walk park.

The atmosphere on the broad promenade hovered at the optimal balance between deserted and overrun by masses of people. As it was a weekend night the balance wouldn't hold for long, but for the moment it pulsed with energy while still allowing plenty of room to move about and claim your own personal space. He noted with interest the outdoor bar to the right, complete with live synth band and raised danced platform. *Not yet. Business first.*

He slipped among the milling patrons until he reached a section of railing at the edge of the promenade to the southeast of the bar. Here the crowd had thinned to a few meandering couples and the music thrummed softly in the background.

The light from the skyscrapers now drowned out the light from the meteors, but he couldn't argue with the view.

A thoroughly modern city to the core, humans having initially set foot on its soil less than a century ago, Cavare glittered and shone like a sculpture newly unveiled. The reflected halo of the moon shimmered in the tranquil water as the river rippled along the wall beneath him, winding itself through the heart of the city on its way to Lake Fuori. Far to his left he could see the gleam of the first arch which marked the dramatic entrance to the lake and the luxuries it held.

It was an inspiring yet comforting view, and one he had spent close to forty years watching develop, mature and grow increasingly more lustrous. He contented himself with enjoying it while he waited for his appointment to arrive.

The message had come in the middle of dinner at his favorite Chinasian restaurant. He hadn't even had the chance to go home yet; the entirety of the belongings he had traveled with were stowed in the rear compartment of his bike. But in truth there wasn't much of consequence waiting for him at the apartment, for it was home in only the most technical sense of the word.

Never have anything you can't walk away from. A gem of advice imparted by a friend and mentor early on in his career, and something he had found remarkably easy to adopt.

⚕

He stowed the bike in a nearby stall he had rented in yet another assumed name and hurried to Bay F-18. He made a brief pass through the ship to make sure the contact points on the charges were solid, then sat in the pilot's chair, kicked his feet up on the dash and crossed his hands behind his head to wait.

They were hackers as much as terrorists. It wouldn't take them long to break the encryption to the bay. The encryption on the ship's airlock was stronger—for they would expect it to be—but not so difficult they couldn't crack it.

Planting enough charges at the headquarters to take it out would have involved significant risk of discovery and ultimate failure. But here, he controlled every step and every action.

The hangar bay door burst open. Three...six...eight initially. He sincerely hoped more showed up before they got into the ship.

His wish was granted when three minutes later seven additional members of the group rushed in. The surface pursuit, he imagined. The initial arrivals were still hacking the ship lock. He gave them another two minutes.

With a last gaze around he pulled his feet off the dash and stood. He headed through the primary compartment and below to the mid-level, opened the hatch to the engineering well, and positioned himself in the shadowy corner near the stairs.

They wouldn't all come in at once, lest they end up shooting each other in the confusion. Three, maybe four to start, plus two to guard the airlock. They would fan out to run him to ground quickly.

The first man descended the stairs. As his left foot hit the deck Caleb grabbed him from behind and with a fierce wrench snapped his neck. He made a point to throw the body against the stairwell so the loud clang echoed throughout the ship.

Two down.

Caleb looked over his shoulder to see Michael Volosk striding down the steps toward him. Right on time. Everything about the man's outward demeanor projected an image of consummate professionalism, from the simple but perfectly tailored suit to the close-cropped hair to the purposeful stride.

He extended his hand in greeting as the Director of Special Operations for the Senecan Federation Division of Intelligence approached. A mouthful worthy of the highest conceit of government; but to everyone who worked there, it was simply "Division."

Volosk grasped his hand in a firm shake and took up a position along the rail beside him. "Thanks for agreeing to meet me here. I have a syncrosse rec league game down the street in twenty minutes, and if I miss another game they'll kick me off the team." He wore a slight grimace intended to hint at the many responsibilities a high-level covert intelligence official was required to juggle…then presumably realized the impression it actually conveyed, because he shifted to a shrug. "It's the only opportunity I have to blow off steam."

Caleb smiled with studied, casual charm. "It's not a problem. I just got in anyway. And if the surroundings happen to discourage prying eyes, well, I appreciate the value of discretion."

Volosk didn't bother to deny the additional reason for the choice of meeting location. "It wouldn't hurt if your coworkers didn't know you were back on the clock yet—and that's one reason I chose you. Your reputation is impressive."

He chuckled lightly and ran a hand through disheveled hair made wild by the wind. "Perhaps I'm not discrete enough, then."

"Rest assured, it's on a need-to-know basis. I realize we haven't had many opportunities to work together yet, but Samuel always spoke of you in the highest terms."

He schooled his expression to mask the emotions the statement provoked. "I'm humbled, sir. He was a good man."

"He was." Volosk's shoulders straightened with his posture—a signal he was moving right on to business, as though it didn't *matter* how good a man Samuel had been. "What do you know about the Metis Nebula?"

Caleb's brow creased in surprise. Whatever he had been expecting, this wasn't it. *Okay. Sure.*

"Well, mostly that we don't know much about it. It's outside Federation space, but we've tried to investigate it a few times—purely scientific research of course. We know there's a pulsar at the center of it, but scans return a fuzzy mess across the spectrum. Probes sent in find nothing but ionized gases and space dust. Scientists have written it off as unworthy of further study. Why?"

"You're very well informed, Agent Marano. Do a lot of scientific reading in your spare time?"

"Something like that."

"I'm sure. The information I'm sending you is Level IV Classified. Fewer than a dozen people inside and out of the government are aware of it."

He scanned the data file. In the background the synth band shifted to a slow, rhythmic number threaded by a deep, throbbing bass line. "That's…odd."

"Quite. The Astrophysics Institute sent in a state of the art, prototype deep space probe—the most sensitive one ever built, we believe. Honestly, it was solely for testing purposes. The researchers thought Metis' flat profile offered a favorable arena to run the probe through its paces. Instead it picked up what you see there.

"Obviously we need to get a handle on what this is. It came to my desk because it may represent a hostile threat. We've put a hold on any scientific expeditions until we find out the nature of the anomaly. If it *is* hostile, the sooner we know the better we can prepare. If on the other hand it's an opportunity—perhaps a new type of exploitable energy resource—we want to bring it under our purview before the Alliance or any of the independent corporate interests learn of it."

Caleb frowned at his companion. "I understand. But to be frank, my missions are usually a bit more…physical in nature? More direct at least, and typically involving a tangible target."

"I'm aware of that. But your experience makes you one of the few people in Division both qualified to investigate this matter and carrying a security clearance high enough to allow you to do so."

It wasn't an inaccurate statement. And if he were honest with himself, it *would* probably be best if he went a little while without getting more blood on his hands.

He slid open the hidden compartment in the wall and climbed into the narrow passage, pushed the access closed using his foot and crawled along the sloped tunnel. When he got to the end he activated his personal concealment shield—which did very nearly make him invisible—and with a deft twist released the small hatch.

He rolled as he hit the ground to mask the sound. The lighting in the bay was purposefully dim, and he landed deep in the shadow of the hull.

As expected, there was a ring of men guarding the exterior of the ship. He waited for the closest man to turn his back, then slipped out and moved to the corner of the bay to settle behind the storage crates he had arranged to have delivered earlier in the day.

He was rewarded by the arrival at that moment of an additional six—no, seven—pursuers. A significant majority of the active members were now inside the hangar bay. Good enough.

They moved to join their brethren encircling the ship—and he sent the signal.

The walls roiled and bucked from the force of the explosion. White-hot heat blasted through his shield. The shockwave sent him to his knees even as the floor shuddered beneath him. Pieces of shrapnel speared into the wall above him and to his right. A large section of the hull shot out the open side of the bay and crashed to the street below.

One glance at the utter wreckage of his former ship confirmed they were all dead. He climbed to his feet and crossed to the door, dodging the

flaming debris and burnt, dismembered limbs. The emergency respond-
ers could be heard approaching seconds after he disappeared down the
corridor.

He didn't de-cloak until he reached the bike. He calmly fired it up,
cruised out of the stall, and accelerated toward the exit.

Mission fucking accomplished.

ᴼᴿ

Caleb nodded in acceptance. "I'll need a new ship. My last one was, um, blown up."

"My understanding is that's because you blew it up." The expression on the Director's face resembled mild sardonic amusement.

He bit his lower lip in feigned chagrin, revealing what he judged to be the appropriate touch of humility. "Technically speaking."

Volosk sent another data file his way. "Regardless, it's been taken care of. Here's the file number and all the standard information, including the hangar bay of your new ship."

He ignored the mild barb and examined this data with greater scrutiny, but it appeared everything had in fact been taken care of. "Got it. This all looks fine."

"Good…there's one more thing. It's no secret with Samuel gone there's a leadership vacuum in the strategic arm of Special Operations. He believed you were quite capable of taking on a larger role. Based on your record—a few isolated excesses aside—and what I know of you, I'm inclined to agree. So while you're out there in the void, I'd encourage you to give some thought to what you truly want from this job. We can talk further when you return."

Caleb made sure his expression displayed only genuine appreciation, carefully hiding any ambivalence or disquiet. "Thank you for the vote of confidence, sir. I'll do that."

"Glad to hear it. Now if you'll excuse me, I have to go get my ass kicked by ten other men and a cocky, VI-enhanced metal ball, after which I get to go back to the office and review the Trade Summit file for the seventeenth time this week."

He grimaced in sympathy. It was impossible to escape the growing media frenzy surrounding the conference, even with it over a week away.

Twenty-two years had passed since the end of the Crux War; it had been over and done with before he was old enough to fight. The cessation of hostilities after three years was officially called an 'armistice,' but Seneca and fourteen allied worlds had—by the only measure which mattered—won. They had their independence from the mighty Earth Alliance.

Now some politician somewhere had decided it was finally time for them to start playing nice with one another. He wished them luck, but…. "If it's all the same, I'd just as soon not be assigned to that one, sir. It's going to be a clusterfain of epic proportions."

Volosk exhaled with a weariness Caleb suspected was more real than contrived. "Don't worry, you're off the hook—wouldn't want to endanger your work by putting your face in front of so many dignitaries. *I*, however, won't get a decent night's sleep until the damn thing's finished."

Caleb sighed in commiseration, playing along with the superficial bonding moment. It seemed the higher-ups had decided he was worthy of being nurtured, at least enough to make certain he stayed in the fold. Bureaucrats. They had no clue how to manage people; if they did, they would realize he was the last person who needed *managing*.

"Well, I'm sorry I can't help you there, sir. But I will head out on this mission once I've pulled together what I need. It should be a few days at most."

Volosk nodded, transitioning smoothly to the closing portion of the meeting. "Please report in as soon as you discover anything relevant. We need to understand what we're dealing with, and quickly."

He responded with a practiced smile, one designed to convey reassurance and comfort. "Not to worry, I'll take care of it. It's what I do." He decided it was best to leave *when I'm not blowing up three million credit ships and two dozen terrorists with them* unsaid.

After all, he fully intended to *try* to return this ship in one piece.

AR

After Volosk had departed, Caleb remained by the river for a while. His outward demeanor was relaxed, save for the rapid tap of fingertips on the railing.

He had been on leave ever since the post-op debriefs for the previous assignment had wrapped up. Whether the vacation had been a reward or a punishment he wasn't entirely sure, despite Volosk's vague hint at a promotion. Nor did he particularly care. He had accomplished what he had set out to do, justice had been served—albeit with a spicy dash of vengeance—and the bad guys were all dead. But it appeared it was time to get back to work.

The serenity of the cool night breeze and river-cleansed air juxtaposed upon the pulsing thrum of the music and swelling buzz of the crowd made for an appropriate backdrop. Time to retune himself.

He had enjoyed spending time with Isabela and her family, especially getting to play the bad uncle and fill Marlee's head with rebellious and unruly ideas sure to drive her mother crazy for months. The little girl had spunk; it was his duty to encourage it.

It had been a welcome respite. But it wasn't his life.

He pushed off the railing and strolled down the promenade to the bar area. The throbbing of the bass vibrated pleasantly on his skin as he neared. He ordered a local ale and found a small standing table which had been abandoned in favor of the dance floor. He rested his elbows on it, sipped his beer and surveyed the crowd.

It was amusing, and occasionally heartbreaking, to see how people doggedly fumbled their way through encounters. All the cybernetics in the world couldn't replace real, human connection, which was likely why physical sex was still the most popular pastime in the galaxy, despite the easy availability of objectively better-than-real *passione illusoire*. Humans were social animals, and craved—

"What are you drinking?"

He glanced at the woman who had sidled up next to him. Long, razor-straight white-blond hair framed a face sculpted to perfection beyond what genetic engineering alone could achieve. A white iridescent slip minimally covered deep golden skin. Silver glyphs wound along both arms and up the sides of her neck to disappear beneath the hairline.

He smiled coolly. "I'm fine, thanks."

She dropped a hand on the table and posed herself against it. "Yes, you are. Would you like to dance?"

He suppressed a laugh at the heavy-handed come-on. "Thank you, but…" a corner of his mouth curled up "…you're not really my type."

Her eyes shone with polished confidence. She believed she was in control. How *cute*.

"I can be any type you want me to be." The glyphs glowed briefly as her hair morphed to black, her makeup softened and her skin tone paled.

So that's what the glyphs were for. A waste of credits born of a desperate need to be wanted. He gave the woman a shrug and shook his head. "No thanks."

She scowled in frustration; it marred the perfect features into ugliness. "Why not? What the hell is your type?"

He took a last sip of his beer and dropped the empty bottle on the table. "Real."

He walked away without looking back.

STARSHINE

AURORA RISING BOOK ONE

AVAILABLE IN EBOOK, PRINT AND AUDIOBOOK AT
GSJENNSEN.COM/STARSHINE

SUBSCRIBE TO G. S. JENNSEN'S NEWSLETTER

*Get an *exclusive* free short story, be the first to hear about new book announcements and more*

GSJENNSEN.COM/SUBSCRIBE

Author's Note

I published my first novel, *Starshine*, in 2014. In the back of the book I put a short note asking readers to consider leaving a review or talking about the book with their friends. Watching my readers do that and so much more has been the most rewarding and humbling experience in my life.

So if you loved **THE UNIVERSE WITHIN**, tell someone. Leave a review, share your thoughts on social media, annoy your coworkers in the break room by talking about your favorite characters. Reviews are the backbone of a book's success, but there is no single act that will sell a book better than word-of-mouth.

My part of this deal is to write a book worth talking about—your part of the deal is to do the talking. If you keep doing your bit, I get to write a lot more books for you.

Lastly, I want to hear from my readers. If you loved the book— or if you didn't—let me know. The beauty of independent publishing is its simplicity: there's the writer and the readers. Without any overhead, I can find out what I'm doing right and wrong directly from you, which is invaluable in making the next book better than this one. And the one after that. And the twenty after that.

Website: gsjennsen.com

Wiki: gsj.space/wiki

Email: gs@gsjennsen.com

Twitter: @GSJennsen

Facebook: gsjennsen.author

Goodreads: G.S. Jennsen

Pinterest: gsjennsen

Instagram: gsjennsen

Find my books at a variety of retailers: gsjennsen.com/retailers

AMARANTHE UNIVERSE

AURORA RHAPSODY

AURORA RISING
STARSHINE
VERTIGO
TRANSCENDENCE

AURORA RENEGADES
SIDESPACE
DISSONANCE
ABYSM

AURORA RESONANT
RELATIVITY
RUBICON
REQUIEM

ASTERION NOIR
EXIN EX MACHINA
OF A DARKER VOID
THE STARS LIKE GODS

RIVEN WORLDS

CONTINUUM
INVERSION
ECHO RIFT

ALL OUR TOMORROWS
CHAOTICA
DUALITY

COSMIC SHORES
MEDUSA FALLING
THE THIEF
THE UNIVERSE WITHIN

SHADOWS & LIGHT
LIMINAL SPACE

SHORT STORIES
Restless I • *Restless II* • *Apogee* • *Solatium* • *Venatoris* • *Re/Genesis* • *Meridian* • *Fractals* • *Chrysalis* • *Starlight Express* • *Extinguishing the Stars*

Learn more at gsjennsen.com/books or visit gsj.space/wiki

Acknowledgments

Many thanks to my beta readers, editors and artists, who made everything about this book better, and to my family, who continue to put up with an egregious level of obsessive focus on my part for months at a time.

I also want to add a personal note of thanks to everyone who has read my books, left a review at a retailer, Goodreads or other sites, sent me a personal email expressing how the books have impacted you, or posted on social media to share how much you enjoyed them. You make this all worthwhile, every day.

About the Author

G. S. JENNSEN lives somewhere in the U.S., in a locale that may or may not be where she lived the last time she published a book (she's a gypsy at heart), with her husband and two dogs. She has become an internationally bestselling author since her first novel, *Starshine*, was published in 2014. She has chosen to continue writing under an independent publishing model to ensure the integrity of her stories and her ability to execute on the vision she has for their telling.

While she has been a lawyer, a software engineer and an editor, she's found the life of a full-time author preferable by several orders of magnitude. When she isn't writing, she's gaming or working out or getting lost in the mountains that loom large outside the windows in her home. Or she's dealing with a flooded basement, or standing in a line at Walmart reading the tabloid headlines and wondering who all of those people are. Or sitting on her back porch with a glass of wine, looking up at the stars, trying to figure out what could be up there.

www.ingramcontent.com/pod-product-compliance
Lightning Source LLC
Chambersburg PA
CBHW051437190726

48289CB00001B/226